RUTHLESS
Bishop

SINNERS AND SAINTS BOOK 3

USA TODAY & INTERNATIONAL BESTSELLING AUTHOR
VERONICA EDEN

RUTHLESS BISHOP

Copyright © 2020 Veronica Eden

All rights reserved.

No parts of this publication may be reproduced, stored in a retrieval system, or transmitted in any form or by any means, electronic, mechanical, photocopying, recording, or otherwise, without the prior written permission of the copyright owner, except in the case of brief quotations embodied in reviews and certain other noncommercial uses permitted by copyright law. For permission requests, write to the author at this website:

WWW.VERONICAEDENAUTHOR.COM

Discreet Series Edition

RUTHLESS BISHOP

SINNERS AND SAINTS BOOK 3

VERONICA EDEN

CONTENTS

Author's Note   vii
About the Book   ix
Playlist   xi

1. Thea   1
2. Connor   9
3. Thea   17
4. Connor   31
5. Connor   35
6. Thea   47
7. Connor   61
8. Connor   67
9. Connor   79
10. Thea   93
11. Thea   107
12. Connor   121
13. Connor   127
14. Thea   133
15. Connor   141
16. Connor   153
17. Thea   165
18. Thea   177
19. Thea   191
20. Connor   195
21. Thea   209
22. Connor   221
23. Thea   225
24. Connor   235
25. Connor   247
26. Thea   261
27. Thea   267

28. Connor   277
29. Connor   285
30. Thea   297
31. Connor   303
32. Thea   307
33. Thea   313
34. Thea   325
35. Thea   337
36. Connor   345
37. Thea   349
38. Connor   355
39. Connor   365
40. Thea   373
    Epilogue   381
    Epilogue   389

    Afterword   393
    Thank You + What's Next?   395
    Acknowledgments   397
    Preview the Sinners and Saints Series   399
    Preview Savage Wilder   401
    About the Author   407
    Also by Veronica Eden   409

AUTHOR'S NOTE

Ruthless Bishop is a new adult high school romance containing dark themes intended for mature readers. The Sinners and Saints series boys are all devilish bullies brought to their knees by a spitfire heroine, so if you love intense enemies-to-lovers type stories, you're in the right place. This mature new adult romance contains crude language, bullying, dubious situations, a stalker/predator, and intense graphic sexual/violent content that some readers might find triggering or offensive. Please proceed with caution.

If you like weak pushover heroines and nice guys this one ain't for you, but if you dig strong females and smug antiheroes, then you're in the right place! Hold onto your hearts, because these guys aren't above stealing.

Each book is part of a series but can be enjoyed as a standalone in any order.

Sinners and Saints series:

#1 Wicked Saint
#2 Tempting Devil
#3 Ruthless Bishop
#4 Savage Wilder

Sign up for Veronica's newsletter to receive exclusive content and news about upcoming releases: bit.ly/veronicaedenmail
Follow Veronica on BookBub for new release alerts: bookbub.com/authors/veronica-eden

ABOUT THE BOOK

THEA

EVERYONE HAS SOMETHING TO HIDE.

I was invisible until I wasn't.

One mistyped number became the catalyst to my hell on earth
when I accidentally sent a risqué photo to the blackmail king of
Silver Lake High. Now Connor Bishop holds it as a bargaining
chip over my head. I've become his doll, at his mercy in a
corrupt castle.

Better do as he says or else, or else, or else...

His thumb is on the send button every time I try to buck his
command. Can I survive a private photo going viral instead of
living this life of torment?

It's not right. Maybe it's time his castle burns down.

CONNOR

SOME LIES ARE MORE DANGEROUS THAN OTHERS.

Meek. Shy. Wholesome.

Thea Kennedy was picture-perfect innocence until she wasn't. The unexpected photo is the juiciest secret to land in my lap in a while. Who knew she was hiding luscious curves under frumpy sweaters?

With one racy selfie, Thea stepped into my world, where I control the board. I'll trap the little mouse and won't let her escape the depraved kingdom I built.

But there are darker monsters than me lurking in the shadows. They want to take a bite out of my little mouse. I don't like sharing what's mine.

PLAYLIST

(Spotify)

Black Mirror—Sophie Simmons
I Know Where the Bodies Are Buried—Adam Jensen
In Cold Blood—alt-J
Bad Kind of Butterflies—Camila Cabello
I Will—Eminem, KXNG Crooked, Royce Da 5'9", Joell Ortiz
Play with Fire—Sam Tinnesz, Yacht Money
Sorry Now—Crimson Apple
Something Beautiful—Tori Kelly
idfc—blackbear
Bad For Me—LOWBORN
Crown—Camila Cabello, Grey
like that—Bea Miller
The King—Conan Gray
Dirty Little Secret—The All-American Rejects
Bad Things—Machine Gun Kelly, Camila Cabello
In the Dark—Camila Cabello
Falling—Trevor Daniel

Sweet Disaster—DREAMERS
ain't love—blackbear
Dazed & Confused—Ruel
Skin—Rihanna
Watch Me Burn—Michele Morrone
I Know Your Secrets—Tommee Profitt, Liv Ash
Somebody—Crimson Apple
Consequences—Camila Cabello
Bury Me Face Down—grandson
Depression & Obsession—XXXTENTACION
Staring At The Sun—Post Malone, SZA
death bed (coffee for your head)—Powfu, beabadoobee
Sunflower—Post Palone, Swae Lee

To the ones who tripped their way through feeling invisible, no matter how big our smiles, no matter how kind our hearts, no matter how big our friendship circles grew.

You are not broken. You are seen. You are loved.

ONE
THEA

Sexy selfie attempt number twenty and I still don't have a winner I totally love on my phone's camera roll.

"Just do it," I mutter, arguing with myself. "Spontaneity is a good thing. He'll like it. Be cool."

I've been going in circles for five minutes, getting nowhere as I pace my bedroom.

My school uniform hangs on the closet door from a funky sun-shaped brass hook, the plaid skirt in the school colors—evergreen and white—and the black blazer with the gold embroidered crest mocking me. At school I'm known by cruel names because I prefer wearing my uniform a couple of sizes too big to hide my body, unlike the girls who wear their skirts short enough their asses almost hang out and their blazers fitted to their petite waistlines. The other students are labelled cool because they break the uniform code with designer fashion, but I'm not because my rebellion isn't worthy in their eyes.

At least most of the time I'm invisible to them.

Narrowing my eyes at the uniform, I turn my back, where the riot of color on the other side of the room makes me smile. The wall is a pastel rainbow of baking-themed art with funny sayings like *bake the world happy* and *happiness is homemade*.

"Okay, focus. Send the photo," I coach.

My stomach protests with a wave of butterflies. All of my positive thinking flees.

I can't believe I'm losing an argument against myself. I blow out harshly, deflating my ballooned cheeks along with my nerve. A wayward auburn curl ends up in my eyes. With an impatient flick, I brush it aside.

It's taken me weeks to work up the courage for this step with Wyatt, the cute lifeguard at the summer retreat my parents sent me to. We had a sort of fling. Well, okay. Not really.

It was fling-like. *Fling adjacent.* We were on our way to flirting.

At least, that's what my friend Maisy assured me between yoga class and gourmet s'mores by the campfire.

The air hisses from my lungs in a soft, flat laugh that caves my chest.

You? Dream on. He was only being polite. As a staff member, he was probably contracted to be whatever the guests needed. Even appearing interested romantically.

I shake my head to dispel the depressing inner voice. Wyatt wasn't only being a nice guy, and I am a damn goddess he would love to be with.

Forget the short-girl-with-an-ass figure it's difficult to find jeans for, the stretch marks on my hips and boobs from puberty growth spurts, and the memories of shopping for bras when my friends were still playing with toys.

"A goddess," I repeat, letting the affirmation give me the mental hug I need to restore my confidence.

My tongue pokes out of the corner of my mouth as I hesitate to click on the message icon in his contact, where I saved his name with waves. As if I'd forget about how he looked in his red lifeguard trunks with a deep golden tan. Maybe I should go for a Facebook message or an Instagram DM first to double check I have his number saved correctly.

I shake my head. "Be bold."

This is my chance to keep our tiny spark alive before it snuffs out. I have to act fast. I arrived back in Ridgeview the week before school at Silver Lake High started, and Wyatt went home to Colorado Springs. The drive down is under two hours if this works out—but I'm getting ahead of myself.

First I have to buck the hell up and send the photo.

I've decided. Senior year is my year. I'm eighteen and it's time I stopped hiding myself from the world.

Mom can spout her crap until she's red in the face, but I'm not listening anymore.

A whine sounds at the locked door, followed by a muffled scratch.

"Not tonight, buddy. Go to your bed," I tell my rottweiler. He's an oversized lapdog that usually shadows me all over the house. He whines once more. "Bed, Constantine."

The dog makes a put out sound as his nails click down the hall.

My grip tightens on my cell phone. The picture I took is all right. Not my best, but like the hundreds of photos in a secret folder, it's the version of the girl I want to be.

Confident, sexy, and owning my curvy body.

Ah, the pipe dream.

I pluck at the sunflower yellow chunky knit cardigan I tugged on over the lace-edged romper that barely contains my breasts. It's designed to drape nicely on elegant bodies with long limbs and chests much flatter than mine. Instead, the romper fits to my big hips and rides up my thighs. Thank god for still photos where I can fake like I'm not trying to pick the material my ass is eating every two seconds.

Mom doesn't know I own the romper, or some of the other clothes hidden in the closet. I have to rotate my hiding spots because she is a notorious snooper.

Photo-me looks up from the phone screen with bedroom eyes, my lashes fluttered low over my blue-green eyes. My dark red curls are tossed over strategically to give my hair that bombshell volume, spilling down my neck and over one shoulder as I lean forward to show off my cleavage. My plump lips are puckered into duck lips. I can't help it, duck lips are my go to when I put myself on the spot in the hopes I'll capture something natural and effortless. It's me, and yet...not.

My gaze slides to the mirror and my shoulders droop as soon as I eye my reflection critically.

Mirrors and phone cameras must have a deal with the devil.

Somehow the reflection and the pictures never match up. Maybe the girl I am in my secret folder of photos exists only in digital format.

Squinting, I lean closer. Is that—? *Yup.* That's flour in my hair. I sink my fingers into my curls with an aggravated sigh and shake them out as I check the photo. Fan-flipping-tastic.

I thought I cleaned myself up after baking the rustic cranberry tarts I've been trying to perfect when I got home from school, but I must have missed some. What else is new? I'm almost always covered in some ingredient with my love of baking.

Okay, attempt number twenty-one.

This time I crop part of my face out of the frame and go for a coy smirk. Once I snap the photo, I drop out of the pose and perch on the arm of the floral print cushioned chair by the window, nudging one of my infinite recipe notebooks onto the seat.

"Not bad." I tilt my head and scrunch my lips to the side. The next dilemma occurs to me and my eyes widen. "Crap."

I'm already being bold with the photo, but should I say anything or just send the picture? What do people normally say when they send selfies revealing their thirst levels to their crush? Oh god, I'm going to screw this up. I'm so bad at this!

The glow of headlights shining through the window distracts me from my momentary panic as a dark silver SUV pulls into the house next door. The Bishop's place. I'm the lucky duck who not only has the school principal for a neighbor but also his vicious son, Connor Bishop. Most of the time he ignores my existence, but on days he doesn't, he's the champion of the crusade against me and my favorite sweaters.

"Oh freaking great," I mumble, ducking down in the chair so he doesn't look up to my window and think I'm creeping on him.

I'm not risking Connor seeing me in this romper, either. No free shows for that asshole.

The headlights cut off as he parks outside of the garage. Their house looks like it belongs in the Hollywood Hills with its sprawling paved terraces, huge arched windows, and terracotta tiled roof. It stands out against the other houses, like mine, that resemble mountain lodges and chalets with stone columns and dark accents. Almost everything in our town matches the same mountain vibe. Our neighborhood is comfortably upscale as far as Ridgeview goes, but Connor's is the biggest on the street.

Curling my fingers over the back of the chair, I peek past the sheer lavender curtains and watch him slam the door of the Lexus GX with a bag of soccer balls hooked over his shoulder. It makes his bicep flex, stretching his green varsity soccer shirt taut.

Why do mean boys always have to look like that? He's an angel-faced demon in disguise with his striking gray eyes, floppy light brown hair, and a dangerous, dazzling smile he uses to melt the panties off of his adoring fangirls. Not that I know what his charm-up-to-eleven smile looks like up close. I only get the cruel smirks directed my way when I have the misfortune of catching his attention.

Collapsing back into the chair, I bite my lip and push Connor Bishop from my mind. I'm a girl on a mission to flirt. He isn't messing this up for me.

As I tap my nails against my phone and tug my lips side to side in thought, different options scroll through my mind. *Hey cutie?* I shake my head. *No, that's too much. Hope you're having a good day?* I groan, scrubbing a hand over my face.

"Why are words so hard?"

The stuffed sea lion on the bed doesn't answer. I'm terrible at this stuff. A 4.0 GPA and all my baking skills, yet I can't flirt for shit. It's like I'm defective, missing a social skill or two because I listened to all the things Mom has always warned me about boys, and ran in the other direction when one spoke to me.

Except for one. But that didn't end well.

I cock my head to the side as a thought occurs to me while I'm wallowing in self pity. What would Connor say in this situation if he was going to sweet talk a girl he wanted?

My gaze flicks to the window where his bedroom light is

on. I only know it's his room because he refuses to change with the curtains closed, the self-obsessed exhibitionist. I may have caught sight of his bare chest—*briefly*—a time or two over the years. He has abs, and that's just completely unfair.

Dropping my voice into a lower register and pretending to be all macho, I shoot my stuffed sea lion a sly look and say, "Baby, you light up the sky with your pretty smile."

A beat of silence passes before I make a sound like a dying animal in my humiliation. I sink further into the seat, wishing for the ground to open up and swallow me. Thank god no one actually witnessed that train wreck.

"I'm hopeless!"

With a sigh I scoot up and type out *missing your smile.* I chew on my lip. It's not bad. Maybe an emoji? But then again, emojis change meaning by the day.

"Ugh. No."

I jab the delete button, erasing the message letter by letter. Frustration mixes with a heavy bubble in my chest. It swells until it chokes me. Before I finish deleting the text, I let my phone slip from my grip to plop in my lap, rubbing at my stinging eyes. The mascara I applied is probably smearing, but I don't care. I can't get this right, so why does it matter anymore?

An innocuous computerized *whoop* sound makes me freeze. Oh no. Oh no, no, no. *Shit.*

Mortification crashes through me as I scramble to flip my phone. The evidence of my clumsy mistake glares back at me, punching through my stomach and making it plummet faster than concrete shoes dragging someone to the bottom of the ocean.

Thea: Missing you [Photo attachment]

The message sent. There's no way to unsend texts, because

the technology gods like to laugh at us unfortunate souls who send embarrassing shit and regret it the minute it transmits. Maybe I'll get lucky and he won't see it.

How will I know, though? Wyatt never struck me as the type to leave his read receipts on. He could look at the text and I would never know.

"Fuck," I drag out in a harsh whisper.

What if Wyatt does open it and hates it? I already see three things wrong with my photo. I wish more than anything I could yank it back. Erase it from existence. Keep it tucked away in my secret folder.

I try to suck in a slow meditative breath through my nose like Maisy always instructs, but it catches in my throat while my pulse thunders in my ears.

A million thoughts scramble through my head. Pictures, too. *Thanks overactive imagination.* I see Wyatt with his long-time girlfriend when he reads my text. In my head, they laugh and I feel like the world's biggest idiot.

Squeezing my phone with sweaty palms, I search the internet, scanning articles and results with a jittery focus.

Does the throbbing-prickly sensation in my palms mean I'm experiencing an adrenaline surge?

How do I unsend a text message?

Can I delete a photo from someone else's phone before they see it?

In the middle of my fruitless searching, a notification banner pops up at the top of my screen for a few seconds before disappearing. Wave emojis bracket his name.

My heart stops.

He texted back.

TWO
CONNOR

My life is great from the outside. I'm the life of every party.

Until I'm forced to return home and face reality.

After dumping the bag of soccer balls from practice in the garage, I head for the kitchen. There's nothing good in the fridge when I raid it, but I snag a can of Coke. I need it after that practice and I'll likely be up late tonight.

"Connor," Dad acknowledges as he strolls past me, pausing to check his reflection in the microwave. "How was practice? The team shaping up to have a good year?"

I grunt in response, narrowing my eyes when I pick up a whiff of his cologne. It's not his usual, this one something heavier on the musky notes. My grip tightens on the can in my hand and I blow out a sharp breath, eyeing him up and down.

Dad's salt and pepper hair is slicked back and he has on a new tie, which he straightens in the murky reflection. I roll my eyes and turn my back on his stupid primping. If he's given up, he doesn't need to make it so fucking obvious.

A faint giggle drifts from the second floor hall, followed by a deep murmur.

My brows pinch together and I drag a hand through my hair, digging blunt nails into my scalp.

This family is such a fucked up nightmare.

Then again, who am I to judge my father when Mom does nothing to hide what she's doing either?

A year and a half of this shit and it still feels like the first time I walked in and found her on the kitchen counter with her campaign manager's pale ass pumping between her legs. My stomach rolls at the memory, the traumatic image permanently burned into my brain. At least back then she kept it a discreet secret. Now Damien eats dinner with us and spends almost every night in my mother's bed. Everyone on the block waves at our dear *family friend* when he comes around.

It makes me sick.

"Going to bed. Have a good night, Dad."

"Oh, Connor, don't forget." Dad gestures toward Mom's insane anal retentive calendar on the wall. Well, her personal assistant is the micro manager, I suppose, but Mom's no better. She trains her people well, and the rest of the world falls in line or faces the wrath of a socialite who fancies herself a self-made political woman. Dad peers over his shoulder. "Appointment tomorrow. Meet me in my office. I have a morning budget meeting with the school board, but I'll still be able to take you."

My lip curls. I cover it with a deep gulp of soda.

"Never forget." With a tight smile, I wave my phone, where

the calendar reminder Mom's assistant programmed will go off soon. "Night."

I don't hang around for an answer before going up to my room and slamming the door behind me.

My athletic bag gets tossed in the corner as I cross over to my desk by the window, booting up my computer. I change into sweatpants and a t-shirt.

The quiet hum of my custom built tower and the glow of my double monitors sets my mind at ease. Soccer is fun to obsess over and keeps me in killer shape, but this right here is my real ticket to leaving my parents before they can leave me in the dust like they seem hell-bent on achieving this year once Mom's re-election campaign is over.

They're throwing everything about our family away, including me.

Fuck 'em. I don't need them if they don't want me. The trust fund granddad set up for me isn't accessible until I turn twenty-one, so I have an insurance plan in the meantime.

I won't rely on anyone. The only person I can trust to look out for number one is myself.

While the computer powers through the loading sequence at top speeds, I set my Coke down, open the desk drawer to retrieve my stash, then drop into the high-back orange and black gamer chair. The wooden box has a design on the lid of a trippy night sky burned into the grain that I thought was sick as hell when I was fifteen and a bit of a dweeb. Now I think it's kind of lame. Whatever, it keeps my bud dank.

Mom got all pissy when she found my old stash jar. We live an hour from Denver for fuck's sake, yet she still has a stick up her ass about smoking as if she wasn't sneaking into granddad's conservatory to get away from boring society parties doing the same thing when she was my age. I found her stale leftovers out there when I was exploring the estate during brunch years ago. I know what's up.

Smirking, I hold up a rolled joint. "Hello, beautiful."

The first puff after lighting up has me relaxing back in the chair, hooking an arm over the headrest as I hold the smoke in my lungs for a long beat before exhaling, sending it curling overhead. I take another hit and close my eyes, humming in relief. This is what I needed to unwind.

When my limbs tingle pleasantly and the edge of stress I carried throughout the day ebbs away, I get down to business. The joint dangles between my lips as my fingers fly across the keyboard. I run through my normal checks—bitcoin investments, skim a few Reddit threads, and a social media sweep for anything unsuspecting idiots dump online and later delete that I can save as receipts when I need to put them in their place.

An automated web crawler script I run when I'm not at the computer hasn't turned up much today, so I also do a manual scan to hunt down anything the script missed.

The corner of my mouth lifts when I come across one of the Coyote Girls on the cheerleading squad. Kamile, I recall, picturing last weekend when she drunkenly explained she was *kammy with a K* as she straddled my lap, trying to get with me at a boat party on Silver Lake. In the Facebook photo, she's posing with two teammates with a bright smile, but a telltale dusting of white powder by the corner of her nose means she'll be deleting this within the hour once someone points it out.

It's not powdered sugar.

Don't people know by now? The internet is forever.

Screenshot.

I pull up the program I coded myself to keep track of the dirty little secrets I collect. Maybe the encrypted dossiers are serial killer levels of detailed, but I'm not the king of blackmail because I half-ass it with word-of-mouth rumors. That's child's play. No, I keep extensive proof to back it all up. Every skeleton in the closet, every corrupt truth, I keep it all.

With a few keystrokes, I've made a new file for Kamile, populating it with notes on her extracurriculars, her GPA, and the screenshot with the direct URL address. She can buy me out of using it against her, but it will cost a steep amount. Doesn't mean I delete what I find. Knowledge is power and all that. Mine's backed up twice and protected by my secure protocols to ensure I'm the one holding all the cards.

"Tsk, tsk, Kammy. The hard stuff isn't worth it if it fucks with your future. Keep it herbal, girl. And this side of legal if you're going to post evidence of being a bit of a bad girl." As I'm doing a low-level search of the city for her name, a LinkedIn article pulls up for her mom, profiling the high-end rehab resort she heads in Ridgeview catering to celebrities and trust fund fuckups. A snort shakes my shoulders. "What will your mommy say?"

I knock back the last of my Coke and ash my joint in the empty can.

It's fear of what I know that keeps people on my good side. Not just the students at school, but the teachers, too. Hell, I even have a profile on Holden Landry's dad, Ridgeview's chief of police, and the first entry I ever put in my black book of information.

This all started when I was turning seventeen. I wanted to figure out how I wound up with a slap on the wrist after getting arrested on serious assault charges with witnesses. When I uncovered the truth, I needed to know more, until it shaped me into who I am now—obsessed with collecting everyone's secrets and lies. It's almost a compulsion at this point, something I can't turn off.

No one is real. No one is genuinely who they present themselves as. Everyone has something to hide.

The webs are spun all over this town, from my parents' affairs and what they did to keep me out of trouble to the deeper corruptions infecting the picturesque town nestled in the Rockies.

For every truth, there are two lies. And I'm the keeper of it all.

Aren't you proud of what you've turned me into, Mom and Dad?

I huff out a scratchy, deadpan laugh. A bitter aftertaste sits on my tongue at the thought. I take a deep puff on the joint to wash it away in a haze of tangy smoke.

What a twisted kingdom I've built for myself.

At my elbow, the phone screen lights up, the vibration buzzing against the desk. I let my attention flick to read the notification for a fraction of a second, more interested in finishing what I'm doing.

Reminder: *Anger Management Appointment; Doctor Levitt - Tomorrow, 11am.*

"Yeah, I fucking knew that," I grumble.

The corners of my mouth tug down as I grab my phone, intent on flipping it over. I don't need the reminder that I have court-mandated therapy—or why what happened was covered up, and I ended up with a shrink instead of in juvie for assault charges that magically disappeared. That magic being dirty hush money to grease the wheels and bribe the police chief. If I could get out of going, I would've figured out how to do that by now. Court-ordered makes it damn near impossible to escape. Faking it with Doctor Levitt gets me by.

Before I slam my phone face down on the desk, I get a new text. Assuming it's my boy Devlin bitching about sitting alone in his big ass house in the mountains in a roundabout way without saying how lonely he is, I swipe it open without looking. I've already got the perfect GIF to send that will cheer the mopey bastard up before I invite myself over.

It's not Devlin.

The tip of the joint burns down as I tap on the photo to see it full size.

My brows hike up in appreciation of the fine as fuck body this chick has. *Damn, baby.*

Her face is cropped, but I focus on the sexy little smile —*pink* glossy lips, fuck me—and take in the perfect tits practically spilling out of the little number she's got on. What is that, a one-piece nightie? Who knows, but it has lace and highlights every one of her curves.

My hands flex, the desire to grab those hips shooting through me. They look perfect for my hands to grip as I pound into her.

The number isn't one I recognize, but who cares? It doesn't matter if I deleted this chick's number. She's texting me about missing me and I sure as fuck am down to play with her to take my mind off the shit I'm dealing with.

I take one last hit of the joint before putting it out to finish later. Heat coils in my groin, my dick tenting my sweatpants while I admire the babe in the hot little selfie. Blowing out the smoke, I drop my knees open, grinding my semi against the heel of my palm and mumble, "Shit, girl. Wish you were here with that dime body to take care of what you started in person."

There's a birthmark on her thigh, where the material rides up. I tilt my head, tracing my upper lip with my thumb in fascination. It's shaped like a sun.

Too many urges and scenarios run through my head at once, each better than the last. I could call her up and get her ass here now—I bet it will look amazing bouncing on my cock. But first I want to have some fun with the mystery texter.

As I get up and move to the bed, I dip my hand inside my sweats to pump my cock, dropping my head back and groaning with my eyes hooded. She's got me raring to go from one selfie, even with my buzz. Weed dick won't hold me back from enjoying myself with this chick.

I settle on the bed with my legs spread enough to pull the material of my pants tighter, outlining my erection. After clicking on the lamp on the nightstand, flipping up my shirt, and tugging the waistband low enough to show off that I'm trimmed, I rest my hand on my stomach and snap a photo to respond with.

A lopsided smile tugs at the corner of my mouth as I fire off my response.

Tonight just got a lot better.

THREE
THEA

The air feels as if it's been sucked from the room. Or maybe that's the effect of forgetting to breathe while staring at the super sexy photo Wyatt texted in response. My prior worries have flown out the window as I melt into the floral print armchair, eyes locked on the photo like I'm in danger of missing out on his delicious six-pack.

He texted back.

He. Texted. Back.

"Oh my flipping god." The words come out as a strained whisper.

A muffled squeal ekes out of me as I remember to drag in a

huge gasp of air at last, before I pass out like a total basket case. Mark me down on the list of things that faint from overstimulation right below goats and the sweet dog in a viral video I watched from The Dodo who lives with a benign neurological condition.

My mind is the embodiment of the exclamation point on repeat. Several of them. A whole keysmashed parade of exclamation points.

Because Wyatt didn't just reply with an emoji or say he missed me, too.

Nope. Freaking *nope!* Containing the grin on the brink of breaking free is next to impossible. I should text Maisy and spill the good news. *Maise, your girl just successfully flirted and the world didn't die of embarrassment!*

I drop my phone in my lap and hide my face behind my hands, wriggling as I happy dance in place. The rollercoaster of emotions took me from the pits of anxiety and depression to clean off the track, launched into the sky by my elation that the boy I like responded. I can't resist scooping the phone back up and viewing the picture full-screen, biting my lip.

He's reclined on a bed with dark gray sheets, his green t-shirt rucked up to show off his abs and v muscle, his body lean and cut by athleticism. One hand is splayed low on his stomach, toying with his waistband, where I can see the outline of his erection—*and* his trimmed pubes catching the dim light. I swallow thickly. Wyatt's face is mostly cropped out by the angle, but I can still appreciate his jaw line and his playful smirk.

It sends an excited flutter through my belly as I picture his thumb stroking back and forth along the edge of his sweatpants before sliding under to squeeze himself.

Is he turned on because of the photo I sent? I can't know for sure without asking outright, but it's giving me a hell of a boost to think it's true.

The picture has me flustered, my cheeks engulfed in warmth while I wrestle against the urge to look away. Wyatt is a hot lifeguard who owned every one of my fantasies at the summer retreat, but this has my mouth watering on an all new level. The energetic *damn boy* sound clip from TikTok is going off in my head on repeat and it ain't wrong.

My gaze sweeps over his perfect body. He looks like he should grace the covers of magazines. It's not quite how I remember him by the lake, but maybe my memories are blinded by his beaming, boyish smile. He could have been hitting the gym a little harder since I last saw him.

Before I can spend more time dwelling on my memory versus the photo, a new text comes in, making me jump when the phone vibrates in my hand.

Wyatt: Still there, baby?

My eyes widen. *Baby?* A giddy thrill zips down my spine. If I had known it would be this easy to show him how I felt, I would have done this at the beginning of the summer.

"Curse you past Thea." I scold myself in a hush so Mom doesn't come snooping on my business. She thinks I'm studying before bed. "See what happens when you bravely squeeze the day!"

Well, seize the day. But I like my poster with bright citrus fruit and the pun version better. It's more colorful.

I'm still formulating the best way to respond when he sends another text.

Wyatt: Come on, sweetness. Don't show me yours and then get all shy on me when I return the favor.

Wyatt: You got me all warmed up. Are you going to leave me hanging like this? [Photo attachment]

Heat floods my cheeks again. He's grinning now, cocky and confident, and has a hand shoved down his pants. It's blatant and enticingly illicit, sending my heart rate into overdrive. Most of his face is still cropped out to give me a show.

What am I supposed to do now?

He asked a question. So should I respond or do I send another photo? He upped the ante by snapping a pic with his hand on his junk.

I scan myself, debating the most attractive way to match him. Rompers aren't exactly designed for easy access. I could go up the pant leg, I guess, or maybe dropping the straps off my shoulders, but then does it look like I'm too naked? I mean, yes, I would be tits out and everything, though I guess that's kind of the point. It's not like I have anything on under this.

The logistics twist my brain in circles for a few minutes.

I only planned as far as taking and sending the selfie. There was no strategy for what to do next if he answered.

My attention drifts back out the window where Connor Bishop's bedroom light is dimmer, but still on at the house next door. I bet he does this sort of thing all the time with the amount of girls always falling over themselves to flirt with him. An image of him pops into my head from the first day of school, where a pretty girl from the dance squad sat on his lap all through lunch, blushing every time he whispered in her ear. Yeah, with those full lips tilted in a smug curve? He's totally a pro at this stuff.

Maybe I should take a page from him to figure out how to be sexy while texting Wyatt.

A breathy laugh huffs from my lips while I drop my head back against the armchair. "Yeah right."

I can't match Connor for confidence, but W.W.S.F.G.D.? Because Secret Folder Girl—the version of myself I hide away on my phone's camera roll? She'd totally have this situation on lock.

Somewhere deep down, that girl is me.

"I can do this." Sucking in a breath, I nod.

This time it's live instead of when I last tried to flirt with pictures, where I could gather my confidence and walk away when it became too much to email back. But that was years ago now. It wasn't even—

Shaking my head, I push those dark memories aside. I can't let what happened then cloud my thoughts every time I think about other guys. My throat is tight when I swallow. Will it always be like this, the secret I carry following me and tainting every romantic experience?

"No," I say firmly, almost growling the denial.

Determined to get this right, I pop up from the chair and switch to the bed. I move my seal plushie out of the way, stuffing it behind the pillows so Wyatt won't see it and tease me. I'm playing around with different positions, slipping one of the romper straps so it drapes off my shoulder without fully popping a nipple out when my phone pings.

Wyatt: Are you being a bad girl, getting off thinking about me if I was there with you? I'm waiting to see what else you've got. Don't finish without me. Show me how you're touching yourself.

Thea: I wasn't!

Crap. I replied before I could think about whether or not it was protocol. Damn my lack of filter when I get going.

Wyatt: [smirk emoji] You weren't? Are you a good girl, then? Waiting for me to tell you how to make it feel good?

God. Heat pulses between my legs. My thumbs hover over the keyboard for a moment as I gather the courage to reply.

Thea: What would you do if you were here?

Wyatt sends another picture, this one a close up of his parted lips with his tongue licking across the bottom one.

Wyatt: First I'd want to lick that hot little birthmark on your thigh. Anyone ever told you it looks like a sun? I love the taste of sunshine.

I glance at my leg. Huh. I guess so.

It's not what I expected him to say and I tip my chin up, telling him as much.

Thea: Not a kiss on the lips?

The conversation goes quiet for a minute, then he sends a recorded voice clip. Just when I adjust to his pace, he changes it up on me. Holding my breath, I tap play.

"Oh, sunshine. You want me to kiss that sweet little mouth? Mm, I don't know if you could handle it." His deep, raspy chuckle makes my clit throb as his voice rolls over me. *"If that's what you want, I'd kiss you all over...starting with that fucking sexy birthmark."*

I've never heard him sound like this, so in charge and aware of exactly what effect his voice has on me. I'm more used to his kind smiles and enthusiastic laugh. There's a rustle and a faint groan. Is he—? I think he is.

He's totally stroking his dick while recording what he said.

It makes me warm all over, my skin electrified and sensitive to the ruffled material of my purple bedspread. My thighs squeeze together to get some relief from the sensual desire he stirs in me. I glance at the door to make sure it's still locked. Having Mom walk in without knocking right now would suck.

Thea: Then what would you do?

Wyatt: I'd have to touch those tits next. Stroke them nice and light until your nipples are aching from how tight they pucker.

I'm a little disappointed I don't get to hear these words in his voice, but what he says gets me hot anyway. Unconsciously, I've begun dragging my nails over the tops of my breasts, teasing the edge of the delicate lace lining the romper. My nipples demand attention, but I hold out, waiting to see what else he'd do.

Wyatt: Bet those nipples are pretty and pink. They hard for me, baby?

Thea: Yes. I need you to touch them.

Another photo comes through and I suck in a sharp breath. He pulled down his sweatpants just enough to reveal the base of his erection. His thumb and finger are curled around it. I lick my lips and shift around, debating grabbing a pillow to shove between my legs.

Thea: Would you kiss them next?

Wyatt: Yes. Pull down your top so I can suck on them. I'm going to bite them until you cry out.

Releasing a strained whimper, I peel off the thin straps and gasp when the air hits my bare skin. My nipples are pebbled, almost throbbing from how turned on I am. I palm my breast with one hand, pinching each nipple to simulate being bitten. My back arches and my clit aches with need. I almost drop the phone from my other hand.

Wyatt: Tell me how it feels.

A whine gets stuck in my throat while I fumble the phone, my typing getting sloppy as I keep rolling my tingling nipples beneath my palm to feel the tiny electric jolts it sends to my core. I wish he was here, laying next to me so I could smell him, feel his smile against my skin.

My stomach flips when he sends another recorded text.

"Fuck, baby. Can't even type straight, huh? You're so sexy." His voice is a hoarse growl over the faint slap of skin. He's jerking himself off harder. *"Show me."*

My heart thuds as I rub my thighs together to alleviate the tight coil of tension he's worked me into.

Thea: What?

His response is immediate.

Wyatt: Show me how I'm touching you, baby. I need to see you. Take a pic to prove you're being good and doing what I'm saying.

I sink my teeth into my lip. Can I do that?

This all feels so good, way better than I've ever made myself feel when I've touched myself beneath the sheets in the dark. I don't just mean physically, either. Talking to him was scary at first, but it's getting easier once it's clear he isn't waiting to laugh at me.

It's like he sees me, the real me from my secret folder.

My confidence rises and I take a picture of my tits squeezed between my arms, one hand pinching a nipple as my lips part on a gasp. The material of my romper bunches around my waist and the flush in my cheeks is visible.

After I send it, he replies with a recorded text that's a long groan. It takes another minute for him to respond.

Wyatt: Good girl. So good. Now, slide those fingers between those lips and suck them real good.

Thea: Like this? [Photo attachment]

My lips are wrapped around two fingers to the second knuckle, puckered and plump. The way I angled the photo, I left more of my bare tits in the frame than my face and the dirty result drives my confidence higher. I like how wanton I appear.

Wyatt: Holy fuck. Yes, like that. Fuck.

Thea: What next? Tell me how to make myself feel good for you.

Wyatt: Mm yeah, that's good, baby. You're killing me, you sexy as fuck little minx. Need those lips on my cock.

The mental image pulls another gasp from me. I push my fingers back into my mouth, imagining they're bigger and take another photo for him. This time when he replies, I get a dick pic, seeing proof of the effect I have on him. It's shiny, like he spit in his palm or keeps a bottle of lube handy. Pleasure coils deep in my chest because I did that to him, made him hard, made him masturbate to thoughts of being with me. I bite my lip around the shy smile curving my mouth.

Thea: So hot. You going to put it in me?

For a second, I squirm through a frisson of embarrassment. Is that good enough dirty talk? Should I have said cock or something?

The momentary worry disappears when his response comes through.

Wyatt: Fuck yes. So hard for you. Going to fuck your brains out, sweetness. Your fingers nice and wet? They're my tongue. Touch your clit, nice long strokes so you know exactly how I'm tasting you.

My chest caves with my sharp breath. I follow his directions, wriggling out of my romper and kicking the soft material from my ankles. I lay there for a moment, feeling the cool air of my bedroom on my nude body. The throbbing between my thighs is so heady that I don't think I'll last long once I start rubbing my clit. I'm ready to burst from the oversensitivity he's caused with our sexting.

Dragging my fingertips down my belly and stroking my

mound, I let every sensation wash over me. My head tips back when I slide my fingers between my legs and do as Wyatt said, imagining his tongue licking my pussy. Shit, it feels amazing.

I spread my legs wider, getting into it. I've never done it like this, above my covers, the lights on, with total abandon. The world could explode around me, but my focus would only be on my body, on the pleasure I feel touching myself while pretending it's him.

Growing bolder, I bring my phone close and hold down the record audio button, capturing the breathy moans as I rub my clit.

"Wyatt," I whimper. "Feels so good. I'm close."

My thumb slips off the button and I pause long enough to send it before refocusing on what my body demands. The pleasure crests higher. My hips rock as I seek out my orgasm.

Wyatt hasn't said anything for a few minutes, but my brain is so clouded with the fog of touching myself that it takes me a while to notice. Maybe he was close and feels the same as I do, needing to reach oblivion.

The phone pings again, so I could be wrong. Who cares, as long as I keep feeling like this. I press harder, rubbing my fingers in a tight circle over my sensitive clit.

Wyatt: I want more of those sinful sounds you're making. Show me how good it feels, baby. Is your sweet pussy wet for me?

I don't know if it's because I'm so close to coming that I could be convinced of anything, or that I'm flying high on the way this has all unfolded, but I don't feel any shame or nerves anymore. Raising the phone with a wicked little grin, I get a good angle from above of my fingers dipped between my legs, knees drawn together. Just as I fire it off, the hot coil in my core intensifies.

"Ah!"

I drop my head back into the pillows while I stroke my fingers over my folds to gather some of the slickness coating my labia and thighs, gliding my fingers back over my clit. The waves crash over me, the intensity of the orgasm making me clench on the emptiness I wish were full of Wyatt's dick right now as I tremble. It feels incredible, definitely the best orgasm I've ever experienced.

Elation spirals through me, mingling with the aftershocks of pleasure skating over my skin, and I smile at the ceiling, stretching my arms overhead.

The abandoned phone buzzes on the bedspread with a new message. I roll onto my side and rub my thighs together lazily as I reach for it, enjoying the lasting effects of sensitivity and how wet I feel.

I nearly drop the phone with a surprised yelp. Wyatt upped the ante again with a Boomerang. The animated image plays when I open it and my mouth drops open as it repeats. Oh my god. I watch it four times, fascinated and turned on.

In the Boomerang clip he fists his cock with fast strokes and at the last couple of seconds before it starts over, come spills over his fingers.

Wyatt: Thanks babe [wink emoji]

I debate what to say next. Is there something universal that says thanks for the orgasm via text message? And can we set up a time to do it again?

Boldly, I lounge naked instead of getting up to get dressed as fast as possible. The confidence lingers. I roll onto my back and cross one leg over the other, hoping he'll say something first since he seems to be well-versed in this sort of thing.

My face lights up when he does reply shortly after the last of the afterglow fades.

Wyatt: Let me see how you look after you've come.

After everything we did tonight, this one feels easy now. I fluff my hair and recline against my pillows, tilting my face for a cute picture. There's a glow of life in my flushed cheeks and my sparkling eyes. It's one of the very rare times I like how I look in a photo on the first take.

Thea: Goodnight [heart emoji] [Photo attachment]

"Thea!"

A knock at my door makes my heart skip about eighty beats. My life force threatens to leave my body. I can feel the pull for it to float out of my mouth and drift through my ceiling. Poetic that I'd die young, sated, and totally freaking naked.

Mom jiggles the handle and knocks again. "Why is your door locked?"

"One sec, Mom! I'm changing for bed."

I shove my phone under my pillow and kick my romper under the bed. After hurrying into a pair of pink flannel sleep pants and a loose t-shirt sitting on my hamper, I check the mirror and hope she can't tell.

Unlocking the door, I peek through the crack. "Did you need anything?"

"Just wanted to make sure you remembered to study for your math test."

Mom crosses her arms, scrutinizing me in that silent motherly way that feels as if she's eating me alive. I shift on my feet, keeping my expression blank by sheer force of will. *Project calmness and she won't demand to come inspect the room.* Her gaze flicks over my shoulder, peering into what little I allow her to see of my room with me blocking the door.

"Of course I studied for it. I'm all done for the night," I assure her. Crap, is my voice still a little breathy? I clear my throat. "Anyway, goodnight."

I give her a kiss on the cheek and scurry back into my room, diving beneath the covers. A giggle bubbles up in my chest and I hide it in my stuffed sea lion when I fish him out.

Tonight was amazing.

FOUR

CONNOR

I'm either still lightheaded from smoking weed and jerking off, or going batshit fucking crazy because the photo my hot little mystery texter sent looks way too familiar. She's leaning back against a pile of purple pillows that are frilly, or some other girly shit, with auburn curls spilling around her beautiful face. The look she's giving me is...fuck, it makes me want to get off with her again.

Something about her prods at me as I languor in my post-orgasm haze with one arm tucked behind my head, feeling really damn good.

"Wait."

I sit the fuck up, dick still out and everything. Because I do know those blue-green doe eyes. Normally they're sweeping over me with sharp sparks of scorn when I tease her about the frumpy ass sweaters she wraps herself in. Not just scorn, but judgment, just like her nosy bitch of a mother.

"Well, shit." I drag the word out, followed by a short laugh of disbelief as I stare at the girl I've only ever known as my nerdy neighbor, Thea Kennedy.

A shy girl at school I love to torment just to watch her blush.

The same sexy as fuck little minx I just had an awesome sext jerk off session with.

I trace a finger over my lips and glance at my window. Her bedroom faces mine. I've caught her peeking once or twice while I changed, thinking those sheer curtains hide her. Might've even put on a bit of a show for her once I knew she liked to watch. Blinds are for pussies.

Who knew under those lumpy, shapeless sweaters in every color of the rainbow, she hides a body like that, with those luscious, seductive curves? It really is the quiet ones that are the biggest surprise.

I scroll back through our messages to admire the nudes and smirk. Her voice recording is still there, because she's a naïve thing that doesn't have them set to expire after listening. How cute. Between the photos and the recording, I could have an entire field day blackmailing her to do whatever I wanted.

The way she responded to me, obeyed me, makes it a strong temptation. My best friend Devlin would probably do it in a heartbeat, but he's a dark and twisted fucker. I maintain a rep that I could implode lives on a whim, when really I prefer to have a reason to destroy someone with the dirt I keep on people.

As I press the replay button, her breathless voice fills my room again.

"*Wyatt*," Thea whimpers, innocent and sinful all at once. Her soft tone stirs my cock for another round. "*Feels so good. I'm close.*"

It had thrown me the first time I heard it, long enough to stop stroking my dick. She'd called out another man's name and a righteous bout of jealousy surged through me. I'd never been possessive over my hookups, but something about her in that moment made me want to hear *my* name falling from those plump pink glossy lips before she came.

Now things click into place with the blood flow returning to my brain. This is all a case of mistaken identity. She texted the wrong number. Whoever this Wyatt guy is, he's not me. And if I have anything to say about it, he won't ever get to hear Thea moaning his name like that.

The games I play with her at school are out of petty boredom. I need more of this side of Thea. Things just got a lot more interesting.

The next time she makes those sounds, it'll be because I drew them out of her.

My mouth curves in a mean smirk. I bet it will piss off her neighborhood busybody mother if she ever finds out her shy, mousy little daughter is naughty under those good grades and oversized granny sweaters. It's time for some revenge for what that woman did, sticking her nose where it didn't belong.

If I'm going to do this, I have to be strategic. I can't reveal myself yet. It will end this game too soon. Thea is the shy type who likes to get freaky in secret. She'll piss her pants and take off running if I come at this too hard.

No, I have to take it slow and steady. Figure out my play and the next three possible moves ahead to find the right moment to unveil that it's been me all along.

For now, I save her number to my phone and take care of the dirty tissues I dumped on the floor after cleaning myself up.

Thea doesn't know it yet, but with one racy selfie, she stepped into my world.

FIVE
CONNOR

By the next week, I've settled into a new routine. Wake up, text the little mouse that lives next door, take care of my morning wood with help from photos of Thea's sleepy eyes sparkling with mischief, shower for school, text her again—and so on throughout the day until I'm coming before bed to the image of Thea's perfect tits. The best part of the game is passing Thea in the halls or in classes we share, completely unaware I know how she sounds when she's about to come.

I've been keeping up the pretense that I'm this Wyatt guy she believes she's messaging.

On Tuesday, the soccer team has a practice scrimmage after school. Half of us play positions to cover one team, and the rest play against us. We're tied 1-1, but we're coming up on the end of the game.

There's nothing like the feeling of driving the ball toward the goal, the sweet grass-scented breeze in your hair, every nerve ending fizzling with energy. I love playing soccer. Always have, since my dad first put a ball in front of me.

My boy Devlin only has his head half in the game. I've pulled him up on it as captain once, but he keeps watching the girls track team. More specifically, the school's charity case sitting nearby like she's being subtle. Devlin got her kicked off the team because she pissed him off. Those two are bound to be fucking by the end of the year if they aren't yet.

"Dev!" I shout, dribbling the ball while avoiding two mid-fielders. "You better quit making moon eyes at Davis when I make this pass."

I check my periphery for him. One guy playing against us tries to break my footwork, but Devlin appears out of nowhere, like the lightning-quick devil I know, and picks up the pass I send him.

Satisfied laughter bubbles from my chest as Devlin's attack turns merciless, whipping past the other team's defenders and punting the ball with insane speed. It's how he got his nick-name, the dark devil of Silver Lake. Together we're an unstoppable pair. The ball becomes a blur, cutting through the air and sailing past their goalie's outstretched hands as he dives for the save.

Devlin turns back to me, a sharp, wicked smirk in place. He jogs to my side at a lazy pace. I shake my head, grinning at my best friend. He's an asshole, but I love him. We get each other in a way the rest of the superficial idiots at this school don't.

"We could've cinched that goal faster if you hadn't been all goo-goo eyes for Davis. I told you last year, bro, you've got to just do her already, get your obsession out of your system." I hook an arm around Devlin's neck and rub my knuckles into his scalp. "Watching you two eye-fuck at lunch is not on my agenda for a second year in a row."

"Fuck off." Devlin shrugs my arm off. "I wouldn't touch Davis' cunt if it were the last one in the world."

I bark out another laugh. "Even you don't have that much self control. Pussy is pussy. You'd cave eventually."

Devlin rolls his eyes. "Whatever, prick. If you're so sure, you go fuck her."

"Nah. You called dibs last year." I hold up three fingers in a Boy Scout salute and solemnly intone, "Bro code is sacred."

I get smacked upside the head for being a good friend. Dick.

"All right, guys," I call. Sticking my fingers in my mouth, I whistle for the team to circle up on center field. They hustle over, wiping sweat from their brows with their practice jerseys. "Trent, you need to dig harder when the ball comes to our backs. Don't slack because it's practice, you lazy shit. Bad habits in practice make for bad habits in real games."

Trent snorts and flips me off while Sean, our other center-back, shoves him with a smirk.

"First official game of the season on Friday. No partying the night before. I don't want to hear any excuses—if I can manage, so can you." I point at a few of the guys who are hard-up to get through the week without getting wild. A few murmurs of assent filter through the team. "Aight. Go shower off the stink, you disgusting fuckers."

The team trickles toward the locker room entrance at the back of the school. Our coach waits for me to check in with him by the sidelines. He lets me run things since I made varsity captain last year, but offers insightful pointers I can't see when I'm playing the game.

Devlin hangs around, fiddling with his phone while I finish

up going over the schedule with the coach. Something distracted him today. Whatever it is, it's been bugging him since yesterday. Maybe longer. He was weird over the weekend —weirder than usual. I'm used to most of his quirky shit after years of friendship, like his penchant for reading boring ass psychology books.

It was easier to weather Devlin's brooding moods when his older cousin was around. Lucas Saint was king of this school last year, a grade ahead of us and this town's golden boy with a golden arm. Too bad he pissed all that talent away to go to art school with his girlfriend.

With Lucas at college, Silver Lake High School belongs to Devlin and me. It's our senior year. He's our Devil Boy with his black hair, mischievous smile, and a wily streak the size of Texas. We're the perfect match of deviants.

"What time does it start tonight?" Devlin asks.

The corner of my mouth lifts. The Ridgeview police chief's son, Holden Landry, is organizing a fight ring. Because I have a copy of a positive drug test that would end Landry's football dreams along with footage of him getting blitzed at a boat party over the summer, Devlin and I are getting a thirty percent cut of tonight's winnings.

This is how things operate with us in charge.

"He's taking bets until seven. Pick me up at nine?" I grab the bag of soccer balls and sling it over my shoulder as we walk to the locker rooms. Devlin is distracted by his phone again, obsessively checking his messages. "I'll be at the usual spot down the block."

"You're like a junior high chick, the way you sneak out," Devlin says absently.

"You know what my mom is like. Most of the time I wish someone would see me sneak out and run a story in the gossip column." I gesture with my hands to highlight a headline. "I can see it now, Chairwoman Bishop's re-election campaign overshadowed by delinquent son." A wistful sigh blows past my lips and I elbow Devlin. "It would solve so many of my problems."

"At least she's around."

I bite back a reply. Devlin's parents duck out on him pretty often. I haven't seen them in three or four years.

Clapping my hand around his shoulder, I squeeze him closer in a half-hug. "Whatever. Tonight's going to be awesome."

The black shadow that passed over Devlin's features clears, replaced by a devious gleam in his dark gaze.

The scent of weed and beer tinges the night air. It's cooler than it was earlier now that the sun has gone down. September is still warm as hell during the day, but as soon as it's nightfall the mountain air turns frigid.

A joint dangles from my lips as Devlin and I move through the crowd, bumping fists with people here and there. A dirty bass line plays from a wireless speaker, the distorted sound flooding the woods at the edge of the abandoned quarry off Blackhawk Road. After it closed it was filled in. Now all that remains is a gravel lot at the base of the mountain. A few Coyote Girls, townies, and chicks from the two public schools dance on truck beds in skintight ripped jeans and cowgirl boots. Laughter spills through the night and a sense of wild debauchery threads through everyone's energy.

It's the perfect place for illicit partying in Ridgeview, the access road rarely used since the new highway was built. The only people that come through hit it up during the day for the old hiking trail that heads up into the Rockies.

I scan the crowd for Landry. Everyone is getting rowdy before the fights start. I've got something on almost every person here in my files, from my soccer teammates to the people who run in my crowd. Everyone is fair game. It's become an ingrained habit, one I don't plan on quitting anytime soon.

Landry is hanging by a classy white Jeep, thumbing through a wad of cash with a guy I don't know while he flirts with the hot girl sitting on the hood. Maybe he's a townie, but Landry hands him the cash, so he must run with him. He looks like an odd match to Landry, a punk with a leather jacket, messy dark hair, and a mean glint in his eyes when they land on me. I have no idea how Silver Lake's starting quarterback and this guy could have crossed paths.

I leave Devlin with the guys and head for the Jeep. The girl Landry's talking to lets her knees fall open and he steps between them with a wolfish grin. I recognize her as a poli-sci post-grad who joined my mom's campaign staff over the summer.

"Did you close out the call for bets?" I ask as I lean against the Jeep. The campaign staffer's eyes go wide when they land on me. I wink at her and tap my nose. "What mommy dearest doesn't know, right?"

"Uh, yeah," she answers with a strained cough.

To be extra welcoming since this is the first I've seen her at an SLHS party, I offer my joint. She hesitates, then accepts it, taking two hits and grabbing Landry to shotgun the smoke into his mouth.

"Nice," I say.

Landry flips me off without breaking the kiss with the campaign staffer. His friend rolls his eyes and stalks off with a grunt.

Being discreet, I record a short video clip of them kissing to add to my blackmail collection. Papa Landry would blow his lid at the scandals his son is wracking up. What would be more interesting is if Landry's younger sister shed her good girl veneer and proved to be even naughtier. With that tight little yoga bod she has, I wouldn't mind seeing what sort of trouble she could get up to.

Cute as little Maisy Landry is, my mind drifts to Thea and those dime curves she keeps hidden under oversized clothes. I thumb into our message thread. The last text she sent to "Wyatt" was a selfie with a cake she baked after school. I didn't give a shit about the cake, more interested in the fact her hair was tied up in perky pigtails. Fucking *pigtails*. I work my jaw as a bolt of heat shoots to my groin.

A surge of cheers drowns out the music, drawing me from my thoughts. People move in droves from where the cars are parked in the gravel lot into the tree line. The headlights spill into a clearing through the trees. I guess the first fight is starting.

Devlin finds me and we head over together. He hands me a beer and lights up a cigarette. We join the crowd circled around two guys duking it out, grunting when their punches land.

Fight Club rules apply, bare knuckles and no shirts. A few guys are positioned around the clearing to deal with any idiot filming for the likes on social media. Landry's leather jacket friend is one of them, pushing a hand through his hair as he narrows his cold gaze on a couple of chicks taking selfies near us.

One of the fighters in the ring is on the student council at school, with string bean arms, cheeks already pink with exertion and they've barely begun. Thanks to my weekly summons from my dad to the school office before therapy, I also know Mr. Student Council was accused of peddling Adderall last week. He swings with gritted teeth and manages to clock his opponent in the chin. The other guy stumbles back a step to regroup, then comes in with a quick one-two jab to Student Council's weakly guarded center.

The underground fighting is about letting out aggression. The betting is fun, but hardly any of us need the money. Ridgeview is a town that hit it rich in the gold rush era and the sun's been shining down on us since.

Devlin snorts, the sound dark and amused as Student Council successfully takes down his larger opponent, using speed against strength to maneuver the force of gravity on his side. The bigger guy goes down and Student Council wails on him, blood staining his teeth from a split lip, pure murderous rage blazing in his eyes.

It's violent, unhinged, and fucking glorious.

Landry steps into the ring and blows on a whistle clenched between his teeth. Grabbing Student Council's wrist and wrenching it into the air, he barks, "Winner. Next challenger in the ring in two minutes, or you forfeit your buy-in."

The crowd shuffles, waiting for the next person to step forward. Once they do, another match starts. Student Council goes down in two hits, knocked out and sprawled in the dirt.

As the following fighter enters the clearing, my phone goes off in my back pocket. Devlin exchanges a curious glance with me as I step away from the crowd. The name on the screen has me grinding my teeth. *Mom.*

I debate not taking it, feeling a muscle jump in my cheek from how hard my jaw locks. If I ignore it, she'll only hound me once I get home. Big fat FML either way. What a pain in the ass.

"I've gotta take this. I'll be back," I tell Devlin before I jog away from the party. Lifting the phone to my ear, I answer, "What?"

"Is that any way to answer your mother, Connor?"

"I could've not answered," I say dismissively as I pass the cars where some people are still hanging out and talking, and head for the old storage building.

"Where are you? It sounded loud when you answered." The judgement is clear in her tone.

Rolling my eyes and scrubbing a palm over my face, I lean against the rusty corrugated metal siding, kicking at the weeds popping out of the gravel at my feet. "People from school. We're hanging out at a friend's house."

She hums on the line, uppity even in her non-verbal communication. That socialite upbringing always shines best when she's disappointed by whatever way I'm embarrassing her now.

I don't have all night for this. "What do you want?"

"Have you checked the schedule? Angela should have updated the mobile calendar. The children's hospital dinner benefit is coming up. This is your reminder that the entire family must be present. We have to show a united family front for the voters."

For the voters. I bring the phone away from my ear to scoff.

Everything she does is for her constituents. It's the only reason she wants me at this charity event and that dinner, all of these bullshit parties so she can trot out the happy family pony show. Meanwhile, that home-wrecker Damien sleeps in our house and makes Mom breakfast. He stupidly offered me coffee this morning and I threatened to dump the fresh pot over his head.

"Connor," Mom says on the line. I bring the phone back to my ear. *"We're almost there. We've worked this hard and all that's left is the finish line when elections come up. Understood?"*

"Roger." She can't see, but I give a sharp salute anyway.

Before she can add any other stipulations, I hang up and

stomp back through the parked cars to the clearing in the woods. Adrenaline and anger rush through my veins. My breathing has picked up and my vision shrinks around the edges, focused on the ring.

Devlin steps in my path. His expression tightens around his eyes when he takes me in. "You good?"

"My mom," I say.

It's all the explanation I need with him. His dark brows hike up and he stands aside. He knows how I get after a call with her. I strip out of my henley and toss it to him.

"Give me your phone, too."

I hand it over and spot Landry's friend edging toward me. Pointing at him, I say, "Nah uh, dude. You might run with Landry, but he's not in charge here."

The leather jacket punk looks to Holden for confirmation. Landry nods and jerks his head to the ring. His friend picks at random and kicks one of the fighters back into the crowd. Before he's done, I'm stepping in, mouth pulled in a jagged, wild curve.

I square up with the guy who entered after Student Council was KO'd. He's bigger than me, bulkier, but he's tired. He swings and I dodge, smirk stretching wider. A flash of worry crosses my opponent's face. He backs off a couple of steps, trying to lure me in. I don't take the obvious bait, instead waiting for him to come at me again. When he does, I pop him in the chin.

A fist comes against my forearm as I block his blow, but I make a mistake in my stance, giving a clean opening for the guy to punch my face. Shit, I don't even care if I bruise. Maybe I'll get real lucky and it'll last long enough to make me look extra good next to Mom for her stupid fucking campaign benefit.

I spit into the dirt and swipe my hand beneath my nose to catch the trickle of blood. It comes away bright red, smeared across my knuckles. A minor blood vessel injury, nothing serious. When I chuckle, the guy backs off again, glancing at Landry.

No one wants to fight crazy. It's different than angry. Unpredictable. Dangerous.

Come the fuck at me, bro.

I lift a hand and wave him back for more. "Come on, I won't bite."

"No biting," Landry's surly friend barks.

A sharp laugh punches from my gut. I gesture to Landry's friend, appealing to my opponent. "See, no biting. It's in the rules. Let's fucking go, big guy. Time to dance."

The match starts back up and I go hard, unleashing everything I've got until I can see the fear creeping into my opponent's wide eyes. We go long enough that every one of his punches result from desperation as the crowd screams and cheers. Their shouts are drowned out by the pounding pulse in my ears.

Sweet oblivion comes when I use my fists to channel the anger out. I'm the kind of fucked up monster that takes enjoyment in making the guy I'm fighting think I might actually kill him with my bare hands. It's not his fault I'm like this, I don't even see his face when I throw a punch. Every time I do, I'm right back to that afternoon I caught Mom and Damien and lost it.

My next hit clocks the guy across his red, swollen cheek and he goes down in a slump. Everyone erupts in a deafening ruckus of screams, celebrating another win. Landry stands off to my left at the edge of the clearing, hands propped on his hips. He's probably pissed I didn't mention wanting in on tonight, only blackmailed him into a cut of the winnings. If he'd known, he would have made a bigger killing.

I stand over my opponent, panting. He's out cold. Damn, I

wanted that to go longer. I glance up, scanning the crowd for the next challenger.

It takes almost the entire two minute allowance, but as the crowd grows restless, hungry for more brutality, someone else enters the clearing.

My mouth curves wickedly and I square up for the next round.

SIX
THEA

Sweat beads along my temples and makes the baby hairs falling from my messy bun curl against my skin, sticking to the back of my neck as I walk Constantine through the neighborhood. *Something Beautiful* by Tori Kelly plays in my earbuds as we amble along in the uncomfortable afternoon heat, the soulful girl power song helping me forget any self-consciousness for my outfit. It's too hot out to cover up, so I'm in high waist yoga leggings and a billowy boatneck crop top over a sports bra.

Luckily, the neighborhood is pretty quiet this time of day. It's shortly after school let out, and too early for people to be home from work, so no one will see me like this. It's just me, my chunky rottweiler, and the sprawling manicured lawns bordered by natural landscaping rather than fence lines to avoid interrupting the effect of money at work. I swipe my arm over my forehead and emit a tiny groan. Maybe I'll whip up homemade ice cream when we get back. Pumpkin ice cream sounds so good right now.

Constantine doesn't mind the heat, happily keeping pace at my side with his tongue lolling out. I laugh when he stops to sniff a garden bed, coming nose to nose with a fat bumble bee that bonks against his snout and sends him into a playful tumble in the grass.

"Oh, Con, you silly boy. Come on. It's too hot to stay out for our usual walk." I give his lead a tug and continue down the sidewalk. "When we get home, we're making ice cream. How's that sound?"

Constantine gives me the cutest head tilt, his black ears perked.

A jogger rounds the corner on the next block and my steps falter. Shirtless, abs and pecs glistening in the sunlight, Connor Bishop looks like a god amongst men. His light brown hair bounces with his effortless running form, his long legs powerful as he cuts his path. Everything about his aura says *confident, knows what he wants, and nothing's stopping him from getting it.* It's an alluring sight to behold, addictive to be around in school—it's no wonder everyone flocks to him. He's really hot, but I could never want him.

No matter how attractive he looks, especially now, running toward me in nothing but basketball shorts, it doesn't forgive how he's treated me the few times he's paid me any attention since we were kids.

I force myself to keep walking toward my house. Self-consciousness creeps back in.

Why are these streets so long? Why are our houses both in the middle? Maybe he'll reach his before me and I won't have to worry about interacting with him. It's not like he's noticed me much this year.

We're almost home free, but Connor catches my eye after I close out of the playlist on my phone once I reach my driveway. I freeze, arrested by the full force of his attention. It's weirdly commanding, without him telling me to wait I'm obeying. He gives me a once over that floods my cheeks with warmth. *Oh my god.*

Does he think I look weird? A crop top is all wrong for me, I knew it.

No.

That's not true. My inner critic can shove it. I have a body and I can dress it any way I want.

I bet Wyatt wouldn't think my outfit is strange. He appreciates me. I'm already picturing taking a naughty selfie later where I lose the sports bra and flash my boobs, holding the hem of the crop top up with my teeth.

Knowing there's at least one person out there who finds me beautiful just as I am gives me the strength I need to face Connor.

Constantine plops onto his haunches by my side, dragging me from being under Connor's controlling spell. His cool gray eyes flick to the dog for a second before flying back to meet my gaze.

"Um," I mumble, twisting the leash in my hands.

Connor takes AirPods from his ear and studies me again, slower this time, dragging his gaze down my body. "Were you looking at me, neighbor? Here? Or maybe here?"

As he taunts me, he smooths a hand over his pec, then down his torso, hooking his thumb in the waistband of his shorts. His knuckles are red and there's a bruise on his jaw. It makes him look more dangerously handsome.

Air catches in my throat when I inhale too sharply. I fling my hands in front of myself defensively. "I—no, I—"

"Relax." Connor's voice is as smooth as the curve of his smirking full lips. He rubs his chin and rakes his teeth over his lower lip. "There's no crime in it." Each brush of his eyes is like a brand as they sweep over my legs and back up, lingering on my chest.

My breaths come faster. It's hard to ignore him when he's making sure I can't look away. Those gray eyes have some kind of magic that keeps me rooted in place. This might be the closest I've ever been to him.

A raspy chuckle drops from his lips. "Look at you, turning red, little mouse. Are you blushing from the heat or—" He steps closer, leaning in, lips nearly brushing my cheek "—because you like what you see?"

I jerk my head back as my heart thuds from his proximity and the rich, earthy scent of his sweaty skin. He really enjoys the sound of his own voice. For a second, his voice almost sounds like Wyatt's, but I brush that aside. It's simply that he's mocking me with his flirty over-sexualization of everything.

"It's human nature to look. You know, with your dumpy clothes I never pictured you were hiding that underneath."

Connor gestures at my midsection, where my curves are on display. I suck in another sharp breath and narrow my eyes.

"Now, just what is that supposed to mean?"

He shrugs. "You should lose the bulky sweaters. They do nothing for you. About as much sex appeal as a bunch of grandmas playing bridge."

I open my mouth to tell him off for being such an ass, but our front door opens and Mom steps out, keeping to the shade behind the stacked stone columns. She lurks there, watching us. When I don't move, she crosses her arms.

"Thea," she snaps.

My mouth purses and I tighten my grip on Constantine's leash. He shifts at my feet, restless from the tension rolling off me. Is she kidding right now? Ignoring her, I swing a glare back on Connor.

"You're very rude."

He blinks, parting his lips like I've surprised him. Maybe he expected me to curse him out or slap him, like other girls at our school might. Loud, confident girls. But that's not me. I only raise my voice if there's no other choice. Bolstered by catching him off guard, I give him another piece of my mind.

"There's nothing wrong with the way I choose to dress, whether it's a potato sack, my favorite sweater, or this." I fist the hem of my shirt, revealing a tiny strip of skin. Connor impresses me slightly by holding out longer than I expected, but his gaze drops to my midsection after a few beats. "And besides all that, I dress for me, not you, or anyone else. You don't like my sweaters? Tough. So you can just leave me alone and go back to ignoring me."

I don't raise my voice, it even quavers a little at the end. Pride burns in my chest, pleased with myself for standing my ground and telling the jerk off.

This bravery has been growing since I first texted Wyatt, because I don't have to live in fear, hiding myself away. I would never have had the guts to stand up to Connor before. Saying how I feel is empowering, both new and unfamiliar.

It's short-lived when Mom appears at my side. My eyes widen as she waves me to follow impatiently.

"Thea, inside, *now*." Mom huffs when I don't immediately snap into motion. She's acting like Connor has a contagious disease with how embarrassing she's being. My life was already hard facing his teasing without her going all psycho mom on me. "I can't believe you went out like—" She cuts herself off with a frustrated sound. "Let's go."

I tug my arm from her grasp when she tries to take my wrist. "What's the matter? I'm coming, okay? Connor and I go to school together. We were just saying hello on my way back from walking."

Her livid expression says it all. God, what is her freaking deal? Doesn't she realize how insane she seems, dragging her grown daughter inside, away from a boy? Her lip curls and she shoots Connor a poisonous look.

"Stay away from this boy, Thea. I don't want you talking to him."

Connor watches the entire exchange with a bored expression, fingers tucked in the sides of his basketball shorts. He meets Mom's nasty gaze with an arrogant grin, like he knows exactly how much he pisses her off.

"See you later, neighbor," Connor says, eyes half-lidded and locked on me.

There's something about the way he says it that makes my skin break out in a ripple of hot and cold.

Mom releases a bitchy scoff and nudges me toward the house, Constantine following. As soon as we cross the threshold, she lays into me, saying what she refused to air in front of our neighbor.

"How could you go out dressed like that?" She flings her hand at me in jerky movements, indicating my top.

My temper rises. I kept my cool with Connor, but Mom sets me off. She never listens to me when I'm quiet. Arguing with her, I don't have any choice but to raise my voice, or she'd never hear me.

"There is nothing wrong with what I'm wearing, Mom!" I unclip Constantine and he trots off toward the kitchen, the sound of him lapping up water filtering through to the vaulted entryway where Mom and I face off with each other. "These are workout clothes and it was hot."

"Thea!" Her disappointed cry follows me as I go into the kitchen, picking out ingredients and pulling out the mixing bowls. Screw the ice cream, I need to shut my racing mind up. "I don't care how hot out it is, boys will see you dressing like that and think you're advertising you're welcome to their advances!"

If Dad didn't travel so much for work, maybe we wouldn't always be at each other's throats. But he's not here to create a buffer, currently away for another regional conference. I'm on my own against her.

"Do you hear yourself, Mom?" I whirl on her, slamming a whisk on the white countertop. Mom startles. I almost jump myself. Being so confrontational isn't my style. The burst of indignation burned hot and fast at what she said, and I just acted. "This isn't the flipping dark ages. No one is going to freak out because I'm walking around in leggings."

"They will if you're only *half dressed!* Your bra straps are—"

"Mom, so help me, if you are about to say something about my sports bra being visible, I will lose it." It's like I can't even breathe when I'm smothered by her. Constantine comes to sit by my feet, leaning against my leg. I turn back to my baking supplies, surveying what I grabbed on instinct as I continue ranting, getting on a real roll now that I've broken the dam. "Besides, boys need to learn to control themselves so I don't have to put myself out and be uncomfortable in the heat in order to keep their eyes off me. And why am I living in fear of a boy looking at me? Why is that so bad? It's human nature!"

Once it slips out, it occurs to me those are Connor's words.

Moving to the other side of the kitchen, Mom hisses at me, "They're out of control. None of them know how to behave."

"Seriously!" I toss my arms up in frustration. Talking to her is impossible when she gets on these topics. She's so backwards.

"That is such a sexist idea that *I* have to change and be the one to protect myself, and that all boys are dick-for-brains animals driven by their impulses. It's a ridiculous argument, Mom, and it's complete crap."

Her eyes bulge and she opens and closes her mouth a few times, searching for some way to respond to my call out. I can't decide whether she's more pissed I said dick or that I disagreed with her. I stand my ground through it all, hands planted on the counter, armed with my baking supplies for fortitude. Having Constantine's solid weight against my leg helps, too.

When she turns a concerning shade of purple, she gives up on whatever she was going to say and rushes out of the room, leaving Constantine and me alone.

"Well," I say, glancing at the chubby rottweiler at my feet. "Let's bake."

Within minutes, I lose myself to the methodical process that quiets my mind and melts away my stress.

Baking cherry turnovers from scratch helped calm me down, but I'm still annoyed at Mom after finishing up my homework in my room later. The corners of my mouth lift as I twirl a pen between my fingers, sitting cross-legged on my bed. As irritated as I am, I'm so damn proud of myself for not only standing up to Mom, but also telling Connor off.

It felt good.

For those few minutes I embodied everything I aspire to be in my secret folder photos, and for once I wasn't sacrificing anything about myself to do it. Usually when I try to become Secret Folder Girl, I'm imitating other women who have made me stop and go wow, because they have that *it* factor.

It's been like that since my early teens, bombarded with

images of the elusive idea of a perfect woman—as if anyone could live up to the fake ideals presented to us. Women are already wonderful the way they are. But I still struggle to accept that myself, even if I can dole out that advice to my friends.

Those old wounds are stubborn, scabbed over but never fully healing.

I shuffle my books to the nightstand and minimize the half-finished English paper for my favorite teacher on my laptop, opening a new browser window. The address I type in is ingrained, my fingers flying across the keyboard with muscle memory to type out my blog address.

The one I hid from Mom.

It loads, showing a feed of my latest posts—old photos of myself posed by the lake in a bikini that Maisy took for me, selfies in my bedroom trying on different outfits with short skirts or tying the tails of my blouse to reveal my stomach, and artsy crops where a hint of bra or panty line edge into the frame. Hundreds of posts blur past as I scroll the history of my blog, each with a photo.

I haven't posted to it in a long time, at least a year and a half. I didn't have to once I found someone to fill the void the blog plugged up in my aching heart.

Looking at these is kind of cringy now, seeing the phase I went through where I did my hair in half-braided pigtails in every photo, or the ones where I put on thick winged eyeliner. The cringe factor only lasts for a few minutes, then it's just like the muscle memory, the old photos from a few years ago reminding me how good they made me feel at the time.

The comments help that feeling.

I click on posts at random, seeing the numerous comments left by **Henry_Your_GoodKnight**.

Henry_Your_GoodKnight: *This is your best color. I'll picture you like this always.*

Henry_Your_GoodKnight: *Beauty beyond measure princess, but what really gets me is the way you smile. Your intelligent eyes say it all, love. You're longing for the world to show you all it has to offer.*

Henry_Your_GoodKnight: *Wish I could be there with you to experience your laugh. You'll always be my princess.*

His words were always like poetry. He seemed so intellectual and cool. The fact he followed me? Wanted to talk to me? It was a dream come true to have someone like him notice me.

I don't always end up deep down this memory lane. Usually I only look at the pictures, but once I read one of his comments, I find myself in an all-consuming black hole. One after the other, I relive being the sad little girl so desperate to love herself, to make sense of her changing body, to experience being wanted, that I latched onto the first person to give me that. A stranger on the internet who found my blog and gave me the attention I was so hungry for.

There's an echoing pulse of endorphins as I read through the emails we've exchanged, where I sent more...risqué photos when he asked for them. Nothing nude, but not entirely innocent, either. He was so good at talking to me, getting me to see things his way. But some part of me is uncomfortable with the idea the suggestive images are still out there somewhere. I couldn't bring myself to ever delete the emails, afraid I might forget the connection we had.

Maybe I'm stupid.

Maybe he doesn't think of me at all, even though he worms his way into my thoughts and brings my entire day to a halt.

Sometimes, when I'm feeling weak, I consider replying to an old email. Even if he doesn't respond, it would be an outlet. The temptation hovers at the back of my mind. I haven't taken things that far, though.

One of the earlier emails catches my eye.

To: Thea Marie <cupcakecutie22@gmail.com>
From: Henry Knight <henry.k.c@gmail.com>
Subject: a knight always comes for his princess

You're 15? Damn. Thought for sure you were older. By the way you talk and those pretty pictures, you seem closer to my age. I would expect to find you entering college with me this semester. That's not a big age difference, though. How do you like older guys? The idiots in your grade sound like their intellect is subpar to yours. They wouldn't understand you the way I do, princess. You must have one of those old souls, something too special to waste on boys your age. The connection I feel to you is unreal, it's hard to believe.

I used to feel just like you do. Tell me more about it. Tell me everything about you. I feel like I could reach through the screen and caress your cheek when you open up to me.

The world will show you what it has to offer you. It brought us together, didn't it? Now that I have you, I can't imagine you not being mine. Trust and it will keep offering you good things.

I guess I should sleep. It's 4am here. Thoughts of talking to you and imagining your laugh always keep me up. I want to touch your hair.

—*Henry*

Any time I talked to him, I felt his pain, too. He was like me. An old soul stuck in a body too mismatched to feel like we fit in with the world.

Henry was my first love. As much as our conversations skewed toward difficult, dark topics, or how many times he had to talk me into sending another photo, and another, and another...my sick heart was happy I had him.

I jolt when I hear Constantine barking downstairs. It's like a switch has flipped in my mind, the happy thoughts of love tainted by the logical side of me that judged myself the older I got. Releasing a rough sound of aggravation, I close out of everything, putting my face in my hands.

This is my crutch. My fall back. These memories are shrouded in shadows from a time I was tripping my way through growing up. If I had been able to express myself without fear of how much Mom would jump down my throat, maybe I wouldn't have turned to the internet for comfort.

I chew on the corner of my lip until it stings. "Ouch."

Pressing my fingers to my tender lip, I sigh. I used to think this was the most confident I could ever feel, but looking back at the old email thread, I feel in my bones how different it is from today, ever since Wyatt texted me back and took our fling to the next level.

I don't need to try to recapture the excitement I used to feel with my online boyfriend as I broke every one of Mom's rules, because now I have the real deal. It's only been a week, but Wyatt and I have messaged each other every day.

Popping off the bed, I put my laptop on the desk next to a stack of filled journals. I go on my tiptoes in the closet to reach behind an old box of binders filled to the brim with recipes I printed out from online to grab one of my secret stashes of contraband clothes. I lift the lid of the box covered in a sunflower pattern and unveil lingerie Maisy and I bought in secret when we went shopping for our summer retreat in the mountains. The material is soft and luxurious beneath my fingers as I touch the pretty bra and a sheer emerald green bodysuit.

I spend a solid half hour taking all new photos of myself, starting in my crop top, picking my mood up off the floor. When I've got several new pictures on my camera roll, I glance at the clock on my nightstand framed inside a porcelain rainbow. Perfect. It's about that time.

Picking the one I imagined earlier, where I've got a playful smile with the bottom of the crop top between my teeth, I send it to him.

My phone buzzes with a response right away. I bite my lip as pleasure fizzles beneath my skin. It's like he was waiting for me.

SEVEN
CONNOR

It's hours after the encounter with Thea at the end of my run, and I'm still obsessing over it. That was the closest I've ever gotten to her. Turns out, she smells like sugar.

And I wouldn't say no to a real taste.

After stripping out of my shorts, I almost texted her. She seemed to need the salvation of release with her bitchy mom breathing down her neck. The way she stood up to me, so quiet, yet so fucking fierce—I was rock hard and even her mom's arrival couldn't dilute the force of desire coursing in my veins. I've had people yell and scream in my face, threaten me, hit me, and all of it pales to the resolute way Thea held her own.

She doesn't fear me by reputation. We'll have to do something about that, won't we? She has no idea who she's getting tangled with.

Quiet, mousy Thea Kennedy interests me. I want to know what else there is behind the nerdy good girl.

I blame the thoughts of Thea when I enter the kitchen to grab something to eat for distracting me from realizing what was happening.

Mom and Damien look up as I pause in front of the fridge. He has a dish towel draped over his shoulder, a hint of a smile tugging at his lips, shirtsleeves rolled up as he dices vegetables at the island. Mom leans against the counter beside him, a glass of white wine raised to her lips. Her cheeks are tinged pink, the way they flush when she's been laughing.

It's domestic and turns my stomach as soon as I lay eyes on them.

"Hello, son," Damien greets.

My knuckles turn white as I fist my hands at my side. *Son.* No. Absolutely not. He has no right after what I caught them doing, after the beating I gave him for it.

I grunt in response, flashing him a glare. He always tries, and I never give him an inch. I'm in court-mandated anger management because he had to fuck my mom in our kitchen.

Mrs. Kennedy is to blame, too. That snooping busybody is the one who called the cops as a *concerned citizen* looking out for the neighborhood. The one thing Mom and I agree on is Mrs. Kennedy's position on both our shit lists. Without her, I wouldn't have been arrested and Mom wouldn't have bribed everyone involved to land me with therapy instead of juvie.

The faint scar at the corner of Damien's eye sends a sickening surge of pleasure into my stomach. I hit him so hard I fractured his brow bone. Mom's frantic screams still echo in my ears.

"How was school?" Mom asks, popping a cherry tomato in her mouth.

The laugh I bark out is jagged and loud.

"Let's not pretend you've ever been mom of the year. Cool? Cool." I wave a hand at the pair of them. "Go back to playing house with everyone who isn't part of this dysfunctional family."

Mom sighs.

Maybe I'd care if she ever acted like a decent parent.

This lovey-dovey scene can fuck all the way off. I have no intention of lingering around them, hell-bent on escaping to my room.

"Connor." Mom's clipped tone stops me in my tracks. Huffing, I half-turn back to her. She gestures to a manila folder sitting on the edge of the island, waiting in the spotlight cast by the pendant lights dangling above it. "Have a look through this. I've been wanting to talk with you about this matter for a while. It's important we go over it before the campaign benefit for the children's hospital."

My stomach churns with an uneasy ripple. She has her politician voice on, the false-sweetness belying the snake waiting in the grass to bite your ankle. Keeping an eye on Mom and Damien, I swipe the folder and flip it open, thinking I'm about to have some accusation thrown in my face. I've been expecting it with the bruise on my face and my knuckles still healing.

What's inside is so much worse than Mom being pissy over undeniable proof of me at an illegal fight ring.

The bafflement grows as I flip through pages of girls' photos followed by resumes, their entire lives profiled to the tits like they're security threats and it's necessary to know every minute detail about them. I suppose anything can be turned into a threat to a politician. My mom is the one I learned the lesson of *knowledge is power* from, after all.

"What is this?"

"Remember when I said we need to put on a united family front? Well, I also need you to have a girlfriend," Mom explains, distracted by Damien offering her a taste of the meal they're cooking. "A nice girl who will fit into the image we're cultivating. Polls are showing a positive rise in my numbers for voters wanting to see a legacy continuing on the horizon. Commitment is something they value and respect. I've taken the trouble of having these options prepared for you to choose from. They're already pre-approved and vetted."

The horizon. The problem with Mom is she doesn't just want to be re-elected to her office. She has a long-term plan. The endgame for her is the big one—the White House.

Controlling my expression to keep it blank is hard as disgust rolls through me, fighting back the urge to curl my lip. The entire folder is full of jersey chasing Coyote Girls. Not a single *nice girl* in the bunch at all, but all of them come from the crème de la crème families in Ridgeview. One elite name after another glares at me from the folder—daughters of old money like granddad's, real estate moguls, and Fortune 500 CEOs. Daughters of the people in Ridgeview that hold positions of power and influence.

Half of them have hooked up with me. Hell, all of them want me to make them my queen. They recognize the power I hold at SLHS without adding in Mom's political clout.

But I don't date. Never have. Every one of the girls who come onto me are only interested in my name or my family's money.

"You can have your pick from any of the selections." Mom gives me a shark's smile. "Isn't that nice of me? It'll be the perfect boost for our family image."

How can she say that when she's standing in front of me with *him*, making a goddamn meal together from scratch?

I lose the internal battle not to show my cards, snarling as I slam the folder down. The contents spill out in a cascade, spreading over the island, some dipping into the prep station Damien has going.

"What family image?!" My voice rises as I jab a finger at Damien. "Your fucking boyfriend is right there, and you think I need someone? Maybe you should stop spreading your legs for that piece of shit and worry about having an actual family! Instead of fabricating whatever the approval polls dictate, wouldn't it be better to earn your votes the honest way?"

Mom crosses her arms and Damien casts a troubled look between us. *Go ahead and try it, fuckface. If you step in front of me, I'm knocking you out again.*

He takes a step closer and I raise my fists to a ready stance. "I won't hesitate."

Damien's eyes go wide. With a menacing smile that makes him shuffle back to put more distance between us, I stare Mom down for a beat before leaving the room.

"You will do this!" Mom calls after me, her voice changing from the saccharine tone to something more forceful, more true to her actual character.

It sends anger racing down my spine, but I stomp up the stairs to my room instead of fighting her. I might get what I want at school, but with her it takes work. She believes she has full control over me because of the money. Everything with her is an endless sequence of moves until I can back her into a corner, proving that the outcome I want is the right one. If I don't have smoke and mirrors, then my strategy blows up in my face.

My ragged breathing doesn't calm down until I've paced

my room, going over possibilities I can present to get out of this stupid ultimatum.

Movement from Thea's curtains across from my window catches my eye and I creep over, keeping to the shadows of my bedroom so she doesn't see me watching. She's sitting sideways in an armchair angled toward the window, her bare legs crossed at the ankle and propped against the wall. Her head is bent, maybe reading something? Her foot bobs—she must be listening to music. There's something about the way she's sitting that amuses me. Is it even comfortable?

Watching her gives me an idea for getting around Mom's girlfriend project, because she won't sleep on this. I know how she gets. If I'm forced to do something, I'll do it on my terms. I might as well have fun with it.

I have the leverage I need to make sure Thea has no other choice but to agree to become my fake girlfriend.

It'll get me closer to her sugar-scented hair. Close enough to really pin her under my thumb and discover what other secrets she has for me to steal.

Her nosy Mom will hate it. If she was freaking out about me standing close to her, talking to her, she'll blow a gasket at how I'm going to make sure Thea is corrupted and debauched in every way possible. I saw it in her eyes. She thinks I'm the worst kind of wild.

The perfect payback to Celine Kennedy has finally presented itself in the sweetest sweater-wrapped bow: her daughter.

Thea might be fun to play with, but everyone is a liar in some way or another. Apples don't fall far from trees.

EIGHT

CONNOR

Third period English is lit this morning.

Devlin is out for blood with his little charity case obsession. She crawled up to him like a lost dog, surprising me by handing over a paper and acknowledging his existence when she usually ignores all of us like the uppity ice queen she is. A hot ice queen.

But I honor dibs, so she's all Devlin's.

I had snatched up the paper she presented to him and made up a love note instead of the essay assignment with his name typed at the top. He got her to do his homework somehow, but he also wasn't taking it, declaring that he wasn't accepting proclamations of love and calling what she wrote sweet.

Now, I don't know what sort of kinky game he's playing with her, but whatever it is, it's brought a light to his eyes I haven't seen since his cousin Lucas left for college. Davis brought his wrath on herself by picking Trent's pockets right in front of us.

The laughter of our crew fills the room as other students filter in for class. Sean leans on Trent, howling with amused tears clinging to the corners of his eyes. Two of our friends from the dance team, Nina and Bailey, coo cruelly at Blair Davis while Devlin and I tag team her.

Fire flashes in her gaze. Yeah, she's a total fighter, even if she stays silent the majority of the time we're messing with her. "Listen—"

Devlin's voice is cutting as he interrupts, wagging a finger at her. "I don't like the way you look at my dick. It's not sexy to think you might bite it off because you mistook it for a hotdog."

"Oh damn!" I choke into my fist at the brutal burn. "Bro. That mental image. My eyes!"

Davis growls—actually growls like the trailer trash animal we call her—ready to fight Devlin. I'm kind of hoping she tackles him to the ground. He can take her, but it would be fun as hell to watch them wrestle. But our Devil Boy has her halting, balling her fists at her side.

"Whatever," she spits. "You're disgusting."

"Oh, come on, sticky fingers." Devlin props his chin in his hand, smirking because he knows he's won, kicking the trash in the mud once again. These two are out for blood this year. "I've heard you get up to way worse for anyone willing to pay. But not me. I don't pay for it, and I sure as fuck am not touching you with a ten-foot pole."

He goes on. The man loves a savage diatribe, but I miss the

rest of it because Thea walks in. Today her auburn curls are braided, a few strands escaping. She hugs her books to her chest as she pauses in the doorway to say bye to Landry's sister. The school blazer is so big on her short frame, the cuffs of her sleeves become like sweater paws.

I want to unwrap her to get to the delectable body underneath. This lie of hers pisses me off, digging beneath the threshold of my patience.

Thea glances at me as she finds her seat at the desk in front of mine. Even more irritating than her fake frumpy armor is that the only recognition for me is indifference. Maybe a hint of judgement because she's caught some of how we're treating Davis.

She doesn't know I'm the one who gets her to come at least twice a day since she accidentally texted me.

Grunting under my breath, I turn my back on Thea to face Devlin at his seat behind me.

Davis sits stiffly in her chair in the next row over, sleek dark hair hiding most of her face as Devlin finishes eviscerating her by saying, "I don't want this. It's pathetic."

Everyone watches as he rips the essay to pieces and flings the torn shreds in the air. They float to the ground by Blair's feet. Our whole crew and the people that cling to us from the outer rings explode in laughter and coyote howls—the student body's way of honoring our school mascot when something goes down.

Devlin takes out his finished essay and sets it on his desk. Damn, he's an evil bastard. I snicker, sticking the tip of my tongue out of the side of my mouth.

Davis stares at the remains of the destroyed essay, her plump lips pinched at the corners as she fights not to react. The only reason we go at her as hard as we do is because she never does what we expect—doesn't cry at the nasty names, refuses to fight back unless it's Devlin, has never broken down, even after Devlin threw her lunch on the floor last year. She's ice through and through, but ice has to melt sometime.

With a restrained bite in her tone, Davis asks, "Are you still going to—"

"You shouldn't treat people like that." A familiar soft but determined voice speaks up.

My mouth curves into a dangerous smile as Devlin, Davis, and I turn our attention to Thea.

She's twisted around in her seat, cheeks tinged pink as she grips the back of her chair with white knuckles, practically touching my desk.

This is how I know she's hiding the same tendencies as her mom. I open my mouth to bite back at my little mouse for intervening where she doesn't belong.

"It's not right." Thea beats me by doubling down before I can snipe at her. She licks her lips, darting her gaze to me. I'm reminded of the encounter in front of our houses, when she told me off. It was cute then, but it's not now, here at school where she can publicly defy us. Her focus shifts back to Devlin and the rest of our crew hovering behind us. "So please stop."

Releasing a ruthless laugh, I lean close to her, clamping a hand over her wrist so she can't escape. Her sugary scent is intoxicating and I shift closer, whispering in her ear. "What's wrong, neighbor? Were you jealous we weren't paying you any attention? Your secret is how badly you want someone to pay attention to you, isn't it?"

She sucks in a breath, pinning me with her big doe eyes, stretched wide with embarrassed horror.

That's right, sweetness. I know everything. I've got your fucking number.

Literally. I smother a snort.

"You want attention?" I mutter. "I'll give you what you

want."

Thea drags the cuffs of her blazer over her hands. Her face is flaming red. I lean back in my chair, smirking. Pulling out my phone, I kick my feet up on the bar on the back of her seat.

Our teacher bustles in, always with that grating go-getter vibe.

Coleman is in his late twenties, with clean-cut thick brown hair, a strong chin, and matching dimples when he turns a proud smile on the girls he calls on the most in class. He's playing at perfect all-American dreamboat, but I'm not buying his act. He's a try-hard phony if I've ever seen one. He turned up out of nowhere in the middle of the year in tenth grade and had the girls panting after him right away. It's always irritated me that Coleman doesn't take my rep seriously, but I haven't found anything on the guy to show him what I'm capable of, like the man is a ghost.

Or he's great at covering his tracks. Whatever the case is, I'll uncover it.

There has to be something serious for all the falsehoods he protects himself with.

"Let's get started," Coleman says.

Instead of paying attention to him, I pull up my messages.

Thea acts all perfect and innocent, when really she's as much of a corrupt deviant as any of us, and I've got the proof right on my phone from this morning when I got her worked up before school, and again before first period because I wanted to know how far I could push her.

If *Wyatt* can text Thea before first period and she sneaks off to a secluded spot to respond, what will she do if her secret sext buddy messages her in the middle of class? Time to find out. I click into our message thread, the corner of my mouth hitching up at the last message from her saying she was late for class and had to go.

Connor: Can't stop thinking about the sounds you made this morning. Your sweet little moans get me so hard, baby. I need to hear you all breathy and on the edge of falling apart again. Want to play a game?

A squeak sounds from Thea. She hunches her shoulders to hide her phone from the teacher as he explains the reading assignment. My cell vibrates.

Thea: Omg I'm in class right now!! [flustered emoji]

Connor: Be bad with me. I promise it'll be fun. Just lean back in your desk, spread those pretty legs and show me what color panties you're wearing.
Connor: Unless you're not wearing any, you naughty girl.

I shift in my seat, getting myself going from toying with her. My dick is half hard at the thought of her doing it. I flick my gaze between the text conversation and her back, inhaling when she sinks into her chair a few inches and slides both her hands beneath the desk.

Shit. I didn't think she'd actually do it. We're in the middle of class and I've got Thea Kennedy taking an upskirt photo. The sense of illicit mischief courses through me and I bite my lip to hide my pleased expression.

My pulse thumps in my ears as I watch every tiny shift of her body, until her legs widen slightly. Then my phone vibrates. Rolling my lips between my teeth, I check it discreetly. It's grainy and dimly lit, but I can make out dainty scalloped yellow lace.

She did that. She fucking did that. For me, during class, with Coleman strolling around the classroom.

A burst of lust mixed with pride rushes through me.

Connor: Good girl. Or should I say, bad girl? [smirk emoji]
Connor: Mm, baby girl, I want to come find you during the day at your school, pull your panties aside, fuck you good and hard until I cream in you, then smack that thick ass and leave you knowing I'll be in you all day.

Thea muffles another strangled yelp, crossing her legs tightly. It's too fun to mess around with her like this, to get her hot right under everyone's noses.

Our game is interrupted when Coleman pauses by Thea's desk as he strolls around the class and directs his question at her. "Can anyone give me their thoughts on the use of literary devices in the text?"

"I—uh, yes, I..." Thea trails off, flipping through her notebook, voice trembling. In her fumbling, she knocks the book we're reading off the desk.

Titters echo around the room. I cover the smug slant of my lips with my hand, propping my elbow on the desk.

"I have some thoughts," I offer. "You know, since she seems unprepared for class. The book uses irony and alludes to things going on in the world to drive the point that the political party twists the truth to exercise control, but I don't think the theme of propaganda is as universally applicable today. With social media always advancing and evolving, more voices are constantly in the mix from all over the world. People aren't complacent to mindlessly listen to manipulative party lines, or believe whatever the headlines read."

Coleman frowns at me, silent for a long beat. He sighs. "Yes. Good."

Thea drops her forehead to her desk and stays like that for a long stretch as the class goes on.

* * *

Before I make any moves, I need more information. I want to know my grip on Thea is ironclad. There's no way I'll let the little mouse escape the trap I'm setting for her.

I dump my athletic duffel in the corner of the bedroom and boot up my computer. As it purrs to life, I drop into the chair and scroll through notes I've compiled on my phone.

She's on my radar, no longer invisible. I'm paying attention to every move she makes, getting a lowdown on her from the classes we don't share, utilizing every access point I have to pick apart her life. From her friendship circle to her daily schedule, she won't make a move without me knowing about it. Holden Landry proved useful once more, giving me a play-by-play of Thea through the lens of her longtime friendship with his younger sister when I used the video of him at the boat party I've been keeping in my back pocket. Until he described a recent sleepover and how she filled out her skimpy sleep set nicely and I decked him.

I'm building a picture of how she presents herself—the studious, quiet good girl.

And I'm betting it's a lie. No one is that pure and innocent. As humans, we're all depraved beasts.

It's instinct. Our base nature. It lives in our bones.

Once my computer is ready, I waste no time getting to work. Hacking her network remotely is child's play. Their WiFi has basic, default firewalls that I break through with ease, allowing me access to connect my computer to any device in their house logged in on the network, dropping malware I've written to give me a backdoor in anytime I want.

There's no challenge, not like the things I faced when I was first developing these skills on my hunt to uncover the depth of Mom's misdeeds to cover up the assault incident. In the short time since that discovery, I've honed my talents in digging through people's lives.

"Gotcha," I mutter as I locate Thea's laptop, currently connected.

Her screen loads on my second monitor, a baking blog and Instagram open in two tabs on her browser. The calendar application is also open, and I grind my teeth when I see *Mr. Coleman's birthday, bake cookies* set as a reminder for tomorrow.

I never really noticed Thea before, but now that I have, it doesn't escape me that she's as infatuated with Mr. Coleman as every other girl in our class. Hell, the whole school. It still rankles when I think of today's English period. Watching her shoot her hand in the air, leaning forward to answer questions once she recovered from her mortification. Like she was eager to prove herself to our teacher. She might have hidden under her baggy uniform, but because I know what her perfect tits look like beneath the deceptive layers, it pissed me off to see her eagerness for any of Coleman's attention.

With a few swift keystrokes, I access the webcam, activating it. Her room appears on my screen.

Clicking my tongue and shaking my head, I lean back in my chair. "Don't you know any better? Come on, everyone knows to put tape or something over their camera these days. It's 101."

Her room is empty, the door ajar. A stuffed sea lion sits in the center of her ruffly purple pillows. It's every inch as feminine as I expected, splashes of color enveloping the whole thing.

The family's rottweiler sleeps on the floor next to her bed. He seems like a chill dog. I once fed him half of my burger when I was hiding out by our pool house, avoiding my parents when he wandered over. Thea shouted for him around the front of her house. He must have gotten out. She wasn't pleased to find her dog cuddled up to me—really, he was trying to push me out of the lounger, total chair hog—while I listened to her search for her dog for close to twenty minutes before she ventured into our backyard.

For the life of me, I can't remember the dog's name. Only her pet names for him. *Wookiee boy.* It made sense when he jumped down from the lounger, stretched his front half low to the ground, and released the weirdest warbling sound before trotting to her side.

I'm in the middle of scanning the colorful posters on the wall, reading their baking puns when Thea strolls in.

The corner of my mouth twitches up.

Flour is smeared across her cheek and dotting her apron. The sleeves of her sweater are rolled up and her hair is tied on top of her head by a big yellow scrunchie with a bow on it. The sun doesn't shine as bright as the excitement in her blue eyes as she leans over the desk to grab a notebook with pastel tabs sticking out to mark the pages. I drink her in, studying what she looks like when she doesn't know someone's watching. She pauses to pet the dog, giving him a belly scratch that has him stretching languidly before disappearing from the room.

Part of me hopes she'll come back. I have half a mind to start up a sexting session with her while I'm accessing her webcam for a double feature, picturing her wearing only the apron and nothing underneath.

But it's better for me if she isn't in the room. Even if she doesn't know how to prevent hackers like me from doing exactly what I'm doing, there's a chance she'd notice activity on her computer while I'm remotely accessing the files. I have to be quick, then I can play with her posing as Wyatt later.

Starting with the browser history, I download it to my files to comb through later. The page with Instagram open is her account—*@theactualsunbeam*. I scroll through the images, clicking at random. The whole thing is a mix of baking and floral aesthetic, mixed with an underlying obsession with positive optimism and self-love quotes. *Thick thighs save lives. Be kind always. Spread love (and cookies) around the world. Local goddess gang.*

She seems like a fucking woodland creature, too wholesome and good for this world.

Except I know the truth.

I unlock my phone, where the real Thea is. Picking a photo from this morning, I stare at what she shows me—the most stripped down, raw version of herself.

"Who are you?"

Shaking my head, I exit back to her Instagram profile and open Facebook. It loads to her account, login credentials saved.

A soft laugh puffs out of me. "It's like you want me to have easy access."

The Facebook feed isn't as personalized as her Instagram, mostly full of video shares of Tasty videos—damn, girl has a real sweet tooth—and tagged photos with Maisy Landry at a wellness retreat resort, some fancy cabin campground that screams glamping instead of real camping.

Skimming through her files, my annoyance rises. There's no protection against what I'm doing. Her security is so lax. This isn't even hard, any creep can learn to do it with shitty spyware.

"Fucking pain in the ass," I grumble, opening a new window to code in.

A short while later, Thea's computer has security protocols in place that rival the ones I installed for my own computer system. The only outside threat able to get into her stuff is me. No other little shit will spy on her with her webcam.

Only me.

NINE
CONNOR

At the end of the week, my good day goes to hell fast. I'm walking down the north building's hallway on my way to class when I stop in my tracks.

Thea stands with Mr. Coleman, chatting animatedly, her eyes all lit up as her hands move. Today's thick sweater is a peach color with bobbles. She almost drops the stack of books in her arms and laughs as Coleman steps closer to help her catch them. Too close. He leans into her space, his attention rapt as she continues talking.

The rush of annoyance rises so fast I almost go lightheaded.

Hell fucking nah, man.

My feet move before I've even formed a plan.

"Hey, baby, I was hoping I'd see you before lunch," I say, interrupting whatever Coleman was about to tell her. My arm slides around her waist and tugs her to my side, away from our English teacher. I nuzzle into her hair, shooting a flat look at Coleman. "Mm, you smell nice today."

"I, uh," Thea chokes out. I back off a little, but keep my arm around her. Her mouth keeps moving, but no words come out. She looks from me to Coleman, confusion etched into her features. "Connor?"

Pinching my collar and flicking, I say, "One and only."

"We can continue this discussion another time, perhaps. I'll leave you with your...boyfriend, Miss Kennedy," Coleman says, disappointment in her threading his voice. "Mr. Bishop, tighten your tie."

Fucking prick. I resist flipping off his back as he walks down the hallway. The milling students give us curious glances as they pass.

"You're still, uh. Holding me?" It comes out as a question. She licks her lips, glancing out of the corner of her eye at the attention we're drawing with this public display of possession.

"Good eye."

A beat passes, then she drags out her question. "Why?"

Yeah, might as well do this now. I've got enough info in place to make my move.

"Plenty of reasons. Your cute expression right now, for one. Felt like it when I saw you. And..." I fish out my phone and show it to her. On the screen is the last message she sent me from an hour ago—her school blouse unbuttoned in a bathroom stall to show me her mouth-watering rack in a lavender bra with ribbon bows. "I like the little game we've been playing, but we could be doing so much more."

Air hisses out of Thea and she sags. I shift my grip to hold her up so she doesn't collapse in the middle of the hall.

"What is that?" Horror fills her tone and the color drains from her face. "How do you have that?"

Releasing a dark chuckle, I put my phone away and cage her against the row of lockers. "What's wrong? You liked it so much before now."

She shakes her head in disbelief. "N-no."

"Yes."

"I don't believe you." Thea sucks on her bottom lip. "I've heard rumors."

I lift a brow.

She huffs. "You copied my phone somehow. Read through my private conversations."

"What makes you think you're interesting enough to be a target for something so elaborate? You're a nobody. Invisible. We don't notice you." I grasp her jaw, narrowing my eyes. "You're the one that started it when you sent me that pic of you in your nightie with your boobs almost spilling out. You wanted someone to pay attention and I did."

"I don't believe you. I think you're just making fun of me again."

A wild grin crosses my face. With a deft move, I pop a button on my shirt, then another. "Want me to strip to prove it? How much do you need to see? Abs?" I lick my lips slowly, making sure she's watching before I drop my hands to my belt. "More?"

In a flustered frenzy, she clamps her hands over mine, squeezing with more strength than I would've guessed. In my periphery, I feel the eyes of people openly staring at the scene we're making.

I laugh. "Feisty, huh? Can't keep your hands off me."

Thea lets go as if I've burned her. I prop my hands on either side of her head and crowd her against the lockers again.

"I'm not bluffing," I say. "I've seen more of you than I bet you've shown to anyone, sunshine."

"This can't be happening," Thea utters, more to herself than me.

"Damn, how horny are you, Bishop?" Sean taunts as he passes us in the hall. "You're hitting up the uptight nerds now?"

Keeping my eyes on Thea, I snort and play with one of the bobbles on her sweater. "I needed a snack and she was the closest chick around."

His sharp cackle makes Thea flinch, the sound grating as he swaggers down the hall. I grit my teeth and grab her, looking for somewhere private to talk. I can't hash this out with her and field interruptions demanding a different kind of show. She follows obediently.

"In here." I herd her into an empty classroom by my grip on her upper arm to get the prying, gossiping eyes off us.

It's one of the science labs, dimly lit by the half-drawn shades on the windows, the main lights off.

I never meant to do this in front of an audience. Humiliating her wasn't part of the plan, I only intended to make sure I had her in checkmate when I revealed myself. But when I saw her smile for Coleman, I just acted. Left my strategy in the dust.

"We're going to be late for next period," Thea says, her eyes flashing at me mutinously.

Christ, that look. You'd think I kicked her dog.

She tugs her arm from my grasp. "Please let me go."

"Who says I want to?"

"Me. I want you to, so you will." She skirts around me, stepping out of range to lean against a lab table in the deserted science room. Crossing her arms over her chest, she lifts her brows. "Why did you wait so long to reveal yourself? Why did you do it at all if I had the wrong number?"

Her soft voice rises, drawing a chuckle from me. I shrug, admiring another photo from our messages. It's one of her tamer ones from the last few weeks, but I love it. Her red hair looks fantastic in thick high pigtails while she sucks icing off her finger, grinning at the camera with a cheeky mischief she never shows at school.

"Because it was fun." I rake my eyes over her. "And hot. All I thought about every night was how you were just a short distance away, getting off with me."

"But I didn't know it was you! This is all wrong. I wanted —" A rough sound tears from her throat and she turns away, hiding her face. "You're disgusting."

"Disgustingly skilled at making you come, you mean." I slide my tongue along my lower lip as I taunt her. "You're so good for me, aren't you? I keep wondering if you'll do the same for anyone who pays attention to you."

I don't say it, but Coleman crosses my mind. The way he was leaning into her space before I interrupted makes me want to punch something. Preferably his smarmy face.

"Stop it." Thea pulls the cuffs of her sweater over her hands, twisting the material until it's stretched out and limp. She looks like I've shattered her world, the crestfallen expression killing her light. I frown, disliking seeing her face so shadowed. Her eyes lift to meet mine, glistening with wetness. "Why are you doing this?"

"Well, I was horny and high when you texted, so I think that's self explanatory, but—"

"Connor!" Thea sniffles, swiping a stray tear. The sight of her tears twists my insides. I don't want to make her cry. I don't know what's wrong with me, I don't normally care how my blackmail affects people. "What do you want with me? Hurry up and spit it out, so I can go."

"Go where?"

She shrugs. "First stop, ladies room so I can clean up."

I guess she means cry her eyes out that the real Wyatt isn't texting her. "And after that?"

"AP Chemistry."

My brows lift in surprise. "Not, like home or to cry to your gal pals under the bleachers?"

Thea wrinkles her nose. "No. The school day isn't over yet."

I cover my face with my hand and groan. "God, you're a nerd."

"Are you threatened by intelligent women?"

I scoff. "Hardly."

"If you have a problem with it, you'll have to suffer. I'm not changing what I do with my life for anyone."

"No. It's nothing." I shake my head. A lopsided smile tugs at my lips. "It's perfect, actually."

Mom won't be able to deny me. Thea is studious, wholesome, and appears innocent. I'm the only one who knows she isn't.

"Perfect for what?"

"For what I need from you. We're going to strike a deal. That's how this works when I have leverage on people around here." I stroll over and hook an arm around her shoulders. She's so short next to me that I could tuck her head against my chest. "You're going to do me a favor, and in exchange I won't tell anyone about this Thea Kennedy." I wave my phone. "Shame, really, she's way more entertaining than you."

Thea's mouth drops open and it's kind of cute, all indignant and affronted. I'm tempted to stick my fingers in her mouth to turn it sexy and bring one of my fantasies to life. They twitch against her shoulder, and I thread them into her hair instead.

"That's—like extortion, isn't it? That's horrible!"

My amused smile stretches. "Well, I'm not paying you.

This is good, old fashioned blackmail, baby. So do as I say, or I'm going to play Russian roulette with my contact list and all the private pictures you've sent." I tsk, tilting my head. "You know, you should really be careful who you send nude photos to. Make sure you trust them and all that. Or that you've got the right number."

"But I...he put his number in my phone, I don't..."

"Damn, that's cold." I'm holding back from cracking up. "Either that was on purpose, or he's an idiot."

Her eyes flash with a burst of fierceness. "Wyatt isn't like that! He's kind and funny and dedicated to his job as a lifeguard." She gives me a once over. "Unlike you."

My eyes roll. "Sounds like a wet blanket. You need to accept that your lifeguard gave you a fake number because he didn't want you, or that he probably couldn't handle you." I poke my tongue from the corner of my mouth as my gaze travels over the curves I know hide beneath her frumpy uniform. "Not like I can."

"You haven't said what you need from me yet," Thea argues.

"It's easy, sweetness. I need you to pretend to be with me. Pose as my girlfriend."

She sputters, trying to get away from under my arm. I hold her tight. When she can't break free, she huffs. "Be your fake girlfriend? What the hell, Connor? I don't ever see you date."

"You're right, I don't. But this is important and it's all I need from you. It has to be you." I don't tell her I can't get out of it, so I'm forced to pick someone. "This is a good deal, so take it. I'm not asking you to memorize my favorite color, or even interact with my friends. You need me to not spread information about you around school, and I need you to do me this small solid until I'm done with you."

"Small! You're talking about a relationship. That's a huge

deal to me!" Thea's mouth works as she formulates a response. After a minute, she flaps her hand. "You're not even asking! You're just demanding I let you control me by threatening me with blackmail so I can't refuse."

She bites her bottom lip and pinches her brows together. I set my phone on the lab table, curling my fingers into my palm to tame the urge to trace her pout.

"You really are as wicked as everyone says," Thea finishes in a hush.

I smirk. "Better fucking believe it, baby."

Horror morphs her pretty features as she leans as far away as I allow while she's tucked beneath my arm. She shakes her head. "Don't call me that. Don't call me that ever again."

"See, that's the thing, baby." I pause, dragging my teeth over my lip. "I'm going to call you that, because I do what I want. And I want you to be my fake girlfriend."

She tosses her hands in the air. "Why can't you ask some other girl! There are so many who would jump at the chance. They're—" Hesitation stops her, cutting off her words. Her blue-green gaze falls to the floor, lashes brushing her cheeks. "They're prettier, and actually want to be around you."

Thea doesn't think she's pretty? How can that be possible? What a load of shit.

This is taking so much work. Not only that, it's cramping my style and putting a wrecking ball through the ruthless cred I've built for myself in the last couple of years. I'm supposed to strike so much fear in the hearts of everyone in this town that I snap my fingers and they jump.

With a scoff, I put my hands on her shoulders to make her face me. "I can't use any other girls because they're all insipid and plastic. They'll read too much into playing domestic bliss for me. Fuck that." I step closer, toying with her hair, sinking my fingers into the strands framing her face.

It's soft as hell, slipping over my skin. Her breath catches and she stares up at me. She smells so nice. "You, on the other hand, my sweet little mouse, are nothing more than a pawn and you know it."

It's heady to be so close after I've been imagining it. So many thoughts run through my head. Does she make the same sounds in person, or will it be different? Better? If I kiss her neck and put my lips on that sun-shaped birthmark on her thigh, will she tremble deliciously?

But instead of melting into my arms or wrapping her thick thighs around my waist, she struggles, turning her face away. Those pink, glossy lips set in a frown.

"Let me go," she demands quietly.

Stubborn little thing. I breathe out slowly.

I've never worked this hard for a hookup. Girls fall onto my dick. Shit, Thea fell into what we were doing easily. If someone wasn't into it, I'd always moved on to the next girl or three in line.

But I want Thea. I need to have a taste of her, and if I'm tying her to my side for the foreseeable future, I'll seduce her.

This close, her honeyed scent makes me want to swing her around, pin her against the desk, and kiss those rosy lips until they're swollen.

Trailing my hands from her shoulders down her back, I snake my arms around her waist, trapping her in my hold. She shoots a wide-eyed look up at me.

"What are you doing?" Her question comes out a little breathless.

This is affecting her, and I've barely done anything.

The corner of my mouth lifts as I lean close enough to press my lips to her ear, letting my hands roam when she stays still. I squeeze her hips and sneak my tongue out to lick the shell of her ear.

Thea sucks in a breath, shoulders shaking in a shiver. She bows her head, hiding behind her hair. "C-Connor."

The bell rings, but neither of us move.

"I'll still pretend to be Wyatt. You'll know it's me, but nothing has to change. I've really liked being your sexting buddy. We can keep what we have going. Why waste a good thing, right?" My lips brush her ear again. "And I make you feel so good."

The whimper that escapes her is music to my ears, drawing a grin from me. She allows herself to lean into me, touching my chest. My lids fall to half mast as she smooths one palm down my torso. I hum in encouragement. Screw next period.

"That's it, baby," I croon, squeezing her ass. "Give in. We'll have such a good time together. We can get started right now." I clap a hand on the high science desk behind me, chuckling when she jumps. She won't be acting like a scared mouse once I get my mouth on her. "Come sit up on this lab table and spread those legs. I want to eat you."

She sways into me, digging her nails into my shirt. Her voice is so soft I have to focus to hear it when she speaks. "You're crazy and entitled."

With that accusation, she launches herself at me, fingers scrabbling. At first I attempt to catch her, thinking she's trying to kiss me—*hell yes*, that's what I want.

But she's not trying to kiss me.

Thea snatches my phone and scampers back a couple of steps, breathing hard as she fumbles with the screen. I blink, trying to process what's happening.

"Damn it," she curses.

"Ah, ah." I wave a finger in disapproval. "You won't get it unlocked to delete your photos or your number."

"Yes I will." She flashes me a determined look, brows flattened.

The fire she keeps tucked away is like an ember at first glance, but it's blistering hot. I like it. Before she can do anything rash, like smash my phone—pointless, because I keep a cloud backup—I push off the desk and capture her in my hold. She makes a sound of protest as I toss my phone aside. It clatters on the lab table while I pin her arms.

Bringing my lips back to her ear, I bite out, "Don't test me. And don't be mad you liked it when you thought I was someone else." She shudders at my demanding tone. When I nip her ear, she fights to free herself, panting. A smoky chuckle rolls through me. "Fight all you want, little mouse. You're mine now."

"No!" Her attention darts to the door as her desperation climbs.

"Hoping if you go tattle to my dad I'll let you off the hook? Nice thought, but no." I rub my nose into her temple, fisting the back of her sweater. "Or...are you hoping if you figure out your real Wyatt's number, he'll respond like I did? Who else is going to give you what you need?"

She turns a glare on me, her mouth set in a mutinous line I'm dying to kiss. "No. You can't bully me into this because you have private photos of me. I'm never going to text you again." Her chin tips up and I grasp it between my thumb and finger, lifting it higher. Her small fists shift against my torso. "I'll—I'll block your number."

"That's so cute. Well, go ahead and try. But neighbor, I'm never far from you." A tiny sound catches in her throat. She shakes her head. I nod, pinning her with my unwavering stare. She needs to understand. "I control everyone's secrets, you know. That's why people are scared of me. You should be, too. Because I own you by knowing yours." I tilt my head and brush my thumb over her jaw. "You can play along like a good pawn and I'll keep taking care of that needy little vixen you keep under wraps—even from yourself, I think—or I can make your life fucking hell."

"Do you ever stop talking, or do you like the sound of your own voice that much?" Thea whispers, eyes bouncing back and forth, studying my face.

A burst of anger erupts in my chest. There's a sadness in her eyes that cuts me—pity. She should pity herself for the position she's landed herself in.

With a cruel laugh, I chuck her under the chin and hover my lips over hers, wrapping a curl around my finger. "You know, I've been really fucking nice about this. Nicer than I am with anyone, and you're shitting all over it with that attitude."

She grimaces, but her gaze doesn't leave mine. Silly little mouse, looking danger in the eye.

I release her, but she doesn't move, waiting to see what I'll do. Picking up my phone, I sigh in a mockery of being put out.

"Well, it's your choice. You've got real brass ones, Kennedy, choosing to face the entire school getting a good look at your tits. Guess I was right about you liking the attention." As I tell her this, I scroll through the address book on my phone. "I'll just keep sending your photos to my contact list until you submit."

"Connor, don't do this." Her throat works as she swallows. "Please."

I look up through my lashes, face bent toward my phone as I pick a number at random and start a new text message. Her gaze drops to my phone, then flies back up, silently pleading with me.

"That's not the magic word. You know what to do. So what'll it be?"

Thea releases a rough cry and rushes me again, catching me by surprise as her body collides with mine. My back bumps into the high tabletop and one arm bands around her automatically while she tries to get my phone a second time. I hold it out of reach above her head.

"Please! I don't want you to!"

My mouth curves into a smile that isn't nice at all and I cradle her face with my free hand, tilting it up. Her eyes are shiny with wetness. I can see how her strength is cracking, panic taking over. I smooth some of her wild curls back from her face.

"I wasn't kidding. You'll learn quick that when I say something, I'm dead fucking serious. Do you understand?"

After staring back at me for a beat, she plants her palms on my chest and shoves hard, wrenching away from me.

"Fine," Thea spits. Her chest rises and falls with each harsh breath she drags in, face flushed. She touches her hair with a trembling hand. "Fine. I'll do it. Just. Don't send my pictures to anyone."

I slide my phone in my pocket and close the distance she put between us. Tucking her hair behind her ear, I ask, "Was that so hard?"

Thea's eyes are consumed by an intriguing fire when she lifts them to face me, even when she's breaking. Quiet, frumpy, shy Thea Kennedy has fight in her. I'm going to have fun toying with it before I tame her.

"See you later, little mouse." I blow her a kiss before leaving her alone in the middle of the dark science lab, whistling with my hands in my pockets.

TEN

THEA

The shock hasn't faded two periods later. Chemistry and French were both complete blurs. At lunch I'm still reeling from Connor's reveal, and his horrible threat if I don't meet his demand.

And I agreed.

I had to, or he was going to send my photos to people. There was no choice, no way to think my way out.

Fake girlfriend. Am I insane? We didn't even go over what that entails, or what the rules are, like when I'm supposed to start playing a role and if we have to act like a couple.

Back in that classroom, I put on every ounce of bravery, but in reality I'm so far from okay with all of this.

By some miracle, I haven't broken down yet. Once he left, I swiped my eyes and went to AP Chemistry, apologizing to the teacher for arriving so late.

Sighing, I pick at the carrots sitting between Maisy and I on the table in the cafeteria. My stomach gives a feeble protest. I'm not hungry for anything else. My insides are too twisted in anxious knots.

My best friend is so good at picking up on my moods. As soon as we met up at the stairwell by the library to walk to lunch, she launched into a story about falling down a YouTube hole of yoga videos last night.

Maisy Landry is a junior in the grade below me, but we've been close friends since the first day of camp when we were in middle school. It was a miracle to find out we lived in the same town. She looks like a stunning model with long tan lean legs, highlighted light brown hair, and warm hazel eyes. She's the kindest person I know. Her inner beauty makes her outer beauty shine even brighter. I've always loved her confident and laid back nature.

Right now I'm thankful she lets me retreat inside my head, unsure if I manage the occasional hum to show her I'm paying attention. I'm totally not listening, like a crappy friend.

"Are you okay today, girl?" Maisy asks, putting a hand on mine after her story ends. "We can move to the courtyard if you want. I can pull up a meditation flow playlist on my phone. It'll be great, we'll zen out before next period. Think we can get away with a nap, too?" She laughs, the sound light and airy, then crunches into a carrot. "My mom would freak if she found out I stopped being her perfect ideal of a goody-goody for, like, five minutes to cut class. I'm missing out on a teenage rite of passage."

My reaction is delayed, but when her words register, I sit up straight. Rolling my lips between my teeth, I widen my eyes and nod at Maisy. "I'm okay. We're already here, we might as well stay. Tomorrow we should do that, though."

"Yes." Maisy drags the word out with a languid smile and wiggles her fingers at me. It gets me to smile. "All right, there's my girl. Want me to make us an appointment at the goat yoga studio this weekend? We haven't been in so long. We need to release our negative energy so we can soak in all the good vibes. And with that look on your face, we need to call in the big guns. Baby goats."

"Okay." I smile at her and take another carrot when she nudges the container toward me.

Maisy winks and a little of my worries ebb away for a minute. She's always had a calming effect, ever since she found me crying in the woods, lost on a hike, and guided me back to the campground.

A round of laughter sounds behind me. I hear Connor's voice, but I won't turn around. I won't.

The curiosity wins out and I peek over my shoulder.

Connor is at his usual table with the most popular students —Devlin Murphy, guys from the soccer team, pretty girls from the dance and cheer squads. He's holding court over his kingdom, talking with his hands, a big grin on his face. His eyes found me once, at the beginning of lunch when I walked in with Maisy. I haven't been able to look his way since, purposely putting my back to their table.

He didn't acknowledge me other than a quick look, so I guess I don't have to put on an act as his girlfriend today.

Blackmail, lies, and secrets. These are Connor's bargaining chips. It's how he and Devlin rule the school. They keep us all in line through strategy with no room for remorse.

Now I'm the latest victim.

My phone sits on the table in front of me, turned over so I can see the cupcake PopSocket on the back. I'm too afraid to scroll through my message history with Wyatt—who isn't even flipping Wyatt, as it turns out. If I look, it will only taint every thrilling memory of the last few weeks. I'll see the depth of how Connor manipulated me, the hot and sometimes sweet morning and evening messages twisted and poisoned by the truth.

How could I have gotten the number wrong?

It's a question I've been asking myself on repeat since the encounter with him.

Never in a million years would I ever want to be with Connor Bishop the way I *thought* I was progressing my relationship with Wyatt, upgrading from fling-adjacent to bonafide boyfriend and girlfriend status.

Goes to show me, assuming without ever talking about it. I'm so fucking naïve, playing right into Connor's cruel hands. My throat hurts, tight with emotion when I swallow.

I fight the urge to bury my face in my arms. It's pointless to hide from the truth—that my bully and my neighbor is the same guy I've been fantasizing about and having phone sex with. Well, text sex. But still. Lots of sexy stuff has gone down between us.

"Oh my god," I mumble in horror when it occurs to me I know what his dick looks like. I've seen him *come*.

This time I give in and cover my flaming hot face.

My hands burn with the urge to knead something to calm my breathing. I wonder if I can spend the rest of the lunch period in the culinary classroom to bake something before my next class starts. I'm in the mood for bread. Maybe Mrs. Horne will let me hide out there for a while.

It would be the first time I've ever skipped a class, but I think the circumstances justify a break before I crumble under the emotional pressure weighing on my shoulders, stabbing at my heart with fresh reminders.

"Oh great," Maisy says in a flat tone, grabbing my attention.

Usually she's hard to ruffle, so it takes a lot to draw a reaction like that from her. Her gaze is locked on the doors and I swing around to see what's got her twisted up.

A tall, imposing boy stalks through the cafeteria. Dark hair hangs over his forehead and he wears a leather jacket and heavy boots, completely disregarding the school uniform. His face is set in angry lines, mouth turned down as he glares at any student that dares look his way.

"Who is that?" I ask, not recognizing him.

"Wilder," Maisy says quietly. "Fox Wilder. He's in my grade, but he's supposed to be in yours. They held him back when he came back."

"Came back?"

"He used to live here." Her expression is distant and sad. "A long time ago, when Holden and I were kids. He was our friend."

Wilder sweeps his gaze over the room, landing on Maisy. It seems impossible, but his face grows angrier. Maisy lifts her hand, waving. Wilder jerks his head and moves to the corner where her older brother, Holden, sits with guys from the football team.

"I don't think he remembers you, Maise," I say carefully.

She remains quiet, sighing and crossing her arms. "Guess not. He's been cold every time I try to say hi, but he's been hanging around Holden since he moved back to Ridgeview. I don't know what I did. It was so long ago, we were only kids when..." She trails off and shakes her head. "Never mind. Oh crap. Drama alert."

Maisy nods with her chin and I glance toward Connor's table. My heart falls when I realize how quiet the center tables have gone, and *why*.

Blair Davis, the dark-haired scholarship student at Silver Lake High that seems like a punching bag for the rich, popular crowd, stands stock still in front of Devlin Murphy. He's sprawled in his seat before her like an evil king, expression hard and commanding. I watch as Blair lifts the water thermos in her hand and dumps it over herself.

What the hell!

Heinous cackles erupt from Connor and Devlin's crowd of friends. Water drips from Blair's hair and her uniform shirt is soaked right through.

"Oh no," I mumble, already reaching for napkins from a holder on the table. "Not again. Why can't they leave her alone?"

"Assholes," Maisy hisses.

The whole cafeteria claps and taunts, cheering the drama on.

It fires me up that no one is willing to act. "I'm going to help."

"Wet dog alert!" Someone shouts from the other tables surrounding the central popular one. They call more vile things and make kissing sounds at Blair's back, like they're calling a dog.

Connor pops up from his perch on top of the table and slides in next to Devlin, muttering in his ear with a matching smirk as his friend.

He's just as vile and arrogant as Devlin Murphy, cruel and cold beneath the mask of the cocky jokester. All I see is someone who uses people and takes amusement in the torment he puts them through.

My chest burns with anger, both for Blair and at the boys at this school who think they can get away with murder. We aren't their toys. I navigate through the tables separating me from the middle of the cafeteria, clenching the napkins in my fist. I've never been one to resort to violence ever, but right now it's too much—his threats were bad enough, but seeing him laugh as his friend bullies Blair makes me snap. I could punch Connor and not regret it.

The bravado that drove me over to the scene wavers as I stand under the full brunt of Connor and Devlin together. They haven't even noticed me, both focused on Blair.

"Um." I offer the napkins to Blair. "I brought you these."

Connor goes stiff in his seat, inhaling sharply. I can feel the press of his eyes against the side of my face as I hold out the napkins.

"Thanks," Blair mutters, accepting my help.

I don't leave her side as she pats herself awkwardly. This is the second time I've stood up for her against them, and I don't doubt for a second that they'd double down in a more cruel way if I walked away. I shoot the pair of them a hard look, hoping they stop treating her so terribly.

As Connor explodes from his seat, I jump, clutching the napkins against my chest. In a blink, he's in my face, towering over me and invading my space.

"U-um, Connor."

"Were you invited over here?" Bishop demands.

I swallow. Is he saying I need to stay away when he doesn't need me to pretend to be his girl? This is so stupid! He should've told me the rules. My knuckles turn white as I grip the napkins tighter.

What if he sends my photos because of this?

The risk is worth it. No one deserves to be treated the way these people bully Blair.

"No. That doesn't matter, though." My chin tips up, spurred on by the fury simmering beneath my skin. It fights with the fear settling in my gut. Connor could destroy me within minutes. Game over. "Blair needed help."

"*Blair* needed help?" Connor mimics, circling behind me.

My heart jolts when his hands clamp on my shoulders in a harsh and punishing grip. "You hear that, Dev?"

I want to whirl and scream at him, ask him what he wants from me if he's going to act like this when an hour and a half ago he said he needed me by his side.

"Sure did," Devlin says, voice like icy shadows.

With a deep grunt, he rises to his feet and I take a fearful step back, pressing into Connor's chest. Between the two of them, the poison I pick to kill me is Connor. He pays me no attention as he stalks into Blair's personal space, staring at her with his scary, dark eyes.

"Did you need help, Davis?"

Blair's jaw tightens, then she answers in a lifeless voice. "No."

Is this really happening? I gape at Blair, baffled that she would take Devlin's crap. I go to take a step closer to Blair's side, but Connor holds me in place, the warmth of his back burning through my sweater. My gaze bounces from Blair to Devlin and I part my lips, thinking I can appeal to him.

"Well—"

"You know," Connor drawls next to my ear, startling me. His fingers skate over my shoulders, down my arms, plucking at my sweater. "The only thing a girl next door is good for is warming my dick." He leans closer, covering my back with his chest, burying his face in my hair as he lowers his voice to a sinister hush. "You offering, neighbor? You can leave your granny sweater on."

Breathing is hard. His words crash over me, driving spikes into my heart. Why even threaten me if he's only going to be an utter bastard to me in front of his friends? I want to cry when I think of our messages, the way he swore I was the most beautiful girl he's ever seen. Making sure I can't forget that it's been him making me feel excited, wanted, *good*.

Tripping over my own feet, I stumble out of his grasp as soon as it loosens. "You... You—"

"Me," Connor declares, sweeping his arms to encompass it. There's no doubt he's thinking along the same lines as me. I can see it in his piercing gray eyes. "All me, baby."

He doesn't spell it out, but he's reminding me exactly who I've been intimate with. Who I've bared myself to. My heart aches, feeling like it's shriveling. Everything was a lie and it finally hits me, making me gasp with pain.

Shaking my head, my face crumbles in anguish. I can't look at him anymore. Turning on my heel, I rush for the double doors, wiping away tears as they stream down my face. Maisy calls for me, but I ignore her and burst into the hall.

* * *

I don't think of my world history class, heading straight for the culinary room, not stopping for anything until I sag against the door. Everything blurs at the edges, tunneling my vision. My chest feels tight and my skin is hot and itchy. I rub at my neck and shove my sleeves up.

Mrs. Horne is seated at her desk at the front of the room. She takes one look at my face, probably puffy and red by now. "Thea? Everything okay?"

It takes two tries to speak. "Yes. Please, can I spend some time in here?"

"Of course. I'll give you a pass when you're ready to go." She waves at the work stations. "Just clean up when you're done."

There's not another class in here until last period, the class I'm in.

"Thank you," I breathe, on the verge of tears again from her understanding.

I feel vulnerable, like a light wind could blow me over into emotional turmoil. The baking supplies call to me. I'm thankful this school has a thriving variety of courses available, because the cooking class is equipped with everything I need. It seems more like the set of a reality baking show than a high school class, but I don't care about it right now.

Losing my sweater and washing my hands at the sink in the back of the room, I grab one of the linen aprons hanging from a hook in the corner, looping the bib over my neck and knotting it around my waist. I put my hair up, borrowing one of the fresh hair ties Mrs. Horne keeps on her desk for anyone with long hair since I left the cafeteria with nothing. Maisy will take my bag with her.

My phone pings, but I'm not ready to look. Locking every stray thought behind a wall in my head, I get to work.

Once the ingredients are mixed, I turn out the dough by hand. As I work, my lungs stop burning and I can draw air in without feeling like I might pass out at any second. Kneading the dough becomes meditative as I follow a recipe I've memorized for a braided cinnamon sugar challah loaf, my favorite soft bread. I need a comforting bake, and the warm scent of cinnamon will make everything better.

I move on autopilot, and slowly my thoughts creep through the wall after I've calmed down from my panic. One by one, they slip free.

I should delete everything—the photos, our messages. And block his number while I'm at it. My breaths turn shallow and I focus on working the dough for a minute.

Sighing, I set it up in the proofing oven so it can rise. I debate mixing another so I can knead something else, brushing my hands off on my apron. My teeth drag over the corner of my lip. I peek at Mrs. Horne, but she's absorbed in grading at the front of the room.

I'm going to do it.

Pulling out my phone from my sweater, I carry it back to the workstation and put it down, bracing my flour-dusted hands on either side of it. Some dough is caked beneath my nails and around my cuticles. I tap my nails, chewing on my lip.

Come on, Thea.

But I can't. I can't bring myself to do it, not yet. My chest collapses as I release a heavy exhale, hanging my head.

"Stupid," I mutter.

My face prickles with heat as mortification slithers in and chokes me with long tendrils I can't escape. It's not just the nudes I can't face, but where I took them. In school, in *class* with that photo of my underwear. And, *god*, Connor was sitting right behind me when he asked for it. I swallow thickly. He's awful.

A bastard playing me for his pleasure, taking the torment to a new level.

"Thea?"

My head pops up. Mr. Coleman leans against the open doorway with a cardboard cup of coffee, mouth turned down in a frown.

"Is everything all right? I thought I saw you run from the cafeteria when I was getting coffee. I've been looking around for you." One of his handsome dimples appears as his mouth curves at my confused blink. He shrugs. "The student cafe serves better coffee than what they brew in the teacher's lounge."

"Oh. Um." I dust my dirty hands against the apron and flutter my fingers against my hair, hoping I don't look like a total mess. "I'm fine."

"Are you sure?" He steps into the room and weaves through the other worktables to get to me. His gaze shifts to Mrs. Horne for a moment, absorbed in her paperwork, before returning to me. With a soft smile, he puts his hand on my shoulder. "You can always come to me if you need to talk."

The heat filling my cheeks now is a different kind. Mr. Coleman is my favorite teacher, even above Mrs. Horne. He truly cares about connecting with us, and I admire him for it.

"Thank you." I'm smiling for the first time since that dimly lit science room. "You're so kind."

"You're at a difficult time in your life," he says, his voice soothing and warm. His eyes sparkle with his smile and his shoulders shake with a short laugh. "It wasn't that long ago for me. I want you to know I understand what you're going through."

I return his smile. I'm about to offer to bring him the second loaf of challah that my dough will yield when I catch sight of someone hovering in the door. My blood turns to ice and it becomes difficult to breathe all over again.

Connor looms in the doorway with a black, dangerous expression.

How long has he been there? Did he hunt me down, waiting for me to emerge?

He meets my eye and crooks his finger to call me over.

Can hearts turn into rabbits? That's what mine feels like, racing around.

He's the reason I ran to my sanctuary at school, and now he wants me to go to him just like that? That unfamiliar, violent urge returns. I draw a fortifying breath and rub my forehead, turning back to Mr. Coleman.

"Actually, I was, um." A nervous laugh escapes me. "Just cooling my head off, but I feel better now. I should get to class."

Mr. Coleman's expression shifts to something harder to read as he glances between us. "I'll write you a late slip. Come with me and we can chat about it on the way."

Connor steps into the room, silent as death. He picks up my sweater from the apron hook where I left it.

Frazzled, I swipe my phone from the worktable. "No, please. I'm okay. My boyfriend is waiting for me."

I pause, closing my eyes. It just rolled off my tongue. What is wrong with me?

Connor stills, too, watching me curiously. He tips his head to the side and lifts a brow. My stomach rolls unpleasantly.

Did I make a mistake? Isn't that what he wanted from me?

I open my mouth, but Mr. Coleman pats my shoulder. "Well, just remember what I said, okay? I'm always here for you, Thea."

With another awkward laugh, I nod and scurry across the room to Connor, where he seems to be kneading the material of my sweater, his hands flexing. He's locked in a stare with Mr. Coleman as I struggle out of the dirty apron, dumping it in the laundry basket.

"Good girl." He mutters so quietly I'm the only one who can hear it as he hands my sweater over.

"Marina, I have dough in the proofer," I say, sad to abandon my challah.

"I'll take care of it so it's ready to bake when you come back for class later," she says.

Connor puts his arm around my shoulders and guides me out of the culinary classroom.

We walk in silence through the hall for a minute before he stops. "We'll start tomorrow. You shouldn't have done what you did back there, the lunch room. You just butted in and..." He pushes out a harsh breath. "I got caught up, but I didn't mean to make you cry." His jaw clenches. "Clean slate?"

As if I could forget everything? Yeah, right.

Worst of all, if he really needed my help—before he broke

my heart—I would have helped him out, no questions asked because that's the kind of person I am.

I huff, crossing my arms. "Are you kidding? You treated me like shit."

"I'm apologizing for it," he growls, turning cold gray eyes on me. "I don't have to. Would you rather I do business as usual and apply pressure until it hurts you even more? Don't forget, I'm the one with all the leverage."

A shiver runs down my spine. "It's a crappy apology. Are you going to spread my photos around?"

"No. As long as our deal stands."

I can't believe him. I've spent the last half hour sick out of my mind worrying my private photos would be all over school by the end of the day. But for whatever reason, he needs me.

Everything is on Connor's whim. This world is one where he does whatever—gets whatever he wants, and the rest of us simply exist to bend to his will.

"You're not forgiven for being an ass," I say, pushing his arm off my shoulder and walking away.

"Where do you think you're going?"

"Away from you." I turn my head just enough to see him from the corner of my eye. "Until tomorrow, when this dog and pony show starts."

He stares for a beat, then snorts and shakes his head. Turning around, he heads in the opposite direction.

"See you tomorrow, little mouse. Be ready."

ELEVEN
THEA

By *be ready,* Connor meant he'd be blocking my driveway in the morning, his dark silver Lexus GX idling as he waited for me, one hand resting over the top of the wheel as I stood there like an idiot.

He's throwing me in the deep end and we haven't even talked about the details. I wasn't inclined to message him anytime soon, so I thought he might find me before school to go over our...agreement. This is ridiculous and frustrating me to no end.

I stay rooted in my driveway, hoping Mom isn't peeking out the window for one of her random checks because I can't explain to her what I don't understand myself yet.

"Let's go!" Connor shouts through the open window, gesturing like *what* as he squints at me. "We're gonna be late if you don't get in the car."

"I didn't ask for a ride." I nod to my blue Mini Cooper. "I have my own car."

Connor snorts. "That is a doll car. Get in, now."

My lips purse. Damn him. He can't control me!

But he's right, we can't keep arguing or we'll be late. Groaning under my breath, I climb into the front seat, dumping my bag by my feet. The car smells like him—earthy and woodsy with hints of spice. It envelops me, making my stomach flip over in a weird way.

"Don't think this will be a regular thing. When are we going over the rules? I'm totally making this one of them."

"We will." He reaches out with his free hand after he pulls away from the curb, taking mine and threading our fingers together. I go still, surprised he wants to hold my hand when there's no one around to put on our act for. "And I am. Boyfriends drive their girlfriends to school. Can't look like a bad boyfriend leaving you stranded."

A sardonic laugh bursts from me. Connor tips his head to peer at me.

"Stranded? Please, I can drive myself. You humiliated me yesterday in front of your friends and made fun of my sweater, now you're holding my hand like you're sweet?" I yank my hand free and tuck it beneath my thigh so he can't get at it. I smooth my green plaid uniform skirt with my other hand, then prop my elbow against the door, resting my head in my palm. "You're still not forgiven. I'm only here because you're black-mailing me. I wouldn't come near you otherwise."

"You certainly were ready to come all over me before." The glare I direct at him drops the temperature in the car by a few degrees. He blows out a slow, strained breath and grips the wheel with both hands. "Okay. Whatever. Noted."

We ride in silence for a long stretch. The drive to school isn't long, and I realize I'm wasting a good opportunity for the details I'm desperate for.

"So what's our deal? Or rather, your deal that I have no choice but to accept because the alternative is...yeah, no thanks. Asshole." I shift a little to face him better as we drive through Ridgeview, turning onto the tree-lined road that leads up to the school. "When did we get together? How did it happen?"

Connor cuts a look at me from the corner of his eye. "We'll keep it simple so it's easy to remember. We've grown up as neighbors. Got together over summer or something. You're the girl next door, what's not to like about that?"

I frown as he hitches a shoulder. "That's unimaginative."

Amusement crosses his face. "We could always use the true version: you sent me a wrong number nude and I was like aight."

"You ass! We are *not* using that. And I wasn't naked."

"Yet. Shortly after?" Connor hums, shifting in the driver's seat. "So gloriously naked."

With a scandalized squeal, I swat his arm, overwhelmed by his proximity and what he's saying. He drives me to things I never do.

He laughs. The corner of his mouth tugs up in a crooked grin as he turns the wheel with the heel of his palm, entering the student parking lot.

"You want a whirlwind romance, or something? I'm just trying to make it easy. It's not like it's real."

The words slice me and I suck in a pained gasp.

It's not real.

Right.

For as big as his SUV is, I'm suffocated by being so near to him while my emotions spiral.

Connor is my first actual boyfriend, but it's all fake. I stare at my lap.

"Is it cool if I drop you off here?"

I look up, blinking out of my depressing thoughts. He took the loop that cuts off from the student lot for pick ups and drop offs up the hill where the school stands flanked by tall pine trees. His friends gather in the parking lot at the base of the hill. Devlin Murphy's flashy red sports car stands out like a beacon, and a few people gather around it as he leans against the side.

We didn't get to cover much on the ride. Not knowing what to anticipate being Connor's puppet is grating on me.

"Don't want to be seen with your nerdy girlfriend? Too big of a dent to your shiny popular soccer captain image? I thought that was the whole point of this." The acidic bite in my voice surprises me.

"I, no," Connor says, furrowing his brow. He drags his fingers through his messy light brown hair. "I just thought—because of yesterday. I didn't think you'd want to show up with me yet."

The hot and cold nature of his cruelty and his unexpected consideration is giving me whiplash.

"Okay." I'm ready to escape the car anyway. I pop the door handle and grab my bag from the floor. "Thanks. Bye, I guess."

His voice halts me when I turn to join the flow of students making their way into school. "Wait for me after homeroom. We'll walk together to first period."

My brows wrinkle in confusion as I spin to face him. "We don't have first period together."

"The way to your first class has the most foot traffic. We'll get the rumor mill going early and by lunch they'll all have heard about it. You should sit at my table today."

"Uh, yeah, no. No thank you."

Did he forget the point he made about my discomfort with his friends? Or do guys just get over stuff that easily and he thinks I'll be dandy by lunch?

His expression darkens. "Yes."

"No." I fold my arms over the open window, lifting on my tiptoes to reach. "I already have standing lunch plans every day with my friends. And yours are very rude, so. That's that."

Connor releases an aggravated sound. "Just be in the hall after homeroom."

He pulls off before I can say anything.

I won't be waiting around for him. He needs to apologize to me for real to make up for yesterday before I play the perfect doting girlfriend. I only got in the SUV because I didn't want to be late.

After I part ways with Maisy at the end of lunch, a hand clamps on my arm from behind and a dark voice growls in my ear, making me yelp in the empty covered walkway between the north and south buildings.

"Somewhere you forgot to be?"

I toss an unimpressed look over my shoulder as my stomach clenches. "I told you I wasn't eating lunch with you."

He squeezes my arm. "I'm talking about this morning. We'll have to do it all over again tomorrow morning. Or—" My body collides with his chest as he spins me around to face him "—we take more drastic measures. Hold still."

Before I register what's happening, Connor tips my chin up, presses his forehead to mine, and holds his other arm up. He flicks his eyes to the side to check, then I hear the digital *click* sound of his camera. He keeps his piercing eyes locked on

111

mine and kisses my cheek. I gasp, pushing against his chest. His arm is like an iron band around me as he licks my damn cheek like an animal, snapping away.

"What—are—you—doing?" With each word I struggle against him.

He chuckles against my temple, the deep and raspy sound unfairly making arousal pulse in my core, reminding me of the recorded voice texts where he'd say filthy things to me in the heat of the moment.

I push away from him, tucking my hair behind my ears to give myself a second to gather my wits.

"And," Connor drawls. "Posted. Hashtag bae. Better follow me back, or that'll look weird."

Annoyed, I whip out my phone and sure enough, I have a new follower notification on Instagram, a friend request on Facebook, and a photo tag with *@BigBadBishop*. Clicking on the post, I find three photos on a carousel. The first one where he kissed my cheek steals my breath for a moment because of how much we look like an actual couple. Then a sigh of relief hisses out of me. He didn't post the one where he licked my cheek.

"Why didn't we just do that in the first place?" I ask. "Seems a lot easier."

"Because my way was more organic. There are algorithms to fight against for visibility. Plus, photos can be doctored."

"If they can, I'll just say that it's not me in the ones you have." I cross my arms. "Easy peasy, we can go our separate ways."

Connor's smile isn't a genuine one, more like an evil shark's, marring his handsome face. That angelic face of his is a big fat lie. "Everyone knows I'm better than that. I'd never be so amateur that I'd spread something photoshopped. The secrets I collect are the real deal, baby."

The second bell rings, signaling that we're both late to class. He takes my wrist and tugs me into the north building, dragging me back to the same empty science lab.

"Do you ever go to class?" I ask, fighting back the memory of the last time we were in here together.

"You keep begging me to have this chat, so here we are." He pulls out a stool and perches on it, propping his heel on the bar. "This is your one and only reminder: you agreed, so you have to play along. No more ghosting on me if I tell you to be somewhere." He ruffles his hair, making it stick up a little, giving him a more boyish look. "What you have to do isn't even *hard*, just be seen with me and shit for credibility."

He makes me so mad. I'm normally level-headed. But around him? I grind my teeth and stalk up to him. Even seated on the stool, he's taller than me, but I don't let it stop me. I refuse to let him scare me as I poke my finger into his chest.

"Listen here, *Bishop*," I say firmly, using the name everyone calls him, "I might have agreed, but I want a real apology for yesterday before we go any further with this ruse. First you shatter my entire world with the truth, then you blackmail me, then the lunchroom! You hurt my feelings and I don't think I can stand to be around you whether you force me to or not until you make some kind of effort to treat me like I deserve to be treated."

In my head, my inner goddess is snapping and clapping at me for getting that out without my voice cracking.

Connor stares at me, his lips working, unsure how to respond. "You are..." He clears his throat, the wonder shrinking back into the shadows behind his mask. His voice hardens. "Something else, huh? I don't normally apologize to the people I blackmail *while* I'm doing it, if ever."

"I'm waiting."

"It won't change anything." His brows draw together.

"You're still on the hook, or I'll start sending out your photos. I'm serious, Thea. I'm not a nice guy and I will hurt you if you cross me."

"You can continue as planned. After you give me a good apology. Then I'll help you." I hesitate, licking my lips, debating if it helps my case at all to tell him. "I would've, you know. Helped you. You didn't have to use any leverage, just asked and I would've."

It feels good to tell him that. Maybe if he understands who he's dealing with, he'll stop acting like a grumpy, controlling ass.

"Is that a trick?" He huffs out a scornful laugh and scratches the back of his head, muttering, "Better not be."

I lift my brows expectantly. He meets my gaze, unwavering. I'll wait all day if I have to.

"I'm sorry. Dick move on my part."

For the first time ever, in all the years I've watched Connor from outside of his luminescent bubble of popularity and fortune, he sounds genuine. Human. It's the small reassurance I need to do this.

"Okay," I say.

"Okay?"

"Yes. You may continue with your power trip."

Connor gapes at me, suspicion bleeding into the edges of his expression.

Checking the time on the clock above the door, I frown. If I miss any more of my classes, I'll be written up and sent to Principal Bishop's office. Setting my bag down, I pull out a notebook and a pen, prepared to take notes.

"What kind of girlfriend am I supposed to be?"

With a tiny shake of his head, he says, "Like a normal one. Just do whatever you usually do."

Easy for him to say.

I hold back a sigh. He's proven he's dangerous to spill my secrets to. I don't want to give him another one by admitting I've never had a boyfriend—a real, in person one, anyway. Swallowing, I consider my old online boyfriend, even though it was brief. There's always something that keeps me from counting him.

With my minimal experience, I don't know how to be in a relationship, pretend or otherwise.

Thoughts fly through my head, whispering to me how I'll fail at being a fake girlfriend as much as I would a real one. That Connor will find out how pathetic I am and probably destroy me worse for it. The ugly thoughts pick away at me, promising I'll never be the confident girl in my secret folder, driving away my inner goddess of self-love.

Fake, fake, fake.

Sad.

Unwanted.

My throat burns and I realize the rattling in my ears is my wheezing breaths.

"Are you okay? You look..."

He'll see it so easily.

Tossing aside my notebook, I close the distance between us in a panic. Connor's eyes widen as he cups my elbows.

"Just how long do you expect me to put on this song and dance with you? You never even told me when or how you want me to pretend. Just snap to it whenever you decide without an explanation."

Yes, I sound crazed. I don't care.

A bark of laughter drops from Connor's lips as he looks me up and down. He rises from the stool, herding me back a step.

"That's enough," he growls, grabbing my hips and pinning me against a lab table. "This goes until I say so. You're at *my* mercy here while I've got your dirty little secret in my power."

Ignoring his alpha male bullshit, I throw my next question at him without missing a beat to stave off the thump of my pulse. The words flood out of me with no way of stopping them when I'm worked up.

"How long is that exactly? I'm not just going to live some indefinite lie with no expiration date when it's your problem." While he's bewildered by my outburst, I wriggle away to pace. "A year? Three years? What about college? What—will it still be going on when we're in our twenties, and we'll be faking a marriage and two point five kids? And—"

Connor catches me around the waist, clapping a big hand over my mouth. His gray eyes are full of fascinated exasperation.

"Jesus. Are you some kind of wind up toy?" He removes his hand carefully, like he's worried I'll get started again. "What the fuck was all that?"

It's like I blink back to reality, once he interrupted the flow. My panic has faded in the shock of him grabbing me. I almost smile. Until I remember why we're here.

"I babble when I'm nervous." Folding my arms, I shrug. He steps back. "Seriously, Connor. I'm not blindly playing along without an end date. You can't keep using your leverage over me to keep me in line forever."

Connor rubs his chin, studying me. I can see the gears in his head turning. "Until graduation, then. We'll part on friendly terms as we prepare to go to college."

"That's it? Then you'll leave me alone and delete my photos?"

He smirks. "I don't get a parting gift for when I'm lonely at night?"

"Connor!"

An amused sound huffs out of him as he blocks my swatting hands, catching my wrists in his grasp. "All right, yeah.

Fair. Although, little mouse, let me offer you some advice. Never trust anyone who has dirt on you. There's always an extra copy."

"Do you have extra copies?"

"Of course. Cloud backups." He taps my nose. "You can smash my phone and I'll still own you."

Biting my lip, I skate my gaze away. "So do I have to meet your parents? Are you going to meet mine?" I gulp the lump forming in my throat. "Look, I've—I've never had a real—"

I gasp. Crap. I wasn't planning on saying it, but then before I was aware, it was half out. Too late now. It's difficult to continue.

Closing my eyes, my words burst out of me all at once. "I've never had a relationship before, okay? I don't know what I'm doing here. If I'm going to do it with you, we need to outline every expectation, or I'll suck at this."

Silence follows my awkward admission. I crack my eyes open, wary of peeking.

Connor has his lips pulled to one side as he considers me. He reaches out, tangling his fingers with mine, playing with my hand. My breath turns shallow as he drags his finger over my knuckles. It feels nice.

"Not yet," he says, watching my reactions while he touches me. The soft caresses get my heart beating erratically. Whatever he sees makes him nod. "We'll take it slow. With the way you were texting me, I thought...never mind." His expression turns curious and calculating. "Have you ever been kissed?"

I shake my head, breath hitching.

He hums and cradles my face with both hands. "Do you want to be kissed?"

The timbre of his voice curls around me. I can't believe I ever brushed it off because I thought I was talking to Wyatt.

The answer was right in front of me all along. Connor didn't modify his voice to hide it.

That deep voice does things I don't understand to my insides. It's the same tone he always used on the phone. The dark, sensual voice of my dreams.

Do I? My throat constricts. It will be my first. Connor will rob me of all my real firsts with this fake relationship.

My lashes flutter as his thumbs glide over my cheeks. He doesn't stop. The rich sandalwood and spicy scent wraps around me as he steps closer, angling his face toward mine.

This is crazy. I should still be angry with him for yesterday, even with the apology I can't get over how he made me feel overnight—being the person both behind my soaring heart and the one to send it crash landing into the ground.

But his touch is so soft and gentle. I picture how his lips might feel on mine and an ache tugs in my chest. I do want it.

"I—yes. But I don't want it to be fake."

Those gray eyes trap me for a long beat. I think he's going to kiss me anyway as his breath fans over my lips. My whole body feels alive, calling out for him.

Then he eases out of my space, back to business in a cool, collected tone. "No kissing. Okay. What about other PDA? It'll be hard to convince people we're suddenly together if I can't act like your boyfriend. Can I still text you?"

I'm dizzy from the almost-kiss not happening. "Like holding hands? That's fine. Um. I don't know about texting. I didn't know it was you. Obviously."

A rumble sounds in his chest.

"Wyatt," he bites out.

I'm no expert, but he sounds kind of jealous. My brows hike up. That can't be right.

"Fine. I'll leave it up to you. Ball's in your court." Connor grants me a cocky smirk. "Just like we started, with that hot little pic of your nightie you sent me."

Flustered, I sail right over the fact that text was never meant for his eyes. "What about when and where? Is this just for school?" I can't see why his reputation hinges on having a girl by his side—me, specifically. "Or outside of school, too?"

His expression closes off. "It's whenever I say it is. You'll do as I say and you're going to behave. Don't think you can get away with a long leash."

"So I'm just supposed to be at your beck and call when you need me to be your doll?" My eyes narrow. "That's not fair. I'm not some toy to pick up and toss aside when you feel like playing with me. I have a life."

In a blink he's in my face, growling as he corners me against the lab table once more. My throat throbs with my fluttering pulse, a spike of fear lashing me.

"And I own it now."

TWELVE
CONNOR

This is all some kind of trick to outwit me.

I'd bet anything on it.

What my little mouse doesn't get yet? I'm not letting her escape the trap I've locked her in. She stumbled into my depraved kingdom, and I'm throwing away the key to strand her here.

I crowd her against the tall worktable, muscles in my arms flexing. She puts on a frightened little expression that I don't buy. I haven't really scared her yet, not with the way she's fought back, a mouse facing off with a lion.

Thea is fascinating as hell going off on tangents in the face of danger, but I saw it yesterday when she stuck her nose where it didn't fucking belong. Apples and fucking trees, man. I can't forget it again. Can't let the cute little way her nose scrunches distract me from the truth. She keeps knocking me off balance, but if she thinks I'm letting her go or allowing her to call the shots, she's sorely mistaken.

She comes off genuine and earnest, but it's all a lie. Pretty wrapping to fool me into trusting her.

My little sunshine daisy has hidden thorns and roots to choke her king. Beautiful, but destructive.

Why do I keep letting her manipulate me when I'm supposed to be holding a guillotine over her head? This girl...

She's shredding my rep.

I have to stop rolling over when she pulls the pretty puppy eyes on me, or throws such sound logic when she should be cowering in terror that I find myself giving in rather than putting her in her place. Like the end date demand—there wasn't supposed to be one. Mom made a point about legacy and commitment, making it sound more long-term, but I had no way to tell her that without looking weak, not the formidable blackmail king she should fear. I can't keep her forever, and I let her steamroll me. I guess I'll figure something else out after graduation.

"Got it?"

Thea nods. "Got it."

"Great. Enough questions."

I shove down the annoying instinct that keeps catching me off guard, the one where I want to protect her. Like when I made her cry and immediately felt like shit for it. This is what lying bitches do, they get in your damn head and twist you up.

Other than Devlin, Thea is the first person to ever talk back to me and not fear me on sight from the image I've cultivated. In the face of domination and demand, she talks back with logic and a bravery I didn't know a shy chick like her could possess.

But after dumping everything in her lap yesterday, now I know how far I can push her before she breaks. It's information for later.

I put a hand on her waist. Damn, I really want to kiss her, need to claim that mouth. All this verbal sparring with her is getting me horny.

But she said no.

"We could be having so much fun with this, sunshine." I groan under my breath and bump my nose against hers. "You sure you don't want to keep playing our game? Advance to the next boss level? There are killer perks and achievements. I want to show you what it feels like to come on my tongue for real."

She makes a delicious sound, like she took me at face value for agreeing to let her make the first move, but can't handle the filthy words I'm whispering.

The inexperience was a shock after the things we've done when sexting, but it's intoxicating to know she's a blank canvas. I want to paint a masterpiece on it, show her what it's like to fuck the way we fantasized about. It's like I met two different girls, one confident and as devious as I am, and the one in front of me, trembling from a few words and my hand massaging her waist.

"I..." She shakes her head. "Connor. This is a bad idea."

My lips trail over her cheek in the lightest brush. "My favorite kind."

She laughs, breathy and soft. It makes my dick harder.

"They'll be your favorite, too. Let me show you how to live, sunshine."

Fuck yes, I think as she puts her hands on my shoulders, pulling me in.

The door bangs open, startling both of us. A shadow fills the door, back-lit by the bright hallway lights.

"Thea? Aren't you supposed to be in your world history class?"

Coleman.

He looms in the door, keeping to the shadows as Thea stiffens beside me.

"Mr. Coleman," she says.

Is that relief in her voice? I swing my glower to her, getting more pissed off by the second at the way she's focused on him.

What the fuck.

It takes a second for my brain to kick into gear, but once it does, Thea has danced out of my arms, drawn to Coleman. He falls back a step, the light in the hallway showing his smarmy face. The satisfied curve of his mouth ignites a rage in me.

What. The. Fuck.

Sure, he's a teacher, but this guy is always around Thea, especially when I'm alone with her. It's improbable he would just happen to be walking by her all the time. I followed him yesterday when he tracked Thea to the baking classroom. This is all wrong, blaring a dissonant clang in every bone in my body.

"Get to class, Mr. Bishop," he says in a clipped command.

I grin without a trace of pleasure. "Sure thing."

"Come on. I'll escort you to your class." He steers Thea down the hall with a hand resting lightly on her back. "You're really surprising me lately with this behavior. It's not what I expect from you."

Coleman walks off with Thea. She doesn't look back at me once. Nothing about this feels right.

Halfway down the hall, I catch her simpering. "I can explain, sir."

My stomach ices over. Goddamn it. I got swept up in her again.

Still suspicious and questioning why Coleman is always around Thea, I rub my jaw as I head for my car to smoke a joint. I have practice later, but fuck being here right now.

THIRTEEN
CONNOR

Practice is gruesome. Two guys have knelt in the grass at the sidelines to puke. A few more are sprawled and groaning across the field. Devlin's got a wicked gleam in his eye from the torture I'm taking out on the guys.

I stand on the center line with my hands on my hips, spitting on the ground. My throat is raw from shouting directions at them for the last forty-five minutes. "Shape the fuck up. This is not the team I know we are."

Which is true, because I'm taking all my annoyance out on them. For once, I don't want to be here, but I can't skip soccer.

All I want to do is get out of here so I can do more digging on Thea. I might be blackmailing her, but I still want to claim those pink lips. We were about to kiss, having a real taste of her was in my grasp. Then Coleman showed the fuck up and ruined it. She flipped a switch so fast, it's got alarm bells going off in my head.

I'll hunt down every secret she's ever hidden so I don't have any more surprises with her. Then I'll fucking devour her.

Devlin is in full Devil Boy mode with his own demons, enjoying the show. Damn sadist. He dribbles a soccer ball, flicking it from his toe to bounce off his knees.

"The hell did we even do?" Sean mutters to Trent as he helps him to the bench for their water bottles.

"Beats me," Trent answers, glaring at me as they pass.

I shake my head, not in the mood for my favorite pastime or my so-called friends. "Can't keep up? Quit popping your dad's oxy pills, then maybe you'll have some stamina. The pros go harder than this."

Trent lunges at me with a growl. Sean holds him back with a worried look, like he's afraid of what I'll spill about him. I grant them both a vicious grin. They back off, exchanging wary glances.

"Fucking psycho," Sean says in an undertone.

He better watch it, or I will spill his dirty deeds. Porn addiction, that one. Nasty shit, too.

"Another lap, captain?" Devlin asks as he cycles the ball from his toe, to knee, to chest, and over again with perfect control. Showoff. "If these guys can gossip on the field, they haven't had enough."

"Nah. Get the fuck out of my face, all of you." Flapping my hand in dismissal, I head for the showers. I don't care. "Game against Ridgeview East Valley coming up. Coach can deal with you."

Devlin follows, lacing his fingers and putting his hands behind his head. "You good?"

"Yeah. Just an intense day."

He pops my shoulder with the back of his hand. "You need anything?"

"I'm good. I just need to cool off. Unwind." I'm going to shower, go home, and pack a bowl. That'll do the trick to kill the edge close to choking me. "It's chill, bro."

"All right, cool. I'll catch you later." Peeling off from the path to the locker room, Devlin heads for the parking lot without showering.

I head into the locker room and rush through a shower. There's something else on my agenda when I get home.

* * *

Thea is what she seems at first glance. Sweet, kind, and all about a positive outlook. But that's bullshit.

Only forest creatures in cartoon movies are that pure-hearted.

She's a liar like everyone else, but despite the lies she gets my dick hard. I want her.

"I'll find you," I murmur as I poke through her search history thanks to the backdoor I left on her WiFi network. "Every secret. It's all mine, little mouse."

The clack of the keys are as soothing and relaxing as the bowl I smoked when I got home. I tore through two bags of Doritos and rode the high until the buzz wore off. Now I'm hunting for anything that will give me more insight into who I'm dealing with.

As I dig through her social media accounts, I find something new. One that wasn't in the recent browser history when I looked before. It's a blog site.

Once it loads, my stomach tightens.

"The fuck?" I mutter, bombarded by post after post of pictures.

She's younger, her face a little rounder. The newest post has a date stamp of almost two years ago. I'm guessing she's around fifteen or sixteen in these, but the blog archive goes back three years before that.

"For a girl who goes unnoticed, you sure did want to be seen."

By a rough count, there are hundreds of posts. Maybe thousands. When it was active, it looks like she was posting at least three times a week.

There's nothing too wild, but my brows jump up when I see a few that are questionable. Even though we're the same age, I feel skeevy looking at these. Sickos on the internet would have a field day with the gold mine she's offering up. It's not even password protected and private. Public fucking everything for all of her accounts.

My first thought is to lock this, but she could notice if she still accesses the site. It was in her search history, so she looked at it recently.

I was right. She was hiding more secrets. Everyone lies; haven't I learned that lesson enough times by now?

Somehow, victory doesn't taste great. A bitter tang fills my mouth as I click on a few of the posts, skimming the comments. It's a small relief that the blog seems inactive, but if she pulled it up recently, she might be thinking about using it again.

So help me, if she posts any of her pictures to this shit now, I will put her on lockdown and fry her devices so fast.

Ironic, since I'm using her nudes to blackmail her. A snort shakes my shoulders. Whatever, semantics.

My eyes narrow as I scroll through. Most of the comments

make me scoff, but some of the creepier ones have my skin crawling. One username catches my eye.

Henry_Your_GoodKnight: *Beauty beyond measure princess, but what really gets me is the way you smile. Your intelligent eyes say it all, love. You're longing for the world to show you all it has to offer.*

"Yikes."

That one has internet predator written on it in neon blinking lights. I'm about to doxx this fucker for being all over her blog, on every post with multiple comments. The law can suck it. I'd be doing them a favor. Thea better not have given this guy the time of day.

Why the fuck would she subject herself to this for so long without blocking these basement-dwelling neckbeards?

I knew her security was lax as hell when I first hacked her computer, but doesn't she understand how easily this creep or any other on the internet could find her? She didn't even block her photos from download permissions or hide the metadata, putting her location on blast to any dickhead with half a brain.

Shaking my head, I close out of the window.

This girl is going to get me in a mess of trouble, throwing wrenches into my carefully laid plans. I'm supposed to be biding my time until I can break away from this place. All I needed was a fake girlfriend—one of my choosing—to show up when I needed her.

The plan was never someone seducing me with her curvy body, her addictive scent of fresh baked cookies that clings to her skin and hair, and that bright smile. How has a girl that exudes so much sunshine gone under my radar from so long?

Because it's all a lie. A girl like Thea is too good to be true.

I set an alert to notify me when she pulls this site up so I can keep an eye on her like a corrupt guardian angel.

Those protective instincts kick back in, rearing up with the urge to bust down her front door and stand between her and the world.

FOURTEEN
THEA

Sitting in the middle of my bed, armed with my stuffed sea lion, I'm throwing a pity party. I can't kick the down and dirty feeling. It's clung to me all day, ever since Mr. Coleman found Connor and I in a compromising position.

One where I was definitely about to kiss him.

How can I want to kiss my bully after all the crap he's put me through?

He's blackmailing you, girl!

My inner voice of reason sounds like Maisy today and I nod in miserable agreement. "I know."

But I did want that kiss. I would have thrown away my first

on a fake, though, and that doesn't sit right with me. It's a good thing Mr. Coleman showed up when he did.

I flip my phone in my hands a few times, playing with the cupcake grip on the back. Messaging him has been on my mind, or at least reading back through it all. I think I'm ready to see it now.

"Right."

Taking a breath, I unlock my phone and scroll to the beginning.

After weeks of talking to him, the first photo I sent seems so tame. As I skim through the message history, my body warms up, my clit throbbing when I get to one of his dirtier messages.

Can't stop thinking about those sweet sounds you make. You make my cock so hard, I want to bury it in you so deep you'll never get me out, baby. Just you and me, fused together. How does forever sound to you?

"Oof," I mumble, cheeks on fire. "The boy knows how to use his words."

But I did, too. I thought it might make me cringe to read it back, knowing it was Connor on the other side of the screen, but some of it surprises me. Secret Folder Girl showed up, confident, aware of what she wanted. Talking to him like this—well, having phone sex—was easier.

I keep expecting my phone to ping. That's been the weirdest part in the madness of the last two days. I got used to anticipating his messages, got excited at the notification sound on my phone. But he's kept his word, leaving it to me to text him first.

It was hard enough to work up the courage to text *Wyatt*. I don't know what to say knowing I have to face him at school, that he's right next door.

What I need is familiar. Comforting. Safe.

I need to know I can walk away for a minute without

someone like Connor breathing down my neck. Tossing my phone aside, I lean over to grab my laptop from the end of the bed and drag it over. Once it's loaded, I go to my old blog.

The beauty of posting these pictures was that I didn't know who was on the other side of the screen. It was an escape. The distance and sense of anonymity are what gave me the courage to be this version of myself, where I could experiment with the girl in my secret folder without judgement because no one knew me in person to realize how different I was in reality.

How much I fall short of the mark.

A comment on the second post catches my eye. It's from two days ago, but the last time I posted to this blog was years ago. "What?"

Missing these intelligent eyes and talking to you. Where have you gone, love? Do you miss me, too? I dream of finding you, coming to steal you away for the whirlwind romance the world has to offer you. It's me, I'm your world. If I held out my hand, would you take it? The thought consumes me.

Clicking on the other posts, I find a new one on each of them. It's the same username. **Henry_Your_GoodKnight**.

It's him. My old online boyfriend.

Mixed feelings swirl through me. It gives me a sense I'm wanted, desired, *seen*. But at the same time, there's something about the comments that makes my blood run cold and my heart beat faster.

Time has given me a different perspective on the nature of these comments. He was only a few years older, but still. The age I was in these photos and when I was enthralled with our late night emails? A cold sweat breaks out on the back of my neck and I work to swallow past my dry throat.

Opening a new tab, I find the folder in my inbox where I saved our emails, clicking on the last one I never answered.

To: Thea Marie <cupcakecutie22@gmail.com>
From: Henry Knight <henry.k.c@gmail.com>
Subject: ramblings to a princess in a tower

Love, you're all I think of. It's been so long, I fear I'll forget your perfect, porcelain face. Those innocent lips and your sea-blue eyes haunt my sleep. Why won't you answer me? I'll keep sending you messages. I won't stop. Ignoring me won't work.

Answer me, love. Talk to me.

I'll tell you what I really want. At night I sit up thinking about our conversations, the things you've told me. I want to hear your voice. Let me call you. We'll talk all night.

Once I hear your voice, I know you'll stay in my heart forever. If you do this for me, I'll reward you for being my princess again. We'll do what we talked about. I'll come find you, I promise. We'll live the life we planned out. I'll meet your every desire and give you what you ask for in those big sea-blue eyes.
—*Henry*

My breathing is ragged. I fan my fingers over my chest, rubbing.

I stopped because Mom was getting suspicious, and I was so scared of getting in trouble. There was no way I could let him call me in the middle of the night, with my parents asleep down the hall.

Closing the laptop, I climb to my feet. Pity party officially over. I will not sit around dredging up weird old memories to compare to the new ones.

The only comfort I need right now is comfort food.

* * *

A short while later, I'm elbows deep in baking to relieve the stress. The kitchen smells amazing. Two trays of finished double chocolate chip cookies sit to the side of our wide kitchen island, ready for baking once the first batch comes out, while Constantine sprawls at my feet, occasionally peeking up with a tiny whine to beg for scraps.

"I don't know," I tell Maisy on FaceTime, the kitchen iPad propped on the recipe stand.

She's in her airy bedroom, running through yoga poses with her hair in a sloppy bun. I finally broke down and explained I've been weird for weeks because of a mystery texter who wasn't Wyatt.

"I think I might've gotten myself into hot water. He's so zero to a hundred." I slice through butter, crumbling it with my flour and salt to make a batch of pastry dough. By the time I've baked through my feelings, I'll have enough for a full on bake sale. Maybe French club can host a fundraiser this week. "I mean, I'm crazy to agree to this whacky boyfriend and girl-friend thing with Connor, right?"

Maisy loses her balance and tumbles out of the handstand. "What!"

"Uh—"

Shit. I got wrapped up in talking while I was baking on autopilot. The plan was to tell her about the mistaken number debacle and keep Connor's name out of it.

Maisy freaks out, kicking her limbs in the air in a goofy dance. "Thea Kennedy has a boyfriend! What! And it's Connor *fucking* Bishop!"

She devolves into squealing while I shush her, frantically trying to muffle the volume on the iPad before Mom overhears from the other room where she's watching a docuseries on a big cat zookeeper.

"Shh, jesus!" I make a pained face as I flail my butter and flour covered hands around the iPad. "Oh my god, I'm going to end you! Please be quiet!"

"Okay." Maisy sits up, leaning toward her phone. "But for real?"

Blushing, I say, "Well, yes and no? It's not real. We're pretending. His idea."

"Tell me everything, girl!"

I laugh and wipe loose curls back from my forehead with my forearm, hesitating to figure out what to say.

Because that's the thing—I can't tell her everything. This is only the second time, ever, I've wanted to hide anything from her. She's my best friend and we've never held back from each other. We've pretty much been synced up on the same monthly cycle, both getting our first periods within days of each other the second summer at camp. Good times.

Despite our open friendship and deep connection, the only other time I've kept something from her was when I had my online boyfriend. I was vague on the details, calling Henry a pen pal instead.

Checking around the corner to make sure Mom is still absorbed in her show, I keep my voice low. "So, he asked—well, no. He's Connor," I start, laughing nervously. "He demanded I pose as his girlfriend because he doesn't date and doesn't want a real one, but he's got my pictures so what am I supposed to do? It's not like I knew I was texting those photos to him. Now he says I'm his until graduation."

"What? Why?"

"Right?" I shake my head. "It doesn't make any sense. I told him to pick someone else, but he, uh...was really convincing."

I suck on my lips, ignoring the tendril of heat when I think about how close I was to kissing him.

Maisy squints at me, her face filling more of the frame as she scoots across her floor. "You know his reputation, don't you?"

Sighing, I nod. "Yeah. Anyway, he wouldn't tell me when I asked for details. It kind of made me mad."

As I add cold water and mix the ingredients into a sticky dough, my anger grows. I frown when I look down and find I've taken it out on my dough. I pat it in penance.

"Sorry," I murmur.

"Are you talking to the food again?" Maisy snorts. "Goob."

"That's not what you say when I feed you my rustic tartlets."

Maisy moans and rolls onto her back, folding her hands over her stomach with a blissful expression. "They're so good. Screw school. We'll run away together, head for Venice Beach. You'll open up a trendy bakery, and I'll teach yoga. We'll live in a really shitty one-room apartment, but it'll be close to the ocean, so who cares? It'll be *glorious*."

My breath puffs out on a laugh at her elaborate fantasies of leaving Ridgeview in the dust. "Yeah, I'll make you some soon."

"Goddess." Maisy blows a kiss at the screen. She pops up on her elbows. "Ugh. Mom's calling. I've got to go."

I grimace in sympathy. Both of our mothers are a lot to handle. "Good luck, girl."

After she ends the video call, my thoughts turn as I roll out and turn my pastry dough. A new sense of purpose fills me. I'm determined to get to the bottom of why Connor is so adamant he needs me by his side.

FIFTEEN
CONNOR

When I meet Thea in the morning, blocking her driveway so she has no choice but to get in, I'm prepared for battle. It turns out I don't need to be. Other than rehashing the same argument about the merits of her doll car, she eventually gives in.

A few days pass where we settle into this new routine. I pick her up in the morning, she kicks up a cute little fuss about it, then when I remind her the clock is ticking she hops in. She still asks a deluge of questions, but is no longer resisting the deal. Her questions have my guard up. She's probably looking for any way out, but now she's approaching me with more logic and strategy.

Good luck, little mouse. You're going up against a master. You can't outsmart me.

She's acting like she genuinely cares and wants to help, but I can't believe that. I'm blackmailing her. Why would she help me?

Doctor Levitt would spout some crap about harboring trust beginning with small steps, like believing someone means what they say instead of looking for the lie, but people suck. We're all wired to save ourselves. Thea can't be as honest and straightforward as she seems.

As soon as we pull into the student lot in the morning, she scurries off before she's seen. Without meaning to, I've been arriving before the rest of my crew. Somehow, she gets me to consider her. She gets under my skin, bending me to her will. It must be that inexplicable instinct to protect her.

For now it's enough to add a few Instagram posts together to lay the groundwork. We can stay pretty DL until I need her on my arm for Mom's campaigning, but she stays in my head all day and my dreams at night.

Devlin's starting to notice. He busted my balls about it last night before our soccer match. He should focus on his own shit. I've seen glimpses of the kinky game he's playing with Blair Davis.

It's my fault anyway for pulling out my phone and looking at one of her photos in the locker room.

My days seem quiet and bland without her messages. I think I miss them, if that's possible. Me. Torn up over a chick. Unbelievable.

All I keep wondering is if she misses what we had, too. It wasn't always about getting off—she'd show me her baking, or slip in comments about her day. An amused sound punches out of me because she's really chatty for such a quiet girl once she breaks past her line.

The move is hers to make, but I hope it won't be long before she craves it too much to care that it's me. I wasn't kidding, I'm betting I'm the only one who can give her what she wants. Her stupid Wyatt couldn't handle her, not like I can.

I might not believe her word, but the physical chemistry between us? It's a firecracker.

Thinking about her texting me, *knowing* it's me this time... I trace my lip and cock my head. Anticipating the satisfying thrill is almost too much to handle.

I'm stalking the halls, looking for Devlin before first period when he didn't show in the parking lot, but something else makes me halt. Some underclassman crashes into my back and I swear I can see his soul leave his body when my scowl lands on him. The kid squeaks out some apology and disappears. I turn my attention back to what made me stop.

Thea. Standing awfully fucking close to Coleman.

Her secret blog I discovered flashes in my head. Is Thea better at this than I gave her credit for, putting on a good girl act to get attention? I knew it. No one's that naïve. And here I was, all protective over her when I saw those creepy comments. But she clearly has no qualms throwing herself at men.

Fake girlfriend or not, *teacher* or not, no chick of mine should be seen cozying up with another man. I need to do a deeper dig on Coleman to find something—anything on him that will keep him away from Thea. My suspicion from the other day hasn't faded.

She touches his arm for a brief second with a big smile, then gestures to the pastry-filled table beside them. Vague recognition crosses my mind. There was a new Instagram post Thea made this week of her kitchen exploding with baked goods with the caption *bake your feels away* followed by a yellow heart and a sun emoji.

To make matters worse, she's wearing the same sweater

from the photo I was looking at last night. My hands ball into fists and my teeth clench. How many guys would she send a photo like that to, pulling the edge up to show off her stomach and a hint of her tits?

I've seen the fucking blog. That was a couple of years ago, but maybe she's had good practice since then and upgraded to the way she was with me.

Jealousy is an irrational emotion, but there's nothing I can do to stop it surging, calling on the vicious anger threatening to break free, threatening to break Coleman's face for looking at her. I don't fucking share.

I stalk the length of the hallway. If he didn't get the message the two times he's seen me all over her, I'll make it crystal fucking clear this time. She's mine and he needs to stay away.

"I think you'd be a perfect fit to head the winter formal planning committee," Coleman tells her, waving at the table. "You organized this so well. What do you say?"

"I don't know," Thea murmurs, blushing a pretty shade of red. "I'm not a great public speaker."

"This wouldn't be like that. I was the faculty advisor last year, and the students kept it informal, more like a club meeting. I think you'll do great."

"Really?"

Christ, she's so starved for attention, she needs him to praise her? I'm going to put my fist through a locker.

Thea spots me as I stop a few feet away and goes still. She picks up a wrapped pastry and takes a step toward me.

Acid feels like it's boiling beneath my skin, seconds from exploding. I have to get out of here. I might not listen much to that quack therapist every week, but the coping methods keep me in check.

Without acknowledging Thea or Coleman, I keep walking down the hall to cool off before I deal with them.

* * *

After I skip first and most of second period to go for a long run on the track, then grab a shower, I'm late to English class. Exercise helped, but I'm still on edge as I enter the room. The sight of Coleman is enough to have me teetering close to the uncontrollable anger again.

What's so great about him that the girls are always eating out of his palm? Until Thea, I didn't care about a young teacher getting his rocks off with the ego boost of high school girls fawning over him.

Coleman's eyes harden at my interruption. That all-American veneer cracks under pressure. Come on, everything about this guy screams creepy. How do the girls want anything to do with him? Their red flags should be flying around him.

"You're late, Mr. Bishop." Coleman pretends to be authoritative, but I'm not taking it seriously. "Care to explain yourself?"

My skin feels too tight. I almost lost complete control earlier. The thing about being a little unhinged is the breaking point is always a hairline trigger away.

"No," I snark, eyebrow raised.

"Excuse me?"

Coleman doesn't find my backtalk amusing. The urge to laugh bubbles up in my chest and I push it back down with serious effort. The humor helps cut through the red haze of rage.

A few muffled snorts sound to my left. Devlin and Blair have their hands covering their mouths, eyes sparkling. Everyone loves a little bit of anarchy to break up the monotonous bullshit of high school.

Their gazes meet in mutual interest and something passes between them. See? Fucking told him he had the hots for her.

Thea doesn't seem as impressed with my antics, a disapproving, worried frown marring her pretty features. I'm reminded once again why I shouldn't trust her. Why I can't want her like I do. Why does my dick not behave when I need it to? Maybe everything she does will stop messing with my head if I can hit it once and get her out of my system, like the mystery of what she tastes like when it's not my imagination is driving me insane.

Then I could get back on track.

Ignoring Mr. Coleman, I stroll by like I'm not late, enjoying the strangled sound of indignation he can't quite muffle. The closer I get to Thea, the more this morning grates on my nerves. Over and over it replays in my mind: her hand on his arm, her bright smile. I glare at her as the betrayal burns in my gut.

I should destroy her for that act of disloyal defiance. Blast her photos to the whole damn school. She's more trouble than she's worth to have my way against my mom and hers. I swear, I've never put so much effort in with a girl. No one ever fights me, questions me, defies me the way she does.

The brunt of my glare is a blow. Thea slouches down in her seat, shoulders hunched over.

As I drop in my chair, an aggravated sigh explodes out of me. Everything has gone to shit today.

It takes a minute to register the complete silence in the room. Glancing up at Coleman, I wave my hand.

"Well?" I snap my fingers, impersonating Coleman when he wants us to pay attention. The enraged look that flashes on his face has me biting back a smirk. "I'm here to get an education."

As titters move through the class, I feel Devlin nudge me from behind in support.

Mr. Coleman's jaw works. "Let's get back to the lesson.

Can anyone tell me your thoughts on the protagonist's passage on page forty-three?"

Things are fine for the fraction of a second between the end of the question and Thea's hand shooting in the air, flailing her arm with an eager tremor to answer. Then the irrational anger rises like a tide in a hurricane, flooding through my system.

"Yes?" Coleman calls on Thea.

"I think the passage means that it's important to be true to yourself," she answers softly, her arm still hanging in the air.

I suck in a sharp breath. To rub salt in my open wounds, all I smell is sugar because she sits in front of me.

Be true to yourself? Something I know she isn't. The proof sits on my phone and that blog. Thea is full of secrets.

"Yes, Thea," Coleman praises, flashing his gleaming white teeth in an energetic smile. His praise earns a laugh from her, the sound pleased at his attention. "Excellent."

The pencil I choke in my grip breaks when I gouge it against the blank page in my notebook. I picture it's Coleman's face I'm stabbing. Bouncing my knee, I have to rein myself in before I grab Thea and drag her into my lap like I'm some deranged caveman. That's not my style, but she drives me to madness.

If I have to sit through an entire class like this, I'm going to end up with another assault charge to cover up. Thea will probably be the one to call the police this time, just like her Mom. Yeah, fuck this. I explode from my seat.

Coleman drops the pretense and stares at me with contempt, like I'm a bug under his boot he wants to crush. *Feeling's mutual, asshole.*

"Mr. Bishop," he snaps coldly. "You're disrupting—"

"Fuck off," I bite back. "I'm out of here."

"If you leave class, you'll earn detention."

Boo fucking hoo. I'll have Devlin erase it, or I'll do it myself with Dad's access credentials. Tossing up my hands, I make my way to the door, kicking Thea's bag out of the way. The door slams hard behind me, blanketing me in blissful silence.

It's broken by Thea's muffled squeak. I hear her through the door, like my stupid body is attuned to her. I stomp away from class, not interested in listening to her try to get class back on track.

She's messing with my head too much. This isn't good. If I can't keep a level head, my strategizing flies out the window.

Thea was hiding everything under her wholesome home-spun wrapping. The desire for her is twisting me up and clouding my judgement. She's got an ass I want to take a fucking bite out of, luscious curves I could lose myself in, thighs I want to bury my head between and live there for eternity, and full tits I need in my hands or my mouth at all times. Like, damn. She is fine as fuck underneath those frumpy ass granny sweaters and her wallflower demeanor.

But behind it all, she's as much of a liar as anyone else. Because she's not really a wallflower, not with the way she challenges me. She's not shy and wholesome when I can see how she looks at Coleman.

My jaw aches from how hard I clench my teeth. The back of my neck is boiling hot.

The door opens and closes behind me. I don't turn around.

"Connor." Thea has to shuffle double time to catch up to my long strides. Her breath is short. "Connor, wait!"

I whirl on her, eating up her startled yelp. "What are you doing here, little mouse? Shouldn't you be in class like a good girl?"

The fear clears from her face, replaced by stubbornness. I hate that it excites me. That I'm anticipating her fight.

Want outweighs logic when it comes to her every time.

"I was worried. You didn't seem okay back there, and I

haven't seen you since this morning when you walked past me without saying anything." She takes a step closer and puts her hand on my arm tentatively, like I'm a wild animal that might bite her. Smart. I am wild and I will bite her. "Are you all right? Do you need—"

I grab her shoulders and push her back until she bumps into the lockers, caged by my body. "What I need?" A dark laugh escapes me and I lean in. "I need you to stop with this innocent act. You're quite the vixen behind the nerdy exterior, huh?" I close the distance even more, leaving almost no room between us, growling, "I bet you think about being Coleman's teacher's pet, sitting on his desk with your legs spread for *him*. That make your pussy wet? You better not have fantasized about our teacher while you were my favorite little secret, and you damn well better not do it now. He can't have you, little mouse. You're all *mine*."

This is insane. I know I'm acting crazy and possessive, but this is what she does to me. It's impossible to control. I don't understand why she throws me off my game when no other girl has ever gotten me this hung up before.

Does she know the effect she has on me? Is this on purpose? I've been so tangled up, I kept forgetting to remember the strong possibility of her playing me while I was focused on the board, planning my next five moves.

"Mr. Coleman?! W-what, I'm not—I *wasn't* thinking—" She can babble all she wants. I don't miss the way her pupils dilate. She claws at my shirt in her blustering protest. "Why do you always say the most depraved things when you're jealous? Is your ego that fragile? I'm not even your real girlfriend, you territorial ass."

Liar, liar, pants on fucking fire, Thea Kennedy.

I chuckle, the sound rough and dangerous. That damn sugar-sweet scent is intoxicating.

Thea looks at my lips. A growl rips from my throat and I crash our mouths together, kissing her hard. She lets out a surprised sound, then melts into me as my tongue swipes over her mouth. God, her taste. It's better than I pictured. I release a tortured groan as she lets me in, kissing her deeper. My hands slide down her arms and I hold her waist, crushing her body to mine.

It's so much better than what I imagined.

The kiss is hot and demanding. She's a little clumsy at first, unfamiliar with the movements, but she kisses me back and that's all that matters. I cup her face, tilting her head and her arms wrap around my neck.

I'm beyond screwed because Thea Kennedy is an ocean I would gladly drown myself in.

The anger bleeds away, lost to the oblivion of glossy pink lips. It's never faded so fast before.

This calming effect she has on me pushes past every one of my defenses. It demands more of me than I've given anyone, even my closest friends.

A door slamming in the distance brings us back to reality. I don't know how long we made out for, but I want more. She tastes sweeter than the sugary way she smells.

Thea pulls back, blinking up at me in a daze. It's my new favorite look on her. My heart gives an odd squeeze.

Leaning against the lockers for support, she touches her lips, stunned. "That was my first kiss."

"Want a second?" I rasp. With a crooked grin, I move in again, touching her cheek.

Her small hand plants on my chest, stopping me. Her voice is quiet, but serious. "I can't do pretend with my emotions. I won't. Either I'm your pretend girlfriend and that's it, or..." She shakes her head. "We'll need to talk about the texting stuff, I guess. Maybe we can't ignore it and forget it happened. Right now, I can't trust you."

Trust.

Is this real? A strange sensation in my chest quivers and expands. Hope? Thea might be genuine in what she says. The thought bowls me over, painting my defensive actions today in a different light.

Swallowing, I move back, letting her go. Thea sidesteps me. Instead of returning to class, she walks down the hallway, lost in her head.

Maybe she's not trying to play me after all. Could she be as honest as she seems? The concept is foreign to me.

I watch her retreat, well aware of how fucked I am.

SIXTEEN
CONNOR

Wednesday. My least favorite day of the week. Not because of cutesy hump day memes; those are hilarious.

No, on Wednesdays I'm treated to pure torture. My weekly appointments with Doctor Levitt. Worse, a standing lunch with my parents follows, something Dad insists on so we can spend time as a family. Total bullshit. An ice spike to the skull would be less excruciating.

Appearances.

All part of our happy family show.

The only reason Mom makes a point of joining us is because it gives her a boost in numbers when her campaign photographer follows us around and her social media manager posts to her official profiles with an update of how important family time is to Vivian Bishop. I swear it's her only motivation for anything she does. Damien waits in her back seat while we suffer through cardboard conversations.

Mom's been all over my case because the dinner at the children's hospital is this weekend. I still need to tell Thea.

But first, I need to smooth things over with her.

Yesterday surprised me. The kiss and Thea's words didn't leave my mind all night. At first I tried to go back to what I know, looking for the part where she pulled the curtain back. But it didn't feel right. I didn't want it to be.

I think this is what Doctor Levitt means about believing someone at their word. I only find that in her office, and even then it was a hard road to get to the point I wasn't bucking against everything out of my therapist's mouth. Therapy might be dull as shit, but some of it has stuck. It's nice to have someone speak their mind. I allow few people past my guard where I can take them at face value.

If Thea is showing me I can believe what she says, maybe I should try something new: apologizing.

Idling outside her house in the morning, I drum my fingers on the back of the passenger seat, waiting for her and dreading that it's a Wednesday.

What if she doesn't want a ride? Should I give her space?

It's not a concession I'd ever give anyone else. Things go my way, or they don't at all. But with Thea, it's different.

Once my anger faded, I was able to think clearer. I felt like a bastard because it wasn't her fault. And there was no way she faked that kiss. I was wrong. She's not playing me.

The kiss from yesterday repeats in my mind and I lick my lips. That wasn't an act for me, either.

I just wanted her, my secret vixen.

She's right about it. There's no forgetting what we've done.

I never wanted it to stop, but she can't ignore what's between us either.

No, we need to discuss this before the benefit dinner.

Thea seems surprised when she emerges from the house, darting a glance behind her before hurrying to the SUV and climbing in. Her cheeks are pink.

"Hi," she says.

"Hey," I respond, putting the car in gear.

The air goes stale for a few minutes while I navigate onto the main road out of our neighborhood.

Planning to talk and actually doing it? Two very different moods. I'm wasting precious minutes trying to start a conversation, not used to thinking how what I say can affect the girl I want to talk to instead of just laying it out like the law.

"Listen, I—" Clearing my throat, I squeeze the steering wheel. *Come on, man, just spit it out.* "I'm sorry for being angry. That wasn't right or fair to you."

"Okay. Thank you."

She's distracted by braiding her wild auburn curls. Sighing, I continue reluctantly.

Doctor Levitt always says once I'm calm, I need to express my anger. Even if I don't want to be there, some things have stuck in my head.

"The thing is, I have trouble with my temper. You were right, I was jealous," I admit. My stomach tightens. I haven't told anyone other than Devlin about this. With a sidelong glance, I find Thea watching me. My throat bobs as I swallow. "I see a therapist. I have an appointment today. Every Wednesday."

I leave out that it's court-mandated therapy. It's strange to give up one of my cards after spending so long hunting the ones that belong to others. I hold so many of hers between her secret blog and the nudes, it's only fair to give her some of mine to prove I'm serious. I realize the tense set of my shoulders is because I'm bracing for Thea's judgement, but it never comes.

After a long pause where she peers at me curiously, her hand rests on mine on the center console. "I'm glad you have someone to talk to about how you're feeling."

"Yeah." I didn't expect this. She just rolls with it, taking me at face value. She trusts that I'm being honest without question, even after I've tricked her multiple times. "So. I'm sorry for what I said and how I acted. You deserve better, so I'll do my best."

She hums and squeezes my hand. "If you ever want to talk about anything, you can tell me. I'll listen if that's what you need. We might not be a real couple, but I'm here."

I don't love the reminder this is all fake, by my own doing no less, but I'm glad we're cool.

The acceptance feels so good, I'm out of it for the rest of the drive to school, my thoughts cleared and peaceful for the first time in I don't know how long. Thea's like a balm of warm light on my constantly shifting mind.

On my way to the office around mid-day, I curse, remembering an important thing I needed to tell Thea this morning. I got so caught up in sharing one of my own secrets with her, the benefit slipped my mind.

I thought we would have more time to ease into faking a relationship for the reporters and voters, but the event is this weekend. We've been wasting time with so much back and forth and fighting against the sexual connection distracting us.

I'm not supposed to text her, but I forgot to tell her this morning, too focused on apologizing. This is important and it can't wait.

Don't be too mad, sunshine.

Connor: Showtime this weekend. It's a formal event. Do you have that covered, or do you need money to buy something?

It takes a long time before three dots appear.

Thea: Don't think I don't notice how you're texting me. Your apology this morning doesn't change your promise.

Connor: Yeah, well. Not much choice when you pull a disappearing act all day and I need to get a hold of you. Do you need to borrow my credit card or not?

Thea: Shopping spree on your dime? That's big sugar daddy vibes. [laughing emoji]

My stomach dives off a cliff. Is she...flirting? She must not be that mad after all. Hope sparks to life in my chest.

Connor: You wanna be my sugar baby? Hell yes to those perks.

Thea: No! I don't know why I said that. It was a JOKE!

She sends me an army of emojis, filling the screen with the monkey covering its eyes. My mouth quirks up. It's cute when she embarrasses herself.

Connor: I'll give you more details on the drive home.

Thea: Ok [peace sign emoji]

A second later, she sends a selfie. She's in the library with Maisy Landry, a pair of earbuds shared between them. They make goofy faces for the camera. I'm warm all over, staring at Thea in wonder.

Since our kiss, things feel like they're clicking into place more easily.

The good mood Thea put me in evaporates as I walk into the administrative office. A scowl settles on my face while I wait outside Dad's office. My hands are shoved in the pockets of my black slacks, my school blazer tied around the strap of my messenger bag. The office secretary I flirted with to get Devlin out of a pinch when he was in the student records room eyes me in disapproval.

Suck it, Debbie.

I'd much rather drive myself over to the appointment, but Dad has always insisted. His door opens a minute later, and he emerges, buttoning his boring blue suit jacket. Seriously, whoever he's been seeing must have standards through the floor for Dad to jump right over their bar.

"Ready to go?" Dad asks.

I grunt, whirling to trudge from the hive of offices. Dad falls into step beside me. Outside, he clears his throat and I roll my eyes. Here it comes. The weekly lecture.

"Dad, save it. Come on."

We reach his Escalade and get in. He starts the ignition and sighs.

"I'm serious. This isn't like a few weeks ago when you stole the car for a prank." He pats the wheel in indication.

Devlin and I had the idea for mischief after school. Getting back at both our dads was glorious, stealing the Escalade from his parking space and going for a joyride to Denver to crash a college party. Dad was pissed. It fucking rocked.

I snort, slouching back in the leather seat. "What did I do wrong now?"

It's always me. True, I'm not an angel, but how are my actions always under a magnifying glass when I have two parents cheating on each other?

Maybe what I need to do is fake a private investigator profile and slip a tip to reporters on the local elections circuit. I've always thought about doing it, but not until Mom runs for something bigger, like Senate. I'll do it up with the works, a real pro job that'll fool anyone. The problem is, I don't want to be the one to take the seedy photos of my double home-wrecking parents. It's the same dilemma that trips me up every time I think out this plan.

Dad puts the car in gear and grimaces. "There're photos. Illegal fighting, Connor, really? You know how important appearances are to your mother. I don't have to remind you. A bad story like that could linger and be a roadblock in her political career."

Grinding my teeth, I draw in a slow breath. It was up to Landry and his boys to make sure no photos or video got out. Idiots.

"Yeah, Dad. It's only shoved down my throat every day." I jerk my head in annoyance. Great. I made progress with Thea, but today's session will probably suck worse than usual with my mood blackening like an oncoming storm. "Message received."

He sighs. "It's an important election year, son. You can't have any missteps."

How he can be so weak and pliant to Mom's scheming political shit is baffling. Maybe he got used to the silver spoon life and is too afraid to challenge her. After all, she's the reason he's the principal of an elite private school, and he enjoys the money we get from granddad on top of their cushy incomes.

The urge to punch the nearest thing strangles me. "So she

gets to have everything she wants, and the rest of us better fall in line?" I smack the dash in frustration. "Why the hell are we putting up with this? It's stupid."

Dad grants me a sober look. "It's your mother. We have a good life because of her work. You'll go off to college next year thanks to your grandfather's money, so just do as she says until then."

"What the fuck ever."

How great is our life, really? It doesn't seem so peachy. Our family is fractured, all three of us just existing in the same house.

"She wanted me to ask if—" Dad cuts off and frowns. "Did you mother talk to you about finding a date for this weekend and, er..."

What he doesn't say is do I have a pretty puppet to play house with for the rest of the campaigning season.

"I have it covered." I should've never dragged Thea into my mess. Goddamn it. My jaw clenches so hard a muscle jumps in my cheek. "My girlfriend will be there."

I never told Mom I found someone and that I had no intention of picking from her folder. I guess part of me is trying to protect Thea from her, not prepared to subject her to the force of nature that spawned me. I'm a twisted fucker, but I learned from the best, I suppose. Apples and their goddamn trees.

When this started I was ready to throw Thea to the sharks, the same as I would anyone else. It didn't matter before, but now? I'm not so sure.

At first it was routine blackmail, playing with a pawn. Except I've had a real taste of my little mouse.

I'm going to earn her trust so that I can keep her after we get through this charade together. She can be an ally instead of a pawn.

* * *

Thea waits by the coyote statue in front of the school sign after the last bell.

Therapy wasn't as bad as I thought. Doctor Levitt was pleased when I explained how I worked through an episode and talked it out in the morning with Thea. She was on my mind all through the stilted lunch with my parents, helping me tune them out.

When Thea sees me, she smiles shyly, giving me a tiny wave. As I reach her, I put my arm around her shoulder.

"Is this okay?" I ask, steering her across the terrace.

Thea is hesitant, glancing around. People look, because I'm around and that's what they do. She doesn't seem used to being in the spotlight. "Yes. It's good to practice being comfortable with touching for our big debut. What sort of dress do I need to wear?"

Practice. Right. "Uh, I don't know. It's black-tie, so a fancy one."

"Fancy. Got it." She shoots me a shy smile. "Do you clean up nice in a tux?"

The corner of my mouth lifts. "You bet your ass I do. You ain't prepared, girl."

"Will there be dancing?"

"No, it's like." I gesture with the hand around her shoulder, then play with her hair. "A dinner thing. There's a cocktail hour and a banquet. The people going buy their plate and the funds are split between the campaign and the charity. It's boring as fuck. I snuck out for two hours last year."

Thea laughs. My smile grows. A few people watch us curiously as we cross the pavement on our way to the steps down to the student lot. As we pass, I give a few fist bumps to people that I recognize. Thea goes quiet and bows her head.

"What's wrong?"

"Nothing. It's just weird being so close to your popularity." She shoots me a wry look. "How do you get down a hallway to make it to class on time?"

She's joking with me. It makes me want to get in the car and just drive with her, go somewhere we can be alone.

Before we reach the steps, Coleman walks by. Thea stops.

"Have a wonderful evening, Thea."

"Thanks, Mr. C," she says, abandoning self-consciousness.

I grind my teeth, not liking the way he looks at her. "Come on, babe."

Thea turns her attention to me. Keeping half an eye on Coleman, I lean down and kiss the corner of her mouth, squeezing her close with my arm resting over her shoulders. She muffles a surprised sound, putting her hands on my stomach.

Possessive? Yes. Don't fucking care.

Coleman clears his throat. I pull back, smirking at the pretty shade of pink in Thea's cheeks.

"Gotta split, Mr. C." I mimic Thea's moniker for him in a sarcastic drawl. "My girl and I have a big date this weekend to plan out."

Coleman's look is unreadable, but I know I've won this round. He doesn't have a leg to stand on. I'll cut him off at the knees. Thea might be eighteen, but he's a teacher, so he needs to step about eighty steps back from her before I fucking snap.

"Thea," Coleman rumbles before leaving us be.

She narrows her eyes. Her defiant expressions are too adorable to resist. "Was that necessary?"

"Yes. Where were we?" I nudge her and we descend the steps to the lot full of top of the line rides. "How great I look in a bowtie, I think?"

Thea snorts. "So full of yourself."

"I'd rather be full on you, sunshine." I lick my lips and toss her a wink. She makes a delicious, scandalized little sound. "Say the word and I'm going to devour you."

"Connor." Her cheeks turn from pink to rosy. It's too easy to rile her up.

I unlock the car with the fob and open her door for her. She hops up and I climb in on the driver's side.

"What's the event for?" Thea asks, clicking her seatbelt.

"Children's hospital. A fundraiser benefit, sponsored by Mom's campaign. She gives a speech, blah blah blah." The engine rumbles to life and I pull out of the lot. "Really boring stuff. I hate that I have to go at all."

"So why do you have to?" She chews on her lip and tilts her head.

"Her platform and approval ratings center on her being a family woman. A leader, a mother, a wife." I scoff, knowing how much of it is manufactured to keep her numbers high over the guy running against her. "Pretty much everything comes down to politics. Trust me, I've tried to get out of these things. She's...difficult. Persistent."

Thea hums. "I know what that's like. Mine is always breathing down my neck."

My grip on the wheel tightens. I want to tell her I know all about how her mother is, but we've just got to a good place and I already gave up one piece of myself today.

"So if it's all about family stuff, why is it important for you to show up with a girlfriend?" She fiddles with the radio and stops on a song she must like, because she bobs her head to the upbeat music. "Is that why it's a fundraiser for the children's hospital?"

Thea is being nosy again, but it doesn't stir the same ire. In fact, I like her curiosity. She's asking good questions, strategic ones I would pose myself.

"Yeah. Real flimsy, if you ask me." I cock my head as I turn onto our street. "She doesn't have other children, so if I show up with you, it sends a subliminal message of her being a grandmother someday. Nurturing a legacy."

"Oh, so now we are having those two point five fake kids?" Thea taps my arm with a light swat. I park in my driveway. She certainly took that better than I expected. "You should've told me, dear. That will affect my outfit."

I sit back in my seat, angled toward her, totally aware of the crooked, dopey smile on my face. I don't do a damn thing to wipe it off. She keeps surprising me.

Thea winks—or, she tries to, it's sort of a pained blink with both eyes that does things to my heart that shouldn't be scientifically possible—and hops out of the car. "See you tomorrow."

"Bye, sunshine." I sit in the car, watching her all the way to her house.

The girl next door has me under her spell.

SEVENTEEN
THEA

Raised voices catch my attention late Friday afternoon as Constantine follows me out of the house. I stopped at the store to restock the baking ingredients that were getting low. Mom is out for the weekend on a spa retreat, and Dad is on a trip to Salt Lake City for a conference. It's just Constantine and I, which means the kitchen is all mine, so I've got all my bakes lined up until I need to play girlfriend for Connor tomorrow night. It worked out perfectly that my parents are out of town, so I don't have to explain the dress hanging up in my room or where I'm going.

"You need to keep him away from me." Connor sounds

pissed as he stalks across his lawn to his Lexus GX. "I'm not playing. I don't want anything to do with him. Not eat his food, not talk about his day, not play happy family when we're dysfunctional as fuck! This is bullshit!"

Mrs. Bishop stands with her arms crossed, and the younger man I recognize as their family friend who comes to their house several times a week is beside her.

"Come back inside, where we can discuss this." Mrs. Bishop's tone is sharp enough to cut and her platinum, sleek bob sways. There's something about the set of her features that's disconcerting, like they're too perfect. "You're making a scene."

Constantine lets out a low *boof* and plants himself between me and our neighbors, standing sentry while I grab groceries from the trunk of my Mini Cooper. I shake my head with a wry smile. He's a seventy pound overprotective lap dog. He's not fooling anyone.

I grab the last bag from the car and catch Connor's eye. The turmoil in his gray gaze shocks me. He looks away, jaw working.

Is he embarrassed? I didn't think he cared what the world thought of him.

His mom gives me a shrewd once over, hyper aware of my presence. When she speaks again, she regulates her tone, sounding kinder. "Why don't you come inside, sweetheart? Dinner is almost ready."

I'm gripping the bag of flour and sugar, debating with myself. *Don't get involved.* But I can't ignore it, can I? It might not be my place to intervene, but damn it, the look on Connor's face like he's the only one in his corner hooks my insides and tugs hard. I won't stand by while he's hurting.

Not when I know how hard it can be to deal with parents.

Setting the bag of ingredients on the hood of my car, I cross the driveway to stand at his side. Constantine follows, laying down in the grass in front of my feet.

"Hi." I take Connor's hand and kiss his cheek, rising on tiptoe to reach. Turning to Mrs. Bishop, I wave. "I'm Thea. Connor's girlfriend. I live next door and go to school with Connor."

He's stunned silent, watching me from the corner of his eye. I'm standing so close, I feel it when his chest caves with the force of the relieved breath hissing out of him.

Okay, maybe that was rash. Oh my god, why did I kiss him in front of his mom before introducing myself? I clutch his hand tighter.

Mrs. Bishop's eyes narrow slightly, taking me in with a once over. I can't help but feel she's sizing me up and finding what she sees lacking.

Connor drops my hand, but before I can run to hide for being silly and intervening, his arm wraps around me, almost clinging to me. He's strong and warm, engulfing me in his rich earthy scent.

"Well," Mrs. Bishop says. Her eyes dart around the empty street. "We're having a family discussion before dinner."

"Mom," Connor snaps. He rubs my shoulder, hugging me close. His voice is hard, but his touch is gentle. "Thea is my girlfriend. She's my date for tomorrow night."

Mrs. Bishop's lips purse and she exchanges a look with their family friend. I've heard his name before—something with a D? She turns her attention to Connor, crossing the lawn to inspect me closely. She stops a short distance away, glancing at Constantine as he pops his head up. The vibe between her and Connor is charged.

Instead of cowering into his side, I put my arm around his waist so we're a united front, lifting my chin as she sniffs. That's a bitchy non-response if I've ever seen one, worse than my mom's false-sympathetic hums.

"You said I needed to bring my girlfriend," Connor says

smugly. "Remember? Over that nice meal you were preparing with Damien."

The way he says Damien is almost a growl.

"I didn't realize the neighbor girl is who you were planning to bring." Mrs. Bishop folds her hands in front of her. "I thought you were seeing Nina Goldman. Or was it Anette Rossi?"

Popular girls far more perfect than me, ones that hang out with Connor's crowd and come from money, status, and power in Ridgeview. Not me, a nobody.

The effect of her dismissal is...wow. Is this what it's like to appear polite while silently screaming *fuck you?*

Message received.

Message shredded.

Putting on my sweetest smile, I lean into Connor's side. "We've only been dating since school started, but we have a really special connection."

Her eyes flash. I can see where Connor gets his haunting gray eyes. His are impossible to look away from. Hers are just disconcerting. It doesn't impress her, I guess, since I'm talking back.

I see you, Mrs. Bishop. I know what kind of woman you are.

Hopefully Connor doesn't mind I used the timeframe from when I first texted him. Mistakenly, but whatever. It's the truth.

"The heart wants what the heart wants. Doesn't it?" Connor snorts, caressing my arm. I don't shy away, melting into his touch. "I'm sure you and Damien agree."

If I thought she was intense and intimidating before, it's nothing compared to the deadly look that crosses her face now. Nothing changes about her plastered on smile, but the edges twist and shake, hinting at what lurks beneath.

Constantine remains on alert, watching Mrs. Bishop with

an unwavering focus. I nudge him with my foot and he rumbles, laying his head on his feet. His ears are still perked, only pretending to be at rest. If I needed him, he'd protect me in a second.

"I'm looking forward to the benefit," I say. Connor kisses the top of my head. I thought the PDA might freak me out since we've been at odds until recently, but it feels right. "What a great cause your campaign is supporting."

"Is that right? I hope Connor informed you there's a dress code."

"He did. I have a gown." I smile wider. "It's all ready."

"Wonderful." She watches us for a beat, then turns to go back inside without saying anything.

Damien follows behind her. Once they're both gone, Connor winds both arms around me, burying his face in my hair. I slide my hands up his back, holding him. We stay like that for a minute, just hugging.

He peels back far enough to tip my chin up. "Thank you."

I'm about to lean up for a kiss when he squeezes my waist and lets me go.

Connor backs up a few steps, keeping me locked in his gaze, then he gets in his car and pulls out. I'm left alone in the middle of the lawn with Constantine.

"Come on, Con," I call, going to grab the grocery bag from the hood of my car.

He trots after me, panting happily as we go inside.

Later that night, I'm wrestling with myself, chewing my lips raw. A restlessness has settled and even baking for hours into the night didn't help me calm down.

The thing I need I don't want to do by myself.

"This is a bad idea," I mumble, staring down my phone as I pace my room. "Bad, bad idea."

My favorite kind, Connor's voice echoes in my head.

Blowing out a breath, I pick up my phone and do what I've been arguing with myself about all night—I text him. The contact no longer says Wyatt with wave emojis. Now it's updated with Connor's name bracketed by black heart and crown emojis.

The black-hearted king of secrets.

My secrets.

Thea: Hi. Are you up?

The response is immediate, sending my stomach into a wobbly flip of nerves. He doesn't bother with words, just sends a photo of himself, shirtless and sprawled in bed. I can see the edge of his lazy smirk. Just like the first time.

Licking my lips, I take a pic. My curls frame my face and I'm wearing a white bodysuit with illustrated peaches on it. On the backside it reads *peachy keen* across the butt. Maisy saw it when we were shopping and squealed, insisting I get it because it made my ass look amazing. Into the contraband box it went. Until now.

My heart skips a beat as soon as I send it.

Connor: Fucking hell, sunshine. I want you so much.

A nervous laugh escapes me. There's nothing like this, the way he makes me feel. A thrilling buzz travels across my skin as I settle on the armchair by the window, so I can peek at his across the way. Not only are the lights on, but I'm throwing caution to the wind. It's daring, being out of my bed.

I'm home alone and an aching need burns in my core.

Thea: What do you want me to do?

Connor: Touch yourself. Slide those fingers over your tits and down between your legs.

My breath punches out of me as I follow his command, stroking over my pussy. Sinking my teeth in my lip, I hook a leg over the floral-print arm and slip my fingers beneath the body-suit. I'm soaking them already, feeling so turned on.

Connor: You wet for me?

Typing one-handed is always hard, but I manage.

Thea: Yes.

Connor: Mm. Slide one inside. I'm going to suck your finger clean and taste you.

I tip my head back, eyes fluttering shut as I work my index finger in slowly. My hips rock as I push deeper and pull it out, swirling wetness over my throbbing clit. Turning my head to the side, I see a shadow filling Connor's window. My breath hitches and my whole body pulses.

Instead of a text message, my phone vibrates and Connor's name fills my screen with a FaceTime call. We never got that far before he revealed himself. The closest we came were the Boomerang clips and voice texts.

"Oh my god," I whisper, fumbling with my phone. "Shit."

I answer.

Connor's face appears on my screen as the video connects. When he sees me sprawled in my chair he pushes out a breath. "Fuck, baby. Look at you. Eyes all bright and hungry."

He puts a fist over his mouth, leaning against the window frame. He's naked and hard—I can see his erection bobbing from the way he angles the camera. Those gray eyes flick away from the screen, toward my window, before coming back to sweep over me. Desire flares in his gaze, sending my stomach into a pleasant dip.

"I, um." I'm trembling, certain my blush spreads from head to toe. "Hi."

"Hi, sunshine," he rumbles. "You texted me."

"I did," I breathe.

"What do you want?"

"I—I want to come," I choke out.

God, this is harder to do when it's live and I have no time to think about what to say. But Connor grins.

"Prop the phone on the windowsill and turn your chair." Swallowing, I get up to do it. "Good girl. Now, as cute as this peachy little number is, I want you to lose it. Bare yourself for me, baby."

I squeak, holding my breasts as I lean close to the phone. "Naked?"

"I've seen you before, remember?" He drags his teeth over his lip. "Strip."

Not moving right away, I put my hands on my hips. "I want to see you first. I..." The words clog my throat, but I push them out. "I want to watch you touch your cock."

The heat in his gaze grows hot enough I can almost feel it blistering my skin through the phone and across the distance between our windows.

Connor smirks at the camera as he shifts back to fill the

frame with his incredible body. The muscles in his forearm flex as he takes his hardness in hand and strokes it, watching me.

"This what you wanted to see? Proof of what you do to me?" He twists his hand and he grunts. "With your sexy body and the way you always challenge me. Mm. Now strip."

Driven by the confidence and hot pleasure filling me at seeing how I turn him on, I peel out of the body suit, keeping my gaze locked on him through the video connection.

"That's it," Connor encourages with a deep rumble, working his hand faster. "Now you're going to sit back in your chair. Hook your legs over the arms and show me how wet that pussy is."

My heart stutters as I fall back in the chair. It takes me a second where I need to gather my wits. Connor moans as I absently play with my hard nipples.

"Want to break into your house and drive into you, shit."

I laugh, a little delirious before we've even done much. "This feels a lot different. I know you're watching me."

"Hell yes, baby. I'm not taking my eyes off you. It's just you and me. There's nothing to be embarrassed about," Connor croons. "Show me."

With a shaking breath, I spread my legs, resting them over the arms of my chair. Connor goes still, staring at me with such intensity, it's like I can feel him in the room with me. His eyes drink me in.

"Thea," he whispers hoarsely.

The reverence in his tone gives me courage to let go. I coast my fingers down my stomach, over my mound, and stroke my slick folds. I tip my head back with a soft sigh.

"That's it. God, I want to lick your pussy until you cry. But I won't stop, I'll keep going until I've made you come so much, you're wrung out."

My heart pounds and I shift my hips to roll against my fingers as I rub my clit. "Ah. Feels good."

"Yeah. Keep going."

I push a finger back inside and imagine it's Connor fucking me on his long fingers. My brows pinch. I need more. "Please."

"I'm right there with you, sunshine. You hear me? I'm kissing your neck and sucking on your nipples while I thrust my fingers in you."

Gasping, I pinch a nipple and buck against my hand.

"God," Connor bites out as his hand fists his cock. "See this?" Connor moves the phone so I can see how he's leaking pre-come over his knuckles. "This is you, baby. So hard for you."

A ripple of pleasure crests over my body and I cry out. Distantly, I'm aware of Connor cutting off a curse and groaning while I ride out my orgasm. As I come back down to earth, Connor chuckles. He's moved to his bed, covering his lap after tossing aside a used tissue. Blushing, I scramble for my discarded body suit and shift around to curl in the chair with more modesty.

"You feel better now?" Connor asks. His eyes are bright with amusement. "All ready for me to tuck you into bed?"

"I, um." It hits me hard. I just had phone sex with Connor. And I started it. So do I want him? Blinking, I push my hair out of my face. "Yes?"

His shoulders shake as another amused sound rasps out of him. "Sweet dreams, sunshine."

Whether he can tell I need the space after taking things so far with him, or he got what he wanted and he's eager to get rid of me, he winks and ends the video call. I melt into the chair and hide behind my hands. When I peek between my fingers, his shadow fills his window again, facing my bedroom. He doesn't hide behind curtains as he watches me because he doesn't have them. I close my sheer lavender curtains and dive into bed, not bothering with getting dressed.

"Well. That happened," I say to the empty room.

My heart races. I have to face Connor tomorrow and we just did that. Were my last two brain cells on vacation?

EIGHTEEN
THEA

As I pace by the front door, waiting for Connor to knock when it's time to go, my hands itch to sink into dough. I still don't know what happened the night before. I mean, I know the obvious. Phone sex. Really hot phone sex.

My cheeks heat and I fan my hands to cool myself off so I don't mess up my makeup. The elegant, beaded gold gown I'm wearing swishes as I pace. It's the prettiest thing I've ever worn.

I don't know what I want. I don't know why I started things with Connor last night.

A knock on the door makes me startle. "Oh god."

I open the door and gape. Connor stands there, one hand in his pocket and the other braced on the doorframe. His tuxedo is tailored to fit his body, and his floppy light brown hair has some product in it, styled to make him look even more dapper.

This isn't fair. My heart lurches.

He looks amazing. Irresistible. Then he smirks at me and I lose all breathing capabilities.

Sweeping his gaze over me, his full lips stretch into the charm-up-to-eleven smile I've never experienced the full force of. *Oof.*

"Looking good," he says, offering his hand. "Ready to be thrown to the lions?"

I have every intention of responding, but my tongue gets twisted. Connor takes my hand and tugs me against him.

"Don't worry, little mouse. I'll protect you."

Behind him, an expensive SUV is parked in the street. He waits for me to lock the door, then tucks my hand in his elbow, guiding me to the car.

"I'm nervous," I admit.

Connor pauses halfway down the walkway from my house. "Hey." He cups my face, smoothing a thumb over my cheek. "I'm the one who made you go. I won't abandon you. I'll be with you all night. Okay?"

I nod, feeling better.

My nerves spike again as we pull up to the hotel where the benefit is being hosted. Photographers and reporters line the plush carpet leading into the building.

Isn't Connor's mom running for city council? This is like a movie star or presidential welcome. It's a lot more attention than I expected for a local event, but this is Ridgeview. Everything is a big to do.

Connor squeezes my hand as he helps me out and tucks me against his side. Camera flashes and questions start up immediately as we turn to follow his parents.

"Just keep your head down or look up. Those flashes are blinding," Connor says.

"Councilwoman Bishop, this way! Are you hoping to beat out the funds raised from your election campaign last term tonight? Are you here with your family?" The reporter catches sight of me. "Miss, what's your name?"

Connor holds me close and strides past the press gauntlet without answering any questions while his mother lingers to smile. I peer over my shoulder before he pulls me through the carved lacquered double doors leading into an ornate, Victorian style parlor room.

"Cocktail hour is in here, then dinner through there." Connor indicates another set of doors inlaid with frosted window panes.

"This place is so fancy." I tip my head back to take in the deep colors and the intricate high ceiling, where crystal chandeliers dangle overhead. "Wow."

"I've always thought it was stuffy." Connor shrugs and swipes a piece of fruit from the spread of appetizers. "Remember our story if anyone asks."

"Okay." Interested in the table of puff pastries, I take Connor's hand and pull him over to inspect it. I pick one up and take a bite, moaning as buttery crust, creamy brie, and tart cranberry burst on my tongue. "Wow, this is so good. How did they get their pastry so flaky?"

Connor stares at me intently when I turn to offer him a bite. He parts his lips and I peek around us. He waits until I give in, feeding him. His lips brush against my fingers, sending a shiver racing down my spine. His gaze stays fixed on me as he chews.

"They're the top chefs in the country. Mom has them flown in for the event." His deep voice washes over me as he places his hand on the small of my back. He leans close enough to press his lips against my ear. "Moan like that again where anyone could hear you tonight, and I'll have to steal you away and stuff something in your mouth to keep you quiet."

A gasp tears from my throat as Connor strokes over my pulse with his other hand. Heat pools in my core at his words. "But, don't you have to be seen? They'll wonder where you went."

"Don't care. Not when you're making sounds like that while standing within reach," he rumbles, tracing the strap of my dress, slipping his finger beneath it. "No windows separating us."

How can that simple touch steal my breath and make my thighs squirm together? He watches me closely, granting me a wicked, devious grin. He knows exactly what he just did to me.

"You're so pretty when you blush."

"Connor, it's good to see you." A portly man with a whiskery white beard interrupts us. He holds his hand out for a shake and Connor takes it. I watch him slip on a mask, playing his part of supportive son. "What's next for your mother? D.C. I hope. There's a Senate seat that will open up once her next term on the council ends."

"She only wants to serve Ridgeview's residents and do her best for them right now," Connor says with a laugh I know is for show.

I hope that's the truth. To distract myself from over-analyzing last night, I spent a few hours researching the legislation his mom passed. What I found didn't impress me. Given the choice, she's not someone I'd vote for.

"And who's the lovely lady you're with?" The man takes an interest in me.

"My girlfriend, sir. I'm sorry, you'll have to excuse us. I see someone I was told to speak to." He inclines his head at the portly man. "You know how these things go. All hands on deck to woo the purse strings into bigger donations."

The man throws his head back on a laugh. "Too right."

Connor steers me away and we run right into Maisy's parents.

"Chief! Looking sharp," I say.

"Thea," Mrs. Landry says in surprise. "Darling, you look beautiful! I didn't know you'd be here."

"Oh, yeah. Maisy didn't say?" Chief Landry shakes his head, gazing past me to Connor, standing behind my shoulder with his hand planted firmly on my waist. "This is my boyfriend, Connor. His mom is Councilwoman Bishop."

"We're well acquainted," Chief Landry says, coughing when his wife elbows him.

He and Connor share a look.

"Well, have fun tonight, kids," Mrs. Landry says, ushering the police chief away.

It's deceptive at first glance, but Connor keeps himself between me and anyone we mingle with during the cocktail hour. I don't really get why, since I'm supposed to pose as his girlfriend. He won't let anyone talk to me for long, masterfully but abruptly extricating us from conversations when they get too prying.

When we sit down in the next room for dinner, he pulls my chair out for me. The room drips in splendor, with circular tables covered in white tablecloths and place settings more suited for a ball rather than a political charity fundraiser. This event pulls out all the stops.

Connor doesn't seem surprised as he takes his seat next to me. His parents are already at the table, Mrs. Bishop nodding as Damien leans over to speak in her ear with a tablet in his hand. He appears to be running the show as one of Mrs. Bishop's high up staff members.

"We'll do the speech between the soup and main course. Any later in the meal and I'll lose their attention and their wallets."

Her calculating demeanor changes as soon as the other guests who purchased plates at our table arrive.

"We went all out for you this year, Madam Council-woman." It's the man with the white beard from earlier and he's taking his seat next to me.

Connor stiffens.

"Charles, it's an honor," Mrs. Bishop says. "Your support of the campaign is wonderful."

Connor leans close to me. "Friend of my granddad's."

As Charles sits down on my other side, Connor hooks his hand beneath my chair and gives it a subtle yank so my seat scoots toward him. Mrs. Bishop clears her throat across from us, spearing Connor with a pointed look.

Dinner goes on like that, peppered with awkward moments and tiny rebellions from Connor. His mother is doing a scary good job of keeping her cool. It's almost like Connor is pushing her to see how far he can go before she loses it.

I think it backfires, because all she's done is give me another taste of how she's polite but horrible while they have an audience.

"Charles, has Connor mentioned his plans for next year?" Mrs. Bishop asks as we finish the soup course. "Ivy bound. Maybe he'll be giving your company a run for its money in a few years."

As Charles chortles, he bumps against my chair. He keeps doing that and Connor doesn't like it. "Is he now? Of course he is. Spitting image of your father; I'm sure he's got a mind like his as well."

"What about you, dear?" It takes a second to realize Mrs. Bishop is addressing me. "Is it state school for you?"

"I haven't applied yet," I say.

"Mom. Don't you remember?" Connor laces his fingers with mine when I take his hand beneath the table. He brings our hands on the tabletop so they can all see us unified. "We're getting serious. I fell for the girl next door and finally got her to fall for me after nursing my longtime crush. I'm not about to let her go. Thea and I will get married after graduation and move to Paris for a year. She wants to study from the best pastry chefs. After that, we'll travel. Do humanitarian work."

For a second my heart takes a vacation until I remember tonight is fake. I swallow back anxious laughter.

"How romantic," one of the other table guests coos, about to swoon at Connor's steadfast declaration.

"Married." Mrs. Bishop might as well have said *drink sewer water* with that tone. "I'm thrilled to hear you're so committed to each other. And at such a young age."

God, she's just like my mom.

"I'm always thinking about the future, like you wanted," Connor says. He tilts his head and peers at me. "Always."

"Wonderful. You can apply to Oxford for a year abroad, then."

The tension at the table almost chokes me. Thankfully, Damien appears at Mrs. Bishop's elbow and she leaves to give her speech. Connor holds my hand through it all, stroking my knuckles.

My head is spinning by the time dinner ends. I slip off to the restroom to freshen up. When I come out, a man with a press badge is in my face.

"Can I get a quote? You're here with Councilwoman Bishop's son tonight."

Connor materializes at my side, hand resting at the small of my back. "She is. What's your question?"

The reporter motions for a photographer hovering by a

potted fern. "The policies your mother supported in the last year cut back on the education budget for Ridgeview. As students, how do you feel about that?"

"Oh, I was reading about this earlier. I think—"

"Those policies were put forth by the mayor," Connor says, polite but bland as he cuts me off. When I pinch his side, he deftly maneuvers me into posing for the camera with him. "Will that be all? Great. Bye."

As he guides me away, I dig my heels in and walk over by the coat check. The clerk is on break, so we're alone, shielded from the crowd by tall decorative plants.

"What is up with you tonight?" I demand. "You didn't tell me everything. Tell me the truth. Why am I even here? It doesn't seem like you need or want me at all."

"I'm sorry." Connor kisses me, cupping my face. "It's necessary. It's been harder than I thought it would be to play my part and keep you from getting sucked in by this tar pit. This isn't your world. I never should've gotten you involved in my shit." He rests his forehead against mine, closing his eyes. "I'm not really me tonight and you're not really you. Don't think of me like this."

There's a pleading edge to his voice. He seems unhappy and out of sorts. The pressure of tonight has put a strain on him that has him worn out from fielding questions and dealing with his mom. I've watched it weigh on him all night as tension wound through his posture.

He's reverted to being controlling tonight, closing off when things got hard instead of being the disarming guy who drives me to school in the morning, and apologized when he was wrong. Instead of the one who wished me sweet dreams last night.

It's Connor with his guard firmly up, refusing to let me back in. I thought we were making progress toward understanding each other better, that maybe he was changing his ways for the better.

This environment must be toxic for him, because it turns him into someone I barely recognize. He's that damn blackmail king once more.

I don't like this Connor, but I empathize with him.

I'm not really me tonight and you're not really you.

He wouldn't be here without the strict expectations of his mom. I want to do what I can to take away the look on his face, so I slide my hands up the lapels of his tuxedo and pull him in for another kiss.

Connor takes my mouth with a rough sound, holding me against him.

The kiss gets heated, and he tugs me into the coatroom, slamming the door behind us as we stumble through the muted light, bumping against coats. I clutch his shoulders and he grabs my ass, palming it through my gold dress while his tongue delves into my mouth.

Is this fake, too? Has everything tonight been for show?

The last time we kissed, it was intense. I feel the same trembling restraint shattering as Connor devours my mouth.

I need to know if this is real or not.

Because why am I lying to the people out there while we're hooking up in private? It makes no sense.

"You're the cure to this mad circus act I've been trapped in all night," he murmurs against my lips.

An ache pangs in my chest, but I snap my spine straight and plant my hands on his chest to keep him from diving in for another kiss.

"Wait. I'm not just going to play along and be your secret in private while pretending to be your fake girlfriend in public." As I lay it down, Connor stares at me, his expression hard to read. I prod him in the chest. "Why do I have to cater to you if you're just using me? Was last night anything or another game you'll hold against me?"

"Against you? What have I been doing all—" With a frustrated breath, he cuts off and swipes a hand over his mouth. His gray eyes harden. He's shutting me out, I can feel it. He takes out his phone and pulls up one of my tamer photos he's been dangling over my head. His knuckles turn white as he grips the phone. "You want to keep challenging me? Blackmail it is, then. I always keep my word. If you want out, you know what it means."

I fold my arms. I don't believe he would. "Do it. It's better than you pulling the leverage card when you don't like what I say. I'm a *person*, Connor. You can't control me like a chess piece."

He grumbles under his breath and puts his phone away. I called his bluff and it gives me a sliver of hope. I step close enough my chest brushes his body.

"This doesn't have to be a secret we hide. If you want me, you can ask me out for real and *maybe* I'll say yes."

Silence blankets the coatroom for a beat.

"Does that uptight mom of yours even let you date?" Connor narrows his eyes. "Does she know you're here?"

I lift my chin. "You didn't care before when you bullied me into this deal. I don't need her permission to do what I want."

Connor traces my lower lip. "There's just one problem with your cute little declaration."

"What?"

"I don't do girlfriends, remember? Never have. Wanting to fuck you doesn't change that. This is mutual back scratching to get my mom off my case."

"I don't believe you."

"You don't have to." He kisses me, lips moving slowly over mine. "But you do want this."

186

"Do I?" I sass as he herds me through the room until my back hits a wall.

"You're dying to know. I saw it in your eyes last night." Connor drags his lips down my neck and I gasp, tilting my head. "What do you say, my little mouse? Going to let me show you what it's like to become the irresistible vixen you are behind your phone?"

It's tempting. He's luring out the Thea in my secret folder. I want it, but I'm not done pushing my point. I won't give up. We can have this now, but I'm not letting this go.

Connor covers my mouth with his, nipping my lip. I dig my nails into his biceps. "Well?"

"Yes," I whisper.

The pleased sound he makes is downright sinful as he gives me one more searing kiss and sinks to his knees. He pins me in place with his gaze, gliding his hands under my dress, up my bare legs until he teases the edge of my panties.

It's intoxicating to have him on his knees at my feet.

"If you're such a good girl, you wouldn't have worn panties like that." He holds the hem of my dress at my hips, gaze feasting on what's beneath. "Those are the panties of a girl begging to get fucked."

I lean against the wall for support as he lifts my leg, kissing the birthmark on my thigh he thinks is shaped like the sun.

"Maybe I just like feeling pretty. For myself."

His chuckle vibrates against my skin, dragging a gasp from me. I lose my breath as he peels my panties down and stuffs them in his pocket.

"Now how do you feel? Wild?" He leans back to peek up at me. "Only you and I will know."

I bite my lip. "Free."

Connor grins. "Yes, baby. Hold your dress up."

He presses his face against my thigh as he strokes my folds

with a teasing touch. I shift restlessly, needing more. His teeth sink into my skin and he licks my birthmark, pressing his thumb against my clit.

"Ah!" My head tips back.

"Love your sounds," he rasps. "So sexy."

As Connor teases me, he kisses my birthmark over and over, worshipping it with his tongue and teeth. Then his fingers slide into me and I have to let go of my dress to clap a hand over my mouth, muffling a moan.

"Feel good, sunshine?"

I nod, breathing hard when he pumps his fingers, filling me up. My insides twist into a tight coil of pleasure.

"Who's fucking you right now?" Connor growls. "Say my name."

"C-C—" Before I get his name out, he pulls out to spread my legs wider and descends on my pussy with his mouth. As he sucks on my clit, I whimper. "Connor."

"That's right, baby. Not Wyatt. Not anyone else," he says, making my body wrack from the sensation of his lips brushing my wet folds. "All me. Don't you forget who makes you feel like this." He swipes his tongue over my pussy. "Who gets you wet like this."

My knees shake as I'm overwhelmed by the sensations. It's so much and my toes curl. I can barely contain the sounds escaping me.

"Please," I gasp, angling my hips and reaching for his head, running on instinct and need.

Connor groans, eating me while his fingers dig into my thigh and ass. He pulls back to catch his breath and thrusts his fingers in me again, torturing my clit with his thumb.

"Oh my god," I whine.

"You'll always think of me, sunshine. Years from now, with your sweet college boyfriend who buys you flowers, with your wholesome husband who kisses you good morning—you'll think of me fucking you like this." He curls his fingers, hitting a spot deep inside that makes my body quake with pleasure. "Because you'll always be mine. No one else's," he growls. "I'll ruin you for anyone else, because I'm the only one who fucks you the way you like it, my dirty little mouse. There's no escaping me."

I fall apart on his fingers, tears pricking my eyes, almost losing my balance as I come. It's way more intense than I was prepared for.

Connor catches me in his arms, putting me on his lap as he slumps to the floor. I can feel his hard dick against my ass as we both pant. His hair is a mess. I'm sure I look just as debauched. He gathers me in his arms, in no hurry to take care of himself.

I'm about to speak when a commotion at the door has both of us jumping. Connor springs into action.

"Go. There," he points to the coats.

We shuffle into the shadows as an arguing couple comes into the coatroom. Connor holds me close, shielding me with his body.

"They're starting to notice," a woman hisses.

"You promised." That's a man's deeper voice, angry. "What do you expect me to do when I see you kissing him?"

"He's my husband. I'm still married to him."

Connor tenses, glancing over his shoulder. I can't see past him. He focuses on me once more with a mix of possessive protectiveness.

"I can't deal with this right now. It's already a risk to come in here. We'll talk about this at home. Do not mess this up for me, Damien."

My eyes widen as Connor steps closer, plastering his body against mine. "Shh."

The door slams. I don't dare breathe. Another piece of the Connor Bishop puzzle slots into place.

He cups my face, staring at me with resignation. "Let's get back out there."

"We're not going to talk about that bomb? Are you okay?" I wrap my fingers around his wrist. "Did you know?"

He's quiet for a minute. "I knew. Come on."

We emerge from the coatroom and I stop by the bathroom to check my makeup and cool off from the aftershocks of the earth-shattering orgasm he gave me. As I leave the bathroom, I freeze.

Connor watches me, leaning against the opposite wall. His hair is fixed, my lipstick wiped from his face. Without breaking eye contact, he pats his pocket, where he stuffed my panties.

"Get through the rest of the night and you'll get them back."

"Connor," I hiss. "Are you serious?"

He pops off the wall from his slouch and smirks as he closes the distance between us. He puts his lips by my ear and murmurs, "Be a good girl and I'll do that thing you like again."

Too flustered to respond, I spend the rest of the evening stewing on what we overheard in the coatroom with a million questions running through my head.

NINETEEN
THEA

At the end of the night, Connor walks me to my front door.

Principal Bishop has already gone into their house. Connor's mom and Damien rode in a different SUV, getting away with their secret without suspicion because he's her right-hand man. I can't believe what happened tonight, what we heard them arguing about.

After all my theorizing, I've finally worked out why he was forced to bring a fake girlfriend. I'm part of the elaborate distraction to further hide what Mrs. Bishop has been doing. Sadness pangs in my chest. The truth is worse than all the wacky reasons I thought up.

Connor brushes his knuckles over my cheek. Those intense gray eyes trap me in their hypnotic hold.

"Goodnight," Connor murmurs.

"Bye," I call as he walks away. A second later, I realize he still has my panties in his pocket. "Con—Damn it."

He's disappeared.

Unlocking the door, I slip inside. Constantine greets me, his whole hind end in motion as he tries to wag his tail nub. He dances around me in his excitement.

"Okay, okay. Come on, I'll let you out." I pat his head as I pass by him, kicking off my heels on the way to the back door and sighing in sweet relief as my sore bare feet hit the cool kitchen tile.

So many thoughts swirl through my mind.

On one hand, the girl I hide in my secret folder came out and it was overwhelming...and exhilarating.

I'm not ready to do it again unless Connor and I talk about our relationship, but I did like it. I do want more. Is it messed up that the boy who's been my bully for so long is the same one who gave me my first kiss and so many other firsts? Maybe, but I'm not going to psychoanalyze myself.

I wanted it, so that's all that matters.

Opening the door, I snort as Constantine tries to take off like a bullet, but skids on the back terrace and trips into a clumsy roll. He pops up a second later, perfectly fine and disappears past the pool of light into the backyard. I hear him rustling around as I lean against the open door to wait for him, hugging myself against the chill.

My mind goes to the fight between Mrs. Bishop and Damien we overheard in the coatroom. I know it's important. It feels like the key to understanding Connor and the way his mind works. He said he knew, but for how long? Did he recently discover the affair? My heart aches for him as I picture their family friend over for dinner and how that must have shattered Connor's trust.

He's hiding pain behind those cocky smiles and the way he jokes at school. Does anyone see that? I hope his best friend does, at least. I know how hard it is to hide a big secret eating you up and pretend everything is fine around friends. It's what I did with Maisy when I couldn't tell her about Henry.

Constantine returns in a seventy pound blur and sits at the back door, waiting for my command to allow him in.

"Okay. Come." The dog follows me inside and I offer him a treat from a jar on the counter—homemade peanut butter milk bones from a recipe I tweaked. "Take it."

Constantine crunches down and trails behind me as I climb the stairs to my bedroom. My thoughts turn as I change out of my gown and wipe the makeup off my face.

The light never turns on in Connor's bedroom. I watch from my chair for a while before I get into bed.

If Connor's mother is having an affair, why is she hiding it? She has the whole neighborhood fooled. Why is this a big secret?

I would hate to hide my love like that. But even worse, it breaks my heart that she's sneaking around in plain sight, hurting people. And Connor *knows*.

Maybe her affair has jaded him, giving him reason to avoid relationships.

"I'm going to figure this out," I mumble to Constantine as he snuggles with me in bed. I hug him close, stroking his soft fur. He stretches and flops half on top of me. "You big lump."

My arms circle around him. He's always my favorite to hug when I'm feeling down.

When I figure out what's going on, I'll confront Connor

again to find out why he won't date me if he wants me. Isn't that what relationships are all about? I saw the look in his eyes tonight. It wasn't only lust.

And I refuse to be his pawn any longer.

TWENTY
CONNOR

It's impossible to get Thea out of my head. She's taken root, claiming every other thought as hers.

I was an idiot to think I could have one taste and get her out of my system. What happened in the coatroom was inevitable. It was only a matter of time before the powder keg between us finally went off.

That light in her eyes, the shyness burning away to reveal what she keeps locked up tight...

Thea isn't the kind of girl you hit it once and quit. She's the kind you grow addicted to, the kind that burrows beneath your skin and clutches your heart and your dick.

A weakness I shouldn't indulge in more than I already have.

There's nothing I want more than to keep her, both the secret fiery minx and the nerdy stress baker who babbles nonstop. I want to give her what she asked for—a relationship. A boyfriend. That's not me, though. And I'm sick to my stomach because there's always the chance my biggest worry will come true: that she's just like her mom.

I've been learning to let her in, to trust what she says. But what if I'm wrong?

After what she heard in the coatroom, she could tell someone.

Christ, how can I feel like this about the daughter of the woman who's caused me so many problems?

But I can't stop thinking about the other night, even while I'm supposed to be focused on the Monday night game.

My teammates run and shout around me on the field. The floodlights are blinding. Sweat drips down my temples, stinging my eyes. I'm so out of it that Devlin punches my shoulder lightly as the other team subs out players.

"Dude. What are you doing?" he asks, swiping black hair back from his face. "I've never seen you miss a shot so perfectly set up."

"Suffering." Between Thea and my mom, I'm going crazy. I drag a hand over my head and glance around. Several of our guys throw me dirty looks, as if I'm the only one who can carry the team because I'm the captain. I sigh. "Fuck, sorry."

Devlin squints at me. "Was that benefit shit this weekend?"

I grunt in response, nodding.

"Just get in the game. I've got your back." Devlin claps me on the shoulder. "It's almost over."

He's right. If I can stop dicking around, we'll finish this and stay in the running for the playoffs.

The ref blows his whistle and the game resumes. Family members and a group of Coyote Girls gathered on the sidelines cheer as we pick up the ball, zigzagging across the field to keep it in our possession.

Trent loses the soccer ball to the other team's striker, and I swoop back from my position at the center. Instinct and years of practice kick in as I mark the striker heading for our goal. The cheers and shouts on the sideline become white noise. The other team's player fakes me out with a spin, but I anticipate him and steal the ball before he can defend against me. A few of our guys whoop and holler for me, and the corners of my mouth tip up in satisfaction.

Devlin meets me at center field and together we move on offense, passing the ball back and forth as we cut down the grass toward the opposing team's net. Their goalie has his hands up, glancing between both of us.

This is what we're known for. An unstoppable pair with speed and skill.

As we're closing in on the goal, dodging defensive backs, Devlin sets me up so that the defensive players think he's taking the shot. They go to block him as I swoop in, stealing the ball and kicking it with precision. It arcs through the air into the back left of the net.

The sound of celebration erupts behind me as the timer runs down on the second half. I stand with my hands on my hips, dropping my head back and gasping to drag air into my burning lungs.

It feels good to finish this strong when my head is still so messed up. Thea's worked her unassuming roots into me, making me think she's harmless when she's got me entangled.

"Good finish, man." Devlin claps me on the shoulder, squeezing. "Don't let your parents' shit get to you. It's not worth it. Trust me." He grimaces, jaw clenching. "Just—" He gestures vaguely. I don't think I've ever seen him so at a loss for how to express himself. "Forget them. Find someone—*things* that make you happy."

"Uh huh," I say, squinting at him. "This wouldn't have anything to do with Davis, would it? You've been different ever since you had her in that cheerleader uniform at the last practice. You kissed her in front of everyone, bro. We all saw it."

Devlin shoves me without heat. "Pull your head out of your ass."

"Yeah. Sure." I laugh as we make our way to the huddle of our teammates to shake hands with the other players. "But I told—"

"Don't say it."

"So broody." I clutch my chest like he's caused me a fatal wound. "So cold."

Devlin shakes his head and plants a hand over my face to cut off my fake wailing.

After the match, I convinced Thea to meet me at my pool house to talk. She waits in the shadows cast by the edge of the building, peeking around the corner when she hears my footsteps drawing close.

"How was your game?" Thea asks, tucking a loose lock of hair behind her ear. She's wearing a thick tan sweater beneath a pale blue denim overall dress. Her white tennis shoes have hand-painted rainbows on the toes.

"We won." I unlock the door, running through what I need to talk to her about in my head, willing myself not to get distracted by her sweet scent.

"I've never seen one of your games. Are you good?"

I throw a cocksure grin over my shoulder. "I made varsity

captain last year. I'm good. Our team is, too. Dev's a damn sight to behold, wicked bastard."

"Devlin Murphy?"

I hum in response as she follows me into the pool house. My room might be a sanctuary away from my parents, but I come out here when I need to think. A guest bed dominates the room and white cushioned ottomans are arranged in a small sitting area. In the other corner a large full-length mirror reflects most of the space, giving it the appearance it's even bigger.

Thea peers around while I sink onto the corner of the bed, leaning my elbows on my knees. She pauses by the mirror, blue-green gaze flicking to find me in the muted light through the reflection. A moment passes, crackling with this magic quality.

A tug in my chest feels like it has me tethered to her. The girl I was never supposed to have in the first place. The one I'd never noticed.

But that pull gets stronger until I'm gritting my teeth to stay where I am instead of going to her side.

This is what I mean by she's a weakness I shouldn't indulge in. This is a girl I would destroy, eating up her goodness, her warm light. A girl I shouldn't want, but I do. I've only had one taste, but I'd burn the world to the ground for her, damn the consequences.

That's a dangerous kind of devotion I've never experienced. Girls have always been a means to getting off and having fun. Never this intense storm of emotions I can hardly pick apart.

Learning to trust her is scary enough. But wanting her? I can't escape it.

Thea turns around and comes to stand between my knees. I swallow, cupping the back of her legs. Looking up at her, I skim my fingertips beneath the hem of her skirt. She shivers, placing her hands on my shoulders.

"You want to do more dirty things to me." She says it lightly.

"I do." I squeeze the back of her thighs, trailing my touch higher and closing my knees to trap her. "Very dirty things. They involve my tongue and your pussy until I have you crying my name."

She combs her fingers through my hair, dragging her nails gently over my scalp. Holy fuck, it feels good. My eyes fall shut and I release a soft groan, leaning into her body.

"We won't do anything else unless we're together. For real."

"Thea," I say firmly. "I told you, I don't do—"

"Girlfriends. I know." She stops touching me and pulls out of my arms. That mutinous fire is in her eyes again, challenging me. "You want me? Then date me. I'm not your hookup, and I'm not faking anything else for you, Connor Bishop."

God, I love it when she says my whole name all indignant and stubborn like that.

With a heavy sigh, I get up to stalk away, hoping to clear my head. It doesn't help; I can still smell sugar cookies and cinnamon. I peel out of my evergreen Silver Lake High soccer zip up and toss it aside.

"If it's because you're afraid, because of the thing with your mom..." She trails off with a conflicted look when I whirl around. "I just—we aren't our parents. Whatever their mistakes and shortcomings are, those aren't automatically ours, too." She blows out a breath. "I mean, I hope I never turn out like my mom."

She doesn't want to be like her mom. My heart thuds. It's the last fear holding me back with her.

I rub my forehead. Damn her solid logic and reasoning. I don't want to explain my family shit right now.

On top of that, I'm nothing but corruption. I would only taint her with it. Break her.

Staying away from her is too hard. I'm drawn back, taking her by the shoulders. The scent of whatever she's been baking today wraps around me. I lean in, needing to taste her lips.

"I told you." Thea pokes me in the chest to stop me, her voice quiet but not giving an inch. "I'm not the same as you. I can't turn it on and off. I like you. You *blackmailed* and bullied me, and I still like you, because under all that bravado for your reputation, you're hiding the guy you really are."

"I'm not. You're wrong. What you see is who I am. I lied to you. Tricked you because it amused me."

She tilts her head, studying me through her lashes. "You're not as cruel as you pretend to be. If you were, you wouldn't have cared what happened to me at the benefit. Even though you made me go. You put yourself between me and anyone else, keeping me safe in your own way." Sighing, she bows her head. "It's why I want this. Us. But if this is all fake for you, then I'm out of here."

Panic surges as Thea slips out of my grasp, turning toward the door.

"Wait." I grab her wrist. My voice is hoarse and my thoughts race with the burst of adrenaline coursing through my system. "Just—wait. It's not...I do want you." I push my other hand through my hair. "But I don't know how to have a girl-friend either, sunshine. I've only ever gone to girls for sex."

There's a long beat where she gives me her back, and I think she's going to wrench away to leave anyway. Relief pours through me as she turns to face me.

"We'll figure it out together. I'm sure we'll mess up, but I want to do it with you."

My throat grows tight. Why is this so hard?

Just take, like you always have.

I can't though.

"I'll corrupt you." Shaking my head, I step back, releasing her wrist so she can escape me. "I'm not good, Thea. I'm messed up."

I'm so fucked up in my shadows playing god that I spied on her. Toyed with her.

"Isn't that my choice to make? Besides, haven't you already shown me the dark side?"

Thea gives me a smirk that's all mischief. It looks fucking good on her, making my dick hard. That look should be illegal.

She takes my hand, bringing my knuckles up to press her lips against them, peeking up at me. "You said it yourself, I was hiding who I really am. I'm done hiding. Are you?"

A tortured groan tears from me. This girl...

Screw it. I'm done running from my problems and fears. Finished letting my fucked up family keep me from having someone that makes me happy. I tried to keep her away, but I'm not the noble hero. I take what I want, and if she wants me? I'm fucking giving her what she asked for.

Thea's right. This doesn't have to be fake. It never was. I'm a king of misdeeds. She'll be my queen.

The sunshine to my dark moonlight.

Together we make an eclipse.

I'll swallow her golden, warm light in my shadows, but she'll pierce through the blackest parts of my heart.

"Be careful what you wish for," I rumble, tugging her against me. "If we're doing this, I might never let you go."

"Do your worst. I can handle it."

"Yeah?" My cock throbs. I back up toward the bed and drop onto the corner of the mattress, facing the big full-length mirror. "We were interrupted before we could finish what we started the other night, before I devoured you. Come here."

She puts a knee on the bed and straddles my lap, her denim

skirt riding up her thighs. I caress them, then unclip the straps of her overalls, peeling down the material so it pools around her waist. My hands bury under her thick sweater, pushing it up over her head.

Thea captures my mouth in a kiss and it's so sexy. Whenever she popped onto my radar before, I never would've pegged her for a first move girl. She proved me wrong with her mistaken number selfie, but I still thought of her as the kind of wallflower I'd have to coax to show me her petals in bloom.

She yanks on my shirt until it's over my head. Every second I part from her kiss is wrong, and I swallow her gasp when we come together again, both of us shirtless. It's so much better than the rushed coatroom quickie. Now I can take my time with her.

Growling into the kiss, I unclasp her bra, discarding it to the side. I've dreamed of her tits after all the naughty photos she's sent, and I'm finally going to get them in my mouth. Cupping and massaging them, I rip from the kiss to take a nipple between my lips. Thea's head drops back with a tiny cry. As I torture one nipple, then the other with my tongue and teeth, she starts circling her hips, the material of her skirt riding higher as she rubs her pussy on the hard ridge of my cock through my jeans. I suck harder on her nipple, dropping my hands to grab her plump ass, moving with her.

"Oh god!" Thea tenses, burying her face in my neck as her body shakes.

"You come all over my dick, baby?" I speak against her tits, snaking my tongue out to flick the tight buds of her nipples.

She whimpers, bucking against me. I slide a hand lower, between her legs from behind and stroke her soaked panties, watching our reflection in the mirror. We make a sight that has my cock rock hard.

"Mm, baby, you feel how wet you are for me? Turn around, you need to see this."

Thea climbs to her feet on unsteady legs with my help. I make her face the mirror as I strip her denim dress down her body along with her underwear. Her tits rise and fall as I guide her back between my spread knees, gaze locked with hers in the glass as I skim my fingertips over her flushed skin.

Her eyes drop and she turns her head away. A small sound escapes her.

"Hey, what's wrong?" I stroke her sides and can't resist squeezing her ass when it's at eye level. "I thought you were done hiding?"

"I...well, I don't normally have to..." Her stammering fades and she gestures at the mirror. "It's weird."

"It's not weird."

"It is. You've been with so many girls. All I see at school is your charming smile and the pretty girls that fall all over you." She tries to turn, but I hold her in place. "Can't we go back to what we were doing? I want to feel good."

Squinting up at her, I point at the mirror. "Look."

It takes a minute of her peering back at me pleadingly, but she faces her reflection.

"This is who you are, Thea. This is the girl I see. Look at her—*you*. You're beautiful. Forget everything else." I kiss her hip and trail a path to the sun-shaped birthmark I'm obsessed with, biting her skin lightly. With a tug, she lands in my lap. "Come back here."

Tension lingers in her body. I spend long minutes placing feather-light kisses over every inch of skin I can reach, holding her hair up as I focus on the back of her neck and shoulders. Eventually she melts against my chest.

An ember burns around my heart. I will make her see what I do—what I saw that first night we sexted.

While she's relaxed, I nudge her legs wider, so she's spread gorgeously for me. She's no longer paying attention to the mirror, but I am, watching the way her lashes flutter, the way she tips her head back when I caress her tits, and the way she arches when I tease my touch between her legs.

Time slows to a drowsy pace as I finger her, peeking at the mirror each time I grind my cock against her perfect ass. She makes soft sounds when I brush her clit and pump my fingers deeper. I know I'm driving her crazy, working her body with deliberate touches.

"Connor," Thea murmurs, sounding drunk and delirious as I keep her balanced on the edge and walk her back before she can come. "Please. *Please.* It's too much."

"Shh, not yet. It'll be so good, baby, I promise." I kiss her temple, licking the damp sweat beading her skin. "A little longer."

She whines, hips shifting with the slow pace I set, silently begging me to give her more. She's forgotten all about her hesitation with the mirror, all she can think about is the orgasm I'm keeping her a breath away from. With a devious grin, I fall back on an elbow, tugging my phone from my pocket with my free hand and pop back up, hugging her against me.

"Connor?"

"Right here. Now, baby girl," I rasp, smoky and hot against her ear, sending tremors through her body. "I know you want to come so bad, right?"

Thea nods, pushing her ass on my dick, distracting me for a moment. I grab my phone.

"I'll let you come. But we're going to try something. I'm going to play with your perfect tits, and you're going to ride my fingers until you come. Don't look away from the mirror. Cool?"

"I—okay," she says, blushing and biting her lip.

Humming, I kiss her cheek. "Good girl. There's one more thing you're going to do."

"What?" Her voice is husky with need.

I hold up my phone in front of her, setting it up on the camera app. Thea flicks her gaze over her shoulder, a cute wrinkle between her eyebrows.

"I want you to take pictures of yourself. Watch your face when you take your pleasure on my fingers. I want you to see everything I see when you come." Her eyes widen and I draw her into a kiss. "These ones are just for me and you. You can do whatever you want with them after—delete them, whatever."

The hesitation clears from her expression and she takes the phone. I drop another kiss on her shoulder as she shifts on my lap, holding the phone up.

"That's my girl. Don't stop watching."

I take my time working her back to the brink, teasing her sensitive pussy until she's back to whimpering, the click of the camera shutter punctuating her shallow breathing. It's so fucking hot. She's so wet, my fingers slip through her folds and slide into her easily, her pussy practically swallowing my fingers. This time I don't stop her from moving her hips, encouraging her to fuck herself on my fingers.

Heat pulses in my groin and it takes everything in me to let her have this instead of ripping my jeans off and fucking her hard until she screams. She needs this.

"You look so sexy," I say into her neck as I roll a nipple. "You see that?"

"Yes," she gasps, moving faster.

"God, yes, baby. That's it. Fuck my fingers until you come." As she bucks, I rub her clit with my thumb. My wrist cramps in protest, but I'm not stopping. Those high-pitched sounds escaping her tell me she's so close to falling apart. "You look so good."

The camera app clicks with shot after shot. At this point I think she's so far gone she's just snapping away with the burst option, but that's fine. She's focused on her reflection, eyes blazing with desire and pleasure, gasping as she soaks my hand.

With one more flick of my thumb on her swollen clit, she shrieks, falling back against me with a blissed out moan. I catch her with a grunt, falling back against the mattress as I gently stroke her pussy. She trembles and twitches in my arms, the phone slipping from her fingers and bouncing off the bed to the floor. The only sound in the room is our mingled breathing and her murmurs of *oh fuck, fuck, shit* as she rides the aftershocks of a damn good orgasm.

Once she seems coherent, angling her head to peek at me with pink cheeks and parted lips, I flip her over, grinding my cock against her. She cries out, too oversensitive for the rough material of my jeans, but I'm about to blow.

"Sit up," Thea murmurs.

"Baby," I plead, dropping my face into her neck. "Watching you lose it like that, I'm so close."

"You got to pick something and now I want to try something else." She kisses me. "You'll like it."

Grumbling, I roll us to our sides. She gets up, running her fingers through her thick auburn curls, looking sexy as hell. My own personal Aphrodite. I freeze when she kneels at the corner of the bed and motions me over, crooking her finger. As I sit up, I'm sidetracked by the sight of her back reflected in the mirror, her round ass stuck out.

Thea pats the bed. "Come sit here." Her tongue peeks out, swiping her lower lip. "I'm going to suck you."

"I—yes." I scramble to get my jeans and underwear off, sliding to the edge of the bed. Thea looks up at me from between my thighs, holding my dick and hovering her mouth over the tip and, *fuck*, it's my new favorite sight. "Are you sure you want to do it this way? I'll gladly jerk off on your tits if you're not ready for more."

"I want it this way."

Then she takes me in her mouth and I swear I ascend to a higher plane. Her perfect, pouty lips wrapped around my cock are a straight up electric stairway to heaven. She's tentative at first, licking around the tip. I thread my fingers through her hair, groaning as she sucks, taking me deeper. I watch her and the mirror. It's too much, I don't last long. Within minutes she has me coming with her name on my lips.

"Thea," I breathe.

She backs up with a yelp and I release a raspy chuckle, feeling too good to care if I get jizz on the floor. I grin at her, my golden sunshine. There's come on her tits and leaking from the corner of her mouth, a startled but pleased look in her eye.

"You're like a magic little sunbeam," I whisper, brushing a thumb over her cheek.

The shy smile she gives me fills me with warmth.

After we clean up in the bathroom, which leads to another make-out session because I can't resist her, we pull our clothes back on. It's late, after midnight.

On her way out, I give her the key to the pool house and watch as she picks her way across my yard, through hers until she reaches her back door. She glances back at me before slipping inside her house.

A smug curve tilts my mouth as I amble inside, thinking about the cliche of deflowering the neighbor girl.

Fucking worth it.

TWENTY-ONE
THEA

Connor saw exactly who I was in that mirror and made me face it so I knew, too.

He's given me secretive smiles at school this week and sent me good morning and goodnight texts every day. Last night we talked on FaceTime until I fell asleep, and this morning I saw he kept the call connected for another hour.

But I'm still alone at home on a Saturday at the end of the week.

I can't call Maisy to come over because she's out of town. I've already baked my way through lunch. I was ready for more until Mom yelled at me to stop taking up all the Tupperware and storage space in the fridge.

After trudging up the steps, I wind up bored after only a half hour of watching baking videos on YouTube. I roll on my back in the middle of my bed and look at the colorful posters on my wall.

"Maybe Maise posted a story of her yoga intensive." Flipping to my stomach, I grab my phone again.

What I find when I pull up Instagram sinks my stomach. My feed is full of photos. There's a huge party today up at Silver Lake Forest Estates. I don't know anyone that lives in the most elite gated community of Ridgeview, but Connor does. Devlin lives there. And Connor is tagged in a picture with him, armed with water guns.

At first my breath is stolen by how good he looks, shirtless and tan, abs for days and a swimsuit almost painted on his powerful soccer thighs. He's grinning, genuinely carefree. I recognize the smile because it's the same one he gave me in his pool house after he came with my name rolling off his lips.

But then reality sets in, along with my inner critic.

We agreed to be together in the pool house, but if I'm his girlfriend, why didn't I get invited to this party with him? I thought we made some progress. Things haven't changed if I'm sitting at home while he's out with his friends.

You're still his dirty little secret.

Not that I'd jump at the chance for a beach day, but it is unseasonably hot today and I've been baking since this morning. A swim in the cool lake would be nice, even if it means I'd stress over what to wear around the popular crowd.

With a sigh, I remind my inner critic that I don't hate every imperfection and inconvenience of my body. It's beach ready no matter what I wear.

Biting my lip, I spend twenty minutes going through account after account to find more photos, like a stalker. In each one I find, Connor is with one of the dance squad girls. Blair

Davis is even there. I'm kind of surprised to see Devlin Murphy wrapped around her, and the reserved but happy expression on her face. She's cool with him after he made her dump water on herself in the cafeteria while everyone laughed? It wasn't that long ago, yet there they are, sharing an intimate moment someone captured for social media.

The more I scroll Instagram, watching a party I'm not at, the more invisible I feel.

Unseen.

Like always.

Will Connor only ever be mine when the moon is out?

I won't stand for this. I wanted to be together because I like him, not because I was happy to only be trotted out when he needed me.

Closing out of the app on my phone with a frustrated sound, I face plant into my ruffled purple bedspread, letting the darkness swallow me. Once I grant myself a few minutes to wallow, I get up and get my laptop from the desk. As I return to the bed, the positive posters on my wall remind me of my outlook. I turn my back on them and hunch my shoulders as I sink to the floor, opening the laptop.

"I'm not invisible."

Before I've finished typing the address to my blog, I stop. It doesn't feel right. The comments, or even the old emails from Henry aren't what I want right now. It's only a feeble bandage; it won't cure the wound.

I want Connor instead of my secret coping habit.

With a deflated exhale, I lean my head against the side of my mattress. What I want is in Connor's pool house, where we hid away from the world together under the moonlight. Where I felt free to be my true self, no more secret folders, no more splitting myself between who I should be and who I wish I was.

"Are you a clingy girl?" I ask myself, reasoning that I should leave this alone and do my own thing. I don't need him to entertain myself. With another sigh, I shake my head. "But you deserve the universe, so why settle when it doesn't make you feel good?"

Maybe this is one of those things Connor doesn't know to think about. He did make a point about only being with girls as hookup partners before. We're both tripping our way through being in a relationship, the first real one for both of us.

If I don't tell him, he won't know that this made me doubt everything.

After arguing with myself some more, I change out of the ratty old sweats I've been in all day into a stretchy jumpsuit with a pink flower print and sneak out of the house. I avoid Mom by the skin of my teeth as she's leaving through the garage door with sunglasses on. Once she's gone, I creep around the corner and slip out the back door with my phone and the key Connor gave me, cutting across our yard into his.

My heart races as I use the key to get in. Any second I'm ready for someone to ask what I'm doing in the Bishop's yard without an invitation.

Once inside, I leave my key by the door and go to the full-length mirror. It still smells like Connor in here. I lick my lips and sit down in front of the mirror with my legs to the side in a sensual pose, feeling the pinup vibe I have going on right now. I allow one of my straps to slip off my shoulder and angle my boobs forward.

After snapping a few pics, I pick one and send it to him. No caption. It doesn't need one. He'll know where I am.

It doesn't take Connor long to arrive. The door squeals when he opens it in a rush. I haven't moved from my spot by the mirror, and I watch him through the reflection, pressing my fingers to the glass.

"You came," I murmur.

"Did you think I wouldn't when you sent this?" He waves his phone and tosses it on the bed as he crosses the room to me. On the way he loses his black muscle shirt, leaving him in only his short swimsuit and a perfect view of the sculpted indents in his hips. "Shit, I've been thinking about you all day. About this."

He pulls me to my feet and swoops in for a kiss that leaves me breathless. His skin is warm from an afternoon in the sun.

Putting my hand on his chest, I lean back from his kiss. "You know, I opened Instagram to see if my friend Maisy had posted, but I saw the party at the lake instead."

"Yeah?" Connor is distracted, kissing his way down my neck. He hums against my heated skin and makes me shudder.

"Well, I was surprised to see there was a party. That you were there." My breath hitches when he finds a sensitive spot. "And...the girl you were with in the pictures I saw."

Connor stills. "What girl?"

"Bailey? She's on the dance squad." I suck my bottom lip into my mouth as he stares at me. "I'm not the girl you were with at the lake."

"No. You're not."

A sound rumbles in Connor's chest as he wraps me in his arms, picking me up. I squeal when he lifts me off the ground, surprised by his strength. He crosses the room and deposits me on the bed. Another growl leaves him while he fumbles with my jumpsuit.

"Always with the complicated outfits," he mutters, figuring out he needs to yank down the straps.

Once he has me down to my bra and underwear, he descends on the birthmark on my thigh, sucking on it until I'm pretty sure I'll have a hickey. I like that, the idea of him branding my skin with his marks. Proof that we had this moment.

Lifting his head, he pins me with his gray eyes. "If I wanted that chick, I wouldn't be here. Why would I want her when I only want a little beam of sunshine who drives me fucking crazy?" He keeps his gaze locked with mine as he licks my birthmark. "You're who I'm with. No other girl matters to me. Only you, baby."

My fingers claw at the bedding, a hazy fog of desire clouding my head. But this is important and I have to make sure he understands.

"How can I believe you really want me? You only kiss me in the dark." I sit up and face him in only my bra and panties. "The hall when no one was around. The coatroom. In here." My chest rises and falls. "You pretend I don't exist otherwise, like you always have." My voice cracks and my eyes sting. "I can't be invisible anymore, Connor."

"Sunshine," he rasps, cradling my face in his hands as his brow furrows. "I swear, I wasn't keeping you a secret. I'm sorry I made you doubt I want this. What will it take to prove it to you? I'll kiss you at school whenever I see you. You'll be dizzy from my kisses."

The fear clogging my throat vanishes. I give him a wet, breathy laugh. "You don't have to go that far. But a date to the dance would be nice."

"Dance?"

"Winter formal. It's not for a while still, but..."

Connor gives me a lopsided smile and climbs off the bed to sink to one knee. "Well, this is a little impromptu because my girl needs it, but I want you to imagine the flowers I would totally be presenting you with right now. Got it?"

I grin. "Got it. How many flowers?"

"The whole florist supply, obviously. Jesus, what do you take me for, baby? My girl gets the whole world."

For a first time boyfriend, he's definitely got the right idea.

Has Connor Bishop been hiding a secret romantic waiting to be unleashed? The thought makes me smile wider.

"Do I now?"

"Mhm. Now hush so I can ask you a very important question. Thea Kennedy, my bright sunbeam," he starts and I cover my face with my hands. "Hey, look at me. You're gonna miss it." He pries my hands away and holds my hips. "Can I take you to the dance?"

I lean in to kiss him. He lets me for a minute, humming as he sucks on my lip. Then he pulls back and lifts his brows.

"Well?"

"Oh, you wanted an answer? I thought it was a given."

"*Tch.* Girl, please." He pulls a face and clutches his chest dramatically. "You've got my angsty teen heart on the line here. Put me out of my misery."

Laughing, I slide my arms around his neck and kiss his nose. "Yes, Connor Bishop. You can take me to the dance."

"That's my girl. Now where were we?"

Connor takes my mouth and guides my legs around his waist, lifting me from the bed in a smooth move. He carries me back to the mirror and presses my bare back against it without breaking the kiss. I'm dizzy with want, my body thrumming. My hips roll against his muscled torso. He undoes the clasp on my bra with a deft flick of his fingers and buries a hand down the back of my underwear to squeeze my ass.

"Mm, these are nice. Silky. Loose 'em." He lowers me to my feet and smacks my ass. Spinning me to face the mirror, he helps me out of them as I brace a hand against the mirror. I moan as my bra drops along with my panties. "Look at yourself. That's fucking hot."

My skin prickles with excitement.

In the reflection, Connor stands behind me, still wearing his trunks, which are tented as he grinds his hard cock against my bare ass with a groan. He pulls my thick curls off my neck and sinks his teeth into my pulse point, sending a hot burst of pleasure straight to my core. With his other hand, he rolls one of my nipples between his fingers before dragging his fingers down my body to dip between my legs, sliding through the wetness already coating my thighs.

"Oh shit," I gasp, bucking into his touch and back against his hardness. "That feels—ah! So good."

Connor's rough chuckle does things to my insides, twisting them in knots of lust. He makes me wild in a way nothing else ever has. With him, I forget to hate what's in the mirror, only face it with bravery as he pushes the proof of his attraction against my backside. He loses his swimsuit and pulls me against his chest, feeling all of him.

It's unlike anything I've ever imagined, and I'm lost to the heat of his body, his firm muscles, his cock brushing my own flushed skin.

"Watch yourself while I make you come," Connor commands.

My eyes almost flutter shut, too overwhelmed by everything, but he chides me with his lips against my ear, murmuring his encouragement.

"Look, sunshine. See how your pretty blue eyes get all dark when I touch you here?" His fingers circle my clit and it's all I can do to stay standing. "That feel good?"

"Yes! God, yes." I lean my head back against his shoulder, obeying his demand to watch as he kicks my legs a little further apart and cups my pussy. I bite my lip, tempted to rock against the pressure of his palm until I come, my hips shifting restlessly as he teases between my folds. "Connor. Please."

His amused huff fans over my neck in a hot breath. "Listen to you beg for me. So needy."

When he slides a finger in me, I lose my breath, scrabbling

at his arms. He adds another, filling me. I give into the temptation, meeting each thrust of his fingers until my toes curl against the carpet and I'm relying on him to hold me up.

It's too much to take, and as Connor sucks on my neck, I fall apart with a moan. He keeps working me, teasing my clit, my swollen folds, and dipping his clever fingers inside until a second orgasm shocks me. This time I do almost collapse, but he supports me with ease. His heavy-lidded gaze meets mine in the mirror and the slow curve of his mouth into a smirk has me matching his expression.

Pressing up on my toes, I kiss him, smiling into it. The kiss is sweet for a moment while he gives me a second to catch my breath, then it turns heated as I start to tug at his hair. He squeezes my breasts in both hands, trailing his lips down my neck to my shoulder.

In our frenzied kisses and touches, we end up on our knees in front of the mirror. My back is slick with sweat, overheated and sensitive to every touch.

His hand covers my jaw and throat, pulling my head back for a filthy kiss. Our eyes meet and he presses his cock between my thighs, brushing against my throbbing pussy.

"You want it?" Connor thrusts slow and dirty, making me gasp at the sensation of him gliding against my folds between my legs.

"Yes." I moan, leaning against him, my skin burning up. "Please, I want you."

"Easy, baby. Put your hands here." He arranges me how he wants me, hands planted on either side of the mirror on the wall. "Don't look away."

Connor disappears for a moment, rummaging through drawers. I hear a foil packet tear and watch in the reflection as he rolls a condom on. He positions himself behind me, takes my hips, and finds my gaze in the mirror.

"Okay?"

This is nothing like things were with Henry. Connor always checks if I'm into it and doesn't pressure me. If I didn't want this, I know he'd stop and slow us down.

"Yeah." I'm ready, so turned on.

"Good." He grins and bends to kiss the center of my back. "I'm going to wreck you, sunshine."

The first press of his cock at my entrance makes me choke on a gasp, my fingers scrabbling at the wall. He hushes me, dipping a hand between my legs to rub my clit. He takes his time, focusing on working me close to the edge as he eases in. I'm so full. It's tight, his cock thicker than his fingers, but when he moves his hips and presses his fingers harder against my clit, I drop off a cliff into pleasure. My breath fogs the mirror as I press my forehead against the glass.

"Goddamn, baby. Squeezing my cock so good already. Fuck." He starts a slow, torturous pace that draws my orgasm out and grips my hair. "Look at me."

My gaze snaps to his.

Connor looks like a king of debauchery and devious pleasure. His lips are parted, gazing at me intently, gray eyes full of unwavering want. He tightens his hold in my hair—not enough to hurt, just to control the angle of my head. I like it, being at his mercy. His thrusts pick up and my mouth falls open on a silent cry of pleasure.

He falls forward with a rough, possessive sound and my body arches against his, sinking back into his lap as he lowers to the ground to pump into me faster. His scent is all around me, musk mixed with a hint of spice, making me dizzy.

"Fuck, Connor," I breathe, reaching back to hold on to his hair as I roll my hips to meet his thrusts.

"You like that?" Connor rasps in my ear, squeezing my

breasts. He bites the shell of my ear and drops a hand to my clit. "Right there?"

My entire body shakes as my core convulses with pleasure, cresting over my body in waves of ecstasy. I'm delirious and flying high with his arms locked around me. It feels perfect.

Connor groans in my ear and I feel him twitch deep inside my body. He hugs me close, not letting me go for a second as we come back to earth.

"Fucking amazing," he murmurs in my hair, caressing my skin with the tips of his fingers. Gathering me in his arms, he takes me to the bed and kisses my forehead before ducking into the bathroom. A minute later, he comes out and climbs in with me. "Come here. You okay? I wasn't too rough, was I?" He smooths my hair back, taking stock of a spot on my neck he probably left a hickey on. "Are you sore? We can get in the shower or the hot tub if you are."

Shaking my head, I snuggle into his embrace. "No. Just want to lay like this."

"You've got it." He kisses the top of my head and holds me tight.

I fall asleep with his fingers combing through my hair, my head resting on his chest, feeling blissed out.

TWENTY-TWO
CONNOR

A few days later, I can't take the shit in my house anymore. Damien keeps arguing with Mom about the benefit "incident". He means that Mom put on her happy wife mask. Get over it, bro.

Dad's been scarce, most likely off with the librarian from school he's been spending time with, making the house feel like the inevitable train wreck we've all been barreling toward: Damien and Mom getting married. That's what she keeps promising him, anyway.

Damien as my stepdad? No fucking thank you.

It's after one in the morning and they're at each other's

throats. I have half a mind to stomp to the master bedroom and tell them I have school in the morning.

Their shouts filter past my bedroom door and drown out the music I'm blasting. Jesus. I shake my head, entering a new file in my encrypted program full of people's secrets, adding an old incident report of Landry's friend with the leather jacket, Fox Wilder.

"The fuck kind of name is Fox?" I mutter, swigging from my near-empty can of Coke as I input the data.

Holden's dad coughed it up when I pressured him to run a search or I'd start letting his skeletons out of the closet. It didn't turn up much. My access and leverage only extend to the Ridgeview Police Department he heads. There's a report on a car accident that killed his parents and landed little Fox Wilder in the foster care system, whisking him away from Ridgeview at a young age. The rest of the files are sealed or missing, which is weird. I only put a medium amount of effort in before I give up.

Whatever, I have enough to shake him down if he ever steps out of line with me. With that leather jacket and the giant chip on his shoulder, it's only a matter of time before he stirs trouble in this town.

"You're making me crazy, Vivian!" Damien screams. "I've put my entire career at risk because I love you, and you're acting like that's nothing."

Mom's response is muffled by the heavy beat drop on the song playing on my speakers, thank god.

"Why are we still waiting for this? Why am I always the one sneaking around like your mistress? I thought you were in love with me!" Damien wails. Actually full on bleats, the sound of his betrayed misery like some dying animal. Maybe this will be their breaking point. "Divorce isn't going to ruin your political career!"

All right, screw this. I'm not staying in here. I'll head out back to smoke until they've worked out their shit. I know from sickening experience that the bigger their blowouts, the more frenzied their makeup sex is.

No one should have to listen to their mom like that, let alone walk in on it like I did when I first discovered them. It's fucking gross.

I can't wait to save up enough to move out. My trust fund inheritance from granddad won't pay out for a while, but I've got my thumb in a bunch of pies. I won't wait around. I'll do anything I can to get the hell away from my mother's chain leash. The bitcoin investments are growing, and I've been dabbling in learning how to make an app. After I saw Thea's vulnerable security on her computer network, I've been thinking about creating something for desktop and mobile that will protect the same secrets I mine for.

"We're not having this discussion again," Mom snaps as I head downstairs on my way to the back door.

Damien's shouts follow me when I slip out back with a joint, my head pounding. I should leave the back door open so their argument can wake up the whole neighborhood.

Sprawling on a lounge chair, I sigh in relief as I light up, taking a deep drag on the joint. I fold an arm behind my head and play around with making the smoke curl into shapes. As the high sets in, I relax.

I pull my phone out, the joint dangling from my lips as I text Devlin, sending him a GIF of a sad frog in black and white with the lyrics from Simon & Garfunkel's *The Sound of Silence* to convey my despair.

Connor: Darkness is my only friend. [skull emoji]

Devlin doesn't answer, but I'm not surprised. He got Blair Davis to move in with him. I have no idea how he went from

223

dangling dollar bills on fishing wire in front of her at the beginning of school to *living* with her, but that's where they're at. Grumpy bastard is probably balls deep in her, so I tuck my phone away and finish the joint.

My gaze trails to Thea's house and I sit up, surprised to see a light on. I didn't think she'd be up this late.

With a lopsided smile, I stalk across her yard, keeping to the shadows as I creep around. The back door is unlocked when I test it. Sneaking in drives away my melancholy, the mischief putting my mood in high spirits. The smell of warm sugar hits me and I almost groan.

Around the corner, Thea is a delicious mess, covered in flour and dough as she presses a cookie cutter to a slab of cookie dough. Her hair is piled on top of her head in a bun, she has tight spandex shorts on that make her ass look divine, and a loose pink cropped t-shirt. I pause to watch her, my captured sun bathed in moonlight. The light I chased and caught for a few stolen moments.

"Boo," I say, laughing when she jumps with a strangled shriek.

"Connor, what the hell," Thea hisses, flashing a look at the ceiling where her mom probably is. She flutters her messy hands over her shirt, letting out an embarrassed laugh. "You scared the crap out of me."

A deep *boof* sounds and I lift my hands as her rottweiler charges into the room, heading straight for me.

Shit. Maybe sneaking in wasn't my best idea when she's got an attack dog protecting her.

TWENTY-THREE
THEA

My heart is still racing from the jump scare of Connor sneaking into my house in the middle of the night, like some dark prince of depravity.

"Con, wait," I say.

Constantine halts, huffing at Connor.

"Thank you. Bed." The dog lets out a lazy rumble, sniffing Connor's hand as he lowers it to his side, before trotting back to his bed in the corner. "Good boy."

"You mean me, sunshine?" Connor gives me a grin that's all bad boy on his handsome face and traps me against the high counter of the island, arms planted on either side. A thrill shoots through my stomach. He buries his face in my neck, inhaling deeply. "Mm, you smell like fresh baked cookies."

"Well, that's what I'm making. And no, you're not a good boy." I smack his hand as he tries to steal a cookie from the cooling rack. "Those are for the French club."

"But I've got the munchies, and your baking is the best." Pointing to the dog, he wrinkles his brow. "You named your dog after me? Something you want to tell me? Like a crush you've been nursing on your sexy neighbor for years?"

"Wipe that smug look off your face. His name is Constantine, not Connor." I go back to cutting my dough with my set of Paris-themed cookie cutters while Connor goes over to the dog, petting him. When I look back up a few minutes later, he has Constantine on his back, tongue lolling out of his mouth as he gives him a belly rub. "Traitor."

Connor chuckles and returns to my side, sneaking pieces of cookie dough scraps as I get the next batch in the oven.

"What are you doing in here, anyway? It's late."

Connor shrugs. "Saw your light on. Missed my girl."

He shoots me a charming smile, but a tightness lingers around his eyes. I offer him a cookie from the sad pile, and his expression turns more genuine as he takes a bite.

"Oh, god, yes." Connor moans, wrapping me in his arms as he chews. "So good. You should totally make special brownies. We'll get baked and it'll be delicious."

I snort, wriggling out of his arms to get started mixing another batch of dough to pop in the refrigerator before I take out the dough currently chilling.

"What are you doing up so late? You said goodnight two hours ago."

I shrug as I measure out the ingredients into a big mixing bowl. "Couldn't sleep. Baking helps clear my head."

"I know something else that'll help you sleep," Connor

says, planting himself behind me, teasing my arms with tickling touches. He runs his nose up and down the back of my neck, distracting me. His tongue swipes across my skin and he presses his hips against mine so I can feel him, drawing a gasp from me. "Works like a charm."

"I have to finish these."

"Can I help?" Connor picks up the rolling pin, wielding it like a sword instead of a baking tool.

"Here, you can mix this." I set him up with one of the bowls and start another so I can chill more dough at once.

We work in comfortable quiet for a while. Having Connor here is nice, like I'm letting him into my haven, but he's more of a hindrance than actual help. He keeps stealing kisses and eating the dough, and he's much messier than I am. But his muscles come in handy for mixing, since the one thing I don't have is a standing mixer. I'm having a good time with him anyway as we murmur over batches of rolled out dough.

I like this. I like who Connor is here, in the moonlight. He's more real with me alone in the dark, but at school he's still the vicious king of secrets the students and teachers fear. Knowing what I do about his family situation, I think I understand why he's so hell-bent on being the keeper of people's deepest secrets. But I hope he'll drop that wall someday, to share this Connor with the world.

The one who paints Nutella on my cheek so he can hold my face while he licks it off, making my heart flutter with joy.

While we're working, he keeps making vulgar things with the excess dough scraps—boobs, a dick, the poop emoji. He makes me laugh so hard I have to crouch down and muffle my amusement so Mom doesn't hear and come to investigate. Constantine watches our antics from his bed, his deep brown eyes dancing back and forth between us.

As I'm rolling out the next dough, this one a chocolate

shortbread I plan to dip in white chocolate, Connor smacks my ass with flour-covered hands.

"Hey!" Holding my arms up, I twist to find a big flour handprint on my black workout shorts. "I'm so getting you back for that."

"Can't be helped. You've got these hot little booty shorts on."

"You have no self restraint. Just a one-track mind."

With a chuckle, Connor jumps out of reach when I swipe at him with the flour from the bowl by my rolling station. I hunt him around the island and he flashes me a sneaky look as I make my move, trapping me in his arms before I can dump flour down his shirt.

"Got you," he murmurs before kissing me.

I shift around in his arms to kiss him properly, our tongues sliding together. He kisses the curve of my smile, unsuspecting until I smash flour in his hair.

"What the—" Connor's eyes are wide in shock as I choke on my victorious laughter. "Okay, Kennedy. I see how it is."

"Wait—babe, don't!" I retreat before he can retaliate against me with the jar of Nutella, my hands raised in surrender.

He narrows his eyes, but concedes. "Okay, truce. But I get another kiss."

After Connor claims his bounty with another kiss that leaves me breathless, he lets me return to baking.

"You really like this stuff," he says, leaning against the sink as I put another tray of cookies in the oven. "You're good at it, too."

I toss a quick smile over my shoulder, flushed from his praise. "Thanks. I've always loved it. Before I could even reach the counter. When I was little, my grandma used to pull up a chair so I could watch and help while she taught me her recipes." I nod to the notebook I have on the other side of the island. "That one has a lot of her old ones in it. I've tweaked some over the years. I'm always tinkering with them."

His mouth quirks up at the corner as I tell my story. "Is that what you're always carrying around? I swear I see you with a different notebook every day."

"Yeah. I've probably filled hundreds of them by now. Mom used to get so annoyed when we'd be out grocery shopping or whatever and I'd beg for a new notebook I saw." I shake my head. "But I have enough to open my own bakery someday. It's my dream. Feed the world with happiness. And sugar."

"Yeah? That's cool. You'll do amazing at it. Does your grandma approve of your improvements to her recipes?"

A pang pierces my heart. "She did, but she's passed. Right before freshman year."

"Oh. I'm sorry, baby." Connor pops out of his relaxed position and wraps me in a warm hug. "Come here."

"I'm okay. I still miss her, though. We've always shared a love of baking and it just hits me some days that even if I make her signature creamy puff pastry recipe, it still won't be her love going into it, you know?"

He hums and strokes my back in comforting circles.

"What about you?" I tip my head back to meet his gaze. "What do you think you want to do with your life?"

His head cocks to the side. "Something with computers. I like working with them and I'm pretty good. I guess it quiets my head the same way baking does for you."

"Computers?" My nose crinkles with my teasing grin. "You know, I think that qualifies you as a nerd. I seem to remember you calling me that once or twice."

Connor taps my nose. "Takes one to know one."

"Sure," I drawl. "There's no way mister popular soccer captain isn't harboring self-loathing going around calling his sweet neighbor a nerd. Not at all."

"Savage little thing, aren't you?" He nips at my neck in revenge, torturing the sensitive pulse point until I'm putty in his arms.

The timer on my phone goes off and I leave his embrace to take out the final batch of cookies. A tendril of warm pride blossoms in my chest as I survey the room. Every surface in the kitchen is covered in cookies and the traces of our midnight baking. It felt amazing to have him here, even if he snuck in. I can't remember what nasty thought drove me out of bed, my mood soaring high after spending time with my boyfriend doing my favorite thing in the world.

Connor studies me as he leans his hip against the counter. His playful demeanor has shifted to something more serious. "Why don't you ever let anyone see you, Thea?"

The question takes me by surprise and slices into my heart, digging at one of my oldest wounds. *Invisible.* "What do you mean?"

"You're always so quiet, but you have all these opinions about everything." He rubs his jaw and shrugs. "And you've shown me more of yourself, even before you knew it was me."

Heat floods my face. I was so desperate to keep my sputtering flame with Wyatt alive, I really did dive in head first to it when I got a response.

As I'm struggling to respond, Connor adds in a soft voice, "You're brave, so why do you hide it?"

My stomach bottoms out. I take a second to gather my thoughts, wiping my hands clean on a dish towel.

"Well, I'm brave in my own ways. To me, bravery is about showing myself I can do something I'm afraid of. Like standing up for someone when no one else will." My mind flashes to Blair Davis. "It's not about showing off or making myself look good. I don't have to be in front of a crowd to consider myself brave. I don't really care what anyone else thinks, I just answer to myself."

Connor stares at me for a beat, then he huffs out a laugh. "Don't ever let anyone tell you you're not amazing, because you are."

"I don't. I've told you about a hundred times I didn't care what you thought, didn't I?"

My pleased grin stretches when he snorts and mutters to the dog. "You believe this? Boyfriend status and I still get attitude."

Constantine doesn't answer, only continues to snore, deep in sleep after dozing off an hour ago. I bustle around the kitchen, packing the cooled cookies into containers to sort through them for French club. Once I'm done, I gape at the time.

"Wow, it's late. Almost three."

Connor hums, sliding his arms around my waist. "The perfect time for mischief."

"Or sleep." I tip my head back and pucker my lips. He gives me a quick peck, then comes back for more, deepening the kiss. I mumble against his lips, "Need. Sleep."

"Need. You," Connor shoots back, palming my ass. "Come with me. We'll sleep out in the pool house. I don't want to go to bed without you."

It's tempting. I'd love to sleep with his warm arms locked around me and his lips nestled against my skin. Mom would kill me, though. She knocks every morning if I'm not up first, and then she barges in my room anyway.

"I want to, but we can't."

"Come on, baby. I want to fall asleep with you and wake up the same way." He keeps kissing me until I'm dizzy. "Then we'll skip school tomorrow. We'll sleep in, get coffee and donuts, and have an adventure. Run away with me. Sound good?"

I hum, brushing our lips together, entranced by the fantasy of a dreamy date day.

Then the second set of lights flick on and a sharp gasp cuts through my happiness. "What. Is. Going. On. In. Here?"

I fly away from Connor, almost tripping when he's slow to let me go. Mom stands in the arched entrance to the kitchen in a robe, murder in her eyes.

"Do you have any idea what time it is?"

She takes me in and I'm painfully aware of how this looks—making out in the kitchen in the middle of the night, a baking bomb left in our wake, and his flour handprints on my ass. This is my worst nightmare. She's already on my case all the time about what I wear, demanding I dress modestly. Now she discovers me in comfortable but way more revealing clothes than she'd ever approve of me wearing and seconds from climbing my boyfriend like a tree.

Hopefully she can't tell we've had sex, or she'll blow her lid. I've tuned out enough of her lectures about my *sacred gift*—gag. She never listens when I insist virginity is a bullshit social construct designed by the patriarchy.

I have no regrets about sleeping with Connor. None. It was amazing and he treated me like a queen.

"Thea," Mom hisses. I know it's bad when she's so angry she can't even raise her voice. "Get to bed, now. And you." She swings on Connor, pointing at him while she holds her robe closed. "Get out of my house before I call the cops."

"Second time's the charm, right?" Connor gives Mom a cocky smirk.

I stare at him with my eyes wide in terror. *Do you have a death wish?* I ask with my expression. He winks at me. Winks!

Across the room, Mom's nostrils flare. I brace for the incoming rage. Talking back to her never goes well.

"You think I won't? You're trespassing. Get. Out." Mom grabs the landline—the one she refuses to get rid of because 'it works perfectly fine'—brandishing it at Connor. "They should've locked you up before. You're not just a vicious miscreant, you're a troubled boy."

"You flatter me." Connor is still leaning against the counter, not worried that Mom starts dialing. "Tell Chief Landry hi for me. You know, I talked to him earlier? We're good friends now."

A vein in Mom's throat bulges as her throat contracts with her swallow, her face turning a scary shade of red.

"Yeah, yeah." Connor pops off the counter, hands up. "I know you have a real penchant for calling the cops." He lowers his voice to a mutter as he makes a show of gathering his things —things he doesn't have. "Regular ol' Karen you are, Mrs. K."

On his way out the back door, Connor blows me a kiss, sealing my fate as grounded forever.

"I'm sorry," I spit out before Mom can speak. "I won't bring him here again."

I turn to go to bed, but Mom plants herself in front of me. "I told you to stay away from him."

Frustration at being treated like a perpetual child spears through me. Huffing, I square off with Mom.

"You don't get to dictate everything in my life. Connor is my boyfriend." She opens her mouth, but I hold up a finger. "And no, I won't stop seeing him. My life is mine, Mom."

"You stupid girl," she seethes. "Fine. Wait until he breaks you, throws you away. Then you'll see how rotten boys are."

Surprisingly, she doesn't try to ground me.

"Jesus, Mom. Do you even listen to yourself?" Rubbing my forehead, I cast a glance around the kitchen. "I'll clean up tomorrow. I'm going to bed."

Her poisonous gaze tracks me as I leave the kitchen. While climbing the stairs I can hear her fuming to herself.

It makes me sad. I don't remember my childhood being awful, other than her obsession with my body and her little nitpicking comments about my outfit choices, so why is she like this now? She was never overly affectionate with me, but she treated me more human when I was a little girl than she does now.

It seems like she's getting worse and she hates that she can't control me because I no longer cower in fear of whatever she wants to say about my body to keep me in my place.

TWENTY-FOUR
CONNOR

Sticking it to Thea's mom as I strolled out of her house in the middle of the night is one of my top five hashtag swag moments for myself in the last year. I was feeling really damn good about myself, knowing that not only was I pissing her off by my mere presence, but that I also had Thea on my side.

And I know that woman has been fuming about how I'm corrupting her daughter ever since. The next morning she was drinking coffee under their portico, glaring at me as Thea climbed into my ride.

I leaned over and kissed Thea long and hard until she pinched my side. Her mom's face was fucking priceless before I pulled away from the curb.

What can I say? I don't do well with overbearing parents telling me what to do. Celine Kennedy can shove her judgement up her ass alongside the broomstick.

Over the next two weeks, Thea and I spend our time together at night in the pool house as our relationship slowly grows. Her work ethic is bleeding into mine because she won't let me distract her until both of our homework assignments are finished. But once they are? She's all mine.

My friends accept her when we show up to the parking lot in the morning. I miss Devlin being around, but I don't mind that he's been skipping out on us. He's happy and he needs it. I can't fault that. We'll pick up when he comes up for air from his own bubble with Blair Davis.

It feels good to walk into a school I rule with the world's prettiest sunbeam under my arm, talking my ear off about the upcoming dance.

I've already got a plan in the works. She's been putting her all into heading the committee to organize the dance, so I'm going to make sure her night is nothing but magical.

Half-absorbed in my phone as I follow the flow of foot traffic between classes near the end of the day, it takes me a minute to realize the crowd forming ahead is because some drama is going down. The students blocking my way titter meanly at the scene. I don't have time for this.

"What, don't have anything to say? You a mute?"

Some meathead football player pushes someone shorter than him. I can't see clearly through the crowd. A cheerleader I recognize from that boat party before school stands next to him, smirking triumphantly—*Kammy with a K*, my mind supplies.

"Gonna go cry about it?" Kammy teases in a nasty tone. "Should've thought about that before you butted in."

They must be picking on someone. A dealer that shorted them on product, or one of the nerds who make bank selling homework.

I switch directions, planning to take the stairs to the second floor to get to my computer science class, but a familiar voice has me halting in my tracks and flying into protective mode.

"Please leave me alone. I didn't do anything to you."

Thea.

"Move," I demand in a deadly voice.

The underclassman in my way might have shit himself when he saw me towering over him before he scurried out of my path. Others spot me and part, lowering their gazes, too afraid to look a crazed beast in the eyes. By the time I bust through the crowd of onlookers, the football player and Kammy are tugging on Thea's sweater. Fierce rage overtakes me.

Thea stands her ground while they bully her and it eggs them on. They're probably pissed off she's not reacting how they thought. I can see it in their eyes: they want her tears. Her humiliation.

I won't stand for this. No one treats my girl like that.

"The fuck you think you're doing?" I cut in, putting myself between them and Thea. Her hands touch the back of my school blazer. "Messing with my girlfriend?"

"Bishop," the football guy says in confusion. His puny, juiced up brain can't fathom why I'm here. That's what steroids will do. "What's up man?"

"Connor," Thea murmurs behind me. "It's okay."

"No, baby, it's not. I saw what they were doing to you." Swinging back to the other two, I snarl. "Touch her again and I'll destroy your whole life. Then I'll break your arms." Thea tries to sidestep me, but I block her. These two don't even deserve to look at her. My gaze flicks to Kammy. "That goes for both of you."

Kammy and her footballer shuffle back a step at my feral look. I don't have to spell it out for them. Everyone knows when they cross me, whether they realize it or not, I've got dirt that will bury them before their life even gets off the ground.

"All of you, actually." I raise my voice, moving my attention over the crowd watching us raptly. "Thea is off fucking limits. If you mess with my girlfriend, I'm coming for you."

Once I'm satisfied that I've struck enough fear in everyone, I let Thea out from behind me, tucking her under my arm. "Tell me what happened."

She frowns at me. "It's not worth it."

"It is. Tell me."

Her gaze travels over the crowd. She takes my hand and I allow her to lead me away. "Let's just go. The bell's about to ring and we'll all be late."

I toss a glare over my shoulder at Thea's bullies, one that says *I'm watching you*. Kammy's face pales and she yanks on the footballer's arm to get out of there.

Once we're away from the crowd, I dig my feet in.

"What are you—? Hey!" Thea yelps as I tug her into the empty stairwell at the end of the hall. The door clangs shut, enveloping us in its echo that fades into silence.

I cradle her face, examining her.

"I'm fine."

"Tell me what happened."

She huffs. "It's stupid."

"It's not. I'm sorry I wasn't there. I promise I won't let anything like that happen to you again."

Thea lifts her brows. "Yeah? You know, not that long ago that was you, too. It's only been a little over a month since you humiliated me enough to send me running from the cafeteria crying."

Her words stab into my gut in a fatal blow. Fuck, I was such an ass to her. Hanging my head, I give her another piece of myself.

"I'm sorry. I've always been a dick to you because of your mom. I..." Now that I'm saying it out loud, now that I *know* her, it sounds so idiotic. How could I have thought this was okay? With a sigh, I push out the rest of my words. "I thought you were like her. Anytime I noticed you, it was because you were intervening and I took it badly."

Her beautiful features twist in conflict. "What do you mean, because of my mom?"

I rub the back of my head. "About two years ago is when I first discovered my mom and Damien's affair. I walked in on him fucking her in the kitchen."

Her nose wrinkles and she wraps her arms around my waist. "Connor... That must have been awful."

"Yeah, it wasn't peachy." I gather her closer, bolstered by her soothing touch. If she's in my arms, she can't hate me, right? "I lost it. Totally went berserk. I beat the shit out of him while my mom was screaming. It was a whole ass scene."

A sad laugh punches out of her. "What happened next?"

"Well, I was so focused with raging on him that I didn't realize I'd chased him all the way out of the house. I was on my front lawn, punching him until his face was a bruised and bloody mess. Then I guess your mom came out and saw it happening. She called the cops, shrieking like a banshee. You've seen how my mom is with appearances. Not even her own side piece gets in the way of her goal, so you can imagine how she felt that I not only caused this huge scene in front of the neighbors, but that I was pulled off Damien, cuffed, and carted away in the back of a squad car."

It actually feels great to get off my chest. Only my parents, Devlin, and my therapist know the full story. I thought Thea would hate me when I told her the truth about the source of why I bullied her, but it feels right to confess it to her. I'll do whatever I have to in order to make it up to her for being a bastard.

"God," Thea says. "I'm sorry you had to find out like that."

"I'm sorry," I repeat once more. "I took it out on you and that wasn't right."

"I forgive you. We're moving past it now."

A relieved breath hisses out of me as I hug her. After tipping her chin up to kiss her, I feel like I can give her another shard of myself.

"I should've gone to juvie, but my mom bribed Chief Landry and a judge. They made the assault charge disappear, paid a fine for disturbing the peace, and I got slapped with court-mandated anger management."

Thea stretches to brush my hair, trailing her fingers down the side of my face. "I'm glad you didn't have to go away."

The corners of my mouth tip up. There goes my sunshine, lighting up my day with her silver linings and positive outlook.

"Now, are you going to tell me what happened, or do I have to go find out from someone else?"

She snorts, pushing her palm over my face. "No. Don't go bothering anyone, either. It was nothing, I swear. I didn't laugh when he was making fun of an underclassman and told him to stop. He turned on me instead."

I take a step toward the door, intent on hunting down the footballer and putting his head through a locker, but Thea stops me.

"I'd rather kiss you again before I'm late for French class than have you go attack someone to avenge me."

Well, when those are my options, how can I resist giving my girl what she wants?

"Come here then." I herd her against the wall, swallowing her giggle as I seal my mouth over hers.

We're both late to class.

* * *

Later the same week, I'm sneaking around Thea's backyard again.

We started in the pool house, but when she said she had to leave, I wouldn't let her go. So I'm following her, staying low in case her mom is around.

"This is such a bad idea," Thea murmurs for the third time since we slipped out of our haven in the pool house. "I swear, Connor, if you get caught, you're on your own."

"Ouch, baby," I whisper back. "You know what I say about bad ideas."

"Yeah, yeah. Your favorite kind. I know." She peeks around inside the dark house before carefully opening the door. "Just—don't make a sound until we get to my room, or she'll suspect something."

I smother a devious laugh and follow her lead.

Once we sneak upstairs and make it to her room, Thea collapses against the door with a strained sigh.

"Oh my god. I can't believe we pulled that off. She's usually all over me when I come in late."

I plant my hands on either side of her and lean in for a kiss. She goes pliant, releasing a tiny moan. Leaving her against the door, I slowly draw away, smirking at the blissed out look on her face.

"So this is your bedroom. Looks different when I can see

the entire thing, not just your flower chair or your girly bedspread," I tease, taking it all in.

It's the first time I've seen it in person rather than through a phone or computer screen. The room is full of feminine touches, from her positive food pun themed posters to her little rainbow clock on her nightstand. It's got this soft, warm vibe to it that feels like Thea. Bright and welcoming.

"It's not girly." Thea swats at me as she passes by on the way to the closet. She rummages for a moment, then pulls out a hoodie she stole from me last week, holding it to her nose as she sniffs it. "It's just a bed."

I pluck the hoodie from her and she pushes out her plump bottom lip. Goddamn, she's so cute.

"I was looking for this." It's from a concert I went to with Devlin and his cousin Lucas over the summer. I shoot her a sly look. "If I remember right, I sent you home from the pool house wearing this the other night."

"You did." She tilts her head all coy. "I've been wearing it to sleep in. It smells like you."

"Yeah?" I hand it back, eager to see her wearing my clothes. "Make you feel like you're in my arms?"

She nods as she peels out of her outfit to change. I rake my teeth over my lip, dropping on her bed to watch.

As she lifts her hair out of the neck, she catches my eye and squints at me. "No. Don't even think about it. We can't have sex in here."

"Not even a little?" I spread my legs and adjust my dick. She's so hot, wearing only my hoodie and panties. It's big on her, almost hitting her knees. "Leave the hoodie on while I eat your pussy."

She turns red and I chuckle, grabbing the hem to tug her closer.

"You're so vulgar," she says, exasperated. Her hands rest on my shoulders as I tease my fingers beneath the hoodie. "We have to go to bed."

"Baby, that's what I'm angling for." I cup her ass and tug so she lands on my lap, straddling me. "You're so irresistible. I'll never have enough of you, even if I fuck you five times a day."

"We had sex twice in the pool house today." The end of her sentence dips into a moan as I massage her ass and lick the shell of her ear. "Seriously, we can't. She'll hear. There's no way I can be quiet."

I love that I drive her so wild she can't control herself. We fucked in the pool house shower earlier so she could moan as loud as she wanted while I drove my cock into her.

With one last graze of my teeth over her throat, I let her escape across the bed. She takes a minute to compose herself while I kick off my shoes, then shuck my jeans and t-shirt so I'm only in briefs. As I lay back against the pillows, her stuffed sea lion captures my attention.

"Who's this little guy?" I pick it up. It's softer than I expected and I hum, dragging it over her bare leg. "Why a sea lion? I pictured a girl like you would have something magical, like a unicorn or something cute to go with the rest of your bedroom decor."

It's a question I've wanted to ask since I saw it on her webcam, but couldn't without raising suspicion about why I knew she had it.

"It is cute! Give me that." Thea snatches the stuffed toy, her smile fond as she smooshes its lumpy body. "I don't know. I was like, seven, when I got him on a trip to the aquarium. I liked how funny their bodies were. He was round and I liked it."

My gaze goes soft as my heart swells. I might be new at rela-tionships because I wasn't interested in chicks after my family's money or the status of dating me, but she isn't like that at all. She's just herself, this incredible light.

Thea is the only girl I've never hated the idea of letting in, sharing my life with, *keeping*. When I think about the future now, it's one that includes her.

"Ready to fight me for the covers?"

Her question draws me out of my dazed thoughts. She has her fists up in a mock boxing stance. I cover her hands with mine, correcting her so she won't end up with broken thumbs if she ever throws a punch.

"Like this. Remind me to teach you to fight."

"What if I don't want to fight? Make cake, not war."

Thea nods sagely, crawling into my open arms as we settle into a comfortable position. I spoon against her back, nuzzling into her neck.

"For self defense, then." My voice turns drowsy and I stifle a yawn. "Important stuff, baby. Everyone needs to know how to protect themselves."

"Okay," she murmurs, reaching over to turn out the light.

As the room plunges in darkness, I roll my hips against hers, enjoying the feel of her ass tucked against my dick. "Mm, goodnight sunshine."

"Night." She finds one of my hands and tangles our fingers together, holding our joined hands over her heart.

It's the most comfortable I've felt in a long time.

* * *

At dawn, I wake up before Thea, spending a minute enjoying watching her in the pale morning light. Her face is smashed against my chest, and she wasn't kidding about the fight for the covers—she has all of them cocooned around her while I'm left with a measly corner.

I carefully brush her hair back and kiss her forehead before climbing out of bed. Rustling through my pockets of my pants, I take out the small, polished moonstone I've been carrying around, intending to give it to her. I got it when I was a kid, when Dad took me to a nature museum. It was one of our last outings before he began to drift.

The shimmering light blue stone reminds me of Thea. She's my sunbeam, but I love the way she shines at night, like this stone.

After tugging on my jeans, I flip open one of her recipe notebooks on the desk and take a fresh page. I borrow one of Thea's pens to draw a heart on the page, put it on her night-stand, and place the moonstone in the middle.

Resisting the temptation to crawl back into bed and wake her up with my tongue, I slip out of the room and manage to sneak out unnoticed. Once I make it out, I send her a good morning text.

TWENTY-FIVE
CONNOR

After soccer practice finishes, I shower as fast as I can to pick Thea up from the dance planning committee. It's one of the last practices we'll have this season before the playoffs start now that it's November.

"Is your ass on fire?" Devlin jokes as I fly through the locker room.

"Shove it, I'm late to see my girl!" I toss my stuff in my duffel bag as I drag on a clean Silver Lake High Coyotes t-shirt.

"You saw her an hour and a half ago," Devlin points out as he sprawls across the opposite bench. "Made out with her until we had to drag you off her so she could go."

I level him with a flat look. "And where was Blair while this was going down?"

Devlin drops his gaze, grinning stupidly. Yeah, I've got him. I saw the way he was all wrapped up in her in the parking lot when he went to get his gear.

"Aight, I'm out," I call to the other guys in the locker room. "Let's keep it tight and finish the season strong."

A few whoops and hollers follow me as I duck out of the room and head for the one the dance committee is using for prep duties. I can't wipe the dopey grin off my face as I yank the door open, planning to sweep Thea off her feet and kiss her.

I freeze in the doorway, jealousy rocketing through me fast enough to make me sick to my stomach.

Coleman stands too close to Thea, leaning into her space as he points out whatever is on the papers she's presenting to him. Creep.

Dealing with this was hell when we were faking, but now that she's my girlfriend? I'm even more possessive of her. He gives me a bad vibe and I don't want him near her.

Stalking into the room, I make sure I'm as loud as possible, dumping my athletic duffel on the floor. The other students on the committee throw me dirty looks. One of them is Maisy Landry, squinting at me over the clipboard she's marking.

"Hey, babe. Practice finished early. Perks of being captain." I slide in, draping an arm over her shoulder, subtly pulling her away from our teacher. "Ready to go?"

"Hi. In a minute, we're just figuring out the logistics of the refreshment tables and the DJ." She flips through her papers, mumbling to herself.

I touch her hair, pulling it out of her face while she's working. I know I'm being territorial, but I can't help it when it comes to her. Coleman's hand twitches every time I touch her.

"Mr. Bishop, this meeting is for planning committee members and faculty advisors only, I'm afraid," Coleman says in mock-sympathy. Yeah fucking right. He's trying to kick me out so he can perv on my girlfriend. "If you'd like to wait outside for—"

"Actually, come here," Thea says, tugging on my shirt. "I need your help and everyone else is busy with their own tasks."

I smirk at Coleman as she leads me across the room. His lip curls and he looks like he wants to strangle me. Not very becoming for an educator.

"Hold this up for me? Yeah, like that," Thea directs, stepping back and pinching her chin as she studies the balloon archway decoration I'm holding up. "Okay, good. We'll weave the clear ones through to spell out SLHS and fill those with silver glitter. It'll be perfect for the photo op as people arrive."

I peer overhead. "You did all this?"

Thea nods.

"It's awesome."

"Thanks. This is just the test version, but I saw a really cool photo online."

"People are gonna love it. Look, come here." I motion her over with my head as I hold up the archway. "Take a selfie so you can see."

As she holds up her phone, I kiss her cheek. She's grinning in the photo, her face scrunched adorably from my attack kiss.

"There. See?"

"Yeah." Her voice is warm as she studies the photo. "It looks so good. Okay, perfect."

"Send me that one. I'm totally posting it."

Thea shoots me a beaming smile as she shuffles her papers. I set the decoration down and lean over her shoulder to see the logistics.

"Put the tables with food over here and the DJ here," I say, pointing out spots on the page. "Mom made me go to this rally once and that's how they did it. Something about the natural flow."

"Oh! That's perfect." Thea makes a mark on the page, drawing little symbols of her own making. "Awesome, now we can go."

Coleman has been watching us the entire time. While his attention is on us, I take her face and tip it up for a kiss, sliding my gaze to him. A muscle in his jaw jumps.

I wind my fingers with hers. "So are we good to go?"

"Yes." She pulls away to cross the room.

I shoulder my bag and take Thea's as she talks to Maisy. They both come over. Her friend sizes me up.

"Maisy is coming over so we can go shopping."

"Cool." I hold a fist out for her to bump.

She holds out, then taps her fist against mine.

Coleman hovers while Thea delegates last minute questions from the other planning committee members. As she returns to my side, he stands in our path.

"Is there anything else we can knock out today?"

"No, but I'll call the DJ to confirm tonight." Thea doesn't pick up on his intensity. She's too kind to suspect anything is wrong. "We'll move onto the other tasks at the meeting next week."

"Well. I have to say, Thea, I knew you were the right choice for this. You're perfect." His gaze is unwavering as he stares her down, like he's waiting for her recognition. "I have to commend you for a job well done so far."

I exchange a look with Maisy. She's put off by Coleman, too, so I know I'm not imagining this weird feeling.

"Thank you," Thea says.

"I just know that because of your hard work, you'll always have all the world has to offer you," Coleman says in this haunting voice that makes every hair on my body stand on end. "You won't have to wait for it anymore."

What the fuck?

An uncomfortable sense of déjà vu washes over me. I recognize those words. They were one of the creepy stalker comments on Thea's blog.

I'm taking a step before I know it, edging between them to protect Thea. Coleman can't quite smother the frustrated sound that catches in his throat.

"Come on, or we'll totally miss all of our shopping time," Maisy says, hooking her arm with Thea's and ushering her ahead.

I cut a glance to the side, making sure Thea is leaving.

"What? No we won't," she says. "Relax, the dresses aren't going anywhere."

"Let's just get out of here." Maisy twists around. "Boyfriend? Your chauffeur service is required. My brother already left."

I hang back for another beat, meeting Coleman's gaze with a challenge. He seems to snap out of the psycho trance he was in a second ago talking to Thea and sneers at me.

"Get out of here before I give you detention, Mr. Bishop."

I give him an arrogant snort. "For what? Standing?"

Without waiting for his answer, I head out. The slithering feeling knotting my stomach doesn't leave as I catch up with the girls.

"So that was weird, right?" Maisy asks once we reach the parking lot.

"Hmm?" Thea takes her bag from my shoulder, rummaging for her phone. "What was weird?"

Maisy's gaze darts to me and we both look at Thea.

"Do you have conversations like that with any of your other teachers?" Maisy questions. "Seriously, I think what he said to you was over the line."

"I guess not. Mr. Coleman's really cool though," Thea says. "I've always felt like I can talk to him."

"That guy?" I shake my head.

"Thank you!" Maisy looks at me in a new light, no longer judging me for being her friend's boyfriend she doesn't know.

"He's my favorite teacher," Thea says firmly.

"I'm questioning your taste."

Thea pokes my arm. "My taste includes you, too."

"Smile and eyes," Maisy cuts in, studying me. "Twelve out of ten, but butt? Eh, six out of ten."

"What's wrong with my ass? Have you ever seen a soccer player's ass up close, little Landry?"

"Absolutely nothing wrong back here," Thea assures me, biting her lip around a smile and tucking her hand in the back pocket of my jeans, boldly giving my ass a squeeze.

I give her a smile, but it doesn't reach my eyes. I can't shake the dark web of thoughts clinging to me.

We climb into my Lexus GX and I waste no time pulling out of the lot. As soon as I drop them off, I'm setting out on the hunt to dig up the comment triggering my memory to check it against Coleman's words.

* * *

Hiding my suspicion from Thea and Maisy on the ride home was hard. I didn't want Thea to think I was in a bad mood, but I was itching to get on my computer and dig through her blog. A sick feeling has lodged in my gut and I have to double check if I'm right.

My knee bounces as I wake my system from sleep mode, and my fingers pound the keys harder than necessary as I type in my login.

I go straight for her blog, Coleman's words playing in my head like the eerie tune of a rundown carousel ride.

The same thing repeats in the comments.

Henry_Your_GoodKnight: *Your intelligent eyes say it all, love. You're longing for the world to show you all it has to offer.*

Henry_Your_GoodKnight: *Do you trust me, princess? Your knight waits for you. My precious doll. Say you'll take my hand and I'll show you all the world has to offer.*

Henry_Your_GoodKnight: *Missing these intelligent eyes and talking to you. Where have you gone, love? Do you miss me, too? I dream of finding you, coming to steal you away for the whirlwind romance the world has to offer you. It's me, I'm your world. If I held out my hand, would you take it? The thought consumes me.*

The timestamps are recent. My overprotectiveness for Thea goes into overdrive, but I have to know what I'm dealing with first.

Gritting my teeth, I take the IP address and trace it. The search runs for a second, bouncing around before telling me it routes to the Ukraine. That isn't right. I know it.

There's no way in hell Coleman says the same exact thing to Thea that this Henry Knight guy says all over her blog.

"Fucker," I grit out. "Know how to mask yourself with a VPN, huh? I'll find you."

I switch to searching for Coleman instead. One way or another I'll tie him to the Henry Knight username and gather everything I need to prove to Thea she needs to stay away from him. Basic search engines only turn up his LinkedIn and results that don't match him. I slam my fist on the desk, frustrated beyond measure.

How can he have wiped himself from the web? It's damn near impossible these days to fly so under the radar. Leaning forward with a deep inhale, I pull up the Ridgeview School District database and use Dad's password to login to the admin network. Coleman's employee file has to have something. I click through only to find his previous employment history won't open.

Closed records.

"That's not shady at all," I mutter, trying to find a work-around to access it.

All I get is his ID photo and his start date. The name on his file makes me suck in a breath. *Shit.*

H. K. Coleman.

"Too close to be a coincidence. What does H stand for?"

The deeper I search, the more roadblocks I come up against. My hair must be standing on end from practically ripping it out of my head because I'm not getting anywhere.

It's like Coleman showed up without any trace of where the hell he came from. I've never been able to find anything useful on him. No one is that much of a ghost.

When I'm about to give up, a search result on my third try with new keywords catches my eye. Next to the link is a thumbnail of Coleman smiling with a group of students. *Mostly girls,* I note with clenched teeth.

The link says North East Regional Award for Excellence. Beneath that, the description goes on to preview the article.

Local students from Thorne Point Junior Academy commended for their fundraiser work, along with their advisor, Harold K. Coleman.

An icy sensation drags down my back like vicious nails. Harold. If my name was Harold, I'd go by Henry, too. I swear to god, if Coleman's middle name is Knight...

My violent thoughts race too fast to sort out. I click on the link while my heart thuds.

An auto-download triggers.

"Shit!" I fumble with the keyboard and mouse, but I'm too slow to stop it. Within seconds, the file downloads and runs an install package. "Mother fuck—no!"

Goddamn it, I'm better than this. I know not to click on unfamiliar links or download fishy files, no matter how funny an angry desktop goose sounds. Learned that the hard way thanks to a trending TikTok video. Wasn't worth it, twelve out of ten wouldn't recommend.

Whoever this is, they're good. They confused a major search engine to show their download within the results, luring anyone looking hard to find Coleman once they put together enough of the puzzle. That is top level shit. I have no idea how they pulled it off.

An 8-bit crow animation flies across my screen, the little black bird mocking me. The screen goes dark and flashes with a skull. Once the crow lands on top of the skull, the whole monitor display glitches into pixelated distortion before returning to normal.

I'm looking around for the crow, ready to drag its ass to the trash can icon, when a chat window pops up. There's no way anyone should have access to my system. Whatever was in that download package, it infiltrated my firewalls.

Dolos: Looking for info on Harold Coleman?

I hesitate to answer, rubbing my jaw. This whole thing feels hinky.

Dolos: Time's ticking. Answer now.

When I don't respond, they message again.

Dolos: Connor Alexander Bishop. Ridgeview, Colorado. Senior at Silver Lake High School. Varsity soccer captain. Son of city council chairwoman Vivian Bishop. Active social media presence. Girlfriend, Thea Kennedy. Oh, she lives next door. Cute. Should we keep going?

"Jesus." I push back from the desk and scrub my face.

Within seconds they were able to doxx me and get a whole picture of my life. Not just mine. Thea's, through her connection to me. This is a professional who knows what they're doing.

If they're on my system, they could get into my blackmail files or find the backdoor to Thea. Not happening. I drag myself back and release a ragged breath.

Connor: Enough, I get it. I'm here. Nice work on the search result embedding. You got me.
Dolos: Glad you're paying attention.
Connor: You have details on Coleman?
Dolos: We do.
Connor: And??? Give it to me. I need it.
Dolos: That's not how this works. First you need to do us a favor. If you're successful, we'll give you everything you're searching for.
Connor: And if I refuse?

They can give it to me now or not at all. I don't have time to play games. I'll get it on my own.

Dolos: You can try. You'll never find what you're looking for. Coleman has friends in high places with deep pockets that helped him disappear the last time we had him pinned down. We're the only ones with the info. It's no longer public record.

Sighing, I pinch the bridge of my nose.

Connor: Who are you?
Dolos: Unimportant right now. Are you ready to make a deal?
Connor: Yes. Whatever gets me dirt on Coleman.
Dolos: Your task is retrieval. Locate Coleman's house, get it back with proof, then we'll be ready to do business.

An image attachment comes through the chat. It's a necklace. A heart locket with the initials CT engraved on the front. After seeing those comments and the way Coleman's creep factor turned up to eleven today, the sight of the locket makes an uneasiness settle in my gut.

Who the hell are these guys and how are they connected to Coleman?

Connor: Get the necklace and you'll give me what I need?
Dolos: That's the deal. Take too long and it expires.
Connor: Wait! I'll need time. Coleman is evasive and good at covering his tracks.
Dolos: Fine. By the new year, or we'll have to introduce ourselves to that pretty redhead.

I stand so fast to slam the desk, the whole thing almost overturns. A growl tears from me as I grab for the monitor to stabilize it. The desk left a dent in the wall. I type with all the force of the anger coursing through me.

Connor: Touch her and I'll kill you.
Dolos: Better get to work then.

My screen goes black and non-responsive. When I do a hard reset to reboot the computer, the chat window is gone.

"Damn it!" My throat burns as I drag in air, breathing hard to regulate the fury.

Once I have myself under control, I collapse on the bed. The first thing I do is run a search for *Dolos*. My snort jerks my head when the results populate. It turns out Dolos is from greek mythology, a god of cunning trickery and deception. Fitting.

"Edgelords," I mutter.

Next I text Devlin. I'm going to need help to pull this off. I doubt I can get Chief Landry to convince a judge to issue a warrant for Coleman with circumstantial evidence, even if I emptied my investment accounts for the bribe.

Connor: Feel up for some recon?

Devlin: Playing Batman again?

Connor: This is bigger than that. I'll explain. I'm on my way over.

Devlin: Can you give me like an hour?

Connor: This is serious, man! You can get your dick sucked later.

Devlin: My parents just left town again sometime today, dude. You're killing me [skull emoji]

Connor: You can last a few more hours. Bring her with us if you want, Blair might have more insight into what I need to plan.

Devlin: Which is?

Connor: Surveillance. Probably some B&E.

Devlin: [smirking devil emoji] That does sound like something she'll know about.

Some of the tightness loosens in my chest. I knew my best friend would have my back. Grabbing my keys and wallet, I head out the door. On my way, I text Thea to check in on her.

Connor: How's shopping? Find the one?

Thea: Pretty sure I can't show you the dress before the big day.

I snort, leaning against the driver's side of my car.

Connor: Babe, that's a wedding dress. You angling for wifey status?

Thea: [flustered emoji] Stop teasing me!

My heart does a little flip. She always gets me smiling.

Connor: Have fun. I'm going to hang with Devlin. Call you later?

Thea: Ok [heart emoji]

Climbing into the car, I pull out and head for Devlin's place to figure out a plan.

TWENTY-SIX
THEA

The last month has been such a whirlwind. Before I know it, it's the week of the dance. Between my planning committee duties, studying, baking about a million pies for the Thanksgiving dinner at the local shelter, and trying to have a life, time has slipped by me.

Everything is in chaos at school with the semester ending, midterms looming next week, and the excitement for the winter formal at the end of the week to give the students a break before our winter vacation.

Connor and I have barely had time to sneak away to our secret haven in the pool house over the last few weeks. He was wrapped up in his own thing with the end of the soccer season, and being there for Devlin when his relationship with Blair ended abruptly after Thanksgiving.

They're back together now, or at least that's the impression I got when I walked in on them making out in the English classroom before anyone else arrived. Those two burn hot and fast, like exploding stars. I quickly stammered an apology, but I'd already seen Devlin's hand fisted in Blair's hair, holding her head back, and the huge hickey on her neck. They didn't even stop, just gave me matching smirks as I backed out of the room and bumped right into Connor's chest.

The gymnasium is in a state of havoc as the committee members direct our helpers with the decorations. Connor promised he'd bring the soccer team to lend a hand, and I'm waiting on them to drape the silver and white fabric Maisy and I picked out to transform the room into a winter wonderland.

We're both working on lifting a table onto the stage for the DJ, but we're struggling with just the two of us.

"It's too heavy," I say.

"Oh!" Maisy pops up from her squat and heads for the door. "Hang on, I see my brother in the hall. Holden!"

Maisy's brother stops and leans against the doorframe. Behind him, Fox Wilder looms like a deadly shadow, scowling at Maisy.

"'Sup?" Holden asks.

Maisy tugs on his arm, a force of nature of her own making when she wants something. "Come here a sec. We're trying to lift this, but it's too heavy. I need to borrow your football muscles." She peers over Holden's shoulder and latches on to Fox's wrist. "You too, Fox."

She wrangles both of them, but Fox doesn't seem happy about it. His sharp, eerie gaze tracks her as she leads them over.

"How long is this going to take?" Holden asks, dragging his feet. "I'm hungry. We were going to get food."

"Just a minute. You're wasting your own time by complaining about it."

Holden groans, dropping his head back. "You're such a pain in the ass."

"Deal with it, my god." Maisy flips her hair over her shoulder and sticks her tongue out at her brother. "Two minutes, or I'll tell Mom where you've been going on weekends."

"Fine," Holden grumbles.

"Okay, help us get this over there," she directs, kneeling to grab the end she tried to lift with just the two of us.

I get into position as Holden comes to help me support my side. Fox doesn't move. Maisy looks up over her shoulder. Her brows hike up. He towers over her, intimidating as hell with that cold expression, his dead eyes shooting daggers at my sweet best friend.

Maisy is the kind of girl everyone likes, so how can he look at her with so much hatred?

Fox is scary. Bad boy is written all over him, from the motorcycle he rides around town on to his complete disregard for any rules. He looks dangerous in his leather jacket and messy dark brown hair. It's hard to believe this guy is someone Maisy could've been friends with; he's her total opposite.

"Aren't you going to help us?" Maisy sighs. "It won't take long. Then you can go back to pretending I don't exist."

"Maybe we can get it with the three of us," I say, trying to break up the suffocating tension between them. "Right, Holden?"

He grunts, gaze flicking between his surly friend and his sister.

"Fox, come on. Please?" Maisy won't give in, frowning at him when he narrows his eyes. She lowers her voice. "You always used to—"

His furious growl cuts her off. "No."

My heart leaps into my throat. I shift to jump to my feet, but Holden puts his hand on my arm to keep me in place, watching the exchange between Fox and Maisy.

"No?" Maisy sighs, never one to get angry or spiteful. "Okay, it's just...if you helped, we'd get it done faster. Then I'll leave you alone."

Fox moves at last, getting in her face. "Always such a goody-goody."

Maisy's shoulders tense and she hugs herself, glancing away. Fox laughs, the sound an awful, cutting bark.

"Yeah. That's what I thought." He takes a lock of her hair, letting it slide through his fingers. "Didn't your daddy teach you to run from monsters? Get it through your fucking head."

Turning away, he kicks over a bucket of metallic silver paint we need to make the signs. It skims across the gym floor, creeping close to Maisy's flats. Meeting her gaze, he smirks cruelly at the look on her face.

"What are you going to do about it? Cry?" Fox speaks in a deep, biting voice as he mocks her. "That's all you are. All you'll ever be. Maisy Daisy the Crybaby."

Maisy stands her ground, even though I can tell she's upset. She lifts her head.

"What happened to you?" Her whisper is watery. "You were my friend, too."

"Playtime is over," Fox growls. "Fuck off, daisy. Stay out of my way."

He storms off, tearing down a mylar fringe curtain Maisy hung.

"Are you fine being friends with that jerk when he treats your sister that way?" I ask Holden.

"I don't control him. Couldn't if I tried. He's not even my

friend, he just showed up again and started hanging around me."

I shake Holden's hand off my arm and go to her side.

"Holden, get the paint," I say while I wrap Maisy in a tight hug. "Are you okay?"

"Yeah," Maisy says softly, tucking her face in my shoulder. "I don't understand why he hates me so much now."

"Maybe it's best if you stay away from him. He seems..."

"I know." Maisy groans. "I'll go pick up another can of paint."

"Are you sure?"

"Yeah. Holden? Give me a ride to the hardware store."

Holden stops mopping up the silver paint. On their way out, he puts his hand on Maisy's head and ruffles her hair, leaning close to murmur to her. She nods as they pass through the door.

With a sigh, I motion over two students from the planning committee. "Can you two work on this? We'll get more paint for the signs. I'm going to find someone to help lift this."

As I'm pulled in different directions, Connor appears in the double doorway with Devlin and the rest of the soccer team at his back, all dressed down in their SLHS athletic gear. I push out a relieved breath and wave him over.

"Your very hot labor team has arrived," Connor drawls. He captures me in his arms and drops a quick peck on my lips. "Give us your orders."

Smiling softly, I dip my fingers beneath his t-shirt, smoothing them over his skin. "Thanks for helping."

"Of course, sunshine." Connor winks. "What my girl needs, she gets. Ain't that right, Dev?"

Devlin huffs out a laugh, shaking his head. "Yeah. Real attentive lover type, you are."

Connor clicks his tongue and shoots me a finger gun.

"Okay, if a few of you could head to that corner to set up the photo booth station," I say, addressing the soccer team. "We need help to hang the decorations from the rafters, so speak to the custodial staff. Then the rest of you will help with the draping."

"You heard her, guys. Chop, chop," Connor says.

He doesn't move right away, keeping me in his embrace. His gaze darts around, sweeping the room like he's looking for a threat.

"Has Coleman been around?"

"He went to pick up the lighting rental. Why?"

"Just checking." He's being evasive and keeps looking around, as if he expects something to take him by surprise.

Connor is odd like that for the rest of the afternoon, on edge and wary of everything. He barely leaves my side, hovering over me as soon as he finishes the tasks I give him. Despite my shadow, we're able to get most of the decorating done, and I walk out of the gymnasium at the end of the night feeling a sense of accomplishment.

With the logistics taken care of, I can finally allow the excitement for the big dance to creep in.

TWENTY-SEVEN
THEA

Seeing the room all set up and walking in the night of the dance are two different things. It steals my breath as Connor and I pass through the shimmering curtains draped in the entrance.

For once, I feel completely confident. Like the goddess I'm always telling myself to be, dressed in a flowing pink dress that makes me feel amazing, my hair down in soft curls, and my handsome boyfriend escorting me. The flower crown he presented me with when he picked me up helps with the goddess vibes, a beautiful mix of yellow anemones and pink roses sitting on my head. He'd said he wanted to give me the sun, but this was the closest he could get to suit a queen. My heart hasn't stopped glowing with warmth since.

Connor's hair is combed and styled the same as it was the night of the benefit for the children's hospital, and he looks so good in a gray suit that complements his eyes.

"Wow, it really came out nice," I murmur in awe.

"Of course it did. You were the brains behind it all." Connor kisses my cheek. "Nerds, right? The best."

"Oh, now they're the best?" I tease. "Your tune's changed since I found out about you being a computer nerd."

"Like I said. The best."

He chuckles, drawing me toward the balloon installation—a pearlescent white and silver arched confection—to set us up for a selfie. He wraps me in his arms from behind, playing with the material of my dress, and I lift my hand to touch his face as he leans over my shoulder.

Once he takes a couple of us smiling, I turn his face to mine for a kiss. We take a few more photos, then dive into the fray of the dance. It's perfect and amazing.

"Thea! Oh my god, you look so pretty!" Nina, one of Connor's friends from the popular crowd, gives me a big hug. Her friend Bailey holds up her phone and takes a photo of the two of us. "Bishop, take one of the three of us."

These girls were never outright mean to me, but they never made an effort before I began dating Connor, either. I was invisible to them. We've reached a point where we briefly talk in the mornings when we all pull into the student lot.

Bailey hands off her phone and comes to pose on my other side.

"You both look amazing, too," I say.

"Thanks," Bailey says as she squeezes me between her and Nina.

They work it for the camera as Connor obediently captures us. I hesitate for a second, then laugh as we get into it.

"Just what the world likes, hot chicks rubbing up on each other," Connor says.

"Connor!" My cheeks heat.

He laughs under his breath, handing the phone back to Bailey. "Just calling it like I see it."

The girls giggle and go through the pictures he took. More of his friends join us.

When I see some of mine, I peel away from his side to talk to them. I'm in the middle of talking to a girl from my culinary class when Connor materializes next to me, looking annoyed.

"What's wrong?" I follow his gaze to Mr. Coleman, deep in conversation with a girl from our class.

Connor's hand fits to my waist, guiding me further away. "Let's go grab a table over here."

His friends join us. For a while we watch the photo booth nearby, laughing at the funny ideas people come up with.

I'm having a great time, but Connor's good mood chips away as the night goes on.

Not long after, all of his friends have left us alone at the table while they spread out, grabbing refreshments and dancing.

I hold Connor's hand and play with his fingers while he zones out. "Want to make plans for winter break? We haven't had all that much time together lately."

It takes him a minute to register my question. He's distracted, glaring across the room at Mr. Coleman while he hovers at the edge of the dance floor, smiling at the students having a good time.

"What?"

"I was just saying, maybe we could go to one of the holiday markets or something? Like a mini date adventure."

"Uh, yeah. We'll figure something out." He gives me a smile

that doesn't reach his eyes before he settles back in his chair, watching Mr. Coleman while he chaperones.

I drop his hand and rise from my seat to get a drink.

"Where are you going?" Connor's voice stops me before I make it two steps.

"The refreshments table. Do you want anything?"

He gets up and hovers at my back, more like a bodyguard than my date. "I'll go with you."

Getting tired of this putting a damper on our night, I spin to face him, tilting my head. He looks fine, but something is bothering him.

"Are you okay? Things started out great, but you've been weird since we got here."

Connor blinks. He cups my face, his brows pinched. "I'm sorry, baby. I'm fine."

"Are you sure? You can tell me if you're not having a good time. I don't want you to suffer for my sake."

"Yeah, of course. I'm here with you, aren't I?" He bends his head down, kissing me tenderly. "I'm sorry. Let's go dance."

Connor laces his fingers with mine and draws me onto the dance floor as a slow song starts up. The worry plaguing me eases when he smiles at me, a real one this time. Nearby, Blair and Devlin dance together. She looks amazing tonight in her sleek dark gray dress that sparkles when the light hits it, and Devlin looks very dapper beside her in his suit. The two of them are absorbed in each other with twin smiles full of fondness.

"You look beautiful tonight," Connor murmurs, pulling my attention back to him. "Have I told you that yet?"

A slow smile pulls at my mouth. He slides his arms around my waist and rests his forehead against mine. We stay like that through two slow songs, swaying in a tight circle, floating in our own world.

"I'm happy," I whisper, placing my cheek on his chest.

"Yeah? Me too, baby." Connor kisses the top of my head and squeezes me in a tight hug. "All I want to do is make you happy."

"I'm glad Wyatt gave me the wrong number. You're who I'm supposed to be with."

Connor gives me an intent look that pierces through me. The room goes still and my heartbeat speeds up at the way he stares at me.

"Thea, I—" He stops, then takes a breath. "Sunshine, you're my world. I lo—"

Someone bumps into us as the music changes into a faster song, knocking my balance off kilter. Connor catches me.

"Hey! Watch it!" He turns to me. "You okay?"

"Yeah."

The moment we were having is broken. Whatever he was about to say, he lets it go.

Smirking, he says. "You ready?"

"For what?"

"This."

He gets me breathless and laughing as he twirls me around. After a few songs, we're gasping, leaning on each other as we grin bright enough to light the entire room.

"Thirsty?" Connor asks. When I nod, he says, "Be right back."

While he's getting us drinks, I spot Mr. Coleman nearby and head for him.

"Thea. You look lovely tonight." Mr. Coleman's hand lifts for a second, then drops. He curls his fingers into his palm. "Very beautiful."

Blushing, I laugh off his compliment. "I just came over to thank you for pushing me to do the planning committee for the dance. It was fun to work on." I gesture around at all the committee accomplished. "I think the dance turned out really nice."

Mr. Coleman gives me a warm smile. "You're perfect." Clearing his throat, he nods to the dance floor. "Really, I'm so impressed. I knew you'd be perf—"

"Here's your drink, babe." Connor interrupts Mr. Coleman's praise, inserting himself between us and giving Mr. Coleman his back. His face is twisted with tension. "Let's go over there."

Mr. Coleman's expression hardens. Connor ushers me away with a hand at my back, pushing a little harder when I don't move fast enough for him.

"Connor, it's rude to interrupt. And stop pushing me." I step out of reach. "I was having a conversation and you just—"

"Thea, listen," he snaps, then closes his eyes, smothering a frustrated sound. "Sorry. Listen, he's bad news. You have to stay away from him. I turn my back on you for two seconds and you walk right into danger."

"Danger?" I scoff, growing annoyed with his feud with our teacher. "Are you serious? Is this you being jealous again?"

"Don't fight me on this." Connor backs me against the wall, on the outskirts of the dance. His jaw is set in determination. His tone brooks no argument as he lays out his demands. "Stay the fuck away from him."

"How do you expect me to stay away from a teacher I have to see every day for class?" I fold my arms. "He's my favorite teacher. I'm sorry if you feel threatened by that, but I was only—"

"Threatened." The sound that drops from Connor's lips is caustic, far from amusement. "I'm not worried about you crushing on him. I'm worried about what that sick fuck could do to you. It's him I don't trust, not you. I'm trying to *protect* you." He holds my shoulders in a tight grip, pinning me against the wall. "This is serious. I promise, I'll tell you why soon."

I'm not having this. "You don't have to make up wild excuses. If you're determined to ruin our night and not have a good time with me, you can leave."

Connor's jaw works. He's stunned silent. Breathing hard, he balls his fists. "Fine. *Fine.*"

"Hey!" Blair Davis pulls Connor off me.

"Stay out of this!" Connor growls before he registers who he's talking to.

Blair narrows her gaze on him and gets in his face, prodding him in the chest. She's fierce and brave, no longer the girl who let anyone get away with the horrible things they did to her. "Quit being such an asshole! You need to stop acting like a god around here. Got it?"

"You don't know what you're talking about," Connor says through clenched teeth. "You're supposed to be on my side here."

"I know exactly what it looked like: you holding your date against the wall against her will. I don't care what you say," Blair snaps. "Try that shit again, and I'll make you regret it. And I don't give a damn if you're Devlin's friend. I'm not scared of you. Hurt her again, and I'm coming for you, Bishop."

Connor looks so pissed off at the accusation he hurt me. His eyes cut to me for a beat and a muscle in his jaw jumps. He storms off, leaving me feeling empty. Tears prick my eyes as he slams his shoulder into Mr. Coleman's on his way out.

I didn't expect him to actually leave. I only wanted him to stop being so controlling. I thought...

Sunshine, you're my world.

The tears fall, splashing down my cheeks. If he meant what he said, then why did he give up so easily?

Worst of all, I'm worried about what he might do. After he

told me about his anger management, I looked up the symptoms and what could happen if he lost control. I don't want him to hurt himself.

"It's about time I returned the favor for all the times you stood up for me," Blair says. "I thought you guys were together. Did he say something to you?"

I look up from wringing my hands to find her peering at me sadly. My lips part, but no words come out, clogging in my throat. I shake my head, on the verge of shattering.

She sighs. "Are you okay?"

I shrug, a wet breath hiccuping out of me.

"Shit," Blair mutters. She rummages through her clutch and pulls out her phone. "Here, look. This always cheers me up."

On her phone, there's a pug dog account on Instagram.

"Watch the video in the third post."

Despite everything, watching the pug dog fly into a pile of leaves, tongue lolling out, does make me smile. A soft, breathy laugh escapes me.

"Thank you."

"Come on," Blair says. "Let's get something to drink."

She leads me toward the refreshment table, rubbing my back. Without Connor here, the dance doesn't seem as magical. The decorations seem childish.

Mr. Coleman catches my eye, but keeps his distance while Blair is with me. Once I wipe my tears, I'll ask him for a ride home so I can go out looking for Connor.

* * *

Blair helped me calm down, showing me more dog videos and keeping me distracted. When Devlin came to stand at her side, looking at her like she hung the stars in his sky, they insisted on giving me a ride home with them, complete with a pit stop for pizza.

I'm glad I went with them. Getting pizza while all dressed up lifted my mood. They kept my mind off everything as Blair and I argued about the merits of pineapple on pizza against Devlin's firm belief that fruit didn't go on pizza.

The wariness I used to have toward Devlin has slipped away. Beneath his brooding outer shell, he's intelligent and has a wicked sense of humor. Spending time with him, I think I understand him better. Devlin isn't the cold, brutal devil he presents himself as, he's selective about who he lets in past his walls. He and Blair are a sight to behold when they get going, everything about them pointing to *power couple*.

It's nice to see how different they are now. In the back of the limo, they murmur to each other. Devlin holds Blair in his arms.

I peek shyly in my peripheral vision, pretending to mess around on my phone.

They seem happy. The way Devlin looks at Blair makes an ache settle in my chest, both with happiness that someone can love that deeply and with a pang of want. I thought Connor looked at me like that tonight, but the way he left has me questioning whether we're okay or not.

The limo is close to my house. My grip tightens on my phone.

Devlin cuts into my thoughts. "Bishop probably didn't mean what he said. That's why he wanted us to make sure you got home safely. He's..." A sigh escapes him. "I know how his head works. If he loses control, he acts without thinking."

There seems to be something else he's not saying because he shifts around. Blair puts her hand on his thigh and squeezes. They share a look and Blair gives a tiny shake of her head. Devlin shrugs. I blink at the odd exchange.

"Well, thanks," I say as the car pulls up to my house. The lights are all dark. I guess Mom was too tired to stay up late judging me after her snide comment about what boys expect at the end of a dance. She hasn't figured out yet that Connor and I are way past that point. The only thing on my mind is changing out of this dress so I can head out in my Mini Cooper to look for Connor. "I'm sorry I had to cut your night short. I hope you liked the dance."

"It was great," Blair says. "Typical teen scene isn't really my thing, but it was nice to try it on for a while."

Devlin snorts at some private joke between them. He turns his attention to me. "He means well."

I grant him a tight smile and climb from the limo, knowing I won't get any sleep tonight until I know Connor is safe and not doing something self-destructive. Something was bothering him all night and I need to find out what it was.

TWENTY-EIGHT
CONNOR

When the limo pulls away, I step out of the shadows as Thea walks up to her door.

"I'm sorry."

She jumps, hissing out a strangled, "Jesus, Connor." Looking me up and down, she frowns. "I'm glad you're not out doing something stupid. I was really worried about you."

My breath punches from me. I go off like that and she's worried about me?

I'm such an asshole. My girlfriend is right in front of me, stunning in the moonlight in her pink dress and white wool coat. Tonight was the one thing she asked me for and instead of making her night magical, I was on the defensive. I was too focused on the plan to break into Coleman's house in a few days that I pushed her away. It was only for her protection, but now that I see the sadness in her eyes I know I fucked up.

With a sigh, I scrub a hand through my hair. "Sorry. I messed it all up. I didn't mean to ruin the night. I had to get out of there, or I was going to put my fist through the wall, or..." I shake my head.

She doesn't want to hear about me punching Coleman.

I hold out my hand, heart hammering in my chest. "It doesn't matter. I was wrong and I shouldn't have left you alone. I want to show you something to make it up to you. Will you come with me for a drive?"

Thea studies me for a long beat where I think she's going to refuse. She should, after the way I treated her.

"Where are we going?"

I swallow in relief.

"I want to take you to a special place. It's where I go when I need to cool my head."

The wariness in Thea's gaze softens. "Promise me one thing."

"Anything."

"You don't dictate my life. You can't tell me what I can and can't do. You know why I hate that."

My gaze cuts away. I do know. She's told me about her issues with her mom being controlling and conservative. I can't help that in my effort to protect her from the threat Coleman poses, and from the mysterious hacking group using her as incentive to do what they told me to, I became forceful with her.

Controlling is the only way I know how to be. Without it, I turn wild. Learning to give that up when I know I'm keeping her safe is a daily challenge.

She takes my hand in both of hers, her eyes bouncing

between mine when they fly back to her. The sight of her causes a pang in my chest with her flower crown, those big doe eyes, and the tilt of her pouty lips.

I open my mouth to swear to her.

But I can't.

The only choice I have is to lie, and that frustrates the hell out of me. I don't want to lie to her, but I can't freak her out with this, either. Bile rises in my throat, keeping me from betraying her.

This is all for her own good. I can't stop the plan now. Once I get into Coleman's house with Devlin and Blair's help, then this will all be over. I'll give Thea anything she wants afterwards, even if she demands I walk away from her.

It'll kill me to leave her when I'm in love with her, but this will be the last promise to her I ever break.

Thea isn't the meek girl I used to think she was, but I won't hurt her by scaring her with the monsters waiting to take a bite out of her.

It's a huge risk, putting everything between us in jeopardy.

Instead of the promise she wants, I aim for a little honesty, because it's what she'll listen to.

"I can't promise you that yet." At Thea's crumbling expression, I rush the rest of my explanation out. "I want to, baby. So badly. But this is really big. Bigger than dirty politics and cover ups. I swear to you, I would never control you like she tries to. I know you're strong and capable of making your own choices. Please. Trust me?"

"We've had good communication to solve our issues before," Thea murmurs. "I trust you with my secrets, and you trust me with yours. So why are you keeping something from me?"

Damn her logic. She has me there. Forcing out a breath, I scrub the back of my neck.

"Everything I do is to keep you safe. Can you trust that?"

Thea studies me. "I know you'd never hurt me."

"I wouldn't. Just—give me a few days, okay? I swear, I'll tell you everything."

"Okay. As long as you tell me." She gives me that fierce look full of fire that I love. "Don't think I'll forget it."

A weak laugh leaves me as I gather her in my arms, inhaling her sugary scent mixing with the flowers. "You? Never. You're too sharp for that."

I stay like that for a minute, breathing her in while my stomach unknots. I can't mess this up. She's my everything. The only good thing to ever happen to me.

She presses up on her toes, kissing me with so much tenderness that my breath comes out shaky. I lean my forehead against hers and tell her what I wanted to earlier.

"I'm in love with you." Her gasp is soft and she goes still. Before she says anything, I go on in a reverent tone. "I didn't notice you. All these years, and I never looked twice at you. But you were right there the whole time, living next door." I lean back to meet her eyes, tucking her hair as I pour my heart out. "I see you now, Thea. You're so bright, I don't know how I ever missed it. Your light glows, in the day or at night."

"Connor," she whispers, eyes wide and shiny.

The corner of my mouth lifts and fondness fills me. "You make me feel like the moon, desperate to chase the sun. You're all I want to look at, sunshine. All I want to catch."

The smile that breaks out on Thea's face is stunning. A laugh escapes her and she winds her arms around my neck in a hug.

"I love you, too." Her voice is muffled against my chest.

Taking her hand, I back up a step. "Let's sneak out for that drive. I want to show you my favorite place."

We hop in the Lexus and when Thea turns to me, I shoot

out a hand to cover her eyes. "Don't look around. Keep your eyes shut."

She laughs, brushing her fingertips over my knuckles. "Why?"

"Don't want to ruin the surprise I put together for you."

Biting her lip around a smile, she covers her eyes with her own hands.

"Are they closed?" I squint at her.

"Yes!"

"Good. No peeking."

Shifting the car in gear, we drive off, leaving the neighborhood. The streets of Ridgeview are quiet this late. It's past eleven as we drive the winding roads leading up into the mountains that overlook the town. When we reach our destination, I back the car in.

"Keep them closed still," I say as I open my door.

"Okay," Thea drawls, tipping her head back against the seat. With her eyes scrunched tight, she lifts the flower crown from her head and rests it in her lap.

It's cold up at Peak Point. We're the only ones here and I made sure it would stay that way. It's the most popular place to hook up, but I come here for a different reason. I blow into my hands as I round to the back, opening the trunk so we'll have the perfect view. Inside the SUV, I built a nest of blankets, pillows, and a strand of battery powered Christmas lights to make it festive. When I click them on, they blink in multicolor.

Once I'm satisfied with the set up, I go to Thea's door and open it. "Take my hands. I'll guide you. That's it—watch your step."

I want to kiss the crinkle in her nose as I walk backwards toward the rear of the SUV. When I have her in position, I lick my lips.

"Okay. Open."

Thea's lashes flutter and she takes in the sight of Ridgeview lit up at night, tiny lights filling the valley below us from the high vantage point.

"Wow," she breathes.

"Yeah." I'm looking at her instead of the town below. "I know it's just Peak Point, but it's my favorite place. I sit up here for hours when I need to cool my head."

"It's so pretty at night."

"Seeing it all lit up and small reminds me that whatever I've turned into a big problem doesn't have to be in the scope of things."

She turns to me with a smile. "I love it."

"You'll love it more when you turn around. It's too cold." Nudging her by the shoulders, I show her the fort I built in the back of the SUV for us. Her delighted laughter echoes off the tree tops as I help her climb in. "Let's warm up."

"Thank you. This surprise is amazing," Thea says once we're comfortably entwined and burrowed in the blankets to keep out the biting chill. She traces my jaw. "I love you."

"You make me fall in love with you over and over." Cradling her face in my hands, I hover my lips over hers. "The world doesn't matter. Only us. Right here. Only this."

"Only us," Thea repeats, her eyes hooded.

I slant my mouth over hers. She plays with the hair at the nape of my neck as we fall into the pile of blankets, kissing like the world could end and we still wouldn't stop, wouldn't part from each other.

My hands slide into her coat to get at the curves of her body. She arches against me and a faint moan fills the back of the SUV. I take her mouth again, a rough sound catching in my throat.

This is my favorite place now. Right here, with her in my arms.

Layer by layer, our clothes come off as our bodies tangle together. We close the door to engulf ourselves in a cocoon of our own making. The chill from outside is forgotten as we heat up the back of the car.

"I want you," Thea begs as I kiss a trail from her breasts down her stomach, settling between her legs.

"Soon, baby." I stroke her hips and place feather-light kisses over her thighs, then her folds, teasing her until she shakes. I give her a long lick with my tongue where she needs me, enjoying the broken sound that flies past her lips. "First, let me worship you."

Gripping her thighs, I bury my face between her legs, licking and sucking until Thea is crying out, rolling her hips to ride my face. The sounds she makes while she comes have me grinning against her pussy, my face a mess as I flick my tongue against her clit.

"Love making you fall apart like that," I rasp, shooting a cocksure look up the length of her body.

"Please, please, I need you now." Thea tugs on my shoulders, half sitting up to capture my lips in a kiss, moaning into my mouth when she tastes herself on my lips.

Without breaking the kiss, I roll us over, grinding my cock against her. Fuck, her body feels incredible and I can't wait to drive into her. I fumble around for my pants to get the condom, finally forced to stop kissing her to tear the packet and roll it on. She makes me so wild every time, I'm close to the edge before I'm inside her.

Thea sits up on her knees with a spark of determination in her eye that's so sexy. The look in her blue-green gaze has my groin tightening with a coil of heat. Before I can go to her, she straddles my lap, bracing her hands on my shoulders and sinks down on my cock.

We both release a groan, leaning into each other for a

moment. Nothing can touch us. It's me and her, the way I want it to always be. My hands find her hips, squeezing as she starts riding me at a slow pace.

"God, you're incredible." I kiss anywhere I can reach—her neck, her chest, between her breasts as they brush against my jaw. "My beautiful sunshine."

Thea winds her arms around my neck and drops her forehead against mine, meeting my gaze as we move together, making love in the back of my car beneath the moon.

My breath grows shallow and I sink a hand into her hair when the pleasure becomes too much to withstand, gritting my teeth to hold on for her a little longer.

"Thea," I whisper, tensing.

"Yes. Let go with me." She tips her head back with a moan and I feel her squeezing my cock, driving me over the edge.

We're both left panting by our orgasms. I stroke her hair and pull the blankets around us, keeping her in my lap.

If I could freeze time, I'd pick this moment to stay in forever. Right where I belong.

TWENTY-NINE
CONNOR

Weeks of planning brought me here, sitting shotgun in one of Devlin's dad's cars—one of the lower end luxury models to blend in—parked near Harold Coleman's house.

Tonight, I'm breaking into my English teacher's house for a group of mysterious hackers obsessed with crows and skulls.

He lives on a quiet street on the outskirts of the town center, with only a handful of other houses on the block. Most are decorated for the holidays, lit up and festive. His is the only one that's not decked out, except for a sad little lawn sign that says happy holidays with a snowflake on it.

Winter break starts tomorrow. We picked tonight because Coleman would be stuck late at school with meetings to close out the first semester. Blair's tailing him as our lookout, Devlin's the getaway driver, and my job is breaking in to get the locket the Anonymous wannabes demanded before they give me the dirt on Coleman.

"You're sure about this? The time to back out is now." Devlin rests his hand over the wheel. He's a ride or die friend, no matter what I say he's down to back me.

I think about how pretty Thea was the other night at the dance in her gauzy pink dress, then later, even more beautiful beneath blinking Christmas lights in the back of my SUV. My heart squeezes.

"No doubts, bro." Devlin and Lucas both found their queens in Blair and Gemma. I'm doing this to make sure mine has her place of honor by my side. I'll do whatever it takes to protect her. "I'm going in there."

Devlin gives me one of his sadistic grins. He's living for this epic mischief making. This is bigger than any of our pranks.

"What do you think you'll find?" Devlin muses.

I suppress a shudder. I haven't wanted to think about it, braced for the most depraved shit my twisted imagination could think of.

"The truth. Probably a sad as fuck, lonely life."

Devlin hums in agreement.

I haven't told Devlin and Blair everything. I glossed over the details about Thea, but explained how the hackers got into my system when I found something connecting Coleman to a creepy online persona. Devlin is the one who guessed Coleman has an interest in Thea going off my short fuse and his own observations.

Blair's been ready to cut off Coleman's balls ever since, sitting in third period English like she's prepared for battle.

We're waiting for her confirmation in the group chat on our phones before I go. Her criminal tendencies and pick-pocketing talents have come in handy planning out the logistics of tonight.

"What's the psychology behind a predator?" I ask.

Devlin cocks his head in thought. He has a strong interest in psychology, always carrying a book with him.

"It always comes down to power. But in this case, it's like the victims aren't people. They serve their purpose fulfilling a sexual desire. A predator is a hunter. They know to set themselves up for success by working on a victim who is vulnerable and already susceptible to being manipulated into doing whatever the predator wants," he says after a minute. "It's abusive."

The answer has my blood boiling. Thinking of Thea in that frame of mind, her window right across from mine.

Damn it.

Our phones ping at the same time. When I check, I shake my head.

Blair: All this sneaking around brings back memories [smirk emoji]

Devlin's answer pops up in the conversation.

Devlin: [smirking devil emoji] you just wait until we get home, little thief.

"Can you two not flirt in the group chat? You're nauseating with your lovey-dovey sap shit."

Devlin just smirks while Blair sends a selfie of her leather-glove covered middle finger in front of her face to our group text. A minute later, she hits us up again.

Blair: Ok, meeting started. Timer begins now.

With the go ahead, I tug a beanie on and put up the hood on my black hoodie.

"Gloves," Devlin says, handing them over.

"Thanks, man. For everything."

"You're family. We go to war for family."

"You big fuckin' sap. Love you, bro."

"Shut up. Go be a badass."

Saluting him with a crooked grin, I get out of the car and act like I belong here.

The house is quaint, with blue shingles and a porch. It pisses me off how easily Coleman gets to blend in when he's a fucking creep preying on young girls. Who knows how many? The thought turns my stomach. I'm here for a locket, so I can only guess Thea isn't the only honey pot he's tried dipping his claws in.

Gritting my teeth, I check if anyone's around before I slip toward the back door to pick the lock.

Blair let me borrow her kit of picks and drilled me until I could pick Coleman's brand of lock with my eyes closed. It comes in handy that Dev's girl has a history of criminal tendencies. I kneel at the back door and get started, carefully working it until the knob gives way.

"Gotcha." Tucking away the tools, I step inside, leaving the lights off and illuminating the way with my phone.

The inside of Coleman's house tells a much different story than the charming young teacher persona he puts on at school. My lip curls as I move through the dated kitchen to a living room with grime-stained walls. This place looks fine from the outside, but it's a shithole. He must've got it real cheap because it looks like it was a crack den. Empty take out containers and instant dinner dishes sit around, making the place smell rank. They're at least two days old.

"Fucking gross," I grumble, scanning the room.

There are no signs of a partner or roommates. The place is sparsely furnished. Every inch of the house screams shut in bachelor.

Coleman clearly spends a lot of time on his computer. It's a setup like mine and the only corner of the room that seems frequently used. A serious system with big monitors, like a skeevy command base. I picture him sitting there typing that shit to Thea and ball my fists to control the wave of fury crashing over me. Blowing out a breath, I cross to the computer and tap a key.

The display wakes up and I smirk. "Thanks for the easy access."

I plug in an encrypted drive and type in a keyboard shortcut to bring up a command prompt window, giving me admin control. With a few more keystrokes, his hard drive is downloading for me. While that's running, I head into the other rooms to search for the necklace and hunt down anything else I can find.

The house is a single floor bungalow, so there are only so many places for Coleman to hide his sinister corruption. I start with the bedroom, which makes me gag.

Black silk sheets? Is he fucking kidding?

As the creep factor climbs, so does my anger. I take pictures of everything to paint the image of Harold K. Coleman, perverted douchebag degenerate. The darkest monster I've ever met. Considering the secrets I know of the people in this town, that's saying something.

"Going to have to shower eighty goddamn times to get the vibe of this place off me."

The closet has nothing interesting, so I try the bureau, pulling drawers out and rifling through ratty pairs of sweatpants and stained graphic t-shirts. What a man-child.

When I don't find anything, I'm about to look under the

bed, but the third drawer down on the left makes me pause. The grain on the bottom of the drawer is a shade off from the others. I shine the flashlight from my phone closer, furrowing my brow. I pull out the drawer on the right side to compare, putting my hands in both.

"Shit."

The one on the left is slightly higher. It's a fake bottom. I take out the stacks of clothes, taking care not to mess up the order so Coleman doesn't suspect anything. There's a tiny tab at the back. When I pull on it, I'm able to remove the false cover.

My heart stops.

A row of necklaces sits in the drawer on black velvet. All matching.

At first I suck in a breath, thinking I've found the locket. But no, these aren't silver. They're gold plated. Cheap. Each heart pendant sits on a slip of paper with Coleman's handwriting.

Girl's names.

These are disgusting collars of ownership for every girl Coleman is manipulating. He probably sends them as gifts to make the girls feel special, when he's got six other duplicates. If they feel doted on, he must have an easier time controlling them to do whatever he wants.

Acidic bile rushes up my throat.

"Jesus fucking christ." My teeth clench hard enough to crack.

It takes a long minute to control the powerful instinct to punch through the wall as hard as I can as an outlet for the rage.

I snap several photos on my phone, documenting closeups of the name tags, each necklace, and the hidden compartment in the drawer. My phone vibrates with an incoming call, sending my heart into an awful adrenaline spike. It's Thea.

My chest goes tight and my attention drops to her necklace, second in the row. What a cruel twist of fate that she ended up vulnerable and pliant to fall into this monster's trap. "I'm sorry, baby."

I grip my phone tight, rubbing my forehead with the back of my hand, and let her call go to voicemail. I can't afford to get distracted when I need to be ready for Devlin and Blair's signal while I search. If I answered, I don't know if I'd be strong enough to keep this secret from her. As soon as I give the crow guys what they want, I'm telling Thea everything.

And I'll never let her near Coleman again. She'll be safe.

Once I know she's protected, I'm coming for Coleman. The proof of his evil is here. If Landry won't listen to me, I'll go over his head. Whatever it takes to put Coleman away for his crimes.

He won't hurt anyone ever again.

Putting everything back the way I found it in the drawer is one of the hardest things I've ever done. Every part of my being screams at me to grab the necklaces, that it's wrong to let Coleman keep these like he hasn't been caught. With a rough sound, I turn my back on the bureau.

A single nightstand sits beside the bed. I head there next.

For a minute, I stare down at the dark wood, rubbing my fingers to gear up to continue the search. I force out a ragged breath and brace for the worst as I open the first drawer. My nose wrinkles at the tube of lotion mixed in with an inhaler and other odds and ends. There's nothing else, so I go for the second drawer.

At first glance, anyone could mistake it for a junk drawer.

But amongst charm bracelets, a headband, two leather cuffs, and a picture keychain I find a silver locket. *Trophies.*

Before I do anything, I pull up my phone camera and grab several shots of the drawer's contents.

My hand shakes as I take the locket, checking it.

The initials *CT* are engraved on the silver heart.

This is the one.

My gaze flicks from the bed back to the drawer. He keeps them right next to where he sleeps. An uncomfortable shudder wracks my body.

"I will end you, if it's the last thing I ever do," I growl, stuffing the locket in my pocket.

I have what I came here for, but I want to keep going. As soon as I finish the bedroom, my phone buzzes, signaling my time is up. Opening the group chat confirms it.

Blair: On the move. 15min ETA.

A second later, Devlin revs the engine outside.

"Damn it." I cast a glance around the room I was checking.

Connor: 2 mins [sweat smile emoji]

Devlin: Now. Christ, only you would use emojis at a time like this.

Gritting my teeth, I rush into the living room to check the download status. A relieved breath leaves me. It finished. I've got it all. Ejecting the thumb drive and closing out of everything, I put his computer to sleep the way I found it.

Once I'm outside, I cut through the shadows and bushes, emerging on the street as if I was there all along. Moving quickly, I slide into the passenger seat of Devlin's car. He doesn't wait until my door is fully closed before pulling away, peeling down a side street and shifting gear.

It's not until we're five minutes away that he speaks. "Did you find it?"

"Yeah." I stare out the window, fist covering my mouth. "I'll show you when we meet up with Blair."

Devlin scoffs, shaking his head. "Knew he wasn't right."

While he drives, I reach in the back and take out my tablet from the backpack on the floor, plugging in the encrypted drive. I push off my hood and drag off the beanie as the thumb drive connects. My throat goes dry and scratchy once I get into Coleman's files.

It doesn't take me long to find. She's right there in a photo on his local drive, along with other girls. Each photo is labeled with a name. Thea, Charlotte, Jen, Alicia...

My nostrils flare before I finish checking all the names. Some are tame, like Thea's, but others are far less so. I almost throw the tablet out the window, but I control myself. Instead, I put the photos in a folder to separate them from the ones I can stomach, where the girls aren't baring themselves to this disgusting asshole.

With images like these, he could do anything with them. Start a porn site. Sell them. A sharp pain stabs in my gut as nausea rolls through me.

Steeling myself, I sift through what's left in the folder.

In Charlotte's photo, she's wearing the same locket burning a hole in my pocket. She's a pretty blond, around the age Thea was in her blog photos, maybe a little younger.

In Thea's photo, the metadata tells me it's three years old, from when she was fifteen. She's in her room, the colorful baking pun posters visible behind her. She's not nude, but her outfit is revealing and the way she poses is suggestive. I shift uncomfortably in my seat, plagued with the skeeze feeling again.

The thought of Coleman having this photo, and others like

293

it, makes me want to scream and go fucking wild. If I was unleashed on him right now, I'd kill him. No mercy.

It's no wonder Thea started dressing in less form-fitting clothes after going through however long of dressing like this for an older man she didn't know on the internet.

In the same folder, there are saved transcripts from conversations. I can't look at any at the moment, too wired by my anger to face more of Coleman's depravity poisoning these young girls. Regulating my breath is difficult. Thankfully we're almost to the abandoned quarry.

Shame there isn't a fight tonight. Then again, I'm so ready to go off, I might be a danger to myself and others, like Doctor Levitt warned me.

Devlin pulls in, parking behind the rusted old storage building next to the car Blair is leaning against. He cuts the engine and we climb out.

"Did you get it?" Blair asks.

Without a word, I unlock my phone and hand it to her, jaw clenched.

"Shit," Blair hisses, scrolling through the photos. Devlin leans over her shoulder, scowling. "What a sick dickhead."

"I'll kill him." I stalk away, grabbing one of the broken old pieces of steel littering the ground around the building.

"Bishop," Devlin calls.

"Just—give me a minute, man. It's too much. If I don't get it out, it'll eat me up."

He and Blair exchange a glance. They leave me alone as they go through what I found on my phone. Seeing the way Devlin rubs Blair's arms when a chilly breeze moves through the clearing makes me ache to speed across town to tuck Thea in my arms.

Releasing a harsh yell, I swing the metal with all my might against the ground, leaving a deep dent in the gravel. I lose myself in it for several minutes, pouring the torrent of emotions into destruction. By the time I come back to myself, I'm panting.

"Feel better?" Blair asks lightly as I walk back to them.

"Much." With a sigh, I toss the busted up piece of steel aside into a patch of scrubby weeds and drag a hand through my hair. "So. Yeah. Coleman."

"Coleman," Devlin repeats in a dark tone.

"Dead man fucking walking," I utter harshly.

"Exactly," Devlin agrees.

All three of us are pissed off by the pictures I took. I'm glad I have the two of them with me so I don't have to deal with this alone. Now that the adrenaline and fury are under control, I'm itching to get out of here so I can send proof, get the unsealed files from those hackers, and finally tell Thea what I've been keeping from her.

"Did you take the locket?" Blair holds up my phone, showing me the photo of the trophy drawer.

My lip curls. I pull out the necklace by the chain, the pendant dangling in the air.

She leans in to examine it. "What do you think those guys who hacked your computer will do?"

"They seem pretty dangerous." I shrug. "And they wanted it fast. If they don't do something by next week, I will."

"I knew he was a creep, but thinking of sitting through class with him is—ugh." Blair shakes off her shudder, burrowing into Devlin's side. He wraps his arms around her. To anyone else it might look like a normal embrace, but Devlin's knuckles turn white from how tight he clings to her, like he's preventing her from disappearing on him after he almost lost her. "I'm so grossed out right now."

Devlin props his chin on Blair's head and cuts his gaze to me. "Ready to head home?"

"Yes. I have the proof one way or another. Time to do what I do best."

"You're a real piece of work when you go into blackmail mode." Devlin smirks, tossing me a set of keys. "Here, take that one. I'll pick it up tomorrow."

"Thanks," I call to them as Devlin opens the passenger door for Blair. "No one I'd rather commit a crime with than you two."

Blair snorts, glancing up at Devlin.

"Go be the Batman to your girlfriend." He nods to me before he gets in the driver's seat and revs the engine.

I watch as the wheels throw gravel and dust while Devlin pulls out of the quarry.

Getting into the car Blair had been driving, I grip the wheel tight. I'm a man on a mission as I turn the ignition and drive home.

THIRTY
THEA

When my call goes to Connor's voicemail, I hang my shoulders in defeat. I thought things would be better after our amazing night in the mountains, but I haven't been able to get a hold of him for days. Every time I look across the space between our windows, his light has been off.

"You've reached Bishop. You know I don't check this shit, so I don't know why you're bothering. Text me."

There goes my plan to invite him with Maisy and I to the holiday bazaar downtown. Winter break is off to a great start with my boyfriend back to avoiding me.

With a sigh, I set my phone next to the rainbow clock on my nightstand and flop on the bed, hugging my stuffed sea lion.

An unpleasant flutter fills my chest.

Could Connor be bored with me? If he is, why would he tell me...

I close my eyes and just breathe for a second to stop the racing thoughts and nasty inner voice that makes me doubt everything. No matter how hard I try, I can't keep it at bay.

You're not good enough to keep someone like him. He'll forget you soon enough.

I swallow past the lump in my throat. The thoughts chew me up, leaving me raw and vulnerable. Curling on my side, I hug the sea lion tighter, burying my face in the plush fuzziness.

I can't go back to being invisible. Not to him.

After a few minutes of breathing through the thorns twining around my heart, pricking at every insecurity, I get up and pat my puffy cheeks.

"This calls for double chocolate fudge cupcakes."

With a sniffle, I text Maisy before the evening yoga sessions start at the wellness and recreation center she volunteers for.

Thea: Great British Bake Off marathon after your class?

Maisy: You got it, dude. Which season?

Thea: [hiding monkey emoji] All of them...?

Maisy: Oh lordt. Should I cancel class? The yoga moms can survive one day without their warrior 2 and downward dog.

Thea: No, no. I'm going to bake us cupcakes until you get here. See you after class!

Maisy sends me two peace sign emojis and promises not to

eat all the cupcakes this time. I pull on the hoodie I stole from Connor, press the neckline to my nose, and close my eyes. It feels like he's hugging me when I wear it.

Downstairs, Constantine follows me into the kitchen while I tie my hair back in a pony tail. A few minutes later I have the oven preheating, my supplies are out, and the cupcakes are underway.

I'm still feeling sensitive about Connor as I'm mixing the batter when Mom walks in, eyeing me critically. I'm too tired to fend her off if she says anything about wearing my boyfriend's hoodie.

"Mom," I say in greeting while she pours herself a glass of wine. It's not her first of the day.

"What are you making today?" she asks after a minute of stale silence.

An exhale leaves me, unwinding the tension in my shoulders. It's okay. She's going to be normal and not attack me.

"Double chocolate fudge cupcakes. Extra gooey." I direct my hesitant smile at the mixing bowl. "Would you rather have peanut butter or cream cheese frosting?"

Mom says nothing. I look up to find her gaze narrowed on me in disappointment.

"Yeah..." I trail off. "You're right. Peanut butter would probably be too rich with the chocolate. Still, I'm kind of craving it, so I guess I'll make a batch of both."

I'm desperate for a scrap of normalcy with her. It's always made me crazy that I can't have the same bond with her I had with grandma. Part of me wonders if she's resented me all these years because I liked baking and she never did, so grandma and I had something Mom couldn't get from her.

"Are those for that horrible boy next door?" The acid in her voice stings.

A weak protest catches in my throat. I was wrong. She's

primed for attack after all, and I'm too drained to clash with her.

Mom continues before I can push any response out, planting her hands on the island between us. "Look at you, like his little housewife baking away. You have to understand, Thea. Men aren't trustworthy." Her voice drops to a horrible, grating whisper as she tears into me. "His doting is all a lie. He doesn't want you. All of them are the same—only after one thing."

"Mom, can we not?" With a frown, I shut her out, keeping my spine straight as I work on the batter. "I'm so tired of having this argument."

Circling the island, she pinches the sleeve of Connor's hoodie and yanks. "We clearly need to have it. You must've given him what he wanted, so now he'll drop you. If that's all he does, you'll be lucky."

The words cut deep, blow after fatal blow.

She hasn't bothered me with this in over a month, so she must have been bottling it up to dump on me all at once. I clutch the whisk hard enough the handle leaves an indent in my palm.

"Mom, please," I whisper in a tight voice, holding back the tears pooling in my eyes.

I've held out against her for so long, never giving in. But everything she's saying pulls on the same fears that haunted me in my bedroom when Connor didn't take my call.

"You're going to end up just like my sister."

I blink. "Wait—what?"

Mom closes her eyes. "You had an aunt. My younger sister. Momma's favorite."

This is news to me. I knew Mom and grandma had bad blood between them all the way up to when she passed away, but this is something Mom has never talked about.

"She met a boy when she was in high school, about your

age. I'd gone off to college and couldn't keep an eye on her." Mom's lip curls, gulping her wine. Now she's so close, I can smell it on her breath. Her eyes are too bright. "She was always dressing for attention and it caught his eye. He was older, but it doesn't matter. They all want one thing. He got it from her, all right. Left her dead in a ditch for it once he had her body."

"Mom," I breathe. "Jesus."

Everything about her strictness with me, why she's always nagged me to dress conservatively, becomes crystal clear. But it doesn't mean Connor is like the man who hurt her sister.

She's silent for a beat, eyes glassy. "Too infatuated. Thought he hung the moon. Just like you."

"I—Connor isn't like that. He's always been sweet and gentle with me, even when we—" I cut off. Crap. "He's a good guy, Mom."

She folds her arms and nods like she has all the confirmation she needs. "You should've listened to me in the first place."

With the satisfaction of the final word and making me feel small on top of telling me about her sister's death, she takes her wine—the glass and the bottle—and leaves me alone, crying over my cupcake batter.

THIRTY-ONE
CONNOR

There was nothing I wanted more than to go straight to Thea after I left Coleman's place. But first I have to know what the mysterious hackers have on him. Once I get all the concrete evidence, I'll take every damning piece of it to her.

Damien didn't even register as I blew through the kitchen and took the stairs two at a time to my room. Slamming down in the chair at my desk, I hook up the encrypted drive and my phone to input what I found at Coleman's house. I pull out the locket and set it next to the computer as I work.

It occurs to me when I'm halfway through adding the new information on Coleman to the file in my app, I have no idea how to contact Dolos. No sooner does the thought cross my mind, a chat window pops up in the middle of the screen.

"Backdoor? Those douchebags." I try to navigate away or close the window, but the only access I have is the chat window.

An irritated sound rumbles in my throat. This is pissing me off. My system isn't easy to hack. I pride myself on the security measures I have in place to prevent compromises, but they're able to slip past them with ease.

Dolos: Well? We know you infiltrated Coleman's residence tonight.
Connor: The fuck? Were you watching me the whole time?
Dolos: Someone had to check you were doing as we said.
Connor: I thought you didn't know where he lived?
Dolos: We didn't. You found it, we traced your phone.
Connor: Whatever. Give me what you promised.
Dolos: Proof first. Take a picture.

Blowing out a breath, I lift the locket as my webcam connects. I peel off the electrical tape I cover the camera with and hold the locket close.

Dolos: Good.

A second later, a compressed file labeled HKC comes through, along with control of my computer again. I hold my breath as I double click to open it. Once it's ready, air hisses from my lungs.

"Holy shit."

It's all there. Reports, police records, employment history. Between the stuff at his house and the files documenting his previous two employer records—both with complaints of sexual harassment and inappropriate conduct with minors in his charge—I have more than enough to make a move.

I'm so focused on combing through the information in the unsealed files, I almost miss the new message blinking in the chat window.

Dolos: Now we start the next phase. Stay put.

"What? No." My brows pinch as I type.

Connor: Fuck that. Wherever you are, you can suck it. He's here and he's a threat.
Dolos: You will do nothing.

I don't answer to these assholes. I'm getting fed up with them telling me what to do. Screw waiting, it's time to act.

Dolos: Don't be an idiot when you still have that cute little neighbor to think of. We hate making threats against the innocent ones.

Fuck.

Connor: Fine. What's the next phase?

They don't answer. The window disappears and the screen goes black, flashing with a laughing skull being circled by another 8-bit crow.

"Assholes." I reboot my computer once again, really hating their idea of goodbye.

Every part of me revolts at the thought of sitting on my

hands. I've done enough of that. If I don't do something, Coleman has more chances to hurt Thea.

Why should I sit around and wait for whoever the hell these guys are when they're somewhere else and I'm here in town with a monster hyper-focused on my girl?

I'll die before I let the crows or Coleman touch her.

All I want to do is protect Thea. She won't slip through my grasp.

THIRTY-TWO
THEA

In the morning, I feel like a husk. Maisy stayed up with me half the night after we gorged our way through the cupcakes, then ate frosting directly out of the mixing bowl during three full seasons of feel-good bake off competition. She helped me through the shock of finding out I should have an aunt.

Grandma never said anything. Maybe Mom forced her to hide it from me, but my heart aches for her, losing a daughter at such a young age in a horrible way.

Groggy, I roll over in bed. Maisy is starfished, arms and legs spread to take up most of the mattress while I'm curled against the edge. It's funny that such a kind-hearted, giving person can be such a bed hog. I somehow end up fighting her skinny butt for space every time we've shared a bed over the years.

With a groan, I nudge her. "Up. Or move. Whatever you want, just do something because I'm about to fall off."

Maisy cracks one hazel eye open, squinting at me. "Demon."

"Maise." I laugh as she burrows further under the covers.

"The sugar coma I'm coming off of might be the end of me. We had a good run, bestie." She shuffles over, reaching out blindly to drag me closer. "How are you feeling?"

"I'll be okay, I think. Thank you." I massage my forehead. "It was a lot on top of an already emotional state of mind."

Maisy hums, hugging me. "Do you still want to go to the holiday market? Instead we could do a face mask spa day. Meditate it out? Or do I need to pull out the big guns with goat yoga?"

A sleep-tinged, husky chuckle rolls out of me. "Actually, I think I'm going to shower and head next door. I want to see if Connor is home before we go to the holiday market."

"Mind, body, and spirit self-care bonding with a friend passed over for the power of a good dicking," Maisy teases, pinching my sides where I'm ticklish.

I flail in my attempt to escape. "Maise, no!" I wail, clawing my way to freedom while she tortures me with precise attacks. "God, you're the worst! You know it's not like that!"

Laughing, she sits back against my headboard. "I know. The vagina needs its own worship to achieve the zen of self-care, too."

"Oh my god, you're such a weirdo." I flop on my back, head dangling off the bed. "Love you."

"Love you back," she sings. "We'll meet up later by the entrance to the bazaar?"

"Of course."

"Sweet. Dibs on the shower first."

"Go ahead. I'll take one later."

As Maisy heads for the bathroom, I try messaging Connor again.

Thea: Are you around?

No response comes by the time she's done.

An hour later, I'm standing outside Connor's house after lunch time. I don't know what I expected when I knocked on the door, but it wasn't Mrs. Bishop answering instead of him. She's dressed down, rather than the power suits I typically see her in. Maybe she has off from city council duties today.

"Oh. Sorry, I don't mean to interrupt your day, Mrs. Bishop."

Mrs. Bishop leans against the door frame, rather than welcoming me inside. "Vivian, please. What is it?"

"Is Connor home?"

She sweeps her gaze over me, pursing her lips. It's the most expressive reaction I've witnessed since that night in the coat closet at the benefit dinner.

"Come inside." Without waiting, Vivian turns and walks deeper in the house.

I follow, unable to shake the uneasiness clinging to me. "Is he here, or...?"

"No. Left early and wouldn't say where he was going." She stops and turns on her heel when we reach the kitchen. "You can wait here for him. Would you like some tea?"

"Okay." I take a tentative seat at the island. "Thank you."

She smiles without moving the upper half of her face. It's disconcerting. "Be right back."

I'm not waiting long before she returns with a manila folder. She must be working from home. She paces on the other side of the island.

"Sorry again for interrupting." I gesture at the folder she's flipping through. "I haven't heard from Connor in a few days, so I was worried and wanted to stop by to see if he wanted to go to the holiday market downtown."

Vivian lifts a brow with her attention on the contents in the folder, but doesn't answer.

"I'm going to make you an offer," she announces after a stretch of awkward silence.

"I'm sorry?" I lick my lips nervously.

Snapping the folder shut, she plays with it as she studies me with a tight expression. "You've worn out your usefulness for the campaign's family-centered message. Leave my son. Stop seeing him. Don't call or text him."

"What?" The air sucks from the room as I grip the edge of the counter. "Why would I do that? Connor and I—" I close my mouth. It sounds stupid and cliche saying we love each other to his mom while she's trying to drive me away. "I won't do it."

She sighs like I'm a big inconvenience. "How much do you want?"

"You can't pay me to stop dating Connor." I gape at her. "That's horrible."

Vivian coos at me, the sound derisive. "That's how the world works, darling."

I straighten my spine. "No thanks. No matter how much you try to bribe me with, I wouldn't do that to him. I don't like lying."

"Well, aren't you good at playing wholesome?"

"*Playing?*"

I'm about to jump up from the stool when she smirks. "Connor doesn't want or need you. Why do you think he hasn't contacted you?"

Denial clogs in my throat. No. He wouldn't ghost me. He's too proud for it. If he wanted to end things between us, he'd tell me to my face. I shake my head.

Vivian clucks her tongue. "With your...promiscuous proclivities, you don't foster the right kind of image. It's best for everyone if you disappeared from his life."

"Disappeared? Promiscuous proclivities?" My head is spinning. "What are you talking about?"

She tosses the folder across the counter. It lands between us, pages spilling across the gleaming granite. They're...*me*. Photos of myself. Dread seeps into every inch of my skin as I stare at printed pages from my blog.

No. No, no, no. This can't be happening.

"I'll take your stunned silence as agreement." Her words tear me from my stupor. She clicks a pen, poised over a checkbook she pulled out while I was in a daze. "How much will it be?"

What a horrible woman. I'm never voting for her.

Sucking in a fortifying breath, I face her. "If Connor doesn't want me, why would you have to pay me to stop seeing him?"

I'm proud that my voice only shakes a little.

Vivian taps the tip of her silver pen against the blank check. "Insurance."

My lips part. Forget this, standing up to her is pointless. I swipe the pages from my blog and hop down from the stool.

"I have to go," I say.

"Those aren't the only copies, dear. Be smart. Tell me your price, or I'll show my son."

A wild laugh escapes me as I back away from her. "You

think you can blackmail me?" It's kind of hilarious, actually. I wish Connor was here to see this. He would get a kick out of it. "Bye, Mrs. Bishop."

Heart in my throat, I get the hell out of there. On the way, my phone rings. I wait until I'm in the Bishop's driveway before I pull it out. When I see who it is, a sound catches in my throat.

"Connor!" I answer, pressing the phone to my ear in a white-knuckled grip.

"Thea? Are you—? I'm almost home. Can you meet me in the pool house?"

I turn back to face his house, my stomach roiling. The last twenty-four hours weigh on my shoulders after facing off with his mother and my own.

"Yeah." I sniffle, wiping my nose. "Of course. Are you okay?"

"We need to talk."

My stomach drops.

The call cuts off.

"Connor? Connor! Damn it."

I almost drop the phone as the printed pages slip from my grasp, cascading all over the driveway. Doubt engulfs me as I crouch to gather the pages blaring my secret.

Between the ideas both our mothers planted in my head, I dread what Connor needs to talk about.

THIRTY-THREE
THEA

There might as well be a singed path in front of the pool house from the serious, stressed-out pacing I did in the last ten minutes waiting for Connor. The entire time I had myself half-convinced we're breaking up, like both our mothers want.

My inner critical voice wreaks havoc, running rampant with the worst things I think of myself, clawing at my mind with one berating thought after another.

Not enough, silly girl, my mind chants.

The anxiety has ratcheted so high, I'm sure any second I'll puke up all the sugary confections Maisy and I gorged ourselves on last night. Double chocolate fudge cake is coming back for a gruesome revenge.

I threw out the printouts I took from Vivian, but what if she already told Connor?

The tense, resolute expression on Connor's face when he finally rounds the house to the backyard with a laptop and thick file in hand doesn't help alleviate any of those poisonous thoughts. I smother a sound that should belong to a dying animal, not a girl seeing her boyfriend for the first time in days.

The last time we were together, we talked about loving each other. Now I'm certain those were our last happy moments. Something in my bones braces me for the impact of this conversation shattering my heart.

One smile from him could save it.

"Hi," I say hoarsely when he's close.

Connor doesn't smile. The first crack in my fragile heart splinters, catching me off guard.

"Come inside." He glances around, watchful of our surroundings. "We need to talk."

"Yeah, about that," I croak, wringing my hands. "You're kind of freaking me out. Maybe you can put a girl out of her misery over here? I've had a rough couple of days."

"You and me both, baby," Connor rumbles, reaching for my hand and squeezing it.

It's a brief ray of light breaking through the clouds of despair hanging over my head, but it helps me breathe a little easier and soothes some of the anxiety, bringing me back from the brink of an emotional breakdown. Once we're inside, he sits me down on the bed, kneels in front of me, and opens his slim laptop with a grim expression.

The tension is killing me. I haven't fully calmed down from what his mom tried to pull, let alone the bomb dropped on me last night.

"Your mom wants to bribe me to stop seeing you." I put one

thing out there, shoving the weight off my shoulders so I have help bearing it before it crushes me.

Connor stills, dragging his attention from the screen to stare at me. He pinches the bridge of his nose.

"Fucking bitch. Don't listen to her. Whatever poison she tried to feed you, it's bullshit."

My body sags in relief. "I thought—when I couldn't get a hold of you. I thought you didn't want me."

"Thea." He puts the laptop on the floor and slides his palms up the sides of my thighs. "I want you. I love you. Everything I've been doing is for you. All of it. I'm ready to tell you why I've been distant the last few days."

I lean in, resting my forehead against his. The earthy scent unique to him twines around me as he strokes his thumbs against my legs.

After a minute, he taps my thigh and picks up the laptop again. "We have to prioritize this. Time is running out and I'm not waiting around anymore."

"What is it?"

Connor sighs. "You know I'm good at weeding out people's secrets?"

I nod.

"Back when you and I...well, before I revealed myself to you, I did some digging. It wasn't hard to access for someone like me. I told you I'm good with computers."

"What are you saying?"

"It's better if I show you what I stumbled on."

Connor turns the laptop, the screen full of several windows showing photos of necklaces, email transcripts, and Mr. Coleman's photo.

"What is this?"

"Something sinister. Chief Landry won't listen. That's where I was this morning, begging him for an arrest or an investigation after I did all the damn legwork. 'Evidence obtained illegally is useless'." Connor pulls a face, imitating Maisy's dad's gruff voice. "Bullshit, right? Whatever, like hell I'm waiting around. We'll get him ourselves if we have to."

"You're throwing a lot at me," I say, head jumbled by the battering my emotions took and wary of where this is going. Connor has always had trouble with my favorite teacher.

"Coleman," he clarifies, watching me as he taps his laptop screen. He gestures to each of the windows as he talks. "If I didn't have the comments to compare the conversations to, I might not have figured it out, and then he said that freaky shit to you. It threw up red flags."

My lips part to interrupt, but he goes on before I voice my questions.

"I couldn't tie him to the creepy knight username concretely with an ip address match at first—bastard's damn good at covering his tracks—but there are these insane hackers also onto him, and they sent me on a wild goose chase to get one of Coleman's trophies back. They gave me the unsealed files once I did, but I'd already seen enough after I broke into his place."

"Broke in?" I yelp, pushing my fingers in my hair. He broke into our teacher's house? "Oh my god, Connor. What are you talking about?"

"I had to." He squeezes my knee. "I'd do anything to keep you safe."

There's so much to unpack. Between his confusing explanation and the information overload, I'm speechless. One window in particular pulls my focus and my body freezes.

The relief I felt moments ago vanishes. He already knows my secret. An instinctive refusal rears up, leaving me feeling exposed, but I swallow it back, trying to keep a level head.

He sees you. All of you.

"How did you find that?" With a shaking finger, I point at the browser window with my blog loaded.

"I hacked into your computer and it was in your recent browser history." Connor shoots me a look that says *not the important thing here,* and jabs his finger on the screen over Mr. Coleman's face. "I don't care about the blog. Although, really, if it's private you should've password protected it, but what matters is it was key in figuring out—"

"You hacked into my computer." The disbelief spiraling through me is profound. My voice is quiet, but he goes still at the monotone in it. "You spied on me! What gives you the right?"

Connor exhales in exasperation, brows pinched together. "Is that really what you're focused on when I'm showing you all this evidence that Coleman is an online predator? He gets off grooming his victims, knows exactly how to talk to them. He's a psycho."

"A *what?*"

My mind screams in denial at the word *victim.* It's not true. As much as I try to keep calm, a raw anguish overtakes me.

Ignoring the predator accusation for a minute, I hold my head in my hands. It feels like my secret has been wrenched from me, but it was mine to tell, not his to hunt down. "This is too much. If you knew about my blog, why didn't you talk to me about it sooner? Not that I have to explain anything to you, but it's a sensitive and personal escape for me."

Flashes of my conversations with my online boyfriend pop into my head, cut in a harsher light.

I was the one to give us that label. Henry never did. *No.* It can't be.

It hurts too much to think about. The only thing my brain can focus on is the lesser, but still stinging pain of Connor hacking my computer. Desperation to shut those old questions about Henry behind an iron wall has me pushing all of my anger on Connor.

"Damn it, Thea. It was before we were really together. I'm sorry I did it. I wasn't spying. Shit, I know it was wrong, baby. But it helped me find him. What Coleman was doing to you for years. Others, too."

Others. Doing to you. I shake my head, air catching in my throat. I'm not a victim. I stopped answering the emails. I never sent nude photos.

But Henry still controlled you.

The blog was my safe place to escape the nitpicking from Mom about my body. Henry poisoned it, his infection spreading deep until he had me in his web.

A pained noise escapes me.

Connor sets the laptop aside and picks up the thick file, flipping through to show me. "He's taught at two schools before he showed up in Ridgeview. He was fired from both after sexual harassment reports and complaints for inappropriate conduct."

Focusing on the pages as he talks is hard. I barely take in any of the information. My mind keeps chanting *no* over and over.

"He doesn't even hide how he favors his female students. And he was all over your blog comments even though you're inactive, then he's so focused on you at school. Think about when he showed up here. He's going to make you his next prize."

An unpleasant hot and cold sensation flies over my skin. This is insane. How could Henry and Mr. Coleman be the same? It's so much to think about. I can't accept it.

There's only one thing I can control right now: how I feel about the man I love invading my privacy.

Isn't that what Henry did?

Gritting my teeth, I shove the thought back into a mental abyss. *Stop it.*

Connor is acting like he was justified, as long as he got to find out his version of the truth. Forget who it hurts along the way in his search.

I'd rather deal with Vivian Bishop and my mother at the same time than face the truth—Connor spying on me.

This is the blackmail king of Silver Lake at his best.

Is this all I am to you?

"This is serious."

"I know!" Connor shouts. "That's what I'm trying to tell you."

"You had no right to worm your way into my secrets without my permission. Your jealousy of Mr. Coleman is out of control. You've been obsessed with him for months." I give a forceful shake of my head as I grasp at straws, unable to believe. "You could've fabricated photos to get him fired because you don't like him."

"Are you hearing yourself, Thea? You know me. Would I really put that much effort in when I could get rid of him in other, easier ways? I'm telling you the truth. It's far scarier than anything I could've made up about him."

"But you hacked my computer," I repeat, unable to let it go. It's the only thing I can process in this mess.

Twice in the last day I've defended him as a good guy. But he's been lying to me. I swallow, struggling to choose logic over the shaky emotions threatening to drown me. We always talk out our problems, but how can we work out a betrayal like this?

I thought we tore down our walls to be together. If he's still hiding behind his, I can't be with him. I want Connor, not the ruthless blackmail king.

Maybe it's time his whole damn castle burned down.

As soon as the thought hits me, I push it aside. That's not

us. My emotions are wreaking havoc on my mental state. These aren't rational thoughts. If there's one thing I've learned with Connor, we both need clear heads.

He cups my face with one hand and I push out of his grasp. He forces out an aggravated sound. "It was—I'm trying to protect you!"

"I didn't ask you to!" My yell echoes in the pool house.

I'm trying to stay calm, but it's impossible. The evidence he's forcing me to face is slicing me apart at the seams. My mind races in different directions, a base instinct seeking some way to control this so it stops hurting so much, to hide and go back to ten minutes ago before there was a possibility I could be a victim. That's not me. I don't want it to be.

Tears of overwhelm prick my eyes, turning my voice watery. "I've forgiven you for a lot, but I can't look past you invading my privacy and lying about it. I don't believe you. You're just playing god because you're obsessed with everyone's business, just like my mom and yours. You're too afraid to make your own life better, so you just ruin everyone else's!"

Connor jerks his head back as if I slapped him. "Why are you so focused on the hacking? So you kept a blog for your pictures—so what? Doesn't every girl do that these days?"

When he says it like that, it makes the insecurities I've struggled with about my body and feeling invisible seem so small and insignificant. Posting to the blog and finding Henry are the only things that helped me through that time in my life. How can he say it was fine to have my blog but tell me I was groomed by an online predator because of it?

And my abuser is Mr. Coleman? Rejection surges in my head. Maybe what I had with Henry wasn't normal and made me feel weird, but Henry *isn't* Mr. Coleman. He can't be. That would mean—

Before I can face the thought of sitting in class with Henry as the teacher instead of Mr. Coleman, I shut down, going completely numb. I wring my hands, taking unsteady breaths in through my nose to calm myself, like Maisy instructs me when I feel like I'll fly out of my skin.

"Are you okay?" Connor asks, backing off when he sees the state I'm in.

I shake my head, unable to formulate a verbal response.

"Here." Jaw tense, Connor pulls out a photo of a teenage girl that's so similar to the kind of photos Henry would ask for. "He has these on his computer—it's a big set up like mine, dual monitors. I have an encrypted copy of his hard drive, where I found this. I don't know whether he keeps them to himself or sells them or what, but he has more than one. We have to stop him."

Looking at it causes a riot in my body. I shy away.

Every photo I've ever sent Henry flashes in my head, along with the discomfort and uncertainty I felt every time I pushed back, only to be convinced to do what he asked. My stomach hurts. I block every thought about Henry from my mind, too vulnerable to think of those memories.

"Please," I whisper, throat burning. "I don't want to, Connor. I just want it to stop. It's too much."

A rough sound escapes him as he gathers me in his arms. "I'm sorry, baby. I don't want to hurt you with this. Just—fuck, okay, I know I messed up, but I'm trying to fix it. I don't want him touching you." Leaning back, he tries to hand me the evidence again. "Just look at the pictures in the file. He's got these creepy as shit trophies and necklaces with names. *Your* name!"

Another memory floats to the surface, murky and heart-stopping. There was a gift Henry said he had for me. Something special to show he cared. My stomach plummets.

"I have to go. I-I can't be here right now."

Connor growls, fisting his hands in his hair. "Thea!"

Pushing him back, I spring up from the bed. He stands from his kneel, following me as I pace across the room, whirling back, only to spin away again as thoughts run through my head.

"You asked me to tell you," he says. "I swore I would, and now you don't want to hear it."

"This isn't what I thought you'd say! How did you expect me to react to all this? I'm not—I'm not a—"

I can't force the word out. It sits on the tip of my tongue, driving daggers into me.

"Jesus," Connor snaps, throwing his fist into the wall when he can't control his temper.

I jump at the force of it, heart in my throat. I can't stand by and watch him injure himself with self-destructive behavior. It breaks me out of my spiral.

"What are you doing?" I rush to his side, taking his wrist to examine his red knuckles and the damage left behind in the wall. "Why?"

Connor clenches his jaw and a muscle twitches. "Seemed like a good idea."

"It wasn't." Sighing, I drop his hand. "I really can't do this right now."

"Look, we'll start over at the beginning." He holds up the file. "You have to listen."

It's too much to handle with Connor pressuring me to face a truth I can't cope with. I run my fingers through my hair and swallow past the searing heat in my throat. "Please. I can't."

"Thea, *listen* to me." He drops the file on the bed. "Let me explain."

"No! You should've told me right away instead of this. I thought we told each other everything." I'm near a breaking point, lashing out to protect myself from what I can't look at directly. It crushes me to see the disappointment on his face.

My chest heaves and my voice grows small. "I thought we were past the lies and games."

"It's not like you told me about this, either!" As soon as he says it, he jerks his head, holding a hand out to me. "Fuck, I didn't mean that. I'm sorry. All of it was to protect you from Coleman. This isn't what I wanted, baby."

Connor takes my hand as I rush toward the door. I tug free from his grip.

"Don't leave."

"I need to go. I just want to go lay down. I'm supposed to meet Maisy at the holiday market later. I came here to invite you, but...I think it's best if we both cool off. I need time and space to process this."

"Thea, please." He captures me in his arms and spins me around. "I'm sorry I ambushed you like this."

I lean back against the door. Everything feels too confusing. "You hurt me with your lie."

He releases a ragged breath, gray eyes filled with the same anguish plaguing me. "I never want to hurt you. Ever."

Despite the disappointment and anger, for a second I stay in his arms. A lump forms in my throat. I can't turn off the love I feel for him. I allow the safety of his strong embrace to be the balm I need.

"Let me go. We'll talk later. I just need to go be alone for a while. I'll think about what you said."

Connor's arms tighten around me before he steps back. We stare at each other for a beat, then I turn the knob.

"Wait," he says. "Here, take this with you." He pushes the thick file into my hands. "Look at it and call me when you're ready to talk." Taking my chin in his thumb and finger, he stares into my eyes. "I'm sorry I kept this from you. I'm sorry for hacking your computer, for everything. We'll do this together, like we should've from the start."

"Fine. But I need time." I pause on the threshold, glancing back. "Please don't do anything reckless."

The sight of Connor watching me walk away from him, face etched with the suppressed rage he battles against sears into my brain.

It's only once I make it inside my house and step under the blistering spray of hot water in the shower that I let the tears free.

THIRTY-FOUR
THEA

A week that started off with an amazing night in the mountains has turned into the hardest of my life. I had an aunt that lost her life too young. My boyfriend's mom cares more about her political career and image than her son's happiness. My *boyfriend* admitted he spied on me.

And the accusation of something even worse. Someone stalking and grooming me for years.

Victim.

The word causes my chest to cave. Crying in the shower hasn't made my fear of the word fade. Or what I'm blocking behind brick walls in my mind. They're cracking fast, crumbling to dust no matter how much I want to keep hiding from it.

The only thing the shower helped me see clearly was that I shouldn't have lashed out at Connor. I was putting all the blame on him because I was so scared to face questions I've asked myself about Henry.

It hurts that Connor spied on me, but as I pick through the denial with a clearer head, I see the real problem is Henry. What he really was. What he did.

I don't think I can stress bake my way out of this one.

Once the initial anger faded, burning off fast, I understood I was scared in the pool house. Afraid to face the truth beneath the surface all these years.

Some part of me knew it wasn't right, but I always pushed it aside. Now the burn of pain and humiliation is blistering. It's something that could happen to anyone, but I never thought it would be me.

I sat under the spray until it ran lukewarm, leaving my body pink and tender. It didn't wash away the feelings slithering beneath my skin.

Online boyfriend. It was the easiest way to explain away that I was talking about private things with someone I'd met on the internet. Easier to say we were together, because sending photos and having the intimate conversations we did... pretending to act out fantasies. I swallow thickly, shying from the thought. The things I did with Henry were the things couples do. I did them because if I didn't, he'd break up with me. But that doesn't make it okay.

What he did to me was wrong.

He used me. Abused me. Manipulated me when I was vulnerable, making sure I felt like shit if I refused to give him what he demanded. Punishing me for it with his silence until I was running back into his arms like a good little pet.

Henry was not an online boyfriend.

He is a predator.

Not only did he feed on my insecurities about my body—he made them worse. He actively whispered in my ear to knock me back in the dirt whenever I felt strong enough to overcome the negative thoughts, dragging me down with his claws into a pit of despair where he was the one in control of my happiness if he felt like giving it. *If* I did what he wanted.

Fear, that was how he controlled me.

A wheeze cracks my throat as I sit down hard on my bed, digging my fingers into the damp towel wrapped around me.

After a long minute, I lick my lips and take a deep breath.

"I am a victim," I say hoarsely, wincing at the word once more.

Saying it out loud makes it real. I can't run from it when it lives in my bones, lurking in my memories. I tremble on the bed, my knuckles white.

Did I bring this on myself? I responded to his attention in the first place.

As soon as the thought enters my mind, I vehemently refute it with a sharp jerk of my head. "No. I will not blame myself."

Nothing I do will change what happened to me. I was at a vulnerable age that caused a perfect storm. Mom might have driven my negative feelings about myself, but we both aren't to blame for this. Henry preyed on me. He is the only one to blame.

Acknowledgement of it all hurts. It's embarrassing to think a smart girl like myself could be duped. The truth I never dared face rakes me raw.

This is still a lot to think about all at once. I don't know if I can do it by myself without breaking down. Before I'm swallowed by my emotions, I finish getting dressed.

After a quick search online, I find therapists in the area who can help me process this. I save a list of potentials to the note app on my phone. Whether I decide to seek out therapy or not, I want to be prepared when I'm ready to cross that bridge.

For now, I need to get ready or I'll be late. Maisy is expecting me at the market. It's one of our favorite holiday activities to do together. I'm not missing out on it when it's exactly what I need—another afternoon with my best friend, hot chocolate with cinnamon and marshmallows, and something normal to take my mind off of all this for a while.

* * *

In the car on the way to meet Maisy, more memories and thoughts worm their way through the decimated remains of the mental walls, painting everything in a new light. It makes my heart beat hard and my palms sweat.

I want to stop thinking about it, but it's like being dumped in ice water. Every time my mind jumps off it, the wet clothes remind me how tightly they cling to my skin. I don't know how I lasted in denial about this for so long.

Would I ever have figured this out without Connor? Or would I have buried it deep down, pretending it was harmless, when in reality it was a poison flaring up when I least expected it?

Maybe I was an idiot.

With a sigh, I park the car. I'm not an idiot, but my mind is still jumbled. I'm beating myself up for something I couldn't control.

I knew I was uncomfortable in some way talking to Henry, but I always brushed it off in order to please him, too worried to let go of the connection to him. What if I didn't find someone else? I didn't want to go back to being invisible again.

"It will be okay," I murmur.

I grab my bag as I climb out of my car and follow the trickle of people walking to the holiday market. I didn't have time to hide the file I took from Connor before I left, and I couldn't chance Mom snooping, so I left it in my big purse and brought it with me. I might have come to terms with the truth about Henry abusing me, but I still need more time before going through whatever proof Connor handed over. Too much at once is devastating.

Besides, I'm here to take my mind off of this and enjoy the market with Maisy.

As I'm walking with the crowd, a couple catches my eye. I roll my lips between my teeth and push down the pang in my chest. I just need some time with Maisy, then I'll talk to Connor.

"Hey!" Maisy waves at me from the arched entrance wrapped in boughs of fir and festive ribbon. She's wearing maroon yoga pants, knee-high boots, and a vintage boho-style fringe poncho with a dark green fair isle pattern. Once I'm close, she does a double take. "Whoa, dude. Are you okay?"

I put on a little makeup to cover up before coming, but I guess it doesn't do much to help my swollen eyes. If I get into it now, I'll definitely break down again.

"Yeah. Still raw from everything." I offer a smile as I adjust the chunky scarf poking out of the neckline of my white wool coat. "I just want to have a good time."

"One good time, coming up."

Maisy hooks her arm with mine and leads us down the stall-lined main street. The folder sits heavily in my bag. My plan is to ignore it while Maisy and I stroll around the lively market.

The heavenly scents of spiced meat, cider, cinnamon, cranberries, and pine trees fill the air. It's everything *winter* and it smells amazing, lifting my spirits.

Maisy leans into my side, fluttering her lashes as she rolls her eyes back dramatically. "Oh my god, it smells so good."

"It does." This time my smile comes more easily. "First stop, hot drinks and pie pops?"

She snaps her fingers and points at me. "You read my mind."

We veer left toward our favorite stall to kick off our yearly tradition. Maisy gets a hot cider and I ask for extra marshmallows in my hot chocolate. We toast each other, tapping our cherry pie pops before laughing into the huge bites we stuff in our mouths. It feels really good to laugh. The tart burst of fruit on my tongue makes everything feel a little better.

"Ready to roll?" Maisy blows on her cider. "I think for this year's prank gift, I'm getting my mom one of those carvings with moose crap."

I snort as we amble with the flow of traffic, pausing at a few stalls to check out the wares on display. Maisy has a tradition where she tries to annoy her mom by getting her the weirdest gift she can find every year, acting like she really thought her mom would love it. Neither of them will give in or back down, so Maisy forges on with her mission.

"Trying to outdo that hideous cross stitch from last year?"

"She didn't even blink at that! I thought she would, I mean it was so detailed. How do you stitch shading for a bull's balls? A true artist at work."

"That thing still gives me nightmares."

Maisy muffles a proud laugh as she sips her cider.

A couple bumps into me at the next stall, not apologizing for being so wrapped up in each other they don't notice me. My heart gives another feeble pang. The man's cologne smells similar to the earthy one Connor wears. With a polite smile, I sidestep the pair to check out the crystals and gemstones on the shelves. Maisy makes a sound like she found one she likes, and gets lost in a conversation with the vendor about crystals for empowering and boosting yoga practice.

I tune it out as I poke at the pretty stones on one of the tables. The basket at the end of the row stops me. It's full of moonstones, reminding me of Connor once more.

Gulping the dregs of my drink, I slip outside to toss the cup, putting him from my mind. I bump into someone.

"Sorry!" I put my hands up to brace myself and catch my balance.

"Thea." Mr. Coleman gives me a handsome smile. "It's so good to see you outside of class."

"Mr. C." The high-octave surprise in my tone has him tipping his head. My bag suddenly weighs a thousand pounds with Connor's file inside sitting like a brick. All the accusations float up to the forefront of my thoughts. They test the impression of the cool, kind teacher I thought of him as, small fissures running along the facade. An uncomfortable pitter-patter moves through my chest. I edge back a step, putting more distance between us. "Uh, hi. You're here, too."

"I am. The holiday bazaar in Ridgeview is one of my favorites in the area. I'm a real sucker for the mulled wine." He chuckles and reaches out to pat my shoulder. "I hope your break is going well."

He pauses when I flinch and step back again. Henry flashes in my mind and my skin crawls.

Maisy saves me from answering, slinging her arm over my shoulder. "They had such a good deal on rose quartz!"

"That's great," I say in a strained voice. "Well, bye Mr. C. Enjoy the market."

I feel his eyes on my back as Maisy and I keep walking. Can't I get one afternoon away from my problems?

Apparently not, because every couple-oriented ornament, holiday song, and activity at the market bombard me the further we go. Damn Connor for owning my thoughts. One of his hugs would feel so good right now.

"Oh damn, look how long the line is." Maisy motions to the bathrooms, where she pulled us after the last stall. "Don't wait up."

"Are you sure? I don't mind."

"It's fine. Go ahead." She points at me with a sly smirk. "Keep your eye out for a good prank gift for me."

"We can meet up by the tree display in the middle when you're done," I offer.

"Perfect."

Leaving Maisy, I tuck my hands in my coat pockets and continue browsing. I'm looking at a vendor with wooden holiday ornaments when I spot Mr. Coleman again at the next booth, enraptured by the jewelry. The necklaces in particular have his attention.

Uneasiness whispers in my mind. Connor swore he was dangerous.

I abandon the laser-cut ornament with baking tools dangling beneath a pie to sneak closer, observing Mr. Coleman's actions. He touches the jewelry with a meticulous focus, stroking each pendant. It brings up the memory of the necklace Henry planned to send me. After selecting one, he stands in line to pay.

A woman runs the stall, but she hands off Mr. Coleman's necklace to her teenage daughter while another customer asks her for help. I bite my lip as Mr. Coleman's eyes light up. He leans closer to the daughter, talking to her. She's flustered but peeks at him shyly as she packages his purchase. His hand brushes hers as he takes the bag.

The corners of my mouth turn down. Glancing around, I follow him, keeping several feet behind so I can duck out of sight.

Mr. Coleman meets up with a girl from Silver Lake High, a sophomore, I think. She doesn't seem wary as they chat, but I can't stop watching. He gives her a serene smile, all his attention focused on her. Whatever he says makes her giggle.

She kind of looks like me. Similar shade of red hair, same white coat I have on today. I swallow as Connor's voice fills my mind.

He's so focused on you at school.

Maybe it's because I'm used to him in one setting and now he's out of that box that has everything feeling so off. It's not that he's doing anything crazy, but now that I'm watching him with Connor's words in my head, it feels questionable.

He could be Henry. Imagining it sends my stomach into an uncomfortable flip.

I shake my head, sucking in air.

This is ridiculous. I'm hiding behind a large quilt in the middle of the holiday market, stalking my teacher.

I ball my fists, but I don't walk away, tethered to my hiding spot. Because what if it's not as harmless as it appears? Henry is in my past, but if he's not? Then the danger is even more real.

Mr. Coleman gives the bag to the girl. She's delighted as she pulls out the necklace he bought. She tries to give it back, but he must insist because he curls his fingers over hers, closing the jewelry in her hand.

Without hearing their conversation, I'm jumping to conclusions about what's happening. Is it the first time he's given her a gift? Is he grooming her?

I'm lost in my head, but when I zone back in, the quilt hiding me is pulled aside as another shopper debates between two choices. His attention is on me. He caught me. Crap.

Mr. Coleman nods to the sophomore girl and walks over to the quilt vendor before I can brush off following him or give him the slip into another stall.

"Hello again."

"My mom loves these quilts." As soon as the words are out of my mouth, I want to dive under the blankets hanging around the hut. Curse my nervous babbling.

Mr. Coleman's brows lift. "Is that so?" He pinches one of the smaller throw sized blankets hanging behind me, reaching over my shoulder to do it. My spine goes rigid. "Ah, yes. It's made nicely."

He doesn't leave, so I'm forced to make small talk as he fondles the blanket over my shoulder. "Are you enjoying the market?"

Mr. Coleman hums. His gaze slides back to me. "You could've asked to walk with me if that's what you wanted instead of following me. There's no harm in it outside of class, right?"

What? No, that's not what I wanted. It's a really odd response. Back at the pool house I wasn't thinking straight, but face-to-face with Mr. Coleman, I'm on high alert.

The way he's honed in on me that makes my heartbeat spike in a horrible way. I want to walk away.

"I was kinda wandering aimlessly. My friend is in the bathroom line, but we're meeting up. I was just killing time."

He watches me for a long beat. *It's not a fixation*, I tell myself, clinging to desperation. He doesn't have to be Henry. That monster can stay in the past where he can't hurt me anymore.

"Well, enjoy yourself." Mr. Coleman steps back, dropping his arm from feeling up the blanket. "If I don't see you again, have a wonderful holiday."

"Bye." Not waiting, I hurry away, hoping Maisy is already waiting at the tree display when I get there.

I came out today to get my mind off all of this, but it

followed me here anyway. Maybe I should tell her we can come back again another day.

When I make it to the tree display, I circle it twice. She isn't there yet. I check my phone and curse under my breath. The battery is on 1%.

"Seriously? Unbelievable."

Pawing through my bag, I don't find the charger, remembering I left it in the car. I chew my lip. If I hurry, I can grab it and make it back here. The coffee shop has outlets I can use. I shoot Maisy a text before my phone dies to let her know to meet me at the coffee shop instead, then leave the cheery holiday festival behind to return to the parking area.

The late afternoon sun cuts across the street as it falls closer to the ridge line in the distance. I have to charge my phone before it gets dark, or Maisy and I might miss each other.

My plan goes up in smoke when I reach my car. Mr. Coleman is parked a few spots away, and the sophomore girl from before is with him. They climb into his car.

"Oh no."

If Mr. Coleman is Henry, I don't want him to hurt anyone else.

I squeeze my bag against my side, feeling the heavy file stuffed in it. Making a decision, I unlock my car and slide in. Something in me can't leave the girl alone. I'd never forgive myself for abandoning someone potentially in danger if I could do something to help.

As Mr. Coleman pulls out, I follow in my car, hoping he doesn't spot me tailing him in the rearview. The whole way, my fingers tap on the wheel and I scrape my teeth over my lip until it's tender and raw.

"It'll be fine," I repeat over and over.

THIRTY-FIVE
THEA

The drive isn't long. Mr. Coleman pulls off onto a residential road not far from downtown. There are a handful of houses on the short dead end street, a patch of woods beyond that. Most are decorated for the holidays with lights and lawn ornaments, but Mr. Coleman's car pulls into the driveway of the one house on the block without festive trimmings.

Feeling too conspicuous, I park my car a few houses away, scooting low in my seat so I go unnoticed. I hold my breath as they get out of the car, prepared to dart across the street to save my lookalike. Mr. Coleman gestures with one hand as he talks, the other tucked in his coat pocket. My heart shoots into my throat as the girl beams and follows him inside.

"No! Don't go inside! Shit." My knee bounces as my worry rises.

I can't just walk up to his door. He already caught me following him once today. What can I do?

Rubbing my forehead, I finally reach for the folder in my bag. My hands shake as I open it, fully ready to believe Connor.

The name on the records has me releasing a choked sound —*Harold Knight Coleman.* Henry's email was *henry.k.c.* The initials are the same. I frantically flip through the photos and copies of reports in the file as my breathing turns shallow. With shaking hands I lift a photo of myself, one I remember emailing to Henry when I was fifteen.

"Oh my god. No."

I didn't want it to be true, because thinking about it already hurts. The overwhelm crashes back into me and I squeeze the edges of the folder until the pages crinkle. God, I sat in his classroom when he had my photos, *knew* who I was.

A strangled sob escapes me.

The next photo in the file is a row of gold heart-shaped necklaces against dark velvet, each with a name card. One of them has my name on it, just like Connor said. Shit.

I can't run from the agonizing truth any longer.

Mr. Coleman was the monster all along. The one who kept me from growing out of my insecurities, making them fester with his manipulation and abuse. He is Henry, my abuser.

And now he has another young teenage girl in his house.

My chest feels tight.

Connor was right. I wish I hadn't hidden behind denial and listened to him.

I want to tell him, but when I grab my phone, it's dead. I never plugged it into the car charger on the drive over, too worried I'd lose track of Mr. Coleman's car. Now I'm kicking myself. When I try the power button, the battery icon blinks on the screen, mocking me in its uselessness. I can't even call Maisy's dad about Mr. Coleman to make a report about what happened to me.

Glancing from my phone to his porch, I blow out a breath. I can't wait for the phone to charge. The sophomore girl is still inside. He could be trapping her right now. If I leave to get help, will it be too late for her? Maybe I can knock on the doors of other people on the block. But how long will it take?

There's one thing I know for certain: I won't stand by and let Mr. Coleman harm any other girls like he hurt me. I've seen the folder. Hell, I *lived* the folder.

I have to do something.

Stuffing the file back in my purse, I take the bag and grab the all-in-one tool from the glove box Maisy insisted I have. It's for car accidents, but it could do damage as a weapon in an emergency. Climbing out of the car, I shove it in my coat pocket as I hurry to the closest house across from Mr. Coleman's. I knock on the door, but there's no answer. I knock again, shifting restlessly on my feet.

"Come on. Damn it. Why doesn't anyone answer their doors anymore?"

I run to the next house over, trying there. No one answers. This is wasting time.

Shaking out my hands, I head for Mr. Coleman's house. I keep low as I sneak around, peeking in windows carefully. Inside, it's rundown with cracks in the plastered walls. My breath catches at the sight of the dual monitor computer surrounded by an array of old takeout containers. I still don't see anyone, so I continue around the side of the house. Voices from inside drift out through the old, grimy windows.

"...sure you have to go right away? I insist, stay for a quick cup of cocoa," Mr. Coleman says. "It'll warm you up from the chill."

Only part of their conversation is audible as I strain my ears, crouched beneath a window.

"...supposed to get back, but..."

"Don't be silly," he says, closer to the window. I hold my breath. "There's no rush, right?" There's a slight pause, then, "That's the holiday spirit. Never too much cocoa. I'll put on some music, too."

She must have agreed. I shift around, but in the fading light I misjudge the distance between my hip and the recycling cans near the window, accidentally knocking into one.

"Crap, crap, crap," I hiss, steadying them before they make too much noise. Hopefully Mr. Coleman didn't hear that. Or if he did, writes it off as a wild animal.

Holiday music starts playing. I try to peek in another window to see if I can gesture to the girl to warn her off, but it's too dark inside to see anything. Why aren't any of the lights on?

I skirt around to the back door to see if I can hear better. Before I reach the handle, a hand covers my mouth as I'm grabbed.

"*Mmph!*"

Lips press against my ear, making my skin crawl when I hear Mr. Coleman's husky voice. "You came, princess. I thought that was your little blue car in my mirror. Following me, sneaking around out here playing naughty games? Well, if you insist. I'll have to punish you later."

White-hot panic rushes up my spine. I kick and thrash, but he's strong. I try to scream, but his hand muffles it.

When did he come outside? Oh god, this can't be happening!

"Ah, ah. You came to me. I'm your knight, princess. Stop fighting it." His demeanor has changed from earlier, bordering on manic. "I've been waiting for you. I've wanted to tell you for so long—every day in class. Having you chase me at the market was so thrilling. I knew you must have realized it and couldn't stay away any longer." He presses his nose into my hair as I struggle. "But you're making this hard for me by misbehaving."

I'm your knight, princess.

No.

No fucking way.

He's spouting words he's typed to me a hundred times over. A sickening sensation travels through my body.

This is worse than every nightmare I've ever had come to life.

Mr. Coleman keeps my arms pinned tight. I'm too short to crack my skull back into his. I try to bite him, to yell, but he squeezes my face hard enough to hurt.

Everything in my body screams in protest at his harsh grip. I feel violated all over again, worse this time with his hands all over me. His breath is hot on the back of my neck as he grunts against my frantic flailing.

No!

Escaping his hold is impossible, but I manage to worm my fingers into my coat pocket. They slip on the smooth handle of the all-in-one tool. My chest caves with a desperate, smothered cry.

Please, please.

When I have it, I release a wild sound, swinging as hard as I can with limited motion. Mr. Coleman grunts as I catch him in the leg with the hard tip meant for breaking glass. But it doesn't work for him to release me like I wanted. I didn't strike hard enough.

He wrenches the tool from my grasp and throws it aside in the dead grass. That was my only weapon against him!

"Mmph! Mmmph!" My protests come out as muffled grunts.

His voice is a low growl in my ear as he lifts me from the

ground. "You'll behave, pet. I don't want to punish you too harshly, but I will."

Terror spears through my body as he crushes me against the back door, covering my back to pin me there. My nostrils flare with each panicked, labored breath.

He has me inside before I can fight him off. I try to scream again, to warn the sophomore girl, but with his hand over my mouth and holiday music playing, I go unheard.

My pulse races as he shoves me through another door, then down a short flight of steps into a basement off the kitchen. I squirm to reach for something I can use against him. Anything to stun him long enough to escape.

My feet jar as he drops me back to the ground, sending me stumbling from the jolt. A second later, he shoves me against a workbench with shelves of cubby holes. My bag drops to the ground as I try to break his hold. In the struggle, my head knocks into a shelf, spreading a jarring pain in my skull and making my vision swim. Everything goes black around the edges, a strange pulse in my head leaving me woozy.

He watches me with calculating, narrowed eyes, then steps back. Without his disgusting hands holding me up, the dizziness gets worse and I slump against the table, then collapse to the floor. I try to form words with my heavy tongue, but everything goes black.

Open your eyes! Get up!

Cracking my eyes open takes effort. I think I try it multiple times as I sit on the dusty floor because distorted flashes of Mr. Coleman slip through the throbbing in my head. Watching me. Getting a tool and extension cords. His back to me as he climbs the stairs.

Now! Escape now!

When I come to, I'm alone. I don't know how much time it's been. Seconds? Minutes? Hours? I scrub a hand over my face and climb to my feet. My head still hurts, but the dizziness that made me black out has passed.

It can't be long if my head is still tender. I wince, carefully prodding at my skull.

The room grows dimmer as the last of the daylight outside fades into dusk. No lights are on, swallowing me in shadows and darkness.

My chest heaves as my breathing speeds back up. I race up the steps, but the door is locked. The music is turned down lower. I smack my palm against the door.

"Help! Hey! Help me! Let me out!" As I scream, I jiggle the doorknob. No matter how hard I yank on the handle, it doesn't budge. My palm stings from banging so hard.

Mr. Coleman's muted voice travels through the door, sounding far away. I pause to press my ear to the door. "...no problem. Tell your parents they can borrow from me anytime. Goodnight."

The extension cords. That was why she came in? I thought—

Shit! I wanted to help the other girl, but now Mr. Coleman has *me*. How the hell am I getting out of this?!

My nerve endings feel flayed from the dread choking me.

Was it a mistake to want to help? I didn't have any other choice. A swollen lump lodges in my throat as I press my forehead to the door, breathing through the rush of emotions.

Princess.

Repulsion rushes over my body. How could I have thought that pet name made me feel special at fifteen? Now it only sends wave after wave of nausea through me. I'm trapped by my abuser. What will he do to me?

At least the other girl got away. That's the only silver lining I can cling to right now. Mr. Coleman took me instead.

I'm sorry, Connor. I'm sorry I messed up so badly.

If I hadn't shut down in denial, I wouldn't be here right now.

I wish Connor were here. He has stepped in so many times, not trusting Mr. Coleman around me. But wishing for him won't save me.

I have to save myself.

I'll get out of this. I have to.

Be brave.

THIRTY-SIX
CONNOR

After cooling off by beating shit up with my bat at the abandoned quarry for a couple hours to give Thea space and get my thoughts off my major failure, I'm worn out but feeling less like I'm about to split apart.

The late afternoon sun dips low, creeping behind the ridgeline as dusk falls, casting long shadows across the weed-choked gravel lot. Thea asked me not to do anything stupid, so I came out here to work out my frustration rather than put more holes in the pool house wall.

With my head refocused, I'm ready to try talking to her again. I told her I'd let her come to me, but we don't have the time. Two hours to calm down is long enough.

It was a mistake to ambush her with all the information at once, especially after she told me what Mom did to her. I should've come at it from a different angle, starting with Coleman. Keeping everything from her was killing me, so it poured out all at once.

Worse, I hated the panicked look on her face and the tears in her eyes as she left. I hate making her cry.

I sit in my Lexus GX with the door open and call her to find out what part of the holiday market she's at. It goes to voicemail.

"Hi! You've reached Thea. I'm unavailable at the moment, probably because I'm up to my elbows in cake batter. Leave a message and I'll call you back soon!"

I lift the phone away from my ear, scowling at it. I almost never get her voicemail when I call.

A bad feeling slices through me.

When my phone pings with a message, I relax. She's fine, it must be loud at the market. Missed the call. That's all.

But it's not Thea when I open it. The text is from a contact in my phone I don't remember putting in—the name blank except for a skull and crown emoji.

"Those crow bastards," I grumble, opening the video clip.

As the CCTV footage plays, my heart stutters to a stop. *Fuck.*

It shows Thea following Coleman at the holiday market, then talking to him. He's standing way too close to her for comfort. The last angle isn't clear, but there's a girl getting in Coleman's car with him, driving off. She's wearing the same wool jacket as Thea's. My mind jumps to the worst.

Nothing else matters but getting her back.

"Goddamn it!" I pound my fist against the wheel, flying into motion. "This can not be happening right now."

How can Thea be in the exact danger I was trying to

protect her from? How could she get in a car and go anywhere with Coleman after what I tried to show her?

I should've followed her instead of cooling my head. My heart beats in double time as I fight off the sick sensation of failing her.

I can't lose the girl I love.

We have so much ahead of us still, our entire future together.

I pull out of the quarry in a spray of dust and gravel. The tires skip over the road in a high-pitched squeal, and the lingering scent of burnt rubber tickles my nostrils. I push the gas harder, speeding toward my house. I need a weapon before I go save her from him.

And I *will* save her. She's the most important person to me.

If I'm the storm tearing through everything, Thea is the sunlight that breaks through in my wake. A sun captured by the moon, eclipsed by love. She pierces through my darkness with her light.

Thea is it for me. She's the girl I plan to marry. The only queen I want by my side. I'll spend the rest of my life groveling for every mistake I've made if it means we make it out of this.

I'm close to breaking my teeth from grinding them so hard as I take corners too fast. The car screeches as I brake hard in the middle of the street, throwing it in park while I burst from the car to run across the lawn to my house.

Nothing registers but my goal: Dad's gun safe.

It's in his study on the first floor. The door hits the wall when I fling it open, but I don't care. I go to the desk, open the bottom drawer, and punch in the access code. I looked over Dad's shoulder when he was showing it to me before he took me to the gun range to learn how to shoot.

The 9mm Glock sits in the foam casing. Wasting no time, I take it and get bullets from where he keeps them.

Once I'm back outside with the gun tucked away so I don't give the neighbors a heart attack, I get back in the SUV and floor it toward Coleman's to rescue my girl. On the way, I call Devlin.

"*Yo. What's up?*"

"Get the cops to Coleman's," I demand, speeding through a red light at an empty intersection. I need to make it there before I get pulled over for reckless driving. "Do whatever you have to. Call in a suspected shooting. Start a fire. I don't care, just do it."

"*Whoa, slow down,*" Devlin says. "*The fuck are you on about?*"

I smack the wheel. "He has Thea!"

"*Shit. Okay, got it.*"

I push the car faster, hoping I'm not too late.

THIRTY-SEVEN
THEA

While I scramble in the darkness, searching the workbench for another weapon to defend myself, the basement door opens. My stomach lurches. A dim, flickering bulb blinks to life, casting the basement in sickly yellow light.

Oh god. He's back.

"Kicking up all that fuss and not behaving. Tsk, tsk," Mr. Coleman says in an eerie tone as he descends the rickety wooden steps. "I don't know if you deserve this gift or not. But you've always been my special princess, haven't you?"

Shoulders rigid with terror, I spin to face him with a strangled cry, my head throbbing with dull pain from the sudden movement.

Mr. Coleman stands between me and the exit. I feel blindly behind me and wrap my fingers around a small tool handle—tiny screwdriver, maybe? I don't know. It feels like the kind used on computers. I can't look, not willing to risk drawing his attention to it.

It won't do a lot of damage, but it's all I feel behind me without continuing my search.

He reaches the bottom step, presenting me with the same necklace from the file half-spilled out of my purse on the dingy floor. It's a gold heart dangling from a dainty chain.

"Mr. Coleman," I try, my tongue sluggish. Maybe I can talk my way out in order to escape from this monster. "Why are you doing this?"

Ignoring my question, he glides across the floor. "I didn't want to say anything earlier, but your eyes are all swollen and bloodshot. I know the result of crying when I see it. I'll make it all better." He speaks in a soft, reverent tone. "Princess, are you ready to take my hand?"

Fuck, what can I do? He has me cornered. He's too far away to stab without losing the element of surprise, and too strong if I run without diverting him first. I need to get to those stairs.

"The other girl," I whisper.

"Hmm, yes. I thought about keeping her, but then you came right to me. I'd much rather have my prize instead. I knew you couldn't stay away forever. You don't have to be jealous of the others."

He's not just manic—he's delusional. He thinks I want him. A fierce wave of nausea upsets my stomach.

I need something to distract him. There's a paint can on a bench next to the worktable, just out of reach while his attention is on me. An old rolling chair sits at the edge of the pool of yellow light. Maybe I can knock him off balance?

While I'm searching for something else to use against him, Mr. Coleman steps closer. I jump aside in revolt, but he traps me with a terrifying chuckle, his chest touching me as I lean back against the worktable until it digs into my back.

"Where do you think you're going, pet?"

Another panicked noise catches in my throat as I try to edge away. My nails dig into my palm around the screwdriver's handle.

Wrong, wrong, wrong, my mind clangs.

"You...you said your name was Henry," I babble, mind racing to figure a way out of this without ending up like my mom's sister. I'm so scared of what he'll do to me, the fear making it hard to move. Whenever he was mad because I didn't do what he wanted, he would flay me with words once I crawled back. Now, he could do so much worse. "And that you were only three years older than me. We stopped, I-I stopped answering."

Mr. Coleman touches my hair and I flinch with a frightened sound. "Shh, my darling. I know it's upsetting to find out I lied, but they were little lies. Necessary ones. You were so young, so I didn't want to scare you off. Not when our souls were speaking so clearly to one another."

Bile rushes up my throat.

His eyes dance back and forth between mine. He cocks his head. "I know you felt it, too. Every class, I longed to reach out." His mouth curves into an ugly, lopsided grin. "You're always so eager for me."

I shake my head, unable to speak. The tears welling in my eyes wobble, blurring my vision. When I blink, they burn hot paths down my cheeks.

"Don't cry, pet," he says in a light, haunting tone. "I got you this gift, see? I want to show you how special you are to me. You'll wear this and know you're mine."

So special he has several other matching ones for however many girls he's done this to.

As he leans back to fumble with the chain, he spots my purse on the floor with the file sticking from it. One of my photos peeks out far enough to see what it is. He lowers the necklace, staring at the picture.

Ice shoots through my veins.

"What's this?" Mr. Coleman sounds annoyed, sending my heart tripping over a beat in fear I've made him mad. He snatches the bag, digging the folder of evidence out.

"No, don't!"

His face turns to stone as he flips through the file while I'm plastered against the worktable in horror.

"Why do you have this, Thea?" I didn't think it was possible, but his creepy factor ratchets up another degree when he turns his gaze back on me, eyes dead and soulless. He sighs in disappointment. "I can't let you leave here now, princess."

"W-Why? That would be bad. Wrong. Please." My voice trembles. Every part of my body quakes in fear. "It's fine. I won't tell. You can let me go. We'll pretend nothing happened."

He barks out a sharp sound, shaking his head as he comes close again. "Nothing, is it? You're ruining our nice evening together."

"Please," I whisper hoarsely. "You don't have to do this."

"Princess," he says as he strokes my cheek, leaning close enough to nearly brush his lips over mine. With a sharp intake of air, I jerk my head to the side, but he grips my chin in a punishing grip and yanks me back. His touch feels like barbed wire tearing through my gut. "What makes you think I can resist when I have you here? You ran right into my arms."

I shake my head in denial, struggling to free myself from his hold. Maybe if I play along again, he'll let me go. It might give me enough time to grab the paint can if he doesn't think I'm going to run. He was always more receptive when I made clumsy attempts to take initiative in his games. It makes me sick to my stomach, but I can do this. I fight back the nausea rolling through me and force my body to relax.

"It's just..." My voice is scratchy and small. *Come on, Thea. Do this and maybe you get to escape your nightmare and live.* "It's just, my mom. She's strict."

Mr. Coleman coos to pacify my false worries. "We'll sort it all out, princess. We'll leave town if we have to. If no one understands us, we'll just go."

"Or, we could just wait until graduation. My friends are here." I'm grasping for anything to make him disregard me as a flight risk or a threat enough to back off. As soon as I have space, I'll distract him and run. The door isn't locked anymore. It's left open at the top of the steps. "We'll make it like a game. Secret meetings."

Using something so close to my love story with Connor rakes hot coals over my heart, but I'm so stressed out and scared. I'll say anything to appease the man caging me against the worktable.

Mr. Coleman hums in consideration, studying me. I think he likes the idea. "A game."

I nod eagerly. "Yes! No one will know we're t-together. It'll be fun. Our little secret, just like our emails."

"Yes, you're onto something there." He taps my nose and finally takes a step back. "Right under everyone's noses. No one will know I've fucked you on my desk, had you on your knees beneath it with those incredible lips sucking my cock. Mm, princess. This is a wonderful idea. I always knew you were my favorite of my girls for a reason."

His grin stretches into something hideous as I swallow my gag. At last he turns his back on me as he ruminates on his disgusting fantasies of having me. While he's distracted, I snatch the nearby paint can, heart thumping violently. It's not as heavy as I hoped, maybe half-full, but I throw it as hard as possible. It smashes into his head, disorienting him.

The papers in the file spill to the floor as he stumbles, catching himself on the rolling chair. It crashes as his body weight collides with it.

I don't wait, dashing for the stairs to get to the kitchen, still armed with the screwdriver. A grunt and heavy footsteps are right on my heels. I push my legs to move as fast as possible so I can outrun the monster chasing me.

"No you don't!" The sound of his feet pounding on the creaking wooden stairs will haunt me forever if I make it out of this alive.

I scream as his weight collides into my back once I've made it through the basement door, tackling me. We land against the kitchen table, shattering a glass in the fall. It cuts one of my palms as I try to push him off. From this angle, the best I can manage is stabbing the small screwdriver clutched in my grip into Mr. Coleman's leg, squeezing so hard the handle hurts the bones in my hand. He lets out a furious shout as we thrash against the table.

"You're all mine, princess." He hisses into the back of my neck, breath humid. "Your knight will take good care of you."

A heavy bang sounds nearby. Mr. Coleman growls.

Pinned in place with my stalker panting against my neck, I fear for my life. Tears stream down my face while I struggle, my breaths coming short and fast, burning my lungs.

My heart breaks in a splintering mess.

I wasn't good enough. Not strong enough or fast enough. Not brave enough. I didn't escape.

Am I about to end up like my mother's dead sister after all?

THIRTY-EIGHT
CONNOR

Thea's Mini Cooper is the first thing I spot when I whip onto Coleman's street. I park crookedly behind it and check the handgun once I load the full magazine. There's no time to waste. It's past dusk now, making it easier for me to sneak around Coleman's house in the dark.

The cops haven't arrived yet.

"Where are they?"

Five to six minute response time, my ass. I made it in under fifteen minutes breaking every speeding law. With a muffled, aggravated exhale, I circle toward the backyard.

No lights are on in any of the windows. I strain my ears, listening for any sign of life in the house. It's hard to focus when my pulse won't stop pounding over everything. If they aren't here, he could've taken her to a second location.

Thea has to be here.

Keeping low, I creep up to the back door, gun squeezed in my grip.

All bets are off once I hear a shout. The back door is locked when I grab the knob. There isn't a window to smash to reach in and unlock it. Coleman's house is older, maybe I can—

Thea's scream followed by a crash makes my heart stutter.

"Fuck!"

Stepping back to center myself, I kick next to the knob as hard as I can. The old wood cracks, but it's not good enough. Nothing will keep me from getting in this fucking house. With a grunt, I kick again, then another. The frame breaks as I bust through the door.

It's mostly dark, the only light coming from an open basement door, but I make out Coleman pinning Thea to the table in the middle of the kitchen. He wrenches his head up, glaring in my direction. I slap my hand against the wall and flick on the light. Coleman squints as the brightness blinds him momentarily.

"Connor!" Thea screams, desperate and pleading as she struggles beneath her attacker, craning her neck to see me.

"I'm here!"

Coleman snarls, bracing his forearm against the back of Thea's shoulders to keep her in place. There are splotches of blood on her white coat—*hers or his?* She chokes on a sob, nails scrabbling for purchase on the table amidst broken glass.

The sight of Coleman on top of her, the tears staining her blotchy cheeks, her terrified cry, it all makes me wild with the need to protect her.

"Get the fuck off of her!" I lift the gun to make the threat clear, my savage yell echoing in the room. I hope the neighbors hear the commotion of the break in or the goddamn police get here soon.

"What are you doing here? Leave, or I'll call the cops," Coleman sneers. "You're not wanted."

"Nah, man. Not a chance in hell." I bark out a laugh. "The cops? Already on their way. Besides, you think they'll care about busting in your back door when they find out what the fuck you like to get up to? They already know. You're finished." I level the gun, aiming at Coleman. My tone turns deadly. "Now get the fuck off."

Coleman ignores the gun pointed at him and plasters himself over Thea's back, messing up my clean shot. He angles his head and shoots me an evil smirk. "You won't do it. You're nothing but a spoiled, cocky pissant playing hero."

Beneath him, Thea growls, my fierce fighter not giving up. She bucks, but he still holds her easily, keeping her at a disadvantage.

"You think I won't?" I advance two steps, hissing through clenched teeth. I'm done playing around. "I've been itching to kill you for weeks, since I first broke in. This," I gesture with the gun, encompassing the room and the situation, luring him into believing I'm crazy and untrained in handling a firearm, "fucking escalates that mood. I won't even flinch when I put a bullet in you."

My gaze slides to Thea for a fraction of a second, meeting her glistening eyes. She shakes her head slightly, not drawing any more attention to herself. I try to communicate that it will be okay. I'll get her out of this.

Swinging my focus back to Coleman, I take careful aim. "Sunshine, tell this degenerate sack of shit I'm a little unhinged. And the thing is, *Harold*, you're all over my girl. She doesn't seem happy about it. I'm not happy about it, either. You have three seconds. Three...two..."

Before I get to one, I squeeze the trigger. I fire while aiming close enough to Coleman in the hope it will spook him so Thea can get away. The gunshot is sharp and piercing.

Coleman does startle, staggering back against the wall, howling and holding his ear. Thea yelps, rolling away as soon as he moves. She drops to the floor out of sight behind the table. Coleman's hand comes away shining with blood from where the bullet grazed him.

"You little piece of shit." He charges across the room.

I fire again, but miss. Coleman barrels into me. My hip hits the edge of the cheap tile counter, sending a shock of pain through my body as we struggle for control of the weapon. In our wrestling, I get a solid punch in, but Coleman drags me to the ground. The gun slides across the floor when he slams my hand down, weakening my grip.

We both dive, but he gets there first.

Shit, shit.

"Thea, run!" I shout. "Get out of here!"

Her shoes squeak against the floor as she moves.

Coleman jabs the gun under my chin, bruising my skin with the force of it. His expression is crazed, perfectly coiffed hair hanging in his face.

"You're done. All I have to do is get rid of you, then she's mine."

Even if I die here tonight, at least she'll be safe.

I struggle, pushing against his wrists, managing to move his aim. The gun fires and intense blistering agony bites into my upper arm.

"Fuck!" I slam my head forward, glancing off Coleman's chin, then slump over when I put too much pressure on my injured arm.

Holy shit that hurts.

"Connor! No!" Thea wails from somewhere in the room.

"Stop it!"

Damn it, why is she still here? I told her to escape!

Coleman gets up on his knees and points the gun at my face. Fuck, this is it.

Then a loud *whack* has Coleman's eyes rolling back in his head as he collapses to the side, revealing Thea standing over him with a bright blue kettle, panting.

"Oh my god," she breathes as she drops it and crashes to her knees beside me. Her hands flutter over my hoodie where it's warm and sticky. "He shot you. Oh my god. We have to stop the bleeding."

"It's fine, come here." Grunting, I clutch her close with my uninjured arm, stroking her hair. She flinches when I brush over a lump. I'm woozy and aching, but the only thing that matters to me is her. "I'm sorry, Thea. I'm so sorry. I shouldn't have let you leave."

"No, shh, I'm sorry," Thea whispers, hugging me until I wince. "Shit. God, I'm sorry I didn't listen. I should've listened. I came here alone, it was so stupid, but I had to help her. I couldn't let him hurt her like he hurt me, I—"

"You're safe now. It'll be okay, baby."

She fusses over the wound, finding a dish towel to help stem the bleeding, and helps me sit up. I can't tell if it was my shoulder or lower, my whole arm throbs. I can move it, so I don't think he hit bone. If I'm lucky, it was a graze or a clean through and through. We shuffle further away from Coleman's knocked out body.

"Can you stand? We have to get you to the hospital."

"Yeah." I lean on her for support. The red staining her pristine coat catches my eye. "The blood on your coat, are you—?"

"I'm fine. Just a little banged up." She shows me her palm, where a shallow cut has mostly clotted over. "Broken glass. But I stabbed him with a screwdriver I found in the basement."

The corner of my mouth lifts. "That's my girl. Resourceful even in a crisis."

Her lower lip wobbles as she pauses, really taking me in. "I love you so much."

A band constricts around my heart. I almost lost her.

"I love you, too." With a rough sound, I gather her in my arms, kissing the top of her head. "Won't ever stop. My heart beats for you, sunshine."

"How touching."

We spring apart as Coleman climbs to his feet, the gun in hand. I step in front of Thea, shielding her as he takes aim.

"Come here, princess," he commands.

A small sound catches in her throat. She buries her fingers in the back of my hoodie.

"You willing to die for her?" Coleman's voice is creepy as fuck, completely psychotic. "I've shot you once, now I'll finish you."

"I'm not letting you near her."

Narrowing his eyes, he stalks toward us. I back up, keeping her behind me as we move into the next room.

The front door flies open and flashing lights illuminate the shadows in the living room. Shouts come from the front and back of the house.

"Freeze! Hands up!"

About fucking time.

Coleman's eyes go wide as he whirls to face the cop and the gun trained on him from behind. More responders pour in from the front.

"Put the gun down on the floor slowly!"

"Officers, this is a misunderstanding." Coleman shifts his demeanor, putting on his good teacher act. "This punk broke in."

Thea and I shuffle out of the way. I stay in front of her, hands up to show I'm unarmed.

"Drop the weapon!"

I meet his gaze and smirk. "Game over, bastard."

Watching Coleman's expression crack as the authorities disarm and cuff him is satisfying. Thea takes my hand while we are ushered outside. I'm never letting go again.

* * *

It's a madhouse on the quiet residential street outside of Coleman's place a short while later. The road is crammed with squad cars, an ambulance, a news van, and the neighbors watching the scene unfold.

Coleman is in the back of one of the police cars as the cops secure the scene and take our statements.

Thea and I are seated on the back of the ambulance as the EMT patches my injured arm. They cut my hoodie off and Thea wrapped the blanket they gave her around me to keep the frigid night air at bay.

Mom's going to have a goddamn field day when she gets wind of this. Deranged teacher, wounded protecting my girlfriend. Sympathy vote, here she comes.

"GSW, male, eighteen." A paramedic standing to the side checks off on a tablet. "We need to get you to the hospital for a CT scan so they can confirm the bullet isn't lodged in your arm."

The paramedic rolls her eyes as I lift the oxygen mask off and toss it aside.

"Fuck that, I'm not going anywhere. I feel fine." I hold Thea closer, tucked beneath my good arm. I'm not ever leaving her side. "Not without her."

"Connor, they're just trying to help." Thea rests her bandaged hand against my stomach. It shakes slightly, the shock and adrenaline wearing off. Troubled shadows cloud her beautiful eyes and I want to drive them away. "Don't give them trouble."

"I want to see Chief Landry's face when he gets here so I can look him in the eye when I tell him I fucking told him so."

"It doesn't matter now. As long as they stop him from attacking and abusing others." Thea puts her head on my good shoulder and I cradle her close.

I can't stop touching her. It's vital I feel her in my arms, to know she's okay.

"Who are they?" Thea murmurs.

A black SUV rolled up a minute ago, stopping near the ambulance. The windows are tinted. It doesn't seem like regulation, and the car model is way too expensive for a government budget.

"Feds?" I squint as the doors open and one by one the agents get out. "Maybe some kind of elite prodigy squad, they don't seem old enough."

They're not like the FBI agents shown in the movies at all, despite dressing the part with long dark coats and sunglasses at night. All four of them are tall, imposing figures. Tattoos creep up the side of some of their necks and onto the backs of hands as they adjust their sleeves and cast assessing glances around. One with thick, slicked back blond hair gives orders to one of the other guys with inky hair and a contemptuous frown.

"Ten minutes. In and out," the blond agent says curtly. He addresses the most hostile looking guy in the group. "Keep it clean."

A dangerous vibe rolls off them and people give them a wide berth as soon as they move like shadows through the bustling scene, spreading out. Agent Grumpy heads in the house, while the rest follow the domineering blond dude who must be in charge.

The agent stops an officer by planting a hand on his chest. The officer is annoyed until the fed removes his sunglasses and speaks too low for us to hear. Whatever he says, it has the officer heeling to his chain of command, jerking a thumb behind him at the squad car where Coleman is in custody.

He motions to another officer and Coleman is yanked from the car, then marched over to the group of feds. As he gets closer, Thea tenses. I clutch her in a hug. He can't get her now.

Coleman goes willingly enough, until he sees who he's trudging toward. He freezes.

"No." He loses his cool, paling. Struggling against the officers, he tries to get back to the car. "No, no!"

"Is that any way to greet me?" The lead agent asks with a sadistic gleam in his eyes. He holds out his hands. "I told you we'd find you. No point in running."

Coleman hollers in protest as the two other intense agents grab his arms. They have no problem containing him. Their boss gets in Coleman's face, grabbing his jaw and forcing his head back. The curve of his smirk is lethal.

With a sharp nod to his guys, they drag Coleman to the SUV and shove him in the back seat. One pulls out a knife as he slides in with him.

My brows jump up. Are switchblades FBI regulation? Thea finds my hand around her waist and grips it tight. I stroke my thumb over her knuckles to soothe her while we watch.

The lead agent flicks his gaze at us. He motions in our direction, then stalks off toward the house.

After watching his boss' back for a moment, the remaining agent comes over. I blink in surprise when he stands in the pool of light from the open ambulance. This guy can't be much older than Thea and I, maybe two or three years at most. He has tousled dark brown hair and a sick neck tattoo of a crow in flight. His coat is open, revealing ripped black jeans.

There's no way these guys are real FBI.

"Need a statement. Shoo," he says to the EMT working on me. The EMT gives the guy an unimpressed look. He chuckles and nods his head toward the house. "You have a problem with it, you can take it up with him. Trust me, he is in a pissy as fuck mood right now. Rough target for him to finally get his hands on."

"Fine." The EMT points at me. "Don't think about leaving the scene. Coherent or not, you need to see a surgeon as soon as possible."

"He's not going anywhere," Thea assures him, squeezing my hand. "I'll make sure of it."

The fed imposter grins at her, winking. "You're cute as a button."

A growl rumbles in my chest. He lifts his hands in surrender.

"Just sayin', man." Once the EMT moves away, he gives me a once over. "Should've waited. Our way was a lot cleaner than all this fuss. Here."

He hands me a thumb drive and doesn't wait for an answer before walking back to meet up with the other guys.

"Do you know them?" Thea asks.

"I think so."

When I look up, the imposter agents are piling into the SUV with a drawer from Coleman's bureau and the computer tower. All the evidence of Coleman's crimes. The doors slam, then the SUV peels out and speeds away.

Something tells me Coleman won't make it to jail.

Whatever. The only thing that matters is Thea's safety. I lean my head on hers, breathing easier when a hint of her sweet scent hits my nose.

THIRTY-NINE
CONNOR

As the anesthesia from surgery wears off, I wake up groggy in a hospital room. Thea is by the bed, holding my hand as she dozes, her head resting on her folded arm. Her hand is re-bandaged.

"Hey, man," Devlin says from a chair by the window, Blair asleep in his lap with her head on his shoulder and his coat draped over her.

"Time is it?" My tongue moves sluggishly and a gross metallic taste makes me grimace.

"Late. You got out of surgery at eleven and it took a couple of hours for the drugs to wear off."

Out in the hall, I hear Mom's grating voice, followed by

Dad telling her to keep it down. She's arguing about using this to turn around the approval ratings after they took a hit. The gunshot wasn't a fatal injury, but Mom is here to put on her show anyway.

Rolling my eyes at her ridiculous bid for a boost in her numbers, I angle my head to get a look at the bandage covering my upper arm. It's stupid that I'm even in the hospital. I told the paramedic I didn't want to come, but Thea insisted to be on the safe side. I couldn't refuse the pleading look she gave me.

"What's the damage?"

"Stress fracture and stitches, but you're lucky. It went in and out and missed anything vital. Minor fragments and the residue left behind, but the nurse said most of it was the force of impact to the tissue from close range."

"Still hurts like a bitch." I flop my head back to the pillow, easing my frustration by brushing Thea's hand with my thumb. "Did you bring my computer?"

"Yeah, hang on." Devlin nudges Blair, his smile tender as she makes a quiet sound. "He's up. Want to sleep still?"

"No, I'm awake." She moves off his lap, wrapping the peacoat around her shoulders. Her gaze shifts to me. "Glad you didn't die."

I snort, then regret it when it makes my arm throb. "Hi to you, too. Dev, can you also get the flash drive from the pocket of my jeans?"

Devlin gets my laptop out from a bag by his chair, then rummages through the plastic bag containing what's left of my clothes in the corner. At all the movement, Thea startles awake, gripping my hand tighter. Her wide eyes relax once she realizes where she is.

"Hey," I say softly. "Okay, baby?"

"Yeah, I was having a bad dream." She presses her forehead to the back of my hand. "It wasn't real."

"It wasn't." I pat the bed. "Come here."

"No, I don't want to hurt you." She gets up, gesturing with her hands. "You just got out of surgery!"

Gripping her wrist, I tug until she falls into an awkward position, bracing her arms on either side of me.

"Do I seem like I'm a severely injured invalid?" I run my good hand up her side. She no longer has the blood-stained coat on, down to a fuzzy yellow sweater and tan pants. "Come here, baby. I need you close."

"Fine, but if the doctor comes in, I'm not taking the blame for any trouble we get in."

"I'd break every rule just to have you close."

She settles on her side next to me in bed, kissing my cheek. "I'm so glad you're okay."

"I'm more glad that you're okay." I cup her face and pull her closer, capturing her lips in a kiss. Her body trembles as I hug her against my uninjured side, feeling the remnants of tension bleeding away. "It'll all be okay now. He can't hurt you anymore."

She makes a soft sound of agreement, pressing her face into my neck. A hot wetness against my skin makes me squeeze her as tight as I can, trying to pull her pain onto my shoulders to help her bear the weight of what she faced tonight. When things have calmed down, I'll be whatever she needs to support her through dealing with the emotional fallout of knowing she was a victim of grooming.

"Here." Devlin brings the laptop and flash drive over, setting it up on the tray table.

I pull the tray closer with Thea's help.

"What do you think is on it?" she asks.

My brow creases as I open the folder on the drive. From the scraps I know of the guys impersonating federal agents, it could be anything. "Let's find out."

"Financial reports." Devlin leans over my shoulder from the other side of the bed.

Not just financial reports. I jerk forward, trying to sit up, only to grit my teeth at the discomfort it causes. Some of the machines connected to me throw off warning beeps before settling down as I lay prone.

"What's wrong?" Thea bounces her gaze from the screen to me. "Don't move so much, you're going to hurt yourself."

"They're statements of my accounts." I nod to each file. "Trust fund and the private accounts."

The ones I use to grow my bitcoin investments.

"So they're watching you?" Devlin clarifies.

"No. Well, yes, probably. The balances are all tripled from when I looked at them last. That was only a few days ago."

Whoever the hackers are, they're powerful.

Devlin and Thea give me matching expressions, brows rising high. Blair whistles from the visitor's chair across the room. I was close to my goal before, but this is beyond. With this much money, I no longer have to wait to escape Mom's bullshit. A disbelieving laugh huffs out of me.

"Holy shit," Thea murmurs. "That's a lot of money."

I already know what I'll do with some of it. My gaze slides to her. Her dream is to open a bakery. I'll make that happen sooner than she planned.

A commotion at the door draws our attention. Thea's mom bustles in, arguing with the nurse on her tail. Thea tenses at my side.

"No, I will not stay out!" Mrs. Kennedy snaps. She takes one look at the two of us in the hospital bed and her lip curls. "Thea! Let's go. You're coming home right now."

"I'm staying here." Thea sits up, but remains by my side. "I'm where I belong."

"You are not. Get away from that boy right now." Mrs.

Kennedy shakes her head violently. "When I heard from Maisy's father what happened tonight with your teacher, hours later, I—"

"Mom." Thea sighs and squeezes my wrist. Sliding from the bed, she goes to her mom, taking her by the shoulders. "You can't keep smothering me. What you told me yesterday? The way you did it? You should've told me a long time ago instead of the way you handled it." She lowers her voice, but remains firm and strong. "If you had, maybe I wouldn't have questioned everything that was normal about myself. I didn't understand why you were so strict with the way I dressed because you weren't open or honest about your sister."

"Thea," Mrs. Kennedy whispers, throat working. "I only wanted to keep you safe, but you still ended up in danger."

Swiping away tears, Thea goes on. Her voice quivers with emotion. "I'm not blaming you. Or myself. It's no one's fault but Mr. Coleman's for manipulating and preying on me in a vulnerable state. He's the actual monster to blame for hurting me. It was a perfect storm, but I can't go back and change it now."

Pride blooms in my chest watching my girl stand up for herself and not allowing what she went through to bring her down. She's so strong, even when the world is crushing her. I didn't think I could love her anymore than I already do, but the warm glow fills me up from the inside.

Her mom is rendered speechless, expression crumbling. "I didn't hear from you and I was so scared."

"I know. I'm sorry, it was a crazy night and I forgot to call you once it was all over. Learning about the truth and getting attacked by him on the same day was a lot to handle." Thea rubs her mom's arms as she collapses against her, crying into her neck. Thea meets my eyes over her hysterical mother's shoulder. "I'm okay, I promise."

"I'm sorry," Mrs. Kennedy cries. "I'll do better."

"Okay. Shh, it's okay," Thea soothes. "Why don't you head home? You've seen I'm safe. I'm not sure if I'll come back tonight or stay here."

"Will you call me?"

"Yes. We have a lot to talk about."

Sniffling into the tissue Thea hands her, Mrs. Kennedy nods, calming down. The door opens again and my mother steps in, phone pressed to her ear. Dad's right on her tail, going to sit in the visitor chairs with a weary sigh.

She gives Thea and her mom a dirty look. "Damien, I'll call you back. Handle it." Hanging up, she addresses the room. "Here's the story when the reporter arrives in the morning—"

"Mom." My severe tone cuts her off. "Take your image worries and your campaign and shove it up your ass."

"Connor," she hisses, attention swinging between everyone in the room. "Are you cranky from surgery?"

"Vivian, give him a break," Dad complains.

Nice sentiment, but too little too late, Dad.

"The come down's a bitch, but no. I'm done playing your political games. I'm not your dancing circus bear anymore, effective immediately."

"We can talk about this later." She sniffs importantly. "When you're feeling better."

"Now's good for me. The thing is, Mom, you have no way to control me anymore. You want the car back? Take it. I'll buy a new one when I move out."

She narrows her eyes. "With what money?"

It's clear from her expression. She thinks she's got me.

I turn the laptop. "The trust fund from granddad is very generous." He never told her how much he set aside for me. "And from personal investments. I don't need you. You can't keep me under your thumb. If you try controlling me, I'll release the detailed documented account of your affair with your campaign manager."

Color drains from her face and her smug look falls before she plasters another blank mask in place to cover for the slip. It's not as detailed as I make the threat to sound, but my reputation precedes me. She believes my bluff. Still, I go for a final blow.

"Everything. I'll leak it to your political rivals and the press."

"Fine," she snaps.

Thea returns to my side, taking my hand. Together we stand as a united front against my overbearing mother. Nothing has ever felt better.

FORTY
THEA

The finishing touches on the sour cream donuts are perfect. They smell amazing and I can't wait to see Connor's face when I show him my awesome skills icing these gunshot wound confections, especially with my hand still a little sore from the cut on my palm. It's almost healed now, along with my other bumps and bruises from that night.

The donuts are more gruesome than my usual style, but it's worth it to make Connor smile. I set my piping bag aside and lick excess red glaze from my fingers. With the decorating done, I take off the apron protecting my sheer blouse and the high waist fitted goldenrod corduroy skirt with buttons down the front.

Another one of my resolutions: I'm no longer dressing to hide my body. Once I found out the reason Mom was always on my case, it chased away any remaining self-consciousness, allowing me to dress in whatever feels good. I'm moving forward, not letting anything that happened stop me from enjoying my life.

Every day Connor tells me how beautiful I am, echoing my inner goddess of confidence.

I don't have to choose between Secret Folder Girl and myself, I can just be who I am because I'm enough.

Things are finally settling down. It almost felt weird to start the second semester after such a whirlwind over winter break.

When Connor was discharged from the hospital, we combed the internet, news stations, and talked to Maisy's dad for any information on the people who took Mr. Coleman into custody. Almost a month later and we still haven't heard anything.

Connor told me about the necklace he broke into the house to retrieve and how intense the hackers were about it. He is certain those guys killed Mr. Coleman for revenge. They did seem dangerous. But that man is a monster. He won't be free to attack any other girls.

As for myself, I have an appointment with a therapist specializing in cases like mine to begin working through the trauma I went through. The first thing I did the morning after the hospital was call Maisy over and tell her everything I'd kept from her. She hugged the life out of me, promising to be there for me. It felt good to be open with her and get it off my chest. Pushing the truth out was hard, though. It came in starts and stops, interrupted when I couldn't speak from my throat tightening with emotion.

I'm a little nervous to continue unpacking the things I haven't looked at directly about how Mr. Coleman abused me.

The pain is so fresh it sometimes blindsides me out of nowhere. Victim. It's still a weird word in my mouth, as if it doesn't feel like it should belong to me. But does anyone feel like they've achieved the arbitrary required level of trauma before it feels like the right word? Maybe no one ever feels like it's theirs.

I'm learning to accept the shape of it, because I can't erase it or pack it away in my brain behind walls.

Not thinking about it won't make it go away. It's something I have to face in order to move forward. It doesn't have to change who I am or define me.

This is another facet of myself I will learn to treat gently.

I'll find my new normal with the support of my loved ones at my back.

Constantine nudges my leg with his snout, huffing at me when I lift my brows. His big brown eyes dart to the counter and back to me.

"One more piece, you little pig." I feed him a morsel from the broken bits of cake that didn't make the final cut. I scratch under his chin as he chomps happily. "Good boy. Let's take these outside for everyone."

Lifting the tray of bullet wound donuts, I head out back, where Connor and our friends lounge on the terrace around the blazing fire pit. My heart swells at the sight of them all. It reminds me I'm not invisible or alone.

Everyone has a quilt wrapped around them, Devlin and Blair curled together in a cushioned loveseat, Maisy sitting cross legged barefoot on a lounge chair, and Connor holding one side of his blanket open for me to nestle beside him.

Constantine comes when Blair calls him, flopping at her side while she grins, snapping pictures with her phone. His tongue lolls out, drawing a laugh from me at his blissed out expression. We've been bonding over our love of dogs. Now when she sends her friend Gemma dog posts on Instagram, she includes me in the group chat and begs me for pictures of Constantine all the time.

"I come armed with baked goods," I announce.

"Yes!" Maisy unfolds her legs and snatches a donut from the tray. She takes one look and cracks up. After taking a big bite of her bloody donut, she hums in bliss. "My sugar queen."

"I think you mean mine," Connor says in an amused tone. "What's so funny, little Landry?"

Maisy points her half-eaten donut at him. "Dude, you have got to drop that. I might be younger than my brother, but I can still kick ass."

"Play nice," I shoot over my shoulder, offering the tray to Blair and Devlin.

He examines the choices with a smirk. "Oh, I like these. Nice eye for detail."

Blair takes two donuts, biting into the first while admiring the second, nodding in agreement with her boyfriend. "Gruesome. These are rad as hell." She closes her eyes and hangs her head back. "Tastes so good."

The corner of Devlin's mouth lifts and he leans into Blair's space to give her a languid kiss. Seeing her enjoying herself always makes his chiseled features soften in fondness.

I set the tray on the ottoman between Connor and Maisy, taking a donut for myself and Connor.

"Come over here." He lures me to his side with a charming, crooked smile that pulls heat into my core. He knows exactly what kind of effect it has on me as he tugs me down onto the wide cushion, enveloping me with the blanket. "That's better."

"What's that?" I ask, nodding to the real estate page he has loaded on his phone. "Looking for an apartment already? I thought you were joking when you told your mom you'd move out."

He tucks his phone away before I get a good look at the

property he was checking out. "It's nothing. I'm just looking right now, but once I find the perfect place, I'll show you."

Narrowing my eyes, I do an impression of one of his favorite memes. "Keep your secrets, then. Donut?"

He takes it while I bite into mine, staring at what I made for a long beat. "Your baking is taking a turn for the gory, huh?"

I try to contain my grin, but I lose the battle. "Do you like it? How does the blood taste?"

"You tell me."

He swipes his finger through the decorative frosting and holds it up to my lips. Cheeks hot, I part my them and dart my tongue against his fingertip. His gaze is locked on my mouth, dragging his teeth over his bottom lip.

"I'm about to haul you off to the pool house."

I tap his chest with a light smack, lowering my voice. "Don't tease me, then!" Wrapping the blanket tighter around us, I drop my hand to his lap, running it over his semi-hard dick. "You brought this on yourself. We're hanging out with our friends."

With a groan, he drops his head back. I break a piece off my donut and feed it to him. He chews for a minute.

"It's delicious, baby. It always is with you."

Maisy, Blair, and Devlin sound off in agreement, reaching for seconds.

There's nothing like feeding the people you care about with something you baked with love. "I'm glad you all like them."

Surrounded by our friends and wrapped in Connor's arms, my heart is full of the brightest joy. It breaks through any shadows, lighting me up with an ember of warmth that makes me feel stronger.

"Face mask self-care day tomorrow. You in?" Maisy points between Blair and me.

"Wouldn't miss it," I say. "Do you like face masks, Blair?"

She blinks, glancing at Devlin. He rubs her arm, dropping a kiss on her shoulder.

"Uh, sure. I've never done one."

"Oh my god! *Girl.* I'm about to change your life. This is it, this is our bonding moment. Come with me." Maisy gets up, taking Blair's hands. "This can't wait. We're doing this right now. Come on, Devlin. You're doing one, too. We'll film it and put it on our stories. Baby's first face mask!"

Leaning against Connor, I laugh at Blair's perplexed expression. "Go on, she doesn't have an off switch when she decides to do something. It doesn't take long and it feels good."

"Take lots of pictures," Connor says. "I want proof of our Devil Boy in his true form."

Devlin flips him off.

Maisy snaps and points at Connor. "You're right. Is your hair long enough for pigtails? They'll look like horns. It'll be bomb."

"Aren't you, like, quiet at school? What the hell?" Devlin asks, bewildered.

"Not around people that know me," she says.

"Never underestimate the quiet ones, bro."

I shake my head. "You did. Look where it got you."

"Yeah?" Connor pulls me on his lap, trapping me in his strong arms as he puts his lips by my ear. "It got me a lapful of this."

I laugh and yelp as he attacks my neck with kisses. No matter what happened before, I'm safe and loved now. The shining truth of it glows in my chest.

"Okay, enjoy the make-out time," Maisy says as she herds Devlin and Blair through the back door. "Don't get too frisky. Or do. You know, self-care. Peace, bitches."

"You heard her," Connor murmurs, angling my head back

for a languid kiss. "Mm, you always smell sweeter when you bake. I love it."

I shift around on his lap so I can face him, looping my hands around his neck. "How does your arm feel? I know you think you're superhuman, but the sling only came off a couple weeks ago."

"It's good." He takes my hand that was cut and brings it to his lips, kissing each of my knuckles. His gray eyes meet mine, full of warmth. He's quiet for a moment, taking me in. "You hold my heart in your hands. Promise you'll take care of it, okay?"

I give him an impish smirk, cupping his jaw. He drops another kiss to my healing palm. "Like take it for walks and keep it fed? Easy, it's just like caring for Constantine."

Connor wraps his arms around my waist with a playful growl, dragging his mouth over my skin. "You know how I like to be fed, baby."

"My heart is yours, too," I say after he stops teasing me. "It always will be."

When he kisses me again, we lose all track of time, warmed by the fire and our love.

EPILOGUE

THEA
December, 11 Months Later

Squinting from the cryptic note Connor gave me to the numbers above the row of shops on the main street in downtown Ridgeview, I huff. After a quick kiss good morning, my boyfriend disappeared from our apartment, leaving behind a handwritten note that sent me on a wild scavenger hunt all over town. He loves these games, and I usually end up delighted by his surprises, but I would have enjoyed it more if we spent the morning cuddling in bed instead of roaming all over Ridgeview.

"This can't be right."

I glance up and down the street, standing in front of an empty storefront with big windows covered in paper. The shop sits between a florist and an art gallery, both decorated for the holidays. It was recently for sale. I secretly passed by it every day on my way to work making pastries at the coffee shop, imagining how nice a mural would look on the wall inside. It would be a big sun and moon celestial painting surrounding the name of my future bakery—Eclipsed Tarts Baking Co.

The sign in the window reads *Sold*.

So much for my big dream. It was too expensive, anyway. Commercial leases in Ridgeview have pretty much put my plans on hold until I sell a kidney to get my startup.

Connor has been offering to get me going. I keep turning him down because he does so much for me. He already pays for our apartment. In a year he's grown his finances even more, officially a self-made man from releasing an app he built that took off for its uses in preventing security breaches and identifying threats, especially predators. He doesn't want what happened to me to happen to anyone else if he can help stop it. He has been amazing in helping me cope with the fallout of my trauma, and I'm proud he put his skills to use for something good to help others.

But his scavenger hunt note led me here, promising my path to the future if I open the door.

"Okay. Here goes nothing." I pull a face, bracing as I twist the knob. "Please don't let me get arrested for breaking and entering."

"You're too cute for that," Connor says, grinning from across the room. He's leaning against a polished wood counter with the sleeves of his henley pushed up, painting a very attractive picture. "You're about twenty minutes later than I expected."

I hold up the paper as I enter the building, glancing around. It's lit in warm muted light by the thin kraft paper covering the bay windows. "Leave better clues, then."

"What? Which one was hard?" Popping out of his slouch, he plucks the note from me as his arm finds its way around my waist. "Number seven? No way, I made that one obvious."

"Number three!" Gripping his biceps, I press on my tiptoes

to kiss him. He tilts his head, a smirk playing in the corners of his mouth. "Hi. Going to tell me what mischief you're up to today?"

"Thinking about it." His hands slip inside my coat, fitting to my waist over my long black skirt with big sunflowers printed on it. He dips into the high slit with one hand as his other teases beneath my cropped sweater, tracing exposed skin. "Thinking about something else, too. Especially when you wear this."

"When aren't you thinking about that." With a sardonic smile, I shrug out of my white wool coat—a replacement from the one I had last year—and drape it over the counter. It looks newly built. I don't remember the photos on the real estate website having anything inside, but now it seems like whoever owns the place has been getting it ready. "Are we allowed to be in here? I saw the sign out front. I know you love bad ideas, but—"

"We're allowed. This is actually one of my better ones."

He follows me as I explore the main room. I imagine how I'd paint the wall, make the one behind the counter a chalk wall with an artistic display of the daily menu, and fill the back one with a similar poster mural of inspiration and positivity just like my old bedroom. I have one in our apartment that grows every time I find something new to add. It would look perfect in my bakery to create an uplifting environment that will make people smile.

"Do you know who bought this place?"

Connor tucks his hands in his pockets. "I do."

"What are they going to put here? It looks like a shop."

He hums as if he's pondering, wrapping his arms around me from behind. "A bakery, I think."

"Really?" My face falls. A second later, I shake my head and turn in his arms. "That's so great. Maybe I can get a job here instead of the coffee shop!"

Connor's smile turns fond. "Baby. The building is for you. I bought it."

It takes a moment for his words to register as I'm lost in the process of how to quit my job. I blink, digging my fingers into his shirt. "Wait what?"

He chuckles, kissing my cheek. "I'm saying it's yours, all of it."

"You..." I gape, gaze flying around the room. "And you built..."

"Yes. You kept showing me your Pinterest vision board, and I had Maisy help me design the style you saved most."

I'm speechless, mouth working helplessly. Tears of joy prick my eyes. "Oh my god."

"I want to give you the world. Help you achieve all of your dreams." He brushes a knuckle under my eye to catch a stray tear. "Do you like it?"

"Like it? I fucking love it, you crazy, wonderful man!" Laughter bursts free as I crash into him, hugging him tight.

"Oh, f-bomb. I know I got it right when you start letting those slip." He kisses the top of my head. "Love you, sunshine."

"I love you, too. This is the best surprise. Oh my god." I can't stop saying it. "I'm opening a bakery."

"You are." Connor grins into the kiss he gives me. "I have one more surprise."

"Okay, but you probably should've led with that one. I don't think you can top this."

His gray eyes gleam. "We'll see. Close your eyes."

Tugging the sleeves of my sweater over my hands, I cover my eyes. A few moments later, Connor is back, cupping my elbow. He takes a shaking breath, drawing my attention. He's usually confident no matter what he does.

"Okay, you can look."

When I lower my hands, Connor kneels on one bent knee

in front of me, thumbs stroking the sides of my legs. My eyes go wide.

"Are you—"

"Not if you interrupt with your classic nervous babbling."

I mime zipping my lips and tossing away the key. It makes him huff out a laugh, a tenderness lighting up his handsome features.

"I've known you're the girl I'd marry since you first challenged me every step of the way with your not so quiet stubbornness and logic. You're my perfect match"

As a watery puff of amusement escapes me, he pulls out a velvet box, popping the lid back to reveal a ring that steals my breath. It's two rings fitted together, a sun captured by a moon. An eclipse, like he describes our love. In the center is a pearlescent moonstone. A lump clogs my throat.

"Connor," I whisper.

He lifts his gaze to meet mine, taking one of my hands. "Thea, I'd wait until the end of time for you. But I need you to know you're it for me. There's no one but you."

I release a garbled, incoherent sound and fall into his arms. He catches me as we collapse to the floor, lips locked together. When we part, he rubs his nose along my cheek, hands cupping my ass.

"What do you say?"

"Yes, obviously."

He snorts, taking my hand once again. With his eyes burning into my soul, he kisses my ring finger and slides the engagement ring into place.

"I love you so much," I say. "I didn't know it was possible to be so happy."

"Let me keep surprising you. I'm not going to stop now." He makes me squeal as he holds me tight, climbing to his feet.

My arms wind around his neck. "We have a lifetime of surprises ahead of us. Together."

Together.

When I'm happy, he lifts my spirits higher, and when I'm aching, he holds me while I cry, offering his strength until I restore my own. He takes care of me and I take care of him.

"As long as I'm with you, I feel like I can do anything."

"You always could." He sets me down on top of the counter and braces his hands on either side of my hips. "You prove that every day."

I bite my lip around a wicked smirk I've picked up from dating him in the last year. "I'm about to prove something else. With my tongue."

"God, yes." Connor steals a quick kiss. "Hold that thought, though. They're all waiting to come in."

"Who?"

"Our friends. They all helped get the bakery together, so keeping the proposal a secret from them was impossible. Gemma wanted to camp out behind the counter all sniper style to capture your reaction."

As he explains, he types out a text on his phone. A minute later, the door opens and everyone in our life spills in. I hop down to meet them, hugging Maisy first before she makes it across the threshold.

"Dude. You're getting married."

"Holy crap," I mumble into her neck.

When we part, the loud rev of a motorcycle cuts into our celebratory moment. We both look up as Fox Wilder glares at Maisy from across the street, sitting on his bike. She stiffens, breaking their tense staring match first.

While she examines her feet, Fox's sneer fades. He meets my eyes for a beat before driving off. Once the roar of his bike dwindles, Maisy sighs.

"Is he still bothering you?" I ask.

"No. Yes? I don't know. It's senior year, but he hasn't grown up from his stupid feud. At least Holden graduated with you guys, so now Fox doesn't seem to be around every corner as much, throwing what we don't have in my face." She shrugs, tucking her highlighted brown hair behind an ear. "I just wish things could be like before, when we were kids...when we were friends. This is so stupid."

"Don't let him get to you. And if he's still bullying you, Connor and Devlin will kick his punk little ass."

Maisy snorts at the fierce expression on my face. "Okay, come on, killer. It's your day. My petty life dramas can wait."

Hooking her arm over my shoulders, she steers me inside where the rest of our friends are elbowing Connor in congratulations. His gray eyes fall on me and his smile grows. He pulls me to his side as Lucas Saint's girlfriend snaps photos with her camera.

Over the summer while they were on break from college, she helped me grow more comfortable with my body by modeling for her any chance she needed me. She has a real eye. When I see myself in her photos, it feels as if I've bared my soul to the lens, never worrying if there's a difference between the mirror and the photo because I love myself, even on the days it's hard and those dark thoughts creep up on me. When they do, I take myself through the affirmations my therapist had me write out to process those painful thoughts.

Blair slides up next to me and Maisy squeezes in on the other side.

Gemma hands her camera off to Lucas. "Group shot, babe. Girls first, then the guys."

"You've got it." He holds up the camera. "Work it, ladies."

Connor elbows Devlin, grinning. "Damn. We are lucky bastards."

"Fucking truth," Devlin murmurs, with eyes only for Blair.

The door opens again and my parents come in. Mom gives me a tentative smile. I motion her over and show her the ring. As soon as Connor and I graduated, we moved out of our houses to live in the apartment he bought for us. Things have been somewhat bumpy and slow learning to be honest with each other, but they're improving. We're getting to a point we can be a mom and a daughter again. Dad is taking less regional jobs and they've started seeing the same therapist as Connor to work through her suppressed grief for her sister.

Someone plays music from a phone and we bring in take out and snacks from one of the nearby shops on the strip. Tucked against Connor's side, I soak in the love our friends and family share with us.

"You and me," I murmur to him, stealing his chip, then a kiss. "Always and forever."

"Ends of the earth, to the moon, wherever doesn't matter. I'll love you."

He takes my hand and pulls me from my seat on the counter he built, leading me to the middle of the room. Our friends cheer and hold up phones to record us as Connor sweeps me into a dance, twirling me in the middle of my future bakery.

EPILOGUE

CONNOR
Paris, 6 Months Later

"Where do you think you're going? Get back here, I'm not done with you yet." Grabbing Thea by the ankle, I drag her across the bed and latch my mouth over her nipple while tracing her sun-shaped birthmark. She squeals, writhing in the sheets as I tease her. "I need to fuck my wife silly before we go anywhere."

"Silly achieved," she breathes, wrapping her legs around my waist and rolling her hips against me. "We reached it three rounds ago, you insatiable monster."

"I can't help it when it comes to you. Marrying you doesn't change that."

I reach across the bed to take another chocolate covered strawberry from the plate by the open window, the Eiffel Tower in view. Warm, breezy June air billows through the curtains, kissing over our sweaty skin. We've been in bed all morning, indulging in alone time. Chilled champagne sits in a bucket beside the strawberries. Eloping in Europe was a damn good idea.

Our friends are out exploring the city today, or shut away in their own hotel room in Blair and Devlin's case, leaving us to enjoy our honeymoon. Devlin married us as our officiant and Gemma photographed the intimate ceremony. Thea has never looked more radiant than she did reading her handwritten vows from a yellow notebook with a rainbow print on it, her promises penned between the pages of her favorite recipes.

The official wedding isn't until September back home in Colorado, but Thea was going crazy planning a wedding and opening a bakery at the same time. It was time I made good on a promise I made over a year ago, when we first began. Even if the idea to whisk her to Paris was something I pulled out of the air, she's been dying to visit real patisseries.

It was worth it for the look on her face. I love surprising her. I'll never stop doing it.

We might be young, but we both know what we want. What's the point in waiting around?

Feeding the strawberry to Thea, I say, "Well, then I'll just have to do my daily worship with my tongue at the altar between your thighs."

She moans as the chocolate cracks, sucking on the juicy strawberry. Her eyes widen and she sits up, flailing her hands.

"Pause! I've just had the best idea for a fun Valentine's day private order adult line. Where's my notebook?"

I sprawl across the bed, propping my head on my hand, enjoying the sight of her naked ass as she moves to get one of her recipe journals. Her auburn hair spills over her shoulder while she scribbles the idea down.

"Babe, the bakery doesn't open for another two weeks and you've already got a whole menu."

"I know, I know. But this is too good." She spreads her hands dramatically. "Chocolate molds of your partner!"

"You're going to make this into a chocolate replica?" I stroke my cock, shooting her a sly grin. "How much testing will be involved?"

After setting her notebook aside, she shuffles back to me on her knees, straddling my hips. "Oh, plenty."

"I like this idea." I skim my palms up her thighs to cup her tits. "Now you're definitely not escaping. I need you again."

Thea's head falls back when my cock sinks into her body. She moans softly, riding my dick at a torturously slow pace.

She's so fucking beautiful it carves an ache into my chest.

I squeeze her waist, bucking up with a sharp thrust that has her mouth dropping open on a gasp. "Like that?"

"Always," she murmurs, bracing her hands on my chest as she leans in for a sensual kiss.

Always. Our whole future together. I can't wait for all of it.

With the girl of my dreams—my *wife*—in my arms, the world is perfect.

* * *

Thank you so much for reading RUTHLESS BISHOP! The Sinners and Saints series continues in Wilder and Maisy's book, SAVAGE WILDER.

AFTERWORD

Writing allows the reader peek into the author's soul. Sometimes there is more shown than a small look. Writing this book drew a lot out of me and big pieces of myself bled into these pages. I honestly feel a little naked putting this one out there. I've been both so excited and *fucking terrified* to share this story with the world because so much of it is close to my heart.

Thank you for reading it.

THANK YOU + WHAT'S NEXT?

Need more Sinners and Saints series right now? Have theories about which characters will feature next? Want exclusive previews of the next book? Join other readers in Veronica Eden's Reader Garden on Facebook!

Join: BIT.LY/VERONICAFBGROUP

Are you a newsletter subscriber? By subscribing, you can download a special bonus scene featuring Thea and Bishop from Ruthless Bishop, as well as bonus scenes from Tempting Devil and Wicked Saint.

Sign up to download it here: BIT.LY/RBFREEBONUS

ACKNOWLEDGMENTS

Readers, I'm endlessly grateful for you! Thanks for reading this book. It means the world to me that you supported my work. I wouldn't be here at all without you! The response to this series and these characters has seriously blown me away. I love all of the comments and messages you send! I hope you enjoyed your read! I'm really excited to bring you more from this series!

Thanks to my husband for being you! He doesn't read these, but he's my biggest supporter. He keeps me fed and watered while I'm in the writer cave, and doesn't complain when I fling myself out of bed at odd hours with an idea to frantically scribble down.

Bre, once again I seriously couldn't have written this book without you. I'm so glad to have you to talk to when the brain gremlins misbehave or when the writing process gets tough. You get my characters on a level that blows my mind. You keep me sane and follow my wild babbling when something clicks. Thank you always for your friendship and support, and I'm sorry my muse likes to visit you in the middle of the night!

Thank you to my fellow authors for cheering me on through this one and always being a sounding board or chiming in with a laugh to keep me going. The indie community amazes me and I love being a part of it with y'all.

Thank you to Ashlee of Ashes & Vellichor for the amazing book trailers for this series! I love the way you can look at something and get it, and I've been in awe of what you've come up with to bring these books to life!

To my beta readers, thank you from the bottom of my heart! This one was terrifying to send out and I appreciate that y'all read my raw words and offer your time, attention to detail, and consideration of the characters and storyline in my books! Without you, I wouldn't be able to see the forest because I'm too busy staring at one tree. You're a dream team and I'm forever thankful for your help! Your time and hard work are much appreciated!

To my street team and reader group, y'all are the best babes around! To see you guys get as excited as I do seriously makes my day. Thank you for your help in sharing my books and for your support of my work!

To the bloggers and bookstagrammers, thank you for being the most wonderful and welcoming community! Your creativity and beautiful edits are something I come back to visit again and again to brighten my day. Thank you for trying out my books. You guys are incredible and blow me away with your passion for romance!

As always, I want to send a big shout out of love to my writing hags, the best bunch around! I always cherish your support and encouragement of my writing, no matter where my heart eyes and the muse take me. Every book I publish is thanks to you guys.

Savage Wilder
Sinners and Saints Book 4
Available Now

* * *

MAISY

THE BOY I KNEW IS GONE.
Rule follower. Straight laced. Goody-goody.

I'm as well-behaved as they get, but then the worst thing ever
happened to me...I caught the interest of the bad boy. Wilder
isn't the same guy I idolized when we were kids. He made that
clear the day he moved back to Ridgeview.

He hunts me, stalks me, surrounds me from all sides. I'm his
new favorite plaything. Again. Last year was bad enough, but
as graduation looms his claws are in me once more and he
refuses to let go.

And worst of all? I think I like it.

FOX

THE WILDER NAME IS A CURSE.
Pristine. Perfect. *Fake.*

Once upon a time we were friends. Then her family destroyed
mine. In return, I'll destroy hers.

I'm the resident black shadow this town fears. Whispers about. Everyone remembers that a Wilder means bad news. My sweet daisy should fear me because she's the key piece in my revenge plot against her crooked parents.

I'm not her friend anymore.

I'll take them all down, starting with her.

One-Click: bit.ly/SavageSAS
Add to Goodreads TBR: bit.ly/GRsavagewilder
Sign Up for Updates: bit.ly/veronicaedenmail

PREVIEW SAVAGE WILDER

PROLOGUE

MAISY
10 Years Ago

"That's not fair!" I cry, chasing after my brother and our best friend. "You can't win just because you're nine, you jerk heads!"

Their laughter echoes as the three of us run down the quiet street where we all live. They're both a year older and bigger than me, meaning the boys can outrun me easily. It makes me so mad! Girls can be just as awesome at things as boys. I'll show them.

"Holden!" I yell at my brother's back as frustration bubbles up in my chest.

"Suck it up, Maisy. You lost!" Holden shoots a mean grin over his shoulder. "Maisy Daisy is a crybaby loser!"

"I am not!" I shout loud enough that a few birds startle and fly away from the towering pine trees behind the houses on the block.

Fox slows down, trailing Holden far enough that I can

catch up. Once I'm beside him, he bumps his shoulder into mine and shoots me a secretive smirk. Some of the frustration leaves me.

"I'm not a crybaby," I mumble sourly.

A huff of laughter escapes him and he gives me a sly look from the corner of his eyes. They're like the ocean, dark blue and mysterious. I really want to see the ocean again someday. Both our families went last summer and it was my favorite trip, hunting for seashells and cool rocks with Fox and Holden as the waves crashed against the beach in California. I loved it so much, I made a bracelet of the stones Fox gave me. I never take it off.

"You're not," Fox agrees. After a pause, his mouth curves into the trickster smile he gets when he wants to make trouble. It's a smile that always draws me in for his sneaky plans. "Let's get him back."

I grin. "Deal."

After high-fiving, he wraps an arm around my shoulder to tug me closer, whispering in my ear. He's warm and smells like the sweet summer grass and a little like the motor oil from his dad's garage. They must have been working on his dad's motorcycle before he came out to play. My nose scrunches at the mix, but I don't pull away.

"You distract him, and I'll find a beetle," he instructs.

I have to cover my mouth to keep my excitement from sneaking out and giving us away. It's a perfect plan. Holden stayed up late one time and saw a scary movie about an army of mutant insects that freaked him out forever. Now he's terrified of beetles because of one of the scenes.

Nodding, I try to wink at Fox, but I end up blinking twice. Lame. He grins, shaking his head and messing with his dark brown hair as he slips away to hunt through the neighbor's bushes.

My brother has stopped running, waiting for Fox and I near the end of the street.

"Holden," I sing-song, skipping to quickly close the distance between us. "If you don't stop being so mean to me, Fox says he won't trade the Flareon he caught in Pokémon last week with you." I stick my tongue out to sell my taunting distraction. "And I won't show you how to build a cool tree-house on Animal Crossing."

"What?" Holden hisses. He brushes the long ends of his floppy light brown hair from his forehead agitatedly. It's the same shade as mine. People used to think we were twins even though he's older. "You both promised. I need those for my challenges!"

Fox walks up, not giving anything away except for his hands tucked behind him. "What are we playing next? You beat us both to the finish line, so you pick."

Holden shakes his head. "Not yet." He whirls on Fox. "You swear you're going to trade your Flareon with me?"

Fox tilts his head. "Yeah, dude."

Holden relaxes and mulls over what he wants to play next.

"Hide and seek?" I suggest, unable to hold back a tiny smirk as I practically squirm with anticipation of what's to come.

"No, you lost. You don't get to pick." Holden sighs. "But hide and seek does sound good."

"Yeah?" Fox grins. "I was thinking the same thing. Can you hold this for me while we hide from your sister?"

Before Holden can finish nodding, Fox grabs his hand and shakes out a round striped beetle into Holden's palm. It's a harmless potato bug, I think. My brother looks down and his brown eyes go wide. A scream tears from his throat as he flails his hand around to get the bug off. The tiny little thing drops to the ground, wriggling in confusion for a moment before scurrying away while Holden freaks out, waving his hand around like it was poisoned.

"Got you!" I cheer, giving Fox a triumphant high five. "That's what you get for cheating."

Holden's face twists in embarrassed irritation. He swipes his hand on his jeans, over his freak out now that the bug is gone. "You guys suck!"

My delighted laughter breaks free, making me double over and hug my belly when a cramp twinges. Fox leans against me for support as we fall into hysterics at our revenge prank.

"Whatever," Holden grumbles, waving a hand to act like he's all cool. We totally got him. "I'm going home to play Xbox. This is boring."

Satisfaction fills me to the brim as I watch my brother jog across the street to our house. Holden can be such a whiny butthead sometimes, but Fox likes him anyway. I do too, because he's my brother, and he's not *always* a jerk. The three of us have grown up on this street since before I can remember. Our mom and his parents work together and they're close friends.

"Maise, come look."

Fox has wandered over to the grassy field at the end of the block. The tree the three of us challenge each other to climb every week sits in the middle. Beyond the tall grass and wild-flowers, the woods stretch up into the hills at the base of the Rocky Mountains. I walk over, automatically reaching up to catch one of the lower branches of the tree and swing back and forth like a gymnast.

"What's up?" I try to get higher, but the bark bites into my hands.

He pops up from the tall grass and reaches for me, tickling my stomach, making me shriek and wriggle until I'm forced to let go of the branch or keep suffering his attack.

Once I'm on the ground, I curl into a protective crouch so he can't mess with me. "What the heck?"

Fox snorts. "You make it too easy."

"There are rules, Fox," I point out, standing up. We have them written down and everything in a notebook with Pokémon stickers on the front. I huff importantly and recite the sacred rule: "No tickling when a climber is in the tree."

The corners of his mouth lift and his eyes are bright. "Yeah, you're right." He taps my nose. "Sorry."

"What did you want me to see?"

"I found this."

Fox holds up a wildflower he picked, his crooked smile turning proud. It's dainty with thin light purple petals, not like the white daisies we usually see. A small gasp escapes me as I take it.

"It's so pretty." I touch a soft petal carefully. "What's it for?"

"You're *my* daisy."

Fox waits until I tear my attention from the flower to look at him in surprise. He's serious, his eyebrows wrinkled as he stares at me. Reaching out, he circles his fingers around my wrist. I watch, wide-eyed as he leans down and places a kiss on the wildflower clutched in my hands.

"I'm going to marry you someday," he promises.

A feeling like butterflies fills my chest as I stare back at him. "Okay," I whisper.

He grins and tugs on my wrist. "Come on. There's something else I want to show you. It's in my dad's garage. I wasn't supposed to find it, but I did when Dad went to answer a call and left me alone." We walk a few steps, then he stops us. "You have to promise not to tell anyone. Even Holden. Got it?"

I nod. "Promise."

Flying on the giddiness making me dizzy, I follow Fox, like I always do.

* * *

A week later my world feels crushed.

I sit outside my house with my knees tucked against my chest and my arms wrapped around my skinny legs. Holden is at the end of the block throwing a football at our favorite climbing tree over and over. Across the street, the crooked for sale sign stuck in the Wilder's front lawn mocks me.

The *someday* he promised me won't come.

Fox Wilder is gone.

ABOUT THE AUTHOR
STAY UP ALL NIGHT FALLING IN LOVE

Veronica Eden is a USA Today and International bestselling author of romances with spitfire heroines, irresistible heroes, and edgy twists.

She loves exploring complicated feelings, magical worlds, epic adventures, and the bond of characters that embrace *us against the world*. She has always been drawn to gruff bad boys, clever villains, and the twisty-turns of morally gray decisions. She is a sucker for a deliciously devilish antihero, and sometimes rolls on the dark side to let the villain get the girl. When not writing, she can be found soaking up sunshine at the beach, snuggling in a pile with her untamed pack of animals (her husband, dog and cats), and surrounding herself with as many plants as she can get her hands on.

* * *

CONTACT + FOLLOW
Email: veronicaedenauthor@gmail.com
Website: http://veronicaedenauthor.com
FB Reader Group: bit.ly/veronicafbgroup
Amazon: amazon.com/author/veronicaeden

facebook.com/veronicaedenauthor

instagram.com/veronicaedenauthor

twitter.com/vedenauthor

pinterest.com/veronicaedenauthor

bookbub.com/profile/veronica-eden

goodreads.com/veronicaedenauthor

ALSO BY VERONICA EDEN

Sign up for the mailing list to get first access and ARC opportunities! **Follow Veronica on BookBub** for new release alerts!

DARK ROMANCE

Sinners and Saints Series

Wicked Saint

Tempting Devil

Ruthless Bishop

Savage Wilder

Sinners and Saints: The Complete Series

Crowned Crows Series

Crowned Crows of Thorne Point

Loyalty in the Shadows

A Fractured Reign

The Kings of Ruin

Standalone

Unmasked Heart

Devil on the Lake

REVERSE HAREM ROMANCE

Standalone

Hell Gate

More Than Bargained

CONTEMPORARY ROMANCE

Standalone

Jingle Wars

The Devil You Know

Haze

Printed in Great Britain
by Amazon